My Family's Survival

by

Aviva Gat

My Family's Survival

A note from the author

I didn't start to get to know my grandmother until after she died. When she was alive, I visited her multiple times, but we could never have a conversation. While she spoke Yiddish, Polish, Ukrainian, Hungarian, Romanian, and Hebrew, I only knew one language: English.

I knew she was a Holocaust survivor. But like many children growing up in America, I didn't really understand what that meant. Of course, I learned about the Holocaust in school and by going to museums, but I couldn't really understand the magnitude of what it was. That changed in 2005, when my family decided to take a trip to Poland and the Ukraine to reenact part of our ancestors' escape during the war. Our family, scattered around Los Angeles, Israel, and even New Zealand, met in Poland to see the place where my grandmother lived before the Nazis came. From there, we hiked ten kilometers through the forest that, at the time, led into Hungary, the first leg in their escape.[1] During that trip, I started to understand a little bit about what my grandmother went through. Being a Holocaust survivor wasn't just some badge that was used to describe my grandmother's background. It was a scar that shaped her entire life.

Unfortunately, my grandmother passed away in 2012—still years before I was ready or able to ask the questions about her experience. Thankfully, she—and several other surviving members of her family—had their stories recorded. Their testimonies are what led to this book. At the time I decided to write their story, only one member of the surviving family was still alive. Yossi, the youngest of the family, was instrumental in helping me get to know his family and their experiences, but there are many questions still left unanswered.

It is important for me to note, that while this book is based on the testimonies given by the members of the Shwartz family, there are parts that are fictionalized or made up. Even with multiple testimonies and documentations, there are still missing details or holes in the story. The parts of this story that sound the most unbelievable are not fictionalized—rather, they are completely true. The fictionalized parts are based on truth, on something that somebody said. This is the story as I believe it happened, from beginning to end.

---

[1] Due to changes with the border after the war, the forest now sits on the border between Poland and the Ukraine.

1943—Rachel

There were a few times that I felt paralyzed with fear— fear that was so strong it coated me like rust that makes metal, that was once limber and flexible, brittle. That moment, with my arms around Abi and Sarah, was one of those times. I was sure that was it. We had been hearing about raids every day, and I knew it was only a matter of time before we were caught in one. We were too lucky, always getting away in the nick of time, and always finding someone who was willing to help us—for who knows what reason. All of that was coming to an end, I thought, when I heard that knock on the door. I gasped and grabbed my throat, trying to stifle the scream. Will it end like this? Thoughts swirled in my head, finally stopping at one agonizing image: Where had my childhood gone— that time not so long ago filled with giggles and promise? . . .

* * *

1937—Rachel

"Rachel!" I heard a hushed scream coming from outside. Rising from my seat, I went over to the window.

"Rachel? Are you coming?"

It was Bina, my best friend. She was wearing a red dress—the skirt fluttering in the wind—under a black shawl that she had tied around her neck.

"Let's go!" Bina whispered, continuing to beckon me.

I smiled and motioned to her that I was coming. I looked down and ruffled my own dress, which was wrinkled from sitting and reading. My mother had made the dress years ago, and she would have been happy to see me wearing it now. I took a last glance in the mirror and headed towards the door of my house.

"Father, I'm going out!" I yelled to my father as I grabbed my own shawl to cover me and flung open the door to an impatient Bina.

"Ready?" Bina said, a mischievous smile growing across her face.

"Let's go!" I said, grabbing Bina's arm as we started to skip down the dirt road. It was getting dark, but the glow of the sun still barely lit the road in front of us.

"Where are you two going?" A voice called, startling us.

We stopped in our tracks to see my older brother Chaim. He was jogging down the road just steps behind us. We looked at each other giggling, and then both looked at Chaim, neither of us answering.

"Come back, I'll drive you." He winked at us, motioning to follow him back to my house.

We all hopped into Chaim's car and he started the engine. Chaim was proud of his car, and took any opportunity to use it. He worked in Krakow and had been saving for months in order to afford it. When he had first come back to visit our little village of Butla, everyone there came out to see his car. It was one of only few vehicles ever to drive down our dirt roads— definitely the first car owned by a resident of Butla. He deserved it. He, like everyone in our family, worked hard, saved money, and knew how to spend it on the right luxuries. Despite his being ten years older than I was, Chaim and I had been close before he left. I was proud of my big brother and loved that our family was the talk of the village when he returned.

Bina and I giggled the whole car ride to Turka, the next village over. The car weaved up and down the hilly countryside, through fields of wheat and other farmlands. When we arrived, Chaim parked in front of the main building at the village entrance. Bina and I jumped out, flattening our hair that had blown messy in the wind. I gently pressed down on the sides of my head to ensure my long braids were still intact. Good. They were.

We could hear the loud music roaring from inside the building and saw the lights flashing as people walked passed the windows. Bina and I squealed with excitement and ran inside as Chaim slowly followed us.

It was packed inside, with girls and boys dancing in the center, and everyone else standing around the sides drinking and laughing. Bina and I quickly moved straight to the center of the room, lining up with the others dancing to the Polish folk music. We knew all the steps, having practiced at home together. Both of us were beaming with excitement as we lifted our skirts and skipped around. I glanced to the front of the room, smiling at the four-person band creating the music. One of the band members—a heavyset man—was playing a cello, while a second member—an older woman—had a fiddle tucked under her chin. In the front, a younger man played the accordion and a young girl sang while shaking a rattle.

"Rachel! What are you doing here?"

I heard the loud voice from behind as someone tapped my shoulder. It was another one of my older brothers, David. He had come here earlier in the night with some of his friends. I wanted to come with him, but he thought I was too young.

"Hi!" I yelled. My feet didn't stop and I continued to twirl. "Chaim brought us!"

David smiled at me and grabbed my hand to twirl me around.

"Rachel, you have to be at least sixteen to come here," he said.

"I will be soon enough," I smiled. I was fifteen—this was the second time Bina and I had snuck into this dance club. The last time, we had walked a full hour to get here and danced the night away before hitching a ride back with a couple of boys we met.

"All right. Well, I am here if you need anything," David said, squeezing my hand before he went back to his friends.

I couldn't blame him for being protective. I was the youngest in our family, with six older brothers. David was the second-oldest brother, age thirty-eight, and the only one who still lived in our small village. He had a house right next door to Father and me, where he lived with his wife, Hinda, and their two children. He was a farmer and had a huge field behind his house where he grew apples and peaches, as well as lettuce and other vegetables that he rotated each season. He also had a few cows who produced the sweetest milk I had ever tasted.

For as long as I could remember, David has been almost like a second father to me, especially since our mother had died when I was ten. Our five other brothers—Shlomo, Meir, Itzik, Zeilig, and Chaim—all left Butla as soon as they could to move to the big cities, find work, and see the world, but not David. He couldn't leave me.

"Rachel!" Bina yelled over the loud music as she got closer to my ear. "That boy over there is staring at you."

I turned to where she was gazing and saw a young boy, probably a few years older than I was. He was leaning against the wall, holding a drink in one hand. His eyes locked into mine and a crooked smile appeared on his face.

"He's cute," I said to Bina, still dancing. I broke eye contact with the boy, knowing that I had looked back at him just long enough for him to know I noticed him.

A moment later, I felt a tap on my shoulder.

"May I?"

The boy was standing behind me, holding out his hand. I smiled at him and placed my hand on his, allowing him to grip it and pull me closer to him.

"I'm Jan," he said, leading me through the Kujawiak folk dance. He moved gracefully and confidently, as if he were used to dancing like this.

"You're a great dancer, Jan."

"Thank you," he said. "So are you. I have never seen you here before."

"Maybe you just weren't looking," I said as he raised his arm to twirl me around.

"I would have noticed you," he said, catching my other hand to stop my twirl.

When the song ended, we stood facing each other. He was slightly taller than I was and had blonde hair and piercing blue eyes. I blushed as we stared at each other . . . until Bina grabbed my arm.

"Rachel, we have to go," Bina said. "Excuse us!"

Bina pulled me away from Jan, who still held my gaze.

"Rachel?" he said. "When will I see you again?"

"Soon," I said, finally breaking his gaze as Bina forced my feet to move away. David was standing near the door of the club, looking unhappy. But what older brother wouldn't be unhappy, seeing his little sister growing up?

"I think it's time to get you home," David said as we approached him. "You have school tomorrow."

"David, we're fifteen; we're not kids anymore," I said, following him out to his car.

"Yes, but you are still my little sister," he responded. "And that means, no matter how old you are, I am still responsible for you."

Bina and I hopped in David's wagon. His horse, Moshe, had been guarding it while he was inside. Chaim's car was still parked in the lot.

"Next time you want to come, tell me and I will take you," David said.

"Really?" I screamed.

"Yes, you're going to go anyway. It may as well be with me," he responded.

Soon we arrived back in Butla. David dropped Bina off at her home and parked the wagon in the grass between our houses.

"Right to bed!" David said when we got out of the wagon.

I smiled at him. "Thank you. I had a lot of fun tonight!"

He laughed. I gave him a quick hug and ran inside.

The next morning, I met Bina on the way to school. Butla was too small of a village to have its own school. It had so few residents that we knew every single person who lived there. Only about a thousand people lived in the two and half square kilometer village on the edge of a great forest.

Every morning, Bina and I walked the hour to school in Turka. Not only was it large enough to have the school and a dance club, Turka even had electricity and indoor plumbing. With almost ten thousand residents, Bina and I had many other children to mix with there.

"So, who was that boy last night?" Bina dove right in.

"Jan." I smiled curtly.

"That's it? That's all you are going to tell me?" Bina said.

"He seemed very nice," I responded, blushing.

"Nice! He seemed more than just nice," Bina teased. She continued teasing me until we got to Turka and walked past the empty dance club from the night before. The building was dark and showed no trace that just hours before it had been full of people, music, and dancing.

We arrived at school and sat quietly in our seats as the teacher taught us arithmetic and Polish. Our third class of the day was religion. For this class, we all got up and went to different classrooms, based on our faith. Bina and I were both in the class for Jews. Other students went to the Roman Catholic class or the Greek Catholic class. While the Greek Catholic class was the biggest, the Jewish class wasn't far behind. In this class, a Jewish teacher taught us about the Torah and the traditions of our faith.

When class started, one of the boys, Getzel, raised his hand.

"Yes?" the teacher called on him.

Getzel stood and cleared his throat.

"I just wanted to tell everyone goodbye," Getzel said. "My family is going to Palestina tomorrow. We're making Aliyah.[2]"

Getzel stood proudly, scanning the room for reactions from the class. The class started murmuring to each other. Getzel was not the first person from Turka to move to Palestina, but he was the first person whom I knew personally.

Over the last few years there had been a lot of talk in Turka about the Zionist movement— about creating a country only for Jews. Every day, the Zionist organization of Turka was getting bigger, and many of the Jews started saving money in order to move to the Holy Land.

I raised my hand, curious about Getzel's announcement. The teacher nodded at me, allowing me to ask my question.

"Why?" I asked Getzel. "Do you not like living here in Turka?"

"No, I like Turka well enough," Getzel said. "But Palestina is the land given to us by God, and we need to go there to create the Jewish country."

"But why do we need a Jewish country?" I pried.

"So we are safe," Getzel said.

His answer took me aback. Jews and Catholics lived in harmony in Turka, Butla, and the surrounding area. Jews were about ten percent of the population in the area, and I sometimes felt that everyone thought we were special because we were so limited in

---

[2] The act of immigrating to the Holy Land. In Hebrew, Aliyah literally means "to go up."

number. I had never felt that safety was a concern for us Jews.

"What's it like there?" another student blurted out.

"It's beautiful," Getzel beamed. "They say it is the land of plenty, where everyone has enough land, money, and food to live comfortably. And because everyone is Jewish, everyone celebrates Shabbos together . . . and everyone helps each other out."

"Getzel, we will all miss you very much," the teacher said. "Be sure to send us a postcard when you get there. Now, class, let's start our lesson for today."

I couldn't pay attention to anything the teacher said. She was talking about the week's Torah portion, but I was still thinking of Getzel's announcement. What place could be more beautiful than here?

When religion class finished, all the students mixed again, sitting together as though we had never been divided at all.

After school, I had choir practice. I had been given a solo for our upcoming recital and was excited to rehearse. As I left my classroom to go to the rehearsal, someone caught my eye in front of the school.

It was Jan, from the night before. He was standing by the school entrance, carefully watching everyone who walked by. After a moment, he saw me and came running in.

"I had a feeling you went to school here," he said when he approached me.

"Were you looking for me?" I teased him.

"You didn't give me another choice, did you?" Jan said. "Was I supposed to wait until I happened to see you again?"

"Why aren't you in school, Jan?" I asked him.

"I'm eighteen," he said. "I work on my family's farm, over there." Jan pointed to the green pastures on the outside of the school.

"Oh," I said. I hadn't realized he was so much older than I was.

"So, can I see you some time?" he said. "What are you doing now?"

"I have choir practice," I said to him.

"Wow, you dance and sing," Jan said. "A woman of many talents, I see."

I blushed.

"And after choir practice?" Jan said.

"You can meet me back here in two hours," I said, before rushing off to rehearsal.

I was giddy when I arrived at rehearsal. The next two hours seemed to go almost in slow motion, but finally we finished practicing and I raced out to the entrance of the school. Jan was there, waiting for me in a small tractor.

"Can I give you a ride home?" he said, offering me a place on his tractor. I hopped on, giggling to myself.

"I've never been on a tractor before!" I said.

"Really?" Jan said. "What does your family do?"

"My father has a vegetable store," I responded. "We do a little gardening. My brother has a farm."

"So where am I taking you?" Jan asked.

"Butla," I responded, happy that I didn't have to walk the hour back home.

"Butla, it is," Jan maneuvered the tractor to the main road that connected our two villages.

"So, Rachel, how much longer are you in school?" Jan asked.

"I'm in tenth grade now," I said.

"And then what?" Jan asked. "I doubt someone like you will stay in Butla to work at your father's vegetable store."

I laughed. "My brother lives in Krakow, so I want to go there and become an actress."

Jan turned to me. "It suits you."

We arrived in Butla and I directed Jan to my house.

"So, can I take you out tonight?" he asked.

I shook my head. "Tonight is Shabbos."

"Shabbos?" Jan asked in confusion. "Are you Jewish?"

I nodded.

"You don't look Jewish," Jan said, confused.

"What does that mean?" I laughed.

"Nothing," Jan responded. "Can I take you out when Shabbos ends?"

"You can," I responded, as I let myself off the tractor. "Saturday at sundown, I will wait for you here."

"I'll see you soon, Rachel," Jan said. "Have a wonderful Shabbos."

Jan tipped his cap and turned the tractor around. I watched him leave, smiling to myself, before turning around towards my house. Aunt Tzipora was kneeling in the garden, but was watching me approach.

"Hi, Aunt Tzipora," I said as I walked towards her. "How are the vegetables doing?"

Tzipora smiled, tilting her head to invite me to kneel down with her. Tzipora was my father's sister and had moved in with us to help out around the house after my mother died. Tzipora was digging potatoes out of the dirt. My mother started the vegetable garden when she was still alive. She planted many kinds of herbs and vegetables all around the house, ensuring that we always had a variety of things to eat.

"Is Father home?" I asked. Father went to Shul every Friday, where he often spent the afternoon hours before he returned home at sundown to do the Shabbos blessings with us. I wouldn't say we were religious. Yes, my father had a beard and wore a yarmulke, but that's what Jews did.

Tzipora shook her head and handed me the potato she had just pulled out. Then she wiped her hands on her apron and motioned to me to help her stand. Tzipora didn't speak. She was mute and had been since I could remember. I don't know why, or if she had been this way all her life, but I knew she was always listening.

I held out my hand to help her up, and the two of us went into the house. I loved coming home on Fridays. The smell of freshly baked challah wafted through the air, and a big pot of soup simmered on the stove.

Tzipora washed the potatoes from the garden and started making cholent, my favorite dish. She diced the potatoes and added them—as well as black beans, kidney beans, chickpeas, and tomatoes—into a large pot where chunks of beef were already browning. I watched her as she filled the pot with water and sprinkled in salt, pepper, and other herbs she had gathered from the garden. She closed the lid and turned the fire down low. The cholent would cook all night and we would eat it tomorrow for breakfast. Tzipora made cholent every Friday, just like my mother had.

I lifted the lid from the pot of soup, and fished out a carrot with my fingers. Tzipora clicked her tongue sternly, shaking her finger at me as I put the carrot in my mouth. Tzipora hated it when I stuck my fingers in pots of food, but what fun is that? The carrot was soft and the broth of the soup squeezed out when I chewed. I loved Fridays—they were just so magical.

Tzipora motioned to me to grab the Shabbos candles to light before the sun went down. I took the candles, placed them in the window, and grabbed a match to light them. Tzipora stopped what she was doing and came up behind me, putting her hands on my shoulders as I struck the match and lit the two candles. We both then waved our hands over the light towards our eyes, welcoming in the Shabbos.

"*Baruch atah Adonai eloheynu melach haolem, asher kid'shanu b'mitzotav ve-tzivanu lehadlik neir shel Shabbat.*"[3] I said the blessing.

A few minutes later, Hinda, David's wife, came in the door with their two children, Sarah and Abi. Sarah, age five, was holding her three-year-old brother's hand as he waddled in behind her.

"Good Shabbos!" Hinda said, placing a chocolate babka cake on the kitchen counter. She came over to kiss Tzipora and me, giving us both a big hug.

"Good Shabbos!" I repeated back to Hinda. Hinda then started helping Tzipora. She grabbed the set of plates and silverware and started setting the table.

I knelt down to hug my niece and nephew. Sarah squeezed her little body into mine, tightly wrapping her arms around me. I kissed her forehead and held out a hand to Abi, who giggled as he handed me a small yellow flower that he had been holding behind his back.

"Wow, thank you, Abi!" I said. I took the flower and placed it behind my right ear, tucking the stem into my braid. "How do I look?"

"You're beautiful, Aunt Rachel!" Sarah exclaimed. Abi put his hand to his mouth and blushed.

"Thank you," I responded, tickling Abi's stomach. I led the children to my bedroom so we wouldn't be in the way for Tzipora and Hinda. Our house was a quaint little space, with just two bedrooms, a kitchen, and a dining room. We had a

---

3 The Jewish blessing for lighting the Shabbat candles. The blessing says Blessed are You, Lord our G-d, King of the universe, who has sanctified us with His commandments, and commanded us to kindle the light of the Shabbat.

little outhouse around the back. Thankfully, I lived here with only Father and Tzipora. When my brothers were younger, they all shared the room that was now mine. Since they left, Tzipora stayed with me in here, and my father had the other room.

"How about I read you a story?" I asked, as Sarah and Abi climbed onto my bed. I grabbed a picture book of mine and snuggled up with them as I read.

A few minutes later I heard my father, David, and Chaim talking outside. They were returning from Shul, and speaking loudly to one another. They always stumbled back noisily after drinking the Kiddush wine at Shul.

Sarah, Abi, and I jumped off the bed and ran to the door to meet them.

"Father!" I yelled when the three of them walked through the door. My father picked me up and twirled me around. While my father was already seventy-two years old, age didn't seem to have slowed him down much.

After everyone hugged and kissed, we all gathered around the dinner table, which was lit by the candlelight. The table was covered with a bright white tablecloth and glistening white dishes that we saved for Fridays and holidays. In the center of the table sat two fluffy challahs covered with a cloth that my mother had embroidered. It said Shabbos Shalom, in Hebrew, and had big flowers cross-stitched around the letters.

My father poured our silver Kiddush cup full with wine and raised it up. He cleared his throat and started chanting the Shabbos blessing, his soothing voice filling the room.

"*Baruch ata Adonai boreh pri hagafen,*"[4] he finished.

"Amen," we all said, and then took our seats.

My father went around to bless his children, first David, then Chaim, and last, me. Finally, he uncovered the challahs, and blessed them.

"*Baruch ata Adonai hamotzi lechem min ha'aretz.*"[5]

"Amen!"

Father then starting ripping one of the challahs, giving each one of us a piece. The bread was still warm, and the insides were soft and sweet. Tzipora then brought the soup to the table, ladling out bowls for everyone.

"So, Rachel, how was school today?" my father asked, taking a sip of soup.

"Good," I responded. "The Weisses are moving to Palestina."

I had been thinking about my classmate Getzel and his announcement all day.

"Really?" my father asked.

"A lot of families are moving," Chaim said. "Even from Krakow; the Zionists are trying to convince everyone to go there."

"They are right," David said. "We need to go if we want our own country."

---

[4] The Jewish blessing for wine on Shabbat.
[5] The Jewish blessing for bread on Shabbat.

17

"It's supposed to be beautiful," Hinda said. "Green pastures, blue seas. I heard it's paradise." Hinda was a member of the local Zionist organization. They met regularly to learn Hebrew and to support the cause of establishing a Jewish country.

"Ha," my father laughed. "Surely it is full with Arabs and the Jews live in huts in the sand." His laugh started to turn into a cough.

"Getzel said everyone there is Jewish, and that they live there like kings," I said.

"And they speak Hebrew," Hinda said, winking at me. "I'll teach you if you want to learn."

"But why should we leave here?" my father asked, clearing his throat. "We have everything."

"Except a country just for us," Chaim said. "Where we never have to worry about anyone who hates us."

"Who hates us?" I asked, surprised.

"A lot of people don't like us, Rachel," Chaim said. "I know here in Butla we live peacefully, but it's not like that everywhere. For example, in Germany, there is a lot of anti-Semitism. Jews cannot own land or work in many professions, or be involved in politics. Also, in Russia, Jews cannot openly practice religion."

"But why?" I asked.

"No reason, really," Chaim responded. "Probably because we're successful. Or because they just need to hate someone."

"Let's talk about something more positive now," Hinda cut in. "It's Shabbos."

18

"Chaim took Rachel to the dance club in Turka last night," David changed the subject.

"David!" I exclaimed. My cheeks grew red from embarrassment.

My father laughed. "Well, David, maybe next time you will take her. She's not a little girl anymore!"

We all laughed. Once we finished our soup, Tzipora collected our bowls and brought out chicken, vegetables, and gefilte fish that she had cooked. We all filled our plates and continued eating and laughing the rest of the evening.

Soon, Sarah and Abi fell asleep and I helped Tzipora clean the dishes in the kitchen. David and Hinda scooped up their children and left, saying goodnight and that they would see us in the morning for cholent. Chaim left with them. He stayed with them, as their house was a little less crowded.

When everything was cleaned and Tzipora went to bed, I stayed with my father in the dining room.

"So, you like dancing?" my father asked.

"Yes," I said.

"Don't ever go to the dance club without one of your brothers," my father said. "You will be safe with them."

My father kissed me goodnight and went to his room. I was also tired, and went into my room. Tzipora was already asleep in the bed and I snuggled in beside her.

When I woke up, Tzipora was already gone. The bright light from the window and the smell of the cholent motivated me to get out of bed. I got dressed and walked over to the kitchen, where Tzipora was setting the dining table.

"Good morning," I said, as I skipped over to the stove and lifted the lid on the cholent. The thick sauce was bubbling and the steam rose up to my face. Suddenly I felt Tzipora lightly slap my hand, forcing me to drop the lid back down. I smiled at her and backed away from pot.

Soon, Hinda came over with the children, and shortly thereafter, the men returned from shul. Again, we all sat down at the table, and Tzipora filled our plates with cholent. I grabbed a piece of challah and dipped it into the cholent on my plate. The bread absorbed the sauce, becoming soft and spicy with the seasonings.

After the meal, I took Abi and Sarah into the forest behind our house. The forest had tall trees that caused the entire ground to be shaded. The ground was moist and covered in green vines and bushes with different-colored flowers. Sarah liked to pick the flowers, which she would take home and hang upside down until they dried. Abi was more interested in finding mushrooms, so I always had to watch him to make sure he didn't put any poisonous ones in his mouth.

A few Saturdays ago, I didn't watch him so closely, and Abi ate a poisonous mushroom. He seemed fine at first, but an hour later he became red with fever and started sweating profusely. As soon as I told David and Hinda what happened, David immediately hooked Moshe up to his wagon and rode with Abi to the doctor in Turka. The doctor, also a Jew who didn't work on Saturdays, was shocked to see David coming in the wagon, and immediately understood it was a life-or-death situation. He pumped Abi's stomach and gave him medicine, which he had to take for a week. That whole week Abi fought the fever, but by the next Saturday, he was good as new. Nobody scolded me for not taking good care of Abi, but I felt responsible. Not only did I endanger my poor nephew's life, but I also made David and the doctor break the Shabbos.

Now, I watched Abi carefully as we walked through the forest. I was singing a song I had learned in my choir practice, and thinking about Jan.

Like all Saturdays, the day went by quickly. We returned from the forest just before sundown. Sarah had a basket full of brightly colored flowers and had even more which I had braided in her hair. Abi had fallen asleep, and I was carrying him back home.

When we arrived at my house, I saw Jan's tractor parked out front. He was sitting on it, wearing a straw hat that seemed like it was almost floating at the crown of his head.

"Hi Rachel," he said as we approached.

"One minute," I silently signaled to him, as I went inside with the kids. David, Chaim, Hinda, Tzipora, and Father were all sitting at the table playing cards.

"How was your walk?" Father asked.

"Look what I found!" Sarah exclaimed, holding up her basket of flowers for all to see.

"It was nice," I said, putting Abi down on the couch. "I'm going out with Bina."

I am not sure why I lied, but it just came out. I had never gone out with a boy before and didn't want to have to start answering questions.

"Don't get into any trouble!" Chaim joked as I ran out the door.

Jan was still waiting patiently on his tractor.

"Hi," I said when I reached him.

"Hi Rachel," he repeated. "How was Shabbos?"

"Great as always," I smiled.

"So, what is there to do here in Butla?" Jan asked.

I laughed. "Nothing really. We could just walk around; there is a big forest behind our house, where it is nice to go."

"I brought a few things," Jan said. "We'll have a picnic there."

Jan jumped off the tractor and grabbed a bag that was sitting next to him. I led him towards the forest, careful not to pass any windows when we walked by my house. It was getting dark, so we stopped right before we entered into the woods.

Jan took a blanket out of his bag and laid it down for us. We both sat down and Jan continued to unpack his bag. He also took out a small lantern, which he lit. He then pulled out biscuits and fruits.

"You sure came prepared," I joked with him.

"I had a feeling there wouldn't be anything else to do here." He laughed as he handed me a deep purple plum.

"These plums are from my farm. I just picked them today," Jan said.

I took a bite of the soft, juicy plum. Delicious.

"So, you didn't tell me about you," I said, wiping my mouth. "Do you like being a farmer?"

Jan laughed. "I don't know, I never thought about it. I guess I would have liked to finish school."

"Maybe one day you will go back," I said.

Jan smiled at me. "Maybe."

"And you?" Jan continued. "You are going to Krakow and will become a famous actress?"

"That's the plan." I laughed.

"You won't forget about all the little people here?" he said.

"Not the important people," I joked.

"You are definitely too good for a place like this," Jan said. "I know you will make it."

Jan and I sat there for a few hours, talking and looking at the stars. He knew some astronomy and pointed out the Big Dipper, the North Star, and Cassiopeia. We lay on our backs and he told me the story of Queen Cassiopeia, who was considered the most beautiful queen in Greek mythology. She was stuck in the sky as punishment from Poseidon because she and her daughter were more beautiful than any sea nymphs. She was forced to spend half the night upside-down, further part of the punishment for her beauty.

When Jan was telling me the story, I couldn't help but think of how cruel Poseidon was for what he did to her. Because of pure hatred and jealously, he punished a poor girl who couldn't help the way she looked or the way she was born.

When Jan finished telling the story, he leaned over on his side and stared into my eyes. I held his gaze, smiling deeply at him. Then, he slowly leaned in and kissed me. It was my first kiss, and the thrill of it sent sparks through my body. After a second, Jan pulled his head back and smiled at me.

"Rachel, you are very beautiful," he said.

I blushed. "I think I should be getting home soon."

"I had a really nice time," Jan said. "Can we do this again?"

I nodded, still blushing. We got up, and packed up the food and blanket. Jan carried the lantern as we walked back towards my house. With his other hand, he gently grabbed my hand, interlocking his fingers with mine.

When we got back to my house, Jan kissed me on the cheek and tipped his hat to me.

"Goodnight," he said.

"Goodnight," I repeated, watching him get on his tractor. When he left, I turned around to walk into my house.

I had expected the house to be empty by now, as it was already late, but when I entered I saw David, Chaim, Hinda, and Tzipora all sitting quietly at the table. Their faces were lit up from the lanterns hung around the room, and I could feel the thickness in air.

"What's going on?" I asked.

"Rachel," Hinda said. She got up from the table and walked towards me. "It's your father. He wasn't feeling so well, so he went to lie down."

"Is he OK?" I asked, searching everyone's faces for an answer.

"I am sorry," Chaim said, looking at me. "He didn't wake up."

Hinda hugged me tight, not letting me go.

"I am so sorry, dear," Hinda said. "I know how close you were."

"He was very peaceful," David said. "He was very old, and had a full life."

"No," I shook my head.

"He was seventy-two," David said. "Most people here are lucky if they reach sixty."

"No, but he didn't seem old," I said, barely able to release the words.

"Don't worry, Dear," Hinda said, still holding me tight. "Everything is going to be all right."

1939—David

After my father's death, my younger sister Rachel came to live with my family. We closed Father's vegetable store—it was too much to manage with our farm—and our Aunt Tzipora left Butla to go live with one of her other brothers in a neighboring village.

Rachel took our father's death pretty hard, but with time, she slowly started to become herself again. She focused on school and her choir, and spent a lot of time with her friends. She was also a much-needed help at home with the kids. I was proud of my sister, who had matured beyond her years. Hinda had just given birth to a baby boy, whom we named Josef, after my father. Yossi, we called him, and he brought new joy into our house.

It was August—sweltering hot and muggy. Rachel had just finished high school, and was helping out at our farm while she was deciding what to do next. I knew she probably didn't want to stay in Butla, but I think she felt she couldn't leave us.

That day, I was going out to the forest to chop wood for our stove. When I got up, Hinda was sitting in a rocking chair with Yossi.

"Good morning," I said to her, kissing her forehead. I put my hand on Yossi's head. It was so tiny and soft. Hinda smiled up at me.

"Rachel made breakfast," she said. I could already smell the biscuits. I went into the kitchen, where Rachel was sitting at the table with Sarah and Abi. I kissed my children and Rachel, before grabbing a biscuit and heading out the door. I went to our shed to grab my axe, passing our horse Moshe and the cow on the way.

"How you doing, neighbor?" I heard when I was walking to the forest. It was Shmuel Nakhman, one of the other men who lived in Butla. We had grown up together.

"Hey Shmuel," I responded, swinging my axe over my shoulder. "How are the crops doing this year?"

"I'm telling you, this heat," Shmuel said, "is killing the tomatoes."

"I can imagine," I said. I would never have planted tomatoes during the summer. They obviously couldn't handle this heat, but I wouldn't say that to Shmuel.

Shmuel was also carrying an axe to the forest. In fact, a lot of the village people had taken up chopping wood. It turns out there was good money in it. The Ukrainians had started coming to Turka to shop, so we could take the wood there to sell it. The forest has designated spots where we could chop down the trees. We chopped near the edges of the forest and tried not to chop down all the trees in one place, so as not to diminish the forest. There were a few other men already there chopping when we arrived. The two of us settled in, helping cut the trunks of trees that had already fallen.

"Did anyone hear what happened with the Fuchs family?" one of them said. "Some Ukrainians came and stole their horse last night."

"Sons of bitches," Shmuel said. "Why don't they just stay in Ukraine?"

"Because they would starve!" another man said. "They need to come here to get food; those lazy people there can't do anything for themselves."

Suddenly we all heard screaming coming from the village. The screaming was getting louder as a man approached us. It was Isroel Rosenberg, another man from Butla. He was breathing hard and put his hands on his knees to catch his breath.

"Isroel?" I asked him. "What is going on?"

"The war! It started!" Isroel said, still panting.

"What war?" Shmuel asked. "What are you talking about?"

"The Germans," Isroel continued, his breathing becoming steadier. "They have attacked Poland."

I had heard about the tension in Germany from my brother Chaim who lived in Krakow. In Krakow, people were much more aware of what was going on outside of Poland. Here in Butla, we mostly were secluded from the outside world.

"Why would they do that?" another man asked.

"Hitler," I said. "He is trying to conquer all of Europe."

Everyone looked at me, eyes wide.

"David, what are you talking about?" Shmuel asked.

I had to excuse their ignorance; they didn't know any better. "Germany has already conquered Austria and Czechoslovakia," I said. "I guess we are next."

The next day we started hearing the bombing. Our family stayed at home, praying that no bombs would fall on Butla. Yossi cried at every boom, but we held him tight. After four days, the bombing stopped.

"I am going to check out the village," I said to Hinda, Rachel, and the children, who had stayed huddled together for the last few days. I opened our front door for the first time in four days. The sun was shining bright, the rays piercing me as though I hadn't seen the sun in years.

I started walking down the dirt road. It was silent. All the houses were still shuttered, yet none seemed damaged. I walked around the entire village. All of it was still intact. My farmland also looked untouched—but overgrown and in need of tending. I started thinking about how I would need my employees to work overtime now to make up for the loss of four days' work. On my way back to the house, Shmuel peeked out his door when I walked by.

"Hey!" he said as though trying to whisper and shout at the same time.

I waved to him to come out. He looked around both sides before slipping through the door and closing it behind him. He jogged over to me.

"How's your family holding up?" I asked. Shmuel had a wife and two teenage sons.

"We're all shaken up, but we're fine," he said. "What's going on?" Shmuel asked me as though I should know the answer.

"Well, I assume that was the Germans bombing Poland," I said. "But it seems they missed us."

"Do you think the bombing will continue?" Shmuel asked, again, looking to me to console him.

"I don't know." I rubbed the back of my neck. "We'll just have to see."

Shmuel turned around and went back to his house. I continued on my way, back to my family. When I opened the door, I seemed to startle everyone.

"What happened?" Hinda asked. She was rocking Yossi on her lap. "How is the village?"

"Everything looks fine," I responded. "We didn't seem to get hit at all."

"How can that be?" Hinda asked. "Why would the Germans bomb all of Poland and not us?"

"Maybe we just got lucky," Rachel said, optimistic as always.

"We'll see," I said. "For now, let's just carry on as normal, but we all need to be careful. If anyone notices anything unusual, tell me immediately."

The next day, I decided to go back to work. After five days of staying inside, I needed to check on my apple orchard and vegetable fields. I hooked the horse up to my wagon and headed towards my farmland. The village was eerily silent and I could see that my neighbors still hadn't been outside. Some of my land was on a hill. I rode up to the top of it to see if I could see anything in the neighboring villages.

Something a few miles away caught my eye. A great body of something, moving towards Butla. It was an army, walking on foot, with some hundreds of soldiers. My heart stopped. They are coming for us. My heart filled with fear.

I quickly turned around and ran back down towards my house. I left the horse and wagon outside, and I rushed into the house.

"Hinda, Rachel," I said, trying to appear calm. "Hide the children. Don't let anyone in the house; don't go near any windows. You understand?"

"What's going on?" Rachel asked. I could see the fear in her eyes.

"I am not sure yet, but we need to stay safe," I said. "I'll be back."

"What! Wait!" Hinda screamed, waking the baby. "Where are you going?"

"It's going to be all right," I responded, hoping that were true. "Don't worry."

I rushed out the door before I gave any more away. I started running towards the entrance of Butla, towards the main road, towards the approaching army. I wanted to see them up close, to get a better understanding of what was about to happen. When I got to the edge of Butla, I started running in the brush on the side of the road, trying to stay hidden. The weeds were almost as tall as I was, but I could easily glide through them, using my hands to make a path for me.

After a few minutes, I could hear the footsteps of the army—the rhythmic pattering on the dirt road, accented by the trot of horses. I slowed down my run and crouched lower in the weeds, hoping to get a glimpse.

Soon, I could see them. They were just meters from me, passing my hiding spot on the side of the road. They were marching in line in their khaki uniforms with long rifles leaning on their shoulders, sticking straight up in the air. My heart was pounding—not just from my run. I turned my head left and right, trying to gauge the size of the army. Suddenly, a red flag caught my eye. A general on a horse was carrying the flag, which fluttered rapidly in the wind, making it hard for me to see exactly what was on it. After a few moments, I noticed the sickle and hammer on the flag.

A Soviet flag! These weren't the Germans after all! It was the Russian army. A wave of relief spread over me, slowing my heart. Thank God, I thought. We were saved. I ran back to the village, to my house, where my family was sitting on the floor in terror.

"It's going to be all right!" I yelled as I entered the house. "You have nothing to worry to about! It is just the Russians."

"What do you mean, 'just' the Russians?" Hinda said. "Why are they here?"

"They must be protecting us from the Germans," I said.

Soon, we could hear the rhythm of the soldiers' footsteps from our house. They were here. I wasn't sure what we were supposed to do, but soon I heard a trumpet, beckoning everyone to come outside.

I told my family to stay put, and I left to find out what was going on. The army was standing completely still at the entrance to Butla, as the village people slowly started to trickle out to find out what the commotion was.

"Who are they?"

"What's going on?"

"They are Russian," I heard everybody whispering to each other as they gathered around.

A general on a horse came forward, looking for the mayor of Butla. The mayor was a stout man—a Christian and a farmer who had been mayor for almost twenty years. He stepped forward to greet the general, who dismounted his horse to speak with him. The two of them shook hands and spoke quietly to each other for a few minutes. When they finished, they shook hands again, and the general propped himself back up on the horse. He shouted something in Russian to the army, and the soldiers started to disperse.

The mayor turned towards us and spoke.

"They come in peace," he said. "And have asked for our hospitality."

The village people were all whispering back and forth between each other.

"Peace?"

"What do they want from us?"

"Why are they here?"

The mayor continued talking. "They are here to protect us and need places to stay. Each family will house two soldiers." He paused, as the whispering from the village people started to get louder.

"House them?"

"They are going to live with us?"

"In our homes?"

"Your cooperation is highly appreciated," the mayor continued. "Thank you."

That was it. The soldiers who would be staying in Butla had already started walking towards the houses in the village. The rest of the army would continue on to other villages in the area. I jogged over to the mayor.

"What's really going on?" I asked him.

"I said what is going on," he replied.

"What did the general say to you?" I asked him.

"That we don't have a choice," the mayor responded, before walking away.

I then jogged over to my house, where two Russian soldiers were about to barge in.

"Hey!" I yelled to them. They turned, seeing me approach. "Let me talk to my family first."

The soldiers seemed to understand Polish and waited outside as I told my family that we would have two guests staying with us in our small house. We only had two bedrooms, one for Hinda and me, and the other Rachel shared with the children. Everyone would move into Hinda's and my room, and we would give the second room to the soldiers.

Hinda stared in horror when I explained. She understood we had no choice, and silently started moving the children's things into our bedroom. Rachel convinced Abi and Sarah to help as well, telling them how much fun it would be for all of us to be together in the same room.

I opened the door, letting in the two soldiers. They were both tall men with broad shoulders. They seemed to ignore me and my family, going straight to the room I offered them and setting down their things.

That night, Hinda made chicken soup for dinner. She tried to kindly invite the soldiers to eat with us, but they were not interested. They gladly accepted the food and took it to their room to eat.

For the first few weeks, things went on uneventfully with the soldiers. We tried to stay out of their way, and they ours, but that was hard in the small living space we had. They ate our food with no thank-yous, and expected Hinda and Rachel to constantly clean up after them.

During the day the soldiers would go out to the field and practice different battle drills. They also stood guard around the village, watching anyone who came in or out. It could be worse, I told myself. We could get used to this. I continued farming and by Sukkot—the Jewish holiday for the fall harvest—had to hire extra employees to help harvest the crops on my land. I stored the crops in my barn, ready to sell them to the merchants who would visit me every harvest season. But, unfortunately, that would not happen this year.

As the harvest was finishing, a Russian general came to my barn, watching me organize the crops in different piles. He cleared his throat loudly as he entered.

"Mr. Shwartz," he said to me with a thick Russian accent. "We need your crops."

"Sure," I answered. "What would you like to buy?"

"No, no," he said. "I don't buy. We need them to feed the army. Winter is coming and we must feed the soldiers."

"My crops are for sale," I responded to him.

"I think you do not understand," the general said, putting his hand on his rifle. "These crops belong to the Soviet Union. The cows as well."

The general had noticed my cows who were grazing behind the barn.

"But what about my family?" I asked. "We need to eat."

"Oh, I am sure you will be fine," the general smiled, gripping his rifle. "You Jews are so very resourceful. If I see you in here again, you can say goodbye to your family."

When he left, the two soldiers who were staying in my house came to the barn. They would be in charge of rationing food for the army and quickly notified me of my trespassing. I left, but only after stuffing my pockets and jacket with as many vegetables as I could. I left the barn and walked towards the house.

BANG! I heard from behind the barn. Then I heard the moo of a cow and understood one of my cows had just became dinner for a group of barbaric soldiers. My family started foraging for food in the forest, but it was getting colder and harder to find food. Sarah and Abi cried as their stomachs growled, and didn't understand why we couldn't eat any of the crops from the farm.

In the spring, the general came back to our house. He banged on the door a few times before I answered.

"We have some recruits coming," he said. "We will need your house."

"We don't have any more space," I said.

"Exactly," the general responded. "That is why you must leave."

I was shocked by the response. "And go where?" I asked.

"Why would I care?" the general laughed. "You have money somewhere, don't you? You have twenty-four hours."

I decided to take my family to Turka. We had friends there, and I had heard things were better there with the Russian army. I found out that day that the Soviets had decided to expel all the Jews. And that we were not allowed to take anything with us when we left.

I knew I needed my horse. When we went to Turka, I would need to find work, and it would be almost impossible without Moshe. I decided to sneak Moshe—and two of the cows that the Russians had confiscated from me—to Turka in the middle of the night. Hinda fought me over this decision, sure that I would get caught and the Russians would kill me, but I had made up my mind. That night, after the two Russian soldiers had gone to sleep and it was pitch black outside, I snuck out to where my horse Moshe was. He flapped his tail at me as I untied him and brought him over to behind the barn where the cows were grazing. I tied up two cows behind Moshe. Then,

I hopped on the saddle and headed towards the forest. The shortest distance between Butla and Turka was ten kilometers on the road. I was taking a different route, through the forest, that was probably closer to twenty kilometers. It also didn't have a distinct path, so I would need to navigate the direction myself.

If it was dark in the village, it was even darker in the forest—so dark that I could barely see my hand if I held it in front of my face. Thankfully, I knew this forest very well, and felt confident about navigating in the dark. The forest was loud in the night, louder than one would expect. I could hear crickets and other insects crying, the wind bustling through the trees, and, every once in a while, a noise that sounded like there were other people in the forest. I prayed the whole time that I would make it to Turka unnoticed, before dawn, and be able to hide my horse and cows somewhere before heading back to my family.

Finally, after more than three hours, I made it. I could see the village through the edge of the trees. I quietly dismounted my horse and tied him up to a tree, just deep enough into the forest that he would be unnoticed. The cows were still attached behind him, mooing annoyedly at me for interrupting their evening. They instantly started grazing the grass under their feet, and I felt confident that I could leave them there for a bit until I figured out where to hide them.

I still needed to get back to Butla; hopefully, I could make it there before the morning. I decided to run back through the forest, where I felt I would be safer. It took me another two hours, but I made it back, reaching my house just as the sun was beginning to rise. I slipped into the house quietly, to ensure that I wouldn't wake the soldiers.

"David!" Hinda whispered when I entered our bedroom. She had been waiting up for me with Rachel. The two of them were sitting at the edge of the bed, holding hands and watching the children sleep.

"Everything is fine," I assured them. "Let's get some sleep before we have to move everything tomorrow."

Even after the difficult night I just had, I knew I wouldn't be able to sleep. I was too worried about someone finding the horse and cows hiding in the forest, and about how we would walk to Turka tomorrow with the three children.

A few hours later, it was time to go. Because the Russians wouldn't let us take anything, the only things we had to carry were the children. Sarah walked most of the way, and I carried Abi on my back. Hinda and Rachel took turns carrying Yossi, who slept most of the way. We walked on the main road, silently. There were other Jewish families walking as well, all empty handed. Some looked even hungrier than we were, thinner, barely able to walk. We were lucky. We were still healthy, even though we had barely eaten that winter. We took breaks every half hour, and I tried to find some fruits off the side of the road for the children to eat. They were tired, too tired to complain or cry.

After several hours we made it to Turka. I had a friend who lived there, Yaakov Weizer, so we went to his house and knocked on the door.

His wife answered, opening the door carefully to peek through.

"Is Yaakov there?" I asked, taking off my hat. "Tell him it is David Shwartz."

When she heard my name, she relaxed. A moment later Yaakov came. He swung open the door to see my family standing a few meters behind me, looking desperate and lost. Without hesitation, he invited us in. His wife made coffee for everyone, and handed a slice of bread to each of the children.

"I have to help my people," Yaakov smiled at me, shaking my hand. "You can stay in our barn out back. There is plenty of space."

So that's what we did. We took the children to the barn and laid out some blankets to sleep on. While Hinda and Rachel were organizing the space, I ran to the forest to find my horse and cows. Luckily, they were still there, still grazing. Moshe neighed and stomped his feet when he saw me. I am sure they were thirsty. I untied them, and led then to the barn, where they would stay with us. Now, we had a space to live and we had cows for milk. I wanted to find work so I could make some money to feed my family. I went to speak with Yaakov, to see if he had any ideas.

"You need a wagon," he told me. "There is a lot of work if you can haul things."

"What kinds of things?" I asked.

"All kinds," Yaakov said. "The Soviet army always needs help hauling supplies. Also, there are merchants from Ukraine and Hungary who come by often and usually will pay someone to carry their goods for them."

Yaakov helped me find a wagon that I purchased from a local farmer. I sold him milk from my cows, and he agreed to allow me to pay for the wagon from the wages I would earn from using it to work. Yaakov was right—there was a lot of work hauling in Turka. I would get up early every morning and go to the local market, where I would find Ukrainians who came to Poland because here they could buy everything much cheaper. They would pay me to haul their goods to Ukraine, which was just a few hours' ride over the mountains. The Ukrainians were cheap, though, and hated Jews. A few times, if a merchant found out I was Jewish, he would try not to pay me, or he would accuse me of stealing from him. It was hard making money hauling from the market. There were many days I spent the whole day out with the wagon, and still came home empty-handed. Other days, I came home with enough food to fill everyone's belly.

Things for us were better in Turka than they had been in Butla. Sarah and Abi even started going to a school the Russians had opened up, and Rachel and Hinda seemed to be making friends with other women in the village.

A few weeks later, I heard about a quarry that was being opened in Turka, and they were looking for workers. It was steady pay, so I went there to work. All the men working in the quarry were Jews. The pay was low, but it was one of the only places in the village that would employ Jews. Every day, we were in the quarry, extracting stones and other minerals from the ground. It was backbreaking work, and once we finished with the axe, we would load up our wagons and take the stones to a storage facility nearby.

I came home every night exhausted, but at least I could feed my family. One morning, on my way to the quarry, I heard a loud BOOM! I knew instantly, the village was being attacked. I turned around and rode the horse back to the barn. On the way, I saw that the village lumber mill was on fire, having been hit with a bomb. Everyone in the village was running, including Russian soldiers who all were making their way towards their base on one side of the village.

Our barn was safe and we huddled together inside, shielding the children, as we heard the bombs dropping outside all around us. After a few hours, Yaakov came into the barn.

"Are you all right?" he asked. He was carrying a bucket of water which he placed on the floor for us. Abi and Sarah immediately cupped their hands to drink.

"Yes, thank you," I answered. "How are you?"

"We're fine," Yaakov said. "David, may I speak with you?"

We went off to a corner of the barn, where we could speak privately.

"David," he started. "The Soviet army is mobilizing and marching to the Hungarian border. They are ready to fight the Germans."

Turka was just a few kilometers from the Hungarian border, and the Hungarians were allied with the Germans. This attack was probably a preliminary action before the ground invasion.

Yaakov continued speaking. "They are drafting men from Turka to fight with them. I just received notice that I must go."

"What about your family?" I asked.

"That is why I am here," Yaakov said, looking down at his hands. "I have no choice but to go with them. I need you to watch over them."

Yaakov had never held—let alone probably even seen—a gun in his life, and suddenly he was being forced to carry one and march alongside one of the world's greatest armies.

"Of course," I responded, feeling guiltily happy that I wasn't actually from Turka, and, therefore, wouldn't be drafted along with him. I hugged him, and he left.

The bombing stopped shortly thereafter, and the Soviet army was now ready for the invasion. The troops, including many of the eligible men from Turka, stood at the Hungarian border, ready for the attack. In the village, we were fine. There was a little damage in the village, but we heard that the bombs were dropped strategically on specific targets and were not meant to destroy our small village. The quarry had been closed since the attack, as there were now very few men who could work there. I spent my time foraging for food that I could bring back to my family and to Yaakov's.

Eight days after the attack, the Soviet army marched back into Turka. The army seemed unscathed, and came back with just as many men as it had left with. Yaakov soon arrived back home. It was a Friday.

"What happened?" I asked when he came into the barn.

"Nothing," he responded. "We waited . . . and waited . . . and nothing."

"So, what now?" I asked him.

"The army is leaving," Yaakov said.

I immediately understood this was not good news. "Where are they going?" I asked.

"Back to the Soviet Union," Yaakov responded. "I don't know what happened. They are retreating. Some of the men from Turka are taking their families with the army back to the Soviet Union. We'll be safe with them."

"Safe with them?" I almost laughed. "The Russians have taken nearly everything from me. They treat us like dirt."

"Yes, but they have kept us alive," Yaakov said. "My family is going with them. If you stay behind, you can stay in our house. Take what you need."

I would not flee with the Russians. Yes, they had kept us alive, but only because they could take more from us alive than dead. Those scoundrels. I didn't trust them, and I worried for Yaakov's family leaving with them.

Yaakov said goodbye and he left. When he marched his family off with the Russians, they were carrying only one small bag for the whole family, as if they were going off for a picnic, rather than fleeing their home.

The Russians left behind two soldiers who were charged with keeping order in the village. Of course, they did nothing but drink all day, and steal from the village people. We had a quiet Shabbos that weekend, unsure of what would become of Turka. The quarry had not reopened and I was still out of work.

That Monday, we started hearing the gunfire. BANG! BANG! I heard coming from the center of the village. I was in the forest gathering food. I was surprised at first, because we hadn't heard an army coming, and it would have been difficult for an army to make it to Turka without anyone noticing. I snuck out of the forest, towards the center of the village to get a glimpse of what was happening.

It wasn't an army. Maybe worse. It was a gang of Ukrainians. Ukrainians are the most barbaric people. A group of about fifty of them were staggering around the village, carrying bottles of vodka in one hand and guns in the other. They were screaming and shooting the guns up in the air.

Soon, the two remaining Russian soldiers confronted them. At this point, many of the remaining village people were watching the scene, all hiding behind trees and buildings, but still trying to get a glimpse of what was happening.

"Put down your weapons!" one of the Russian soldiers screamed.

The Ukrainians laughed, mostly ignoring the Russian soldiers.

"Where are the Jews in this village?" one of the Ukrainians said. "We come in peace. We're just looking for Jews."

One of the Russian soldiers cocked his weapon. "I said, lower your guns!"

BANG! Suddenly the Russian soldier who had spoken crumpled to the floor, a pool of blood seeping out of him. The other soldier immediately turned around and ran, as the Ukrainians shot at him, too, but missed. He soon disappeared, leaving the Ukrainians as the new conquerors of Turka.

"Now, where were we?" One of the Ukrainians yelled. "We need all the Jews in the village center in the next hour. Any Jew who does not appear will end up like this soldier!"

The Ukrainians dispersed through the village banging on doors, rounding up the Jews. I ran back to Yaakov's house, to the barn, where my family was still staying.

"Hide the children!" I screamed. Hinda, Rachel, and I buried the children under hay in the barn. Then the three of us left to the village center. I knew we had to go, to save ourselves and not draw any suspicion to our house or barn.

We arrived at the village center and saw most of the Jews already gathered around. Many had swollen eyes, or fresh wounds with blood dripping out. The dead Russian soldier was still lying on the ground surrounded by blood.

"Attention!" a Ukrainian shouted. "You must take this scum and bury him in your cemetery." The Ukrainian kicked the dead soldier.

"Hurry up! Let's go," he screamed. "All of you!"

No one moved, unsure of what we should do. BANG! The Ukrainian shot his gun in the air.

"Move it now or you will have more corpses to carry!" he screamed.

A few young men hesitantly moved forward to pick up the dead soldier. Hinda gasped beside me and I grabbed her hand. Rachel stood emotionless, watching it all.

Three men picked up the Russian soldier and started carrying him towards the Jewish cemetery. The Ukrainians forced everyone to follow, as though we were holding a parade. We followed the procession, and I was careful to keep us in the middle so we would not be singled out or noticed by the Ukrainians.

When we arrived at the cemetery, the three men put the soldier down and started to dig a hole for him. The Ukrainians laughed and continued to shout at us.

"Sing!" one of the Ukrainians shouted. The others nodded in agreement and started repeating his command.

"Sing something!" "Sing one of your holiday songs!" "Sing like you do on the Sabbath!" the Ukrainians laughed.

I squeezed Hinda's hand. I could see a tear starting to well up in her eyes, but she stood strong. Rachel had a look of anger and defiance on her face. I motioned to Hinda to look at her. When Hinda noticed her stance, she put her arm around Rachel's shoulders and gently kissed her forehead. Rachel's expression softened slightly.

The crowd stood silent for several moments, unsure how to respond to the Ukrainians' commands. One of the Ukrainians then suddenly smacked one of the men in the crowd with the butt of his gun. He hit the man right in the face. The man screamed out in pain, unprepared to take the blow. He crumbled to his knees and covered his face with his hands. Blood started to seep through his fingers.

"SING!" the Ukrainian screamed again.

Shalom Aleichem malachai hasharet, malachai elyon . . .[6]

One man in the crowd started singing, and soon others joined in. The Shabbos song praises God and the angels for bringing peace to the world. The irony was not lost on anyone, but we sang loudly all the same, hoping God would hear our prayer. I couldn't stop staring at the man who was hit. He continued to kneel, but he also joined in the song.

The Ukrainians kept laughing, happy with our enthusiasm for singing. Soon the men finished digging the grave. Then they started to move towards the dead soldier to lower him into the grave.

"STOP!" one of the Ukrainians screamed. The others looked to him, excited to hear about his new idea. The man cleared his throat proudly. "Kiss the soldier."

The other Ukrainians started nodding in agreement, as if to say "Great idea!" The grave diggers' faces turned white under the dirt that covered them.

"Everyone!" another Ukrainian screamed. "Line up to kiss your Russian friend goodbye!"

---

[6] A traditional Jewish song usually sung on Friday evenings. It means "Peace unto you, ministerial angels, messengers of [the] Highest, from the King, king(s) of the kings — the Holy, blessed be He.

Again, the crowd hesitated. The Ukrainians were getting impatient and one cocked his weapon and pointed it at one of the grave diggers.

"You first," the Ukrainian said, smiling.

The grave digger was a young boy, probably only eighteen. He was tall and muscular, and breathing heavily. I didn't recognize him, but I felt like I knew him at that moment. The boy lowered his head and walked over to the dead soldier lying on the dirt. He bent down, closed his eyes, and lightly kissed him on the cheek.

The Ukrainians roared with laughter. Then they started herding the rest of us in line to kiss the soldier. Hinda was crying silently, tears streaming down her face. I was afraid they would notice her tears and someone would punish her for it. I leaned over to her and kissed her on the forehead.

"You are strong," I whispered to her.

One by one everyone knelt down and kissed the soldier. I watched a young woman cry as she knelt down to kiss him. Then she threw up before she could even stand. As our turn approached, I could smell the corpse. It smelled of sweat and rotting meat mixed with perfume. The smell got stronger and stronger, and finally it was my turn. I approached the body and held my breath as I knelt down and quickly touched my lips to his cheek. I stood and moved away as quickly as I could, staring at Hinda and Rachel who were next in line. Both of them were white with fear.

Hinda came and closed her eyes. She knelt down and kissed him, and then ran over to me. I held her in my arms as she buried her face in my shoulder for a second before pushing me away as she knelt down and vomited. Her vomit was clear and yellow, as there was nothing in her stomach to throw up.

I patted her back and watched Rachel, my beautiful little sister, approach. I could see her lips moving as she approached the body and kissed the soldier. She then came over to us, and also held onto Hinda, whose violent stomach pangs did not seem to abate.

When everyone had kissed the soldier, the grave diggers slowly lowered the corpse into the grave and buried it. The crowd was silent, save for the sound of vomiting throughout the crowd.

The Ukrainians were happy with the spectacle. They told us we were free to go; however, they needed all the men to report to the village center the next morning. They were reopening the quarry and wanted to build new houses for themselves in Turka. All Jews would be forced to work for the Ukrainians.

The three of us ran back to the barn to the children. It had been several hours since we left them, and the three of them were still lying motionless under the hay. Even Yossi, less than two years old, seemed to understand that he needed to be silent. We hugged them all, and told them how proud we were of them.

"Mother," Sarah said to Hinda, noticing her white face and red swollen eyes. "What happened?"

Hinda held Sarah tight.

"Everything is fine, Darling," she told her.

The next day, I reported to the village center for work. Hinda and Rachel would stay inside with the children. I told them not to leave, as I didn't trust the Ukrainians wandering around the village. I was sent to work in the quarry. The Ukrainians didn't give us any pay or food for working, and we were forced to work long days without breaks.

The Ukrainians were enjoying their power, but it didn't last long. Two days later, the German border police showed up.

1941—Hinda

Yit'gadal v'yit'kadash sh'mei raba. Amen.
We were at the cemetery again, for the daily burial.
Saying the mourner's Kaddish was becoming routine,
and I almost felt like it was starting to lose its
meaning.

b'al'ma di v'ra khir'utei v'yam'likh mal'khutei
b'chayeikhon uv'yomeikhon uv'chayei d'khol beit
yis'ra'eil ba'agala uviz'man kariv v'im'ru: amen.

It was already hot and sticky outside. We
finished the prayer, and the crowd started to disperse.
Every morning, the Jewish community in Turka
gathered at the cemetery to bury those who had died
over the last twenty-four hours. Today was a good
day, there were only ten bodies to be buried.
Yesterday, there were seventeen. The cause of death
was almost exclusively hunger—sometimes overwork,
but that was mostly just another cause of starvation.

I stared at the new grave—the fresh dirt that
covered the bodies—and pushed my way through the
leaving crowd in order to approach the grave. I bent
down, picked up a small stone, and placed it on the
dirt. After a minute, I turned around and followed the
crowd.

The funerals were all early in the morning, as all
the men and women had to go to work after. That

morning, David skipped the funeral. He didn't have the strength, especially before having to work a long day in the quarry afterwards. I couldn't skip it. I had to go. If I didn't, who would come when it was my turn to be buried? Or Sarah's? Or Abi's? Or Yossi's? I pushed that thought out of my head.

I also had to work. I did laundry for the Germans. Every day I washed their dirty uniforms and bed sheets. The uniforms were often crusted with blood and dirt and scrubbing them clean made my knuckles raw and swollen. But I was lucky to work. Working means I received 180 grams of bread every day. That was 180 grams more than those who were buried this morning.

I arrived at the laundry and quickly took my place at a wash basin. One of the other women, Esther, had already collected the laundry from the Germans' living quarters and was handing it out to all the launderers. She threw a bag at me. As I opened it, a rancid smell started to seep out. The other women nearby also seemed startled by the smell coming from my bag, and all started to stare at me.

I pulled the laundry out of the bag. A uniform of a young man. He must have soiled himself. The smell got stronger as I laid out the uniform and started to wash it piece by piece. Scrubbing. Scrubbing. The smell stayed strong as I used my nails to try to scrape away the stains.

The day went by slowly. I finished my cleaning and left my day's work of laundry hanging up to dry. The next morning, I would press the uniforms and sheets and they would be returned to the Germans' houses, good as new. It was already getting dark, and I was ready to go home, but we hadn't yet received our bread.

I waited there, with the other women. We all sat silently, just wanting to go home. After waiting another hour, Yosl, the head of the Turka Judenrat,[7] showed up carrying a basket of bread.

"Sorry, ladies, for the delay!" he said enthusiastically. "It was a busy day today as you can imagine. Please stay at your stations and I will bring you your rations."

I knew Yosl when he was a boy. We went to school together. He was never the brightest kid, nor did he have many friends. How things have changed for him. As the head of the Judenrat, he was the most powerful Jew in Turka. He decided who worked, who got which job, who received bread every day. He was in daily contact with the German leaders in Turka, and had the power to determine any Jew's fate. He loved every minute of it as well, I am sure. He ate and fed his family with the bread he withheld from others. He also never came to the morning burials, saying that they interfered with his morning meetings with the Germans. I bet he was too ashamed to show his face. He was a murderer, just as the Germans were, but he still pretended he was one of us.

I watched him carry his bread basket as he went station to station and checked that the laundry hung up at each station was clean. If the laundry passed his

---

[7]Judenrat were Jewish councils established in order to enforce the Nazi's orders.

inspection, he handed the woman a slice of bread. One station before mine, he stopped during his inspection.

"Do you expect to return this uniform to a soldier?" he asked the woman. Her name was Chava.

Chava looked at him fearfully. Silent.

"Answer!" Yosl screamed.

"Yes, yes sir, it is clean," she stuttered.

"Clean?" Yosl screamed. "If I allow this to go back to the soldier it belongs to, they will kill me! Do you understand?"

Chava started to cry.

"And you as well," Yosl continued. "I am protecting you. You need to reclean this. Tonight."

"Please!" Chava screamed. "I will clean it again right now, but please, can I have my slice of bread?"

"The bread is for those who work effectively," Yosl said, his eyes gleaming with power. "Maybe tomorrow."

Chava held her head down sobbing. Yosl moved on, unaffected by her. He now approached my station.

"Hi, Hinda." He smiled at me. "How are you doing?"

"Hi, Yosl." I forced my face to smile at that wretched piece of dirt. "I am wonderful, thank you for asking. How is Ita?" I asked about his wife.

"She is great; I will send her your regards," he said. "Here." He handed me my slice of bread, without even inspecting my laundry.

"Thank you," I said to him, as I took it. I wrapped the bread in my handkerchief and put it in my pocket. "Have a nice evening."

When he moved onto the next station, I looked down at the floor. I could hear Chava still sobbing. My instincts told me to go to her, to hug her, but I knew that wouldn't be smart. When Yosl finished handing out his rations, he left and all the women got up to leave. Chava also stood up, to reclean the uniform. I walked over to her, and pulled my handkerchief out of my pocket. I unwrapped it, and broke the slice of bread in half.

"Take it," I said, handing half to her. Chava had five young children. Her husband had already passed away—a plank of wood fell on him while he was working to build the German headquarters in Turka. I felt greedy that I could only give her half my slice, but I had to think about my children.

She hesitated as she took the bread from me. "Thank you," she whimpered, and shoved the bread in her pocket, as though she were worried I would change my mind.

I knew David would be upset when he saw I returned with just half a slice, but what could I do? She needed it more than I did. She was one person, providing for five children. Our family was lucky—we had three providers.

I left the laundry and started walking home. It was already dark when I arrived and David was there with the children. David stood up and kissed my forehead when I arrived. We were still living in the barn. The house had become property of the Germans, and they let us stay in the barn in peace. The three children were sitting on the ground. All three of them with swollen bellies and sunken faces. I was relieved to see them all still breathing. Every day, it was a relief to come home.

I knelt down to hug and kiss all three of them. They were all tired, I could see, drained of energy and hungry, but they never complained. Sarah was already nine, but she was so much more mature.

"How was the day?" I asked Sarah, who took care of her little brothers.

"Fine," she answered, like a teenager. "I read to them."

Sarah had one book. She would read the same book to her brothers every day. They listened quietly, as though the story might change one day. The children stayed inside the barn all day. They knew they needed to stay quiet and to not leave for any reason.

A few minutes later, Rachel arrived. Rachel was working in the field, harvesting crops. She was young and strong, and able to spend the long days bent over in the sun. It also meant that she sometimes had the opportunity to steal a few fruits or vegetables to bring home.

Rachel knelt down and kissed the children. Then she sat down next to me.

"I have a surprise for everyone today," she smiled mischievously. She then dug her hands into her pockets and pulled out three peaches.

Abi gasped and immediately began to giggle. Sarah also smiled and her mouth started to water.

"Rachel!" David screamed. "Three? You have to be more careful! What if someone saw that you had something in your pocket?"

"No one saw!" Rachel said. "I am very sneaky."
She winked at the children, handing a peach to Sarah
and Abi. The third, she cut into small pieces, handing
them to Yossi one at a time. I couldn't help but smile,
watching as he sucked the juice out of the pieces
before chewing them.

I was proud of Rachel. She was so strong. I don't
know how our family would have survived without
her. After the children ate their peaches, we split the
bread that each of us had received from work. I was
ashamed to only have brought home half a slice, but
David wasn't angry. In fact, he said he was proud of
my humanity, and that I did the right thing. The bread
was black and stale, and I ripped it into small pieces
before putting each in my mouth one by one, savoring
each bite. Our family sat together, feasting on our
small dinner, happy to have finished another day, still
together, still alive.

The next morning when I awoke, Rachel was
already gone. Work in the field started early, so she
was always the first to rise. I got up silently, and began
my morning routine. First, I checked the children.
Everyone was still breathing and sleeping silently.
Then I went outside to the outhouse to relieve myself
and on the way back I stopped by the well to bring
some water for the children. Then, I left and headed
for the cemetery, for the morning burial.

Today there were nineteen bodies to be buried.
Six of them were children under the age of five. I
stood there in the crowd watching the bodies being
lowered into the pit. There was no crying—not even
from the families of the dead. There was no strength

to cry, just disbelief. After the mourners' Kaddish, the crowd started to disperse, but then Yosl ran to the grave and loudly cleared his throat. Everyone stopped, watching him as he stood waiting to get everyone's attention.

When he felt satisfied with the number of eyes on him, he spoke:

"Good morning, everyone," he said loudly, scanning the crowd to see who was there. "Today there is a special decree from the Germans. Everyone is to turn over all their gold, silver, bronze, diamonds, or jewels to the German headquarters today."

He paused to look around. "Tonight, the Germans will be doing a house check to ensure that you have followed these directions. Anyone caught with any valuables will be severely punished. Thank you for listening, and I'll see you at the headquarters!"

People in the crowd started whispering to each other. "Severely punished?" I heard a woman scoff. "What is a worse punishment than what they are doing to us now?"

"Who still has any gold?" I heard someone else say. "I traded all my valuables for bread already."

I headed back to the barn instead of going straight to work. I still had my gold wedding ring, and a bronze samovar that my mother had left me. I would take these to the headquarters on my way to work. I felt lucky that I had held on to these valuables. Surely, any family who didn't turn in any valuables would be suspected of hiding things from the Germans.

"Mother!" Sarah screamed when I arrived at the barn. The children were surprised to see me. They normally didn't see me until I returned late at night. Abi was sitting quietly on the floor, playing with the dirt, while Sarah was holding Yossi on her lap, playing peek-a-boo.

"Good morning, children," I said to them, hugging and kissing all three. "Mother missed you and wanted to come say hello before work."

I sat with them for a moment, and then went to the corner of the barn, where we had buried our valuables. I dug and found the samovar and the small box with my wedding ring. I opened the box and the ring was still shining. It was a plain gold band, beautiful and classic. I tried to put it on my left ring finger, but my knuckle was so swollen it wouldn't fit. It's just a ring, I thought, as I put it back in the box and stood up. Sarah was watching me.

"Mother, what are you doing?" she asked me.

"Just taking a couple things," I smiled. "I want to give them a cleaning."

I left the barn, carrying my valuables to the German headquarters. The samovar was rusting, but still I could see that it was beautiful. It belonged to my grandmother, and then to my mother. When I was little, my grandmother would use it to heat water for tea. It was one of her proudest possessions. When my mother was alive, she kept the samovar next to her fireplace. She rarely used it, but as a child, I had been taken by its beauty. I always imagined I would keep it next to my own fireplace one day and, whenever we had guests, I would tell them about how my grandmother made tea.

There was already a line at the German headquarters. Jews were there carrying their valuables and waiting to turn them over. I got in line behind a couple who were carrying jewelry and a gold figurine. I waited patiently as each person handed over their valuables to Yosl, who was recording what each person brought. He smiled at me when I got to the front of the line.

"Hi, Yosl," I said to him, placing down my samovar and wedding band.

"What a beautiful samovar!" he exclaimed. "Where did you get this?"

"It was my grandmother's," I said to him.

"A beautiful family heirloom," he said, as he picked it up and took it behind the counter where he was standing. He then inspected my wedding band and took that, too. Then he grabbed his pen and wrote down in his book: Shwartz family: Samovar, wedding band.

"Thank you, Hinda," he said. "You should probably hurry to work. You are very late."

"Thanks," I said and turned around. I started to run to the laundry, not wanting to lose my bread for the evening because of this. I got there and started my daily cleaning. I worked hard and fast, and Yosl gave me my bread that evening. He also gave Chava a slice that night. She tried to give half her slice to me, but I wouldn't let her.

That evening, we had our three slices of bread to feed the family. David, Rachel, and I all split our slices with one of the children and ate slowly, savoring each crumb.

Suddenly we heard barking from outside. Loud barking. The sound of bloodthirsty dogs. Yossi starting crying and dropped his piece of bread to the ground.

"What's going on?" Rachel asked. She got up and went to look through the barn window. I picked up Yossi and rocked him on my lap.

"What do you see?" I asked her.

"The Germans brought their bloodhounds to the Weizer's house," she said. "I can't really make out what is happening."

Suddenly there was a loud scream of a woman. The barking got louder and more vicious and the screaming continued.

David ran to the window next to Rachel. "Get down," he yelled.

"Hinda, did you give the samovar to the Germans?" he asked.

"Yes, and my wedding ring," I responded.

"Good," he said. "Itzik said they weren't going to hand over their valuables."

Itzik Weizer worked with David in the quarry. He had a wife and a baby girl. They had been known as a wealthy family, and it must have been suspicious that they didn't bring anything at all to the headquarters.

After ten minutes of the screaming and barking, the Germans left their house and started coming towards our barn. Soon, there was a knock on the door. David answered it, opening it to a group of about ten German soldiers. In the back was one soldier holding leashes of three bloodhounds. The dogs were drooling and foaming at the mouth.

"David Shwartz?" one of the soldiers said.

"Yes," David answered, sounding strong.

"Today, your family turned in a wedding band and a samovar," the soldier said. "Is that correct?"

"Yes, sir," David responded.

"You have nothing else?" the soldier asked, looking in through the door to the barn.

I was watching from the floor, holding Yossi tightly. Rachel was now sitting next to me, her arms around Sarah and Abi.

"Sir, we live in a barn," David responded. "If we had anything of value, we would have traded it for a decent place to live."

The soldier looked at David, up and down, deciding what to do.

"Very well, then," he said. "Have a good night."

The Germans left without another word and went on to the next house. Throughout the night, we heard screaming and the bloodhounds barking. The children barely slept. I could see that Sarah was starting to understand what was going on, and she had fear in her eyes. Abi and Yossi both were scared, but from the noises—this was a simpler fear to hold.

When morning came, I got up to go to the cemetery, Itzik's wife was there, her face bruised and scratched. She carried her baby and stayed close to the grave, as the body of her husband was lowered down. I watched her during the mourner's Kaddish. Her lips were pursed in anger, and she was silent.

When the Kaddish was over, ten German soldiers rode up on horseback to the cemetery.

"Last night, during our search we found this in someone's home," one of the soldiers yelled in German. Yosl ran up to the German guard and translated into Polish. The soldier held up a big picture of Joseph Stalin, the leader of the Soviet Union.

"This is an inexcusable offense!" the soldier continued. "And for this, everyone here will pay."

The German soldiers started to surround the group of Jews in the cemetery. There were about 300 of us, and we were being pushed and shoved closer together. The Germans started to beat the people around the edge of the crowd, hitting them with their guns or fists. I was in the middle of the crowd, and started to pray.

"Please, God, let me get home safe today," I prayed aloud. There were screams all around me, as people started falling to the ground. The Germans were making their way through the crowd, beating everyone they could reach. They were getting closer to me, and closer, and then suddenly, they stopped.

The leader of the German unit showed up on his horse. He screamed something in German and the soldiers quickly backed away from the crowd, and the group of them headed back to their headquarters. There was chaos in the cemetery. Jews were running. Wounded people were screaming, family members were crying. I pushed my way out of the crowd and ran back to the barn.

When I arrived, David was just leaving. He saw me running, and immediately came towards me.

"What's wrong?" he said, grabbing me and holding me in his arms. I cried into his shoulder, still in shock from the morning.

"I want to get out of here," I cried to him. "We can't stay here." I started thinking about Palestina, how I had dreamed of going there when I was young. I was a member of the local Zionist organization. We used to meet to help families who wanted to make Aliyah. We had weekly Hebrew lessons and other classes to prepare families for the journey. Before I married David, I had always thought that I would end up going to Palestina. But then, life happened. David's business was doing well, we had children, and the dream started to seem farther and farther away. Why didn't we go when we had the chance?

David held me tight. "Ok," he said. "I will take care of it. Try to go to work like normal; I will figure it out."

David kissed me, and went towards the quarry. I took a few deep breaths and headed to work myself. That evening, David didn't come home. Rachel and I shared our bread with the children and put them to bed. David still wasn't back. Where could he be? Would we be burying him tomorrow? My heart was racing, thinking of what could have happened. What could he have done?

After several hours, David came in through the barn door. He slipped in quietly, but both Rachel and I were startled and woke up. He came in and lay down on the ground next to me.

"Where were you?" I whispered to him, wrapping my arms around him and kissing him.

"I was with Yosl," he said. "We're going back to Butla tomorrow. I got us a permit to leave Turka."

"But how?" I asked.

"Yosl is easy to persuade," David responded.

I don't know how David could have persuaded him. With what could he have bribed him? But whatever he did, it worked. Better not to know, I thought. I drifted off to sleep, grateful that we would be going back to our old home tomorrow.

The next morning, we all got up early. While many of the village Jews headed towards the cemetery, we piled into our wagon. David hitched the horse and we drove off to Butla. I felt such relief as we got farther from Turka.

We arrived in Butla after an hour. David parked in front of our old house, which looked empty and dilapidated. The wooden walls were cracked as though they had lost the battle to termites and rain. The grass around the house was overgrown and wild. This was our home. We got out of the wagon and slowly made our way inside the house. The house still had our furniture inside, although it was completely covered in dust. The house had been left a mess, and there were rats scurrying around the kitchen.

Sarah screamed in disgust when one ran across the room right in front of her.

"We will clean," Rachel said. "It will be just like it was before!"

Sarah took her brothers to the back of the house to play in the forest, while the three of us dusted, washed and scraped the floors. After several hours of cleaning, there was a knock at the door.

David got up, and went to open it. It was the village sheriff, Tomasz Wozniak. We knew him from before we had left Butla.

"David?" Tomasz said in surprise when David opened the door. "What are you doing here?"

"Tomasz!" David responded. "We decided to come back."

"That is great news," Tomasz said, shaking David's hand. "But I am sorry to tell you, you can't stay here."

"But this is our house," David said.

"It was your house," Tomasz responded. "But you left. It was the Russians' house. And when the Russians left, the Germans ordered that everything that belonged to the Russians be kept for them."

"Are there Germans staying in Butla?" David asked.

"No," Tomasz responded. "But the German Commanders from Turka come every once and a while to check in. So, we need to follow their instructions."

"Is there any way you can figure out how we can stay here?" David asked. He then reached into his pocket and pulled out money.

Tomasz took the money and put it in his pocket. "I will see what I can do," he said. "Have a good day." He left, leaving us to continue cleaning the house.

"Where did that money come from?" I asked David.

"I had an emergency stash," he responded. "How do you think I got us permission to leave Turka?"

We continued cleaning the rest of the day. I was exhausted, but the house was finally in a state that we could live in. The children came home from the forest carrying some berries and mushrooms that they had picked. We ate their findings and quickly all fell asleep in our old home.

We stayed in Butla as the summer turned into fall. Here, there was no place to work, which meant there were no rations of food, but instead we had a forest full of things we could gather. We mostly ate a type of bread that I would make from nettles and bran wheat we found. The bread was dense and dry, but it was better than the bread we had in Turka. Fall turned into winter, and I thanked God every day that we had left Turka. Winter made it harder for us to find food, as the forest was covered in dense snow. We were cold and hungry, but there were no Germans here.

One morning in January, I went out to gather snow to melt for water, as I did every morning. Many of the women were out doing the same thing at that time, and this was always a good time to speak with others and find out if anyone had heard anything from friends in neighboring villages. I saw Hannah, Shmuel's wife, and waved to her. She waved back, so I went over to her.

"You must be so happy you left Turka," she said as I approached.

"Yes, of course; we feel so much safer here," I responded.

"You are really lucky you got out," she continued.

I smiled at her, not sure what she was trying to say. When she realized I didn't understand, she continued. "You heard what happened?" she asked in a hushed voice.

I shook my head. Hannah looked around to see if there was anyone nearby, before motioning me to get closer. I crouched down next to her, interested in what she had to say.

"A few days ago, the Germans, along with some Ukrainians they ganged up with, captured and imprisoned eight hundred Jews," Hannah said. "They told family members that they could pay a ransom for their freedom, but of course, who can afford to bribe anyone today?"

"What happened?" I asked, holding my breath.

"Yesterday, they piled the Jews in trains, and took them somewhere outside of the village, and they shot all of them," Hannah said.

"What?" I responded in disbelief. "Where did they take them?"

"Somewhere near the forest," Hannah said. "They dug a mass grave and forced the Jews to sing as they shot them, one-by-one."

"How do you know that?" I asked.

"You remember Zelda? The wife of the butcher in Turka?" Hannah said. "She was there. She pretended to be dead and stayed in the grave until nightfall. Then she came here. She knocked on our door in the middle of the night, covered in blood. Her husband is in that grave."

"Where is she now?" I asked.

"She is still in our home," Hannah said. "She is delirious and has a high fever. I don't know if she will make it."

My thoughts immediately went to our friends in Turka. Esther. Chava and her five children. Eight hundred Jews. Before the war, there were about four thousand Jews who lived in Turka. With the number of those dying per day, and now this, that number seemed to be slowly disappearing. How could anybody do this?

I finished filling my bucket with snow, and quickly stood up to run home. I had to tell David what I had just heard. When I entered our house, David was crouching next to the fireplace, adding wood to keep it going. He stood when he saw my face as I entered.

"What happened?" he said, coming towards me.

"They are killing Jews in Turka," I blurted out, almost not believing my own words. I immediately started to cry. "How could they do this?"

David hugged me close. "We're OK," he said, stroking my hair. "Don't tell Rachel or the children; they don't need to know."

"But what if they come here?" I asked.

"We'll figure it out," David responded. "I will always take care of us."

We continued living quietly in Butla. I felt constant fear that the Germans would someday march right into Butla and murder us just as they did our friends in Turka. I had nightmares, and I stopped sleeping through nights. But we continued on. Winter turned into spring, meaning the snow was melting and it became easier to forage for food in the forest. The children had fun finding berries and other things to eat. It became a daily game to see what they could find.

Soon it was summer, and rumors about the murdering of Jews started to run rampant in Butla. Everyday there was news of murders happening all around us. Some said there were no more Jews in Western Poland. Some people talked about ghettos, or camps where Jews were being concentrated. But they were all just rumors. And like all rumors, I didn't know what to believe. Some things sounded so horrible, there was no way they could be true.

One morning in August, Yosl, the head of the Judenrat in Turka, showed up in Butla. His council members rode around the village knocking on every door asking everyone to gather in the village center. David, Rachel, and I told the children to stay quiet at home, and we left, to see what the announcement was.

Shmuel and Hannah were there and waved at us when we arrived. We stood next to them, as the crowd started to get bigger and bigger.

"Have you heard anything?" I whispered to Hannah. She shook her head. We both looked around at the Jews in our village. Everyone looked the same. Thin, dirty, tired, tattered clothing. We were no longer citizens of Butla—we were the village's Jews.

After several minutes, Yosl began his announcement.

"Thank you for coming!" he yelled to the crowd. "Everyone is to report to Turka on Sunday. You can

71

bring up to twenty-five kilos of luggage. If you bring any more, it will be confiscated."

The crowd started screaming questions. "What are we reporting for?" "Why do we need luggage?" "Are we going somewhere?"

But Yosl ignored the questions, and left as briskly as he arrived. The crowd continued talking loudly amongst themselves. I turned to David, trying to understand something from his gaze.

"Let's go home," he said.

We walked home silently, but my mind was racing. It was Friday, meaning we had two days to figure out what to do. Should we go to Turka and do as we were told? Should we stay in Butla? Did we have another option?

Saturday morning, David set off to a village near the Hungarian border. He had friends there. When he used to farm, many of his workers came from there, and they respected him. They were mostly Ukrainians, and not Jewish. He wanted to see what was happening in that village and told us to stay put until he returned.

But I couldn't. The minute he left, I grabbed Rachel.

"We have to leave," I told her.

"No," she responded. "David said to wait for him."

"We can't just wait," I said. "They are coming for us. We need to leave. He will find us."

"Where do you want to go?" Rachel asked, crossing her arms in front of her chest. Sometimes I was so shocked by Rachel. She was 19, but I looked up to her. She was tall, beautiful, and still had a sparkle in her eye.

"We have to go to the forest," I said. "We can hide there. And then we need to go to Palestina."

"Palestina?" Rachel asked. "How do you expect to get there?"

"I don't know," I said. "But that is our only choice. I am taking the children. You can wait here for David."

"I will," Rachel said. "We'll come find you when he returns."

I turned to find the children sitting on the floor.

"Get up," I said to them. "We're going to the forest."

It wasn't unusual for them to spend days in the forest, so they thought nothing of it, other than they were excited that for once I was going with them. It was hot, but I made them bring their winter jackets, unsure of how long we would be there.

"What's going on, Mother?" Sarah asked me while we were walking.

"We're just taking a little trip in the forest," I smiled at her. Sarah sensed something was different. I knew it, but she didn't push the questions. I was carrying Yossi in my arms. Sarah held Abi's hand and they walked together next to me. "I want to see how you have gotten so great at finding berries here!"

We walked deep into the forest. Deeper than the children had ever been before. Sarah kept staring at me as though she wanted to say something, but she was still trying to figure out what that was. We found berries and mushrooms and nettles that we snacked on throughout the day. We were there for a while and even though we were covered by the tree tops, I could see that the sun was starting to go down.

"Why don't we sit down here and rest for a little while?" I said. We were next to a big tree with giant roots that seemed to weave through the ground. It looked like a comfortable place we could rest. Or hide in, if we needed.

Suddenly, I heard rustling in the trees. It started coming closer, and closer. A wild boar? I had heard there were boars in the forest if you went in deep enough. It was footsteps. Someone was coming. We had to hide!

I started digging quickly in the leaves that covered the ground. "Sarah, Abi, help me," I said and they immediately started mimicking my digging. When there was a little space, I motioned for them to sit in the small hole, and I put Yossi in Sarah's arms. "Shh . . ." I said to them, putting my finger in front of my lips. I could still hear the footsteps. They were getting louder and louder with every moment.

I started frantically throwing leaves on top of my children. I was holding my breath. I didn't care if a German came and found me, so long as they didn't find my children.

"Hinda!"

I stopped. Rachel was standing behind me.

"What are you doing?" she asked.

My heart dropped and I laughed. An anxious laugh, because I didn't know what else to do.

"I don't know," I said.

"David sent me to come find you," she said, eyeing the children with leaves falling all around them. She smiled at my failed disguise. "He was in the Hungarian village all day. He wants you to come back."

I suddenly felt defeated. I looked at the children, their eyes wide with fear and hair covered with dirt and crumpled leaves.

"Mother," Sarah said. "Let's go to Palestina."

I smiled at her. Yes, I wanted to tell her. Let's go to the promised land. Let's get out of here. Just pack up our suitcases and go. Why couldn't we?

"We will," I said to her. At the same time, I promised myself that we would get there somehow. "Right now, let's go back and find your father."

Rachel brushed the leaves off of Sarah's and Abi's heads and picked up Yossi, who had been quiet this whole time. We walked back through the forest, stumbling our way as twilight turned into darkness.

Eventually we made it back to the house. I could see a candlelight in the window when we arrived. David was waiting. When we got to the door, I could hear voices. David was speaking with someone. In Ukrainian.

We went inside and there David was sitting with Ilya, a young man who used to work on our farm. Ilya had been a hard worker who looked up to David and aspired to owning his own farm one day. Rachel took the children to the bedroom, and I sat down at the table with David and Ilya.

"Many people from my village are coming here tonight," Ilya said. "They heard of the Germans' orders, and are ready to help enforce them and steal anything they can."

David and I were silent.

"I wanted to tell you, so you could be prepared," Ilya said.

I looked at David, horrified. What could we do? Time was running out. Tomorrow morning, we had to report to Turka and now the Ukrainians were coming to help send us off? David was focused as always, thinking about the solution.

"Ilya, I need you to do me a favor," David said. "My sister Rachel, you must hide her."

David then looked at me. "Rachel will find someone who will help us."

Ilya looked down at his hands. I stared at David. After a moment, Ilya nodded.

"She can stay with my family," Ilya said. "We'll figure something out."

Soon we could hear the Ukrainian hooligans running down the street.

"Ilya!" David screamed. "You must leave! If they find out you were here . . . " He couldn't finish.

Ilya got up frantically and slipped out our back door, running as fast as he could. David went to the front door and cracked it open to see outside.

"Stay inside!" a Ukrainian screamed at us. Then he yelled to his friends, "I think we found us a good family!"

I could hear their crackling laughter outside. David slammed the door and pushed the table in front of it. I ran to the children who were sitting on the floor, frozen in fear. A moment later, David came in the room. We all sat there together, the entire night, without a word. The entire night we could hear the hooligans screaming and running through the village, vandalizing and terrorizing the Jews.

When day broke, David stood up and motioned to me to follow him. We walked to the kitchen.

"This is what we are going to do," he said. "I have a few cigarettes that I have been saving. I am going to go out, and offer them to the Ukrainians. I will chat with them, distract them, and I want Sarah and Abi to run to the forest as fast as they can."

"What about Yossi?" I asked. "And us?"

"We need to split up," David said. He grabbed my hand. "Somebody from our family needs to survive. If we stay together, the chances for that are small. Sarah is a big girl. She can take care of Abi, and we will go and find them when we can."

I nodded and turned around to the children, who could see us from their room. David then put his hands on my face and guided my gaze back towards him.

"Hinda," he said. "We will find them and we will be together again."

He then kissed me, and went over to the children. First, he held Rachel in his arms and whispered something in her ear. Then, he held Sarah tight for a few moments and then Abi.

He then got up and nodded to me. I watched his back as he opened the front door and slipped outside. I could immediately hear the cackling Ukrainians outside, eager to take David's cigarettes. I am sure they were just waiting for us to leave so they could swarm our house like vultures and take any last thing that was inside.

I guided Sarah and Abi to the back door of the house.

"Remember where we were yesterday?" I asked them. They both nodded.

"I want you to go there," I said. "Find a tree that you can hide in and stay there. Your father and I will be there soon, I promise."

I squeezed my two beautiful children in my arms, smelling their hair, touching their skins, trying to memorize the feeling of every part of their bodies. And, then, I opened the back door.

"Run," I whispered. "Run as fast as you can."

Sarah grabbed Abi's hand and bolted, pulling him next to her. I watched his little legs scrambling to keep up with hers. They are going to be fine—they have to be, I kept telling myself. I watched them get farther, get smaller, and then suddenly, I heard a scream.

"THEY'RE ESCAPING! THE CHILDREN ARE ESCAPING!"

I could hear the Ukrainians running around to the back of the house.

"RUN!" I screamed, falling to my knees. "RUN!!"

1942—Rachel

"RUN!" Hinda kept screaming over and over, as though her words could power Sarah's and Abi's little legs. I ran to her, grabbing her as she began to fall to the floor, watching two of her children race into the forest.

Four Ukrainians started to run after them. But they were in no shape to catch up. We stood in the doorway, watching Sarah and Abi get smaller and smaller before they disappeared into the forest. The four Ukrainians followed them, disappearing minutes behind them.

"Please God, keep them safe," I whispered. Sarah and Abi knew the forest well, better than any Ukrainian. I knew they would be safe, but I still prayed.

Three other Ukrainians then came around and pushed us inside the house.

"Trying to outsmart us?" one jeered, spit spraying from his mouth.

We stayed silent. David pushed between the Ukrainians and Hinda and me. He glared at them as they stood guarding our doorway.

"We will find them," the Ukrainian said, his giant nose turning purple with anger.

Hinda and I went into the bedroom and sat on the bed where Yossi was lying down. Hinda was sobbing silently, trying to hold in her pain. I held her, glaring at the monsters in our kitchen.

David sat at the kitchen table and offered the Ukrainians cigarettes. David didn't smoke, but he knew Ukrainians could be easily bought with just one cigarette. The monsters each happily accepted, lighting them right in our kitchen. Hinda never would have allowed that. The Ukrainians finished their cigarettes and started pacing around the kitchen. They paced for two hours, as we all sat silently. I could see they were getting restless, bored of this game they were playing with us.

Soon we could see the four Ukrainians returning from the forest. They dragged their feet as they tried to jog towards the house. Sweat soaked their shirts and mud caked on their legs. When they got to the doorway, they stopped, all four panting to catch their breath.

"Well?" one the Ukrainians who had been guarding us said.

"We . . . " one from the forest started, still panting. "We . . . couldn't find them . . . we . . . we . . . looked everywhere."

"What?" the Ukrainian guard screamed. "You idiots, they are two Jewish children! How hard could it be?"

The Ukrainian guard smacked the one from the forest with the butt of his gun. "How does that make us look?"

"Let's get out of here," one of the other Ukrainians who had been guarding us said.

They all agreed and soon they were gone. What idiots, I thought to myself. Why didn't the ones from the forest just lie? They could have said they found the children and killed them. I thanked God for making Ukrainians such dumb barbarians.

"We need to pack up our wagon," David said.

"What's the point?" Hinda said. "Whatever we bring, they will take from us."

"We're not going to Turka," David said. "Just do as I say. Pack anything that could be valuable."

Suddenly we heard a knock on the door. I looked at Hinda and David, unsure of what to do. David went to go answer it. It was Olek, another Ukrainian who had once worked for David. Olek was standing at the door, his horse and wagon behind him.

"David," he said. "I wanted to lend you my horse and wagon for the trip to Turka. It is really the least I can do to help you. Your horse is weak, and your wagon is not so sturdy anymore."

David waved Olek inside and closed the door behind him.

"That is very generous," David said, holding strong eye contact with Olek. "But I prefer to use ours."

I could see Olek's face change with understanding. "I see," he said. "Then I wish you the best of luck and I hope to see you again."

Olek and David shook hands. Olek nodded at Hinda and me and then left, taking his horse and wagon with him. David called us over to the table.

"Rachel," he said to me. "You are going to stay with Ilya. Once the commotion stops, you must go into the forest and find Abi and Sarah. Take them to Shanke and we will meet you there."

Shanke was a small village on the Hungarian border. It has a forced labor camp, where Jews and other unfortunate people worked for the Hungarians in return for crumbs. However, children of the laborers were often transported to Hungary, a country that the Germans didn't seem set of ridding of Jews just yet. I nodded to David. If there was one thing I had learned over the years, it was never to question my big brother's decisions. He always seemed to know best.

"Hinda," David then turned to his wife. "We will take Yossi and find a place to hide until we can go meet Rachel and the children in Shanke."

With that, we got into the wagon, carrying the few belongings we had left. Hinda held Yossi in her arms. I watched Yossi sit quietly. At three years old, he was more mature than I had been just a few years ago. He didn't fuss, didn't complain, just listened and did what he was told. He had a constant look of fear in his eyes. He seemed to always be looking to please his parents and seemed to think twice before he made any movements. He was so small, except for his swollen belly, filled with gas that comes when you don't eat for long periods of time. His gray eyes sunk into his face and his thin blonde hair was ratty and in need of a trim. My heart felt heavy as I watched him.

"Get down!" David yelled. "You think we are going to a party? Try not to let anyone see you!"

Hinda and I crouched down low in the wagon. I could see through the wooden sides and watched as David started to drive away. Butla seemed empty, like a ghost town. The houses that had once belonged to Jews were ransacked and torn apart. The Christian homes were locked up tight, keeping their families safe from people like us.

Instead of heading to the main road, which would have been the way to go to Turka, David headed around the back of the house. We were headed to the small Ukrainian village where Ilya lived. David drove through the fields towards the edge of the forest. I watched our home get smaller in the distance, and suddenly my mind was overflooded with memories. Here in the field is where my mother planted her first garden before she died, where my aunt Tzipora tended the garden to ensure my mother's creation lived on. The garden was full of weeds now, with no vegetables or flowers in bloom. We continued riding closer to the forest, where Bina and I used to run around, talking about what we wanted to do when we grew up.

I hadn't seen Bina since we moved to Turka. We promised to stay in touch, but I was working hard in the fields and Bina's family stayed in Butla. When we returned to Butla, they were gone. I had asked around about them, but no one would give me a real answer. Some said the family left to go to Palestina, while others averted their eyes and told me it was better that I didn't know.

Soon we passed the spot where I had my first kiss with Jan. It was only five years ago, but it felt like a lifetime. In fact, I felt like it wasn't even a real memory, more like a story I had heard about something that had happened to somebody else. I felt like such an adult then, but when I look back I see that I was such a child. I was so young and silly getting involved with a Christian boy, thinking that our religions didn't matter. After that night, I had only spoken with Jan one more time. He came to our house while we were sitting Shiva for my father. I stepped outside to see him, hoping he would hold me, and tell me that everything would be all right. But he didn't. He gave his condolences without even looking at me. He stared at the ground and told me goodbye. Not the "see-you-later" type of goodbye, but the final goodbye, the type that you know signals the end. When we moved to Turka, I saw Jan often, when I worked in the fields. Us Jews were cheap labor for the farmers there, and Jan's family took full advantage of our need to work for a small slice of bread. When I saw him, he looked right through me, as though he didn't even see me at all.

We continued riding along the tree line. In the distance I could see smog from the direction of the train tracks. It was Sunday, but there were no trains on Sunday. It must have been making a special trip to Turka. After about an hour, we got to the small Ukrainian village. David stopped in front of Ilya's house and I hopped out of the wagon. Ilya had heard us approaching and had already come outside.

"Rachel, be safe," David said to me. He then turned to Ilya. "Thank you."

Ilya nodded and quickly motioned me to follow him. It was not safe for a Jew to be seen here, nor was it safe for a Ukrainian who was harboring a Jew. David quickly rode off, and Ilya led me around the back of his house to a small boiler room.

"You can stay there," Ilya pointed to the room. "I will bring you everything you need."

I smiled and thanked him, then slipped inside. It was hot inside. It was August, which was already warm, but inside the boiler room it was at least thirty degrees hotter. Beads of sweat instantly started forming on my forehead and the small of my back. The room was small, about two square meters. Of course, half the space was full from the boiler. The pipes ran along the walls. I reached out my hand to touch one, and it was burning hot. I sat on the floor and looked up. The ceiling had a big air vent, allowing some of the hot air to escape and light to get inside. I hoped it would be night soon and I could cool off.

Suddenly I heard footsteps and Ilya came and opened the door. He brought a bucket of water and a bowl of soup. He smiled at me as put the bucket down near my feet and handed me the soup.

"Don't worry," he said. "No one will come looking here."

I thanked him, and he left me alone to enjoy my meal. The soup was lukewarm – a broth with a few pieces of carrots and potatoes in it. I soon realized he didn't bring me a spoon, so I slurped up the broth and ate the vegetables with my fingers. It was delicious.

It was almost sunset. I could see the light changing through the vent above me, and the air was finally starting to cool down. I washed my face and cupped some water in my hands to drink before lying down on the dirt ground. I hugged my knees in close to my chest so I wouldn't touch the walls and accidently burn myself from one of the boiler pipes and looked up to the vent, watching the light turn from yellow to orange, to pink, to purple, and then, soon, it was dark. I could just barely see the outline of the vent in the roof before I closed my eyes.

The next morning, I was awoken by bright light coming through the vent. My clothes were soaked with sweat, so I took a few handfuls of water to rinse my face and my body. I could hear Ukrainians talking outside as they walked down the street. I tried to listen, seeing if I could hear anything.

" . . . Turka yesterday?. . ."

". . . loaded those trains?"

. . . "Finally we got rid . . . "

. . . "Poor things."

. . . "Where do think they were taking them?"

I kept getting small snippets of conversations but not enough to fully know what happened. I started thinking of David, Hinda, and Yossi and wondering where they went. What if they had gotten caught? Could it be possible that they had gone to Turka as well? What about Sarah and Abi? Were they safe in the forest? My mind was racing and I didn't know how long I could stay put in the little room. Maybe I should just sneak out and leave. I could go find the children now, or I could try to find out what happened to David, Hinda, and Yossi.

That's what I should do. I need to leave. How could I just sit here? I stood up and started to brush the dirt off my legs when I heard a knock. Ilya opened the door with a fresh bucket of water and a slice of bread.

"Good morning," he said. He looked at me up and down, realizing what I was doing. "You can't leave now. They will see you coming out of here. You need to stay until things calm down."

I took the bread from him and sat back down on the ground. "Thank you," I said. "What happened?"

Ilya hesitated. He looked all around the tiny room before he spoke. "When the Jews arrived in Turka yesterday, they put them all in trains," Ilya said.

"To where?" I asked.

"I don't know," Ilya said. "They said they were taking them to new villages built specially for Jews, so all the Jews could be together."

"Do you believe that?" I asked.

Ilya smiled at me. "I don't know," he said. Ilya then left me alone with my bread and water.

I sat on the ground, picking crumbs off the bread and putting each crumb into my mouth one at a time. When I got through half the bread, I heard a scream outside.

"How could you?" a woman screamed. "You are endangering our lives! You would choose them over your own family?"

Suddenly the boiler room door swung open and Ilya's wife was standing there, red-faced, carrying a broom. A heavy-set woman, she was wearing an apron that had probably once been white. She had dirt

87

smudged on her clothes and face and her hair was tied up in a knot at the crown of her head.

"GET OUT! GET OUT!" she screamed. "DO YOU KNOW WHAT THEY WOULD DO TO US IF THEY FOUND YOU HERE?"

She started shooing me out with the broom, making it difficult for me to catch my footing. I slipped the second half of the piece of bread into my pocket, pushed past the woman, and ran out the door. There were people all around on the street who stopped to hear the commotion. I ran past them, and I kept running, not looking to either side, just straight ahead. I ran and ran until I was out of the village, out of sight, and in the middle of wide-open fields of crops.

When I was running, I didn't pay attention to which direction I was running. Then I stopped to look around to see where I was. Stocks of wheat surrounded me, standing tall almost to my chest. There were Ukrainians working in the field, harvesting the wheat. A few were looking at me, mouths open, but hands still pulling the grains off the wheat stalks. I was careful not to make eye contact with anyone. I didn't want anyone to see my expression, or worse, recognize me. I knew this area well, so it didn't take me too long to orient myself and figure out which direction I needed to go. I started walking through the field, catching my breath. I needed to get back to Butla, to the forest, and find Sarah and Abi. They were waiting for me.

"HALT!" I suddenly heard.

My heart jumped and I turned my head without stopping my feet. At the far end of the field there was an SS officer. I could see him from the waist up, his dark uniform, tall hat, and red armband. I started to increase my pace, moving my feet faster and faster until one of the Ukrainian workers started to scream at me.

"Don't you understand?" the Ukrainian said. "He said, 'Stop!'"

I stopped. Maybe I should just crouch down, pretend to be working, pretend I belong here. No, the Ukrainians would give me away. I watched the SS officer start to walk in my direction. Please God, help me, I started to pray. He is going to ship me off, or shoot me! I will never find the children, or see David or Hinda. They won't know what happened to me. Please God!

The seconds dragged. He seemed to be walking towards me in slow motion, getting closer, and then suddenly he stopped.

"JUDEN!" the SS officer screamed, grabbing one of the field workers by the arm. The worker stared at the officer in shock, shaking his head.

I couldn't stay to watch, I immediately took off running as fast as I could through the field, getting farther and farther from the SS officer.

BANG! I heard a shot. The sound startled me and I lost my footing. I felt myself falling forward until my hands hit the ground, breaking my fall. Did the officer see me running? Was the shot directed towards me? I slowly got up, lifting my head just millimeters higher than the wheat to look around. The officer was lighting a cigarette, his gun slung back over his shoulder. I couldn't see the worker he had grabbed, but through the high wheat I couldn't really see any workers except those near to me. The few around me were staring at me. I couldn't stop myself from looking back at them and I scanned all their faces looking for a clue of what happened, or what I should do. One worker looked at me and pointed in the direction I had been running. He looked young—maybe around my age—but his back was arched from years of bending over, and his face was wrinkled from the sun. He nodded to me as he pointed, moving his head as if to tell me to go. So, I did. I ran, but this time I tried to stay low. I ran with my back bent down trying to stay out of sight of anyone who could see over the wheat.

Soon I got to the end of the wheat field and I was near the main road in the area. If I followed this road, I would make it back to Butla. I looked back. I couldn't see the SS officer or any more Ukrainian workers. My back ached from my bent-over run so I stretched to the sky and started walking. I was about fifteen kilometers from Butla; with any luck, I would reach it by nightfall.

The road was quiet and empty. I walked slowly, feeling the sun burning down on me. I hummed to myself as I continued walking. Every once in a while, a wagon would pass me. The driver would tip his hat and continue on his way. It wasn't unusual for people to be walking these roads—not everyone had a wagon. I had walked here countless times before.

It was dark by the time I reached the edge of Butla. I was afraid to enter the village. If someone saw me they would know I didn't obey the Germans' orders and would likely report me. I decided to walk past Butla and enter the forest from a different side. Hopefully that way, I could travel unseen. The road was dark and I could only see about a meter in front of me, but I kept walking forward, trusting my feet to keep me on the right path. I had walked here before, too, but never in the dark without a lantern.

After another hour or so of walking, I reached the village of Sianky. Like Butla, Sianky was a tiny village that lived off of Turka. I assumed the Jews here also reported to Turka the day before to be sent off in the trains. Here, no one would recognize me if I cut through the village get to the forest. The roads were quiet, and I tried to walk in the direction of the forest. I knew the village was no bigger than Butla, so it shouldn't take more than twenty minutes to get to the other end. But I kept walking and walking, and I didn't seem to be getting any closer to the far edge of village. I must be walking in circles! I couldn't continue like this, I was wasting energy, and I couldn't still be here when the sun started to rise. I sat down on the ground for a moment, to try to think what to do.

"Hey," I suddenly heard a whisper. I turned around to see a woman carrying a lantern and walking towards me. I gasped.

"Are you lost?" the woman asked.

I shook my head, and looked away from her, hoping she would leave me alone.

"It's OK," she said, still walking towards me. "I won't hurt you."

I looked back over to her. I could now see her face, framed by a scarf wrapped around her head and tied under her chin. The woman was probably in her thirties, with a soft face lined with years in the sun.

"Come with me," she said.

I again shook my head. I can't trust her. I can't trust anyone. If she reports me to the Gestapo, she will receive a reward—more money than anyone in this area had ever had at one time. The woman continued walking towards me until she was right in front of me. She stretched out her hand to me, standing still, looking at me.

"Come on," she smiled. "You need water."

I gave up. She was right, I needed water. So, what, she would report me to the Gestapo? I would be dead soon anyways without any water. I grabbed her hand and stood up. She led me to a small house nearby and took me inside. I watched her untie her scarf, revealing thick brown hair sprinkled with gray. She then brought me a cup of water and slice of cake.

"Please," she said, motioning for me to sit at her table. I obeyed and quickly drank the water which she promptly refilled. We sat there silently for a while. I continued drinking and she smiled at me motherly.

I broke the silence. "Thank you," I said.

"It's all right," she smiled back at me. "Do you need help?"

"No," I shook my head. "I should get going."

"Where are you going?" she asked me.

I breathed in heavily, trying to decide how to answer that. The woman watched me intently, patiently seeing if I would respond.

"Why don't you continue in the morning?" she finally said.

"I can't stay here," I said, standing up.

"You can," she smiled. "Tomorrow I will take you to the forest. There are others like you there."

"How do I know that the Germans won't come get me before morning?" I said, challenging her kindness.

"I guess you don't," she said. "So, it's your choice."

The woman got up and grabbed a blanket from a cupboard and placed it on a small cot in the corner of the room. She smiled at me and then went into her bedroom. I looked around the house. It was mostly empty, except for a few small pieces of furniture. I walked over to the cot and laid down on it, using the blanket as a pillow. I would rest here for a little bit and then sneak out before the woman would notice, before she could notify the Germans. As I fell asleep, I thought about Abi and Sarah, spending their second night alone in the forest . . .

I awoke with a hand on my shoulder. I had overslept! My heart pounded as I readied myself to open my eyes to see SS officers standing over me, smiling triumphantly as they captured me.

"Hey," I heard the woman's voice. I opened my eyes to see her standing over me, alone. "We need to go now," she said.

I got up quickly, rubbed my eyes open and patted my hair. My hair was still braided from several days before, but now the braids felt more like knots. The woman handed me a handkerchief with a couple slices of bread wrapped in it and led me out the door.

The sun was just rising, the bright light shining over the village. It was still cool; the sun hadn't yet had the chance to heat the air to the scorching temperature that it would be in a few hours. I hadn't been able to see anything the night before, so my eyes took in the village around me. The dirt road curved through small houses that looked the same as the houses we had in Butla. Only here there seemed to be fewer houses, with even more space between them. I followed the woman down the road. After a few minutes, she turned right, and started walking up a hill on the edge of village. I looked around us, but I couldn't see the forest anywhere. I continued following her up the hill, walking through shrubs and dead plants. There was no path, but the woman seemed to know where she was headed. When we got to the top of the hill, I could see down the other side. In the distance, there was the tree line, the edge of the forest!

"Continue going that direction," the woman said to me, pointing at the trees. "There are others there who can help you. Tell them Mary sent you."

"Thank you," I said, grabbing the woman's hand.

She smiled at me. "I have to go," she said. "Good luck."

She turned around and started walking back down the hill from where we came. I stood there watching her disappear back into the village. Then I turned to where I was going and started to run down the backside of the hill. The forest was so close now! Abi and Sarah, I am coming!!

The forest was farther than it looked, and I soon slowed to a walk. Eventually I got to the forest and started to make my way through it. I had never been to this end of the forest before, and I wasn't sure of my way around. The trees here seemed darker, thicker than on the other side. I walked towards the direction of Butla, shaded from the rising sun by the trees. The dry leaves cracked under my feet and I could hear birds cooing above me. Soon I heard people speaking. I stopped to listen and realized they were speaking Yiddish! I quickly made my way towards the voices and saw a few men sitting around on a fallen log. When they heard me rustling through the trees, they stood up. Each man had a rifle slung over his shoulder. They stood silently as I approached.

"Who are you?" a man yelled to me in Polish.

"My name is Rachel. I am looking for my family," I responded in Yiddish. "Mary led me here."

The men relaxed and welcomed me to sit with them. The men were actually more like boys, but they had matured from hiding in the forest. They must have been around my age, but I didn't recognize any of them.

"I'm Moshe, and this is Adam and Itzik," one of the men said. The conversation returned to Yiddish.

"Nice to meet you," I smiled.

"Where are you from?" Adam asked me, handing me a bowl of water from a jug they had.

"Butla," I responded, drinking the water. "My family is trying to hide from the Germans. We didn't want to go to Turka as ordered."

"Smart decision," Itzik said. "Those Jews are as good as dead."

"What?" I gasped.

"You don't think they were taking them all on a vacation, do you?" Itzik responded.

I shook my head.

"Where is your family?" Moshe asked me.

"My niece and nephew are in the forest," I told them. "I need to find them, and I am taking them to meet their parents in Shanke."

"Why to Shanke?" Adam asked.

"Well, to get to Hungary," I said. "There are no Germans there."

"Not yet," Itzik said. "But it won't be safe there."

"Where else can we go?" I asked.

"Nowhere," Adam said. "It is not safe for us anywhere."

"Where did you get the guns?" I asked.

"We stole them from the Germans," Moshe said. "We need to protect ourselves."

"Oh," I responded. "I see." I paused. "Could you help me find my niece and nephew? They are here in the forest, but closer to Butla. I don't really know how to get there."

"Sure," Adam said. "I will walk you towards Butla."

"Thank you," I responded. I finished my bowl of water and stood up.

"Let's go," Adam said. The two of us started walking deeper into the forest. Adam walked in front of me, looking around constantly, one hand always on his gun. He had dark curly hair, freckles on his face, and broad shoulders that connected with thick muscles on his upper back. His dark shirt was stained with sweat and dirt.

"How long have you been in the forest?" I asked.

"A few months probably," he responded.

"Where are you from?" I asked.

"Sianky," he said.

"What happened?" I asked.

"Same as what happened in Butla," he said. "Except we decided not to listen to the Germans and we came here."

"And what are you going to do now?" I asked.

Adam laughed. "We're staying in the forest," he said. "We're safe here. We know the area and we have weapons to protect ourselves. Eventually things will go back to normal and we will go back home."

"But what about when it is winter?" I asked. "How long can you actually stay here?"

"We'll manage," he said. "I think we can live here forever."

"And how do you know when it is safe to go back?" I asked, having more questions with each one Adam answered.

"Well, we go into villages every once in a while," Adam responded. "And Mary comes to us sometimes with news."

"Do you know what happened to the Jews who went to Turka on Sunday?" I asked. Itzik's comment was rolling around in my head. They were as good as dead.

"Well, yes, actually," Adam said. "We paid a few village people to follow and see what happened."

"And?" I asked. I could see that Adam didn't want to tell me. He looked at me, his eyes hardened.

"Well, about ten thousand Jews showed up in Turka. They loaded all of them on the trains; they were cattle trains—each cart probably had two hundred people shoved inside," Adam said. "When the train started moving, some people jumped out of the windows. They were shot."

"Where did they take them?" I asked.

"To Belzec," Adam responded.

"What's that?"

"An extermination camp," Adam said.

"What do you mean?"

"A factory to kill them," he said coldly.

"I don't believe you," I said.

"You don't have to," Adam said.

After that, we walked in silence. I couldn't believe what Adam said. That just isn't possible. They couldn't do that. We continued walking for a few hours and the forest was becoming more familiar to me. Soon I recognized certain trees and clearings and from there I knew how to get to the spot where I was supposed to meet Abi and Sarah. Adam continued walking with me, now letting me lead. He handed his canteen to me, making sure I took a drink every once in a while.

"We're almost to where they are," I said to him.

"I want to meet them," he said, revealing a crooked smile.

I couldn't help but smile back, blushing as I moved my gaze to the ground.

"Behind that tree is a small clearing," I said. "They are there!"

I started to run, calling out their names, "Abi! . . . Sarah!"

I got to the tree and looked out to the clearing, it was empty. "Abi! Sarah! It's me! You can come out!"

My calls were answered with silence.

"Rachel, they aren't here," Adam said. "It doesn't look like anyone has been here for a little while."

"What? No," I said, running around looking for them. "They are here. I am sure of it."

I began to get frantic. Where were they? Had the Ukrainians actually gotten to them? Did someone else find them? I could never forgive myself. "ABI!! SARAH!!"

"Rachel," Adam grabbed my arm. "They aren't here. You have to stop screaming."

"No, I have to find them," I yelled, trying to yank my arm from him.

"Rachel, please," Adam said. "Come back with me. You can stay with us. We will be safe."

"NO!" I screamed. "I can't."

Adam released my arm. He looked at me with pity as if he were deciding whether I could make my own decision of what to do next.

"Ok," he said. "You know where to find me if you need anything."

"Thank you," I said.

Adam turned and went back the way we came. I watched his back disappear into the trees and then I turned around, thinking about what to do. If I couldn't find the children, I still needed to go to Shanke to meet David, Hinda, and Yossi. David would know what to do. He always did.

Shanke was not much farther from where I was. Maybe another hour's walk, and I knew exactly how to get there. I walked in silence, looking all around me for clues that someone had been there. Maybe a footprint in the ground, a piece of food, a string of clothing, anything . . . but there was nothing.

I was getting closer to Shanke—what would I say to David? How could I tell him that I didn't find Abi and Sarah? I started to walk slower. Maybe I missed something; maybe they were there, but afraid because of Adam. Soon I heard the sounds of Shanke. There was a lumber mill there and a constant grumbling from the wood being chopped and processed. I had to be careful; there could be others in the forest here—others who would be less sympathetic to me.

Suddenly I heard a crackle of a dry twig, and then a rustling of leaves. I gasped and slapped my hand over my mouth, holding my breath. I crouched down low hoping whoever it was wouldn't see or hear me.

"RACHEL!" I heard a scream.

"DAVID!" I screamed back, seeing my brother running towards me.

1942—Sarah

"RUN!" my mother screamed behind us. I was running as fast as I could, pulling my little brother's arm to make sure he could keep up.

Don't look back, don't look back, keep moving forward. I was moving so fast, I was sure any step now I would tumble forward, pulling Abi with me to the ground.

"Come on!" I screamed to Abi. "We have to get to the forest before them!"

"I'm going as fast as I can!" Abi yelled back. "You're hurting me!"

I could hear the Ukrainians yelling behind us, and their clumsy footsteps as they ran towards us. We quickly made it to the tree line and I darted left, startling Abi, who almost tripped as I pulled him in my direction.

"Where are you going?" Abi screamed. "We have to go the other way."

"Ugh," I rolled my eyes. I know my mother said to meet them in the clearing where we were yesterday, but that was straight ahead, and what good would it be to stand in a clearing when the Ukrainians came?

We were weaving through the trees, jumping over roots, avoiding small holes and bushes, all the while still holding hands.

"Sarah!" Abi whined as a branch swung back and hit him in the face. "Stop! We're going the wrong way!"

"We can't!" I whispered sternly. "Just trust me!"

Soon we got to the place I wanted to be. The trees here were bigger than the ones near the clearing. These trees were giants, reaching all the way to the sky. Their large roots jumped above the ground, creating an obstacle course that only someone with much practice could overcome. Here was a small stream, thick with weeds and mud. The murky water flowed through the tree roots bringing all kinds of shrubbery and dead leaves with it.

I could still hear the Ukrainians behind us, screaming. They must have known we turned left when we entered the forest. I looked around the stream and saw a small cove under a giant tree root. Perfect! We could jump in the water and swim there. The weeds would hide us from anyone walking by.

"We're going in there," I pointed to the cove, looking to Abi for agreement. He looked back and forth between me and our small hiding spot. He nodded. "Come on!"

I quickly jumped in the stream, feeling the weeds instantly grab onto my legs, making it hard for me to control my movements. Abi followed, splashing in the mud as he dunked in.

"SHH!" I yelled at him.

Slowly we made our way across the stream to the small cove. There was just barely enough space for the both of us to stay there with our heads above the water. Thankfully, it was shallow and we could both stand. When we were completely under the tree root, I started pulling the weeds around us, blocking any sight of the cove. With the weed covering, it was almost completely dark, just a few sprinkles of light came through. There, no one will find us here.

Soon, we heard the Ukrainians getting closer. They were yelling at each other. I could make out enough of the language to know they were talking about us. I heard a splash and they ran through the stream, passing us by.

I let out a sigh of relief as their voices started to get quieter and quieter.

"Are they gone?" Abi whispered to me.

I shrugged. "We should stay here for a little while to be sure."

We stood there silently, not moving. My feet were sinking in the mud below and every few minutes I had to pick up my feet to make sure they didn't get stuck. I could see that Abi was getting restless from staying here.

My parents and my aunt, they think I don't know what's going on. When they whisper, they think I don't hear. They think I am sleeping, but, really, I am listening to every word. I remember when things were different. I remember going to school with all the other kids in Butla and I remember having huge Friday night dinners with meat and chicken. But then things started to change. I remember the last day I went to school: I was in second grade and in class we were learning math. A boy, Antoni, raised his hand and when the teacher called on him, he said: I can't learn when there is a Jew in the room. I could feel the eyes of the entire class on me, like fire burning my skin. The teacher ignored the comment and continued speaking. A few minutes later, I felt something hit me in the back of the head. I lifted my hand, to feel a wad of spit stuck to my hair. I sat silently until the end of the class and quickly made my way home. The next morning, I walked to school, but there was a sign on the door: No Jews allowed. My teacher was there and told me it would be better if I just went home. I should be in fifth grade now.

Then we went to Turka and lived in a barn with poop all around us. Abi, Yossi, and I sat silently every day when Mother, Father, and Aunt Rachel went to work. During the day, we would chew on straw, pretending it was food until the adults came back with enough crumbs to just stop our stomachs from grumbling. Then we came back to Butla. Nobody went to work, but we spent all our free time in the forest looking for food. Mother and Rachel tried to pretend it was a game, but I liked other games we used to play better.

Now, who knows what could happen? I just have to keep Abi and me safe and pray that everyone else will be all right. I used to believe that my father could do anything, that he would always protect me, but now I was not so sure.

I peeked out of the weeds, looking around the area. I don't know how long we were hiding there, but it seemed like there was no one around. I quietly moved out of the cove and pulled myself through the mud and out of the stream. Abi looked around hesitantly and then followed. When we both were out, we looked at each other and laughed.

Abi's red hair was caked with mud and had leaves sticking out of it in all directions. I reached my hand up to feel my own hair and pulled out a fistful of twigs. Our clothes were soaked and brown from the water and little pieces of dirt were drying on my arms and legs.

"Well, let's keep moving," I said.

Abi and I started walking towards the clearing where we were yesterday. We were silent, except for the squishing of our shoes. We walked slowly, both starting to feel tired from not drinking anything the whole day. It was hot, even in the forest, and our soaked clothes were not enough to keep us cool.

Suddenly I heard footsteps. I gasped and instinctually grabbed Abi's arm. We were caught! I froze, unsure what to do. I looked at Abi. He looked brave, and, for a moment, I wished I could be brave like him.

A few moments later, a boy appeared. It was Lieb, one of Shmuel's sons. Shmuel was our neighbor and friends with our father. Lieb was about fifteen years old. He came to our house sometimes with his father and other brother, Chaim, seventeen years old. Here, he was alone, wandering through the forest.

"Hey," he said when he saw us. He was so tall and strong, with sandy blonde hair that grew wildly in all directions. "What are you two doing here?"

I blushed, unsure what to tell him.

"What are you doing here?" Abi jumped in, returning the question. I was grateful Abi responded.

He may be younger than me, but he was definitely better than I was with other people. He also knew me well enough that he would ask everything I wanted to know.

Lieb laughed. "Getting out of Butla," he said. "I'm going to Shanke. Now your turn."

"We're also going to Shanke," Abi responded. "But first we are supposed to meet up with our parents and aunt."

"Where are you meeting them?" Lieb asked.

"Here, in the forest," Abi said.

"What are you going to do if they don't turn up?" Lieb asked.

I hadn't thought of that. I was sure they would turn up.

"They'll turn up," Abi responded.

"Come with me," Lieb said. "I have friends in Shanke; you can stay with us."

I looked at Abi, who looked back at me. He shrugged and we silently agreed to follow him. He seemed to know what he was doing.

"Where is your family?" I asked Lieb.

"They went to Turka," he responded.

"You didn't want to go with them?" I asked.

"To Turka? No way," Lieb said. "There was no way I was going there to do what the Germans said."

I was silent, but the thoughts inside my head were screaming. What was happening in Turka? Some of my friends' families went there. Lieb's parents went. They wouldn't have gone if it was such a bad thing. Better not to let my imagination think about it too much.

"What is in Shanke?" Abi asked Lieb. I was happy he changed the subject.

"Well, there's work and food," Lieb said. "A few of my friends went there. I visited them a few times."

"Where are we going to live?" Abi asked.

"With my friends," Lieb said. "They have a place."

"Our parents also want to go to Shanke," Abi said.

"Then I am sure we will meet them there," Lieb said, smiling at us.

My clothes were starting to dry off. I started picking at the dried mud caked on my dress and arms. My mouth was dry, and I kept swallowing, trying to make some saliva I could drink. I looked at Abi. He was walking a couple steps behind me. He too was picking the mud off his shirt, concentrating intently as he used his fingernails to scratch the fabric clean.

It was a long walk to Shanke, longer than we had ever walked in the forest. I couldn't keep track of how long we were walking—we just kept following Lieb. My legs were getting heavier and heavier, and the gap between him and me was starting to get bigger. I kept looking back at Abi, who was also falling farther behind. Lieb also kept looking back and stopping every so often for us to catch up. But then he would continue, and the gap would widen.

The air was starting to cool off and the sun was no longer piercing us through the treetops. Shadows were getting longer in the forest. I didn't know how much longer we could continue walking before it would get dark.

"We're almost there," Lieb said, stopping and waiting for us to catch up. "Listen, you can hear the mill working."

We took a few moments to rest and then Lieb said that we needed to keep moving. He wanted to get there before nightfall so we had to move quickly. My legs were now like bricks, and every step took a lot of effort. Soon we could see the forest edge. Through the trees were small huts; some had candlelight through the windows. The hum of the lumber mill made my ears vibrate.

Lieb took us through the scattered huts until he stopped in front of one. They all looked the same to me, and I wondered how he chose which one to stop in front of. He tapped softly on the door and then moved closer, placing his ear on the door to try to listen through it. Abi and I were standing a little behind him. Abi grabbed my hand, squeezing it tightly.

The door slowly creaked open and a man waved us inside. We slipped in quietly to see a one-room hut about the size of our bedroom at home. The hut had a dirt floor and two small windows on each side. The room smelled like sweat and mold. There were a couple of candles sitting on the floor between bodies crumpled all over. There were probably twenty people inside the little room. Most were sleeping, but some were sitting in the corner playing cards or smoking. The man who let us in had a thick beard and a cigarette in his lips that was dropping ash right into his beard. He was thin and wore a dirty shirt that looked like it belonged to his dad before it belonged to him. He shook Lieb's hand before he turned to look at us.

"Who are they?" he asked Lieb, nodding in our direction.

"My neighbor's kids," Lieb responded. "I found them in the forest."

Lieb then leaned into the man and whispered something in his ear. The man nodded knowingly and then bent down in front of us.

"I am Jonathan," he said, extending his hand to shake ours. Abi grabbed his hand first, shaking it firmly. "You can stay here until we find your parents."

I smiled at him and then continued looking around the room. Jonathan stood up and spoke to a few of the people on the floor, asking them to move over to give us a small spot. We squeezed into the tiny area, just big enough for Abi and me to cuddle on the floor together with our knees up to our chins. The dirt floor was cool and soft, and I was happy just to be lying down instead of walking. Lieb came over to us with a cup of water. Abi and I split it, careful not to waste a drop. Then, we both drifted off to sleep.

It seemed like just moments later that there was a rustling around the room. Everyone was moving, murmuring to each other as they started to get up. Abi was still sleeping. I carefully sat up, looking around at all the faces to see if I recognized anyone. The room was still dark, but a weak light was starting to come through the windows. It was just enough for me to make out everyone's faces. They were expressionless. Tired. Unhuman. I was looking around for Lieb or for Jonathan, unsure if we were supposed to do something. Soon I caught Lieb's eye and he walked over to me and knelt down.

"Everyone is going to work in the mill," he said. "I am going, too. They give food to all the workers. We'll be back in the evening. Don't go anywhere."

"I can work," I said. "Why don't I come?"

Lieb smiled at me. "Someone needs to watch your brother," he said. "Don't worry, we're going to eat tonight."

Lieb got up and soon the hut cleared out. It was just Abi and me—alone there. Abi was still sleeping, so I lay back down and stretched out my legs. I couldn't fall back asleep, but I didn't know what else to do. My stomach grumbled; I hadn't eaten anything since before we ran away yesterday. I didn't know if I could wait until Lieb got back to eat. The sun got brighter through the windows and I could finally see the room we were in. It was built from old logs and straw that looked like it could crumble any minute. There were a few blankets scattered around the room and broken pieces of candles. I looked around for a sink, a faucet, or anything where I could get some water, but there wasn't any.

Abi was starting to move and soon he fluttered open his eyes. He looked around, confused to see the room so empty.

"Where is everyone?" he asked me.

"They went to work," I said.

Abi stood up. "Come on," he said.

"We need to stay here." I stared up at him.

"We need water; we can't stay here with nothing all day," Abi said. "Let's go. We'll come back before they notice we left."

I stood up. I also felt like we couldn't sit in that room all day and wait for Lieb, but I didn't know what else to do.

We quietly left the hut and started walking through the sea of huts scattered around the area. All the huts were built of wood and scraps and looked like they might fall over if anyone sneezed too hard. The area was empty. No other people were walking around.

I could see the big lumber mill behind all the huts. There was black smoke coming from chimneys on the roof and the vibrating hum filled the air. I started walking in that direction. The humming got louder as we got closer. Soon I could see people walking around, carrying logs or wheeling buckets full of sawdust and woodchips. Everyone seemed to be moving around from place to place.

My eyes caught a spigot sticking up from the ground near the side of the mill. A few men were standing around the spigot, cupping their hands to drink. I nudged Abi, showing him the spigot. He immediately took off in a sprint and I followed. The men there stopped, startled to see two children running next to the mill.

"Hi," Abi said when he got there, seconds before me. "Can we drink?"

The men moved out of our way, letting us get to the spigot. The water running through it was yellow and smelled sour, but I didn't hesitate to put my face

111

right under it and let it wash over me. Abi stood under me, washing his hands and cupping water to bring to his mouth. We must have stood like that for a few minutes because soon one of the men started talking to us.

"All right, better move along," he said. "You children shouldn't be here."

I stopped drinking and looked at the man.

"Where are your parents?" he said. "If you are caught here, they will send you away."

I nodded, even though I wasn't sure what he meant. I smiled at the man and grabbed Abi, who was still gulping from the spigot. The two of us ran back towards the huts. When we got to the huts, I wasn't sure which one was ours. We started weaving back and forth between them, looking for clues.

"I think it's this one," Abi said, standing in front of one.

"No," I said. I was sure it wasn't that one. But which one was it? I started peeking through windows to see if I recognized the inside, but none looked familiar. All had dirt floors and smelled like sweat inside. Blankets and candles were scattered everywhere, without a single person in sight. I felt like we had been searching for hours, with no luck. Finally, we just sat down on the ground in front of the hut we thought was ours.

Soon, people started returning from the mill. We sat on the ground watching men and even some women walk by us to find their huts. The people were dirty and mostly looked at the ground. One woman looked at us as she walked by. She had a scarf over her head and piercing blue eyes that shot out of her darkened face. She looked like she could have been a mother—like ours. People continued to walk by us, probably hundreds. They would walk through the row of huts and disappear inside one. I stared at all the faces as they passed us, looking for someone familiar.

In the distance I noticed Lieb walking towards us. I recognized his walk and the way his shoulders swung side to side when he stepped. I smiled and stood up as he got closer to us. When he noticed us, he started to jog over.

"What are you doing out here?" he asked.

"We got lost," Abi said.

"But I told you to stay inside," he said. "They don't allow children here."

"We were thirsty," Abi said.

Lieb put his hand on my shoulder and guided me to keep walking with him. Soon he stopped in front of a hut and took us inside. I should have known this one was ours, I thought.

There were already a few people inside, sitting on the floor, eating bread and potatoes. Lieb took a handkerchief out of his pocket and unwrapped a few slices of bread. He handed one to each of us and took a third for himself. The bread was black and hard. I tried to break off a piece but it wouldn't rip with my hands, so I took a bite with my teeth. The hard bread broke in my mouth and chewing made my jaw tired.

Jonathan came over to us and handed us a potato. The potato was soft and warm, and I tore it in half for Abi and me. We smiled as we sat quietly, enjoying our meal. It was the biggest meal we had eaten in a while.

Everyone in the hut was going to sleep. The hut was now as packed as it was the night before, if not even more crowded. Abi and I cuddled on the ground and went to sleep.

The next morning, by the time I woke up, the hut was empty. We sat there quietly, unsure of what to do. After a while I started feeling restless. I went over to the window to look outside. It was empty as I thought, but then, suddenly, I saw someone walking towards the huts from the direction of the forest.

I quickly ducked down, not wanting to be seen. Lieb's warning about getting caught was rolling around in my head. Abi saw me duck down and quickly came over to the window.

"What is it?" he asked.

"SHH!" I whispered. "Someone is coming."

"Who?" he asked.

"I don't know!" I said. "Get down."

But Abi didn't listen to me. Instead he stood up on his toes to get a good view out the window. I grabbed his hand trying to pull him down, but he didn't budge.

"Father!" he screamed, yanking his hand from mine. "It's Father!!"

I jumped up and looked out the window. It was our father. He was walking hurriedly through the huts looking inside them and looking all around to check if other people were around. The two of us sprung from our spot and bolted out the door of our hut.

"Father!" we both screamed as we ran to him. When he saw us, he jumped and also began to run. We both leaped into his arms when we met each other.

"Sarah! Abi!" he said, squeezing our bodies and patting our heads. "I heard you were here. Where is Rachel?"

Abi and I looked at each other and shrugged.

"It's OK," Father said. "We'll find her. Come on, let's go."

My father took each of us by the hand and led us back into the forest. I was so relieved to be with him, and to be leaving that place. Soon we were under the treetops and weaving through bushes and branches, the mill getting farther behind. I could sense that there were a lot of people here in the forest. I heard voices murmuring all around us, some in Yiddish and some in other languages that I didn't recognize. Then I heard a voice I did recognize. Mother!

I started to run and then I saw her through the trees. She was sitting on a log with a few other people. When she saw us, she got up and ran towards us. She was wearing the same dress she had on when we last saw her, but now the dress was dirty and torn.

"My children!" she screamed as she was running. She grabbed me close, kissing my dirty face. She smelled like rotting flowers and fertilizer. Then she grabbed Abi, pulling him into her chest.

When she got up, she brought us over to the group she had been with. Father sat down, instantly becoming part of a serious discussion. The adults stopped talking when we approached. One of the other women there was holding Yossi, who smiled when he saw us. I instantly ran over to him and gave him a hug.

"Kids, go play over there with Isroel's girls," Father said. He pointed to two young girls who were sitting a little way from the adults. Isroel was one of my father's friends in Butla. He had four daughters. I started to wonder where were the other two.

"David, they understand what is going on," Mother replied.

"It's all right," I said, trying to sound mature. "Come on, Abi."

I smiled and picked up Yossi from Ety, Isroel's wife. Abi and I walked over to Isroel's two daughters, Zelda and Ethel. Zelda was about my age, and Ethel was probably about seven. The two smiled sadly at us as we approached.

"Where were you?" Zelda asked.

"In Shanke, in the labor camp," Abi replied.

"They let you stay there?" Ethel asked. "I heard they deported all the children there."

"Deported to where?" Abi asked.

"To orphanages in Hungary," Ethel said.

"Oh," Abi said. "Where are Rosa and Pesil?"

Ethel's eyes started to tear up and her nose turned red. Zelda grabbed her hand; she also had tears in her eyes.

"They didn't make it," Zelda responded.

"Oh, I am sorry," I said, feeling ashamed Abi asked, even though the question had been burrowing in my head. We sat there silently, giving me the

116

opportunity to try to listen to what the adults were saying.

"We should leave tonight," Isroel said.

"We need to wait for Yosl," said Ita, the wife of Yosl, who was the head of the Judenrat in Turka. "He said he would come after the transport left."

"For Yosl?" Isroel said. "The scum working for the Nazis?"

"Oh, he is just doing what is necessary to survive," Ita screamed back. "You would, too, if they offered it to you."

Isroel scoffed.

"We also need to wait for Rachel," Father said.

"Fine, but tomorrow, we're leaving no matter what," Isroel said. "And David, Yossi is too young. He is a liability."

"Excuse me?" Father said. "A liability?"

"Yes," Isroel said. "He is a baby. He could cry, and we would be found. All of us could die. We need to think about saving the majority."

"Have you lost your mind?" Father started screaming. "You must be crazy! You think I would desert my child? I would rather we all die."

Father stood up and stormed off into the forest. Soon he was out of sight. I looked over at Yossi, who was sitting quietly, playing with the dirt. Then I looked at Mother, who was sitting with her head down. The adults were silent, each careful not to look at each other.

The sun was starting to go down and Father had still not returned. I kept looking around at all the adults, wishing someone would do something—make a decision, figure something out. That's what they should be doing!

Then, I heard a rustling in the trees. Father must be coming back! Finally! A few moments later, there he was—with aunt Rachel! I ran to her, happier than I had ever been to see her. Her eyes sparkled when she saw me.

"What happened to you?" she said, opening her arms for me. "I was looking all over!"

"We didn't know what to do," I said, hugging her as tightly as I could.

"It's OK," she said. "I am just glad you are all right, and we are all together now."

All together. How lucky we are that our family was all together. Even if we were here, in the forest with nothing to eat or drink. But we had what so many families didn't.

1942—Abi

BANG! BANG! BANG!

I jolted awake with the sound of shots coming from somewhere in the forest. The steady banging continued, one burst of sound right after another. I was lying on the ground between Yossi and Rachel. My mother was on the other side of Yossi and suddenly reached over and grabbed my hand at the sound of the shots. I lifted my head and looked around without sitting up.

"Mother, what's going on?" I asked, the banging still rhythmically echoing through the forest.

She hushed me and looked over at Father. Father was on the other side of Sarah, who was sleeping next to Rachel. He was alert and looking around the forest, as if searching for a clue. Then, the shooting stopped, but the echo still vibrated through the air for a few moments until it was silent.

My eyes followed his gaze toward the other family that was with us. Isroel, his wife Ety, and two of their daughters were huddled together—the two children in the middle with the parents on either side. The parents had their arms on top of the girls, as if they were trying to shield them from the forest. Then my eyes drifted to Ita, the wife of Yosl. She was sitting up with her back against a tree trunk, hugging her knees into her chest. Her frizzy hair moved with the slight breeze and her eyes darted around back and forth. She had big bags under her eyes that looked like they could have been filled with sand.

Suddenly, I heard someone running. I could hear the panting, uneven breaths, and the stomping of footsteps as they crunched through leaves and snapped branches. I looked over at Father again, who had stood up and was brushing the dirt off of his clothes. His head moved back and forth as he tried to narrow in on where the sound was coming from. A few moments later, I could see the runner. It was Lieb. He was sprinting, turning his head back behind him every few paces. Father walked towards him, but Lieb didn't seem to see him. He turned his head back, and then wham! He ran right into Father, knocking him down and falling right on top of him.

"Father!" I jumped. I scrambled up from where I was lying and ran over to them.

Lieb looked startled by his fall. He took a few moments to understand what had happened, then he pushed himself off my father and stood up, reaching out his hand for my father.

"Lieb!" Father cried as he grabbed his hand to pull himself up. "What's going on?"

Lieb leaned over, putting his hands on his legs right above his knees. He was panting hard and his cheeks were bright red and splotchy.

"They came . . ." Lieb said slowly, still breathing hard. "To Shanke . . ."

"Who?" Father yelled at him. Lieb was still standing there hunched over.

"Who!" Father repeated. "Spit it out!"

"The Germans!" Lieb said. "This morning . . . when we were going to the mill . . . they came . . . and took . . . all the Jews."

"Took them where?" I asked. My father looked at me sternly, but I wasn't afraid. I needed to know.

Lieb looked at me, and then turned to Father to answer. "They took everyone to the forest," he said. "Over there somewhere." He was pointing off to his right. My head followed his arm and I looked off in that direction. It was the direction that the sounds of shots had come from just moments ago.

"They are all gone," Lieb said, standing up straight.

"Is anyone following you?" David asked.

"No," Lieb responded quickly. "I don't think so. No one saw me get away."

"Abi!" Father looked at me. "Go back to Mother and Rachel over there."

I looked him back in the eyes, almost challenging him. I wanted to hear what Lieb had to say, about what the Germans did with the Jews, why they took them into the forest, what happened. After a moment, I gave in and turned around, walking back over to where my family was sitting. As I walked, I caught Ita's eyes. She stared at me, unflinching, and I held her stare back until I sat down next to my mother, who was now sitting up with Yossi on her lap.

I started thinking about all the people in the hut we had stayed with the night before. About Jonathan and the others who played cards and curled on the floor around us. Were they all Jews? Were they all dead? I had so many questions I wanted to ask Father, but I could see he wanted to think I didn't understand. Maybe that made it easier on him. I watched him and Lieb standing face-to-face speaking quietly to each other. Father looked concerned and placed his left hand on Lieb's shoulder. Lieb lowered his head, still breathing hard.

Then Father and Lieb started walking back towards us. I looked away, pretending that I wasn't trying to read their lips the whole time they were talking.

"We need to stay hidden today," Father said when they reached us. "Tonight, we are going to start our trek to Hungary."

"What's in Hungary?" I asked.

"For now, safety," Father responded. "We need to be quiet until nightfall."

Nightfall—that was hours away. We just woke up. I started thinking about all the things I could do here. There was a great big tree nearby I could climb. It had branches that were low enough for me to jump and grab onto. From there, I could pull myself up, from branch to branch, until I would reach the tree line. Then I could see everything. I would probably be able to see Shanke and all the little huts crowded next to each other. Maybe if it was clear enough, I could see Butla, or maybe even Hungary, even though I wouldn't even be sure what that looked like. Probably I could find a stream nearby where I could go fishing and catch lunch. I was quick enough that sometimes I could catch a fish with my bare hands. It wasn't the best method, but sometimes it was only option. But I would do none of that. Father was clear that we were to be hiding—staying quiet—until the darkness could shield us.

I looked around at what everyone was doing. Rachel was sitting up braiding Sarah's hair. Well, it looked like that was what she was trying to do. Rachel kept running her fingers through Sarah's frizzy hair, pulling through the knots and gently tugging her head backwards. Sarah sat quietly, with Yossi in her lap facing her. She was quietly playing with him, clapping his hands together and smiling at him. Yossi smiled back, silently clapping his hands and watching Sarah's head bob back and forth as Rachel braided. I watched Yossi for a while, thinking about what it would be like to take him fishing. One day I would teach him, but not with our hands. I would make a fishing rod special for him and I would show him how to cast the line and tug it at exactly the right moment to hook the fish. I smiled thinking about it.

I looked over at Mother, who was sitting quietly, also watching Rachel braid Sarah's hair. Mother's eyes shone, but she had a sad smile on her face. I could see years of worry stamped on her forehead, as though she had aged significantly in the last few months. I remember when she used to laugh, when she and Father used to kiss and hold hands, but now she constantly seemed alert and on edge.

Father and Lieb had gone over to speak with Isroel. The three of them were huddled together whispering to each other. They looked intently at each other as they spoke, as though trying to absorb the others' words. A few meters away, Ety was sitting up with her two daughters lying on either side. She stroked their hair, as they continued trying to sleep.

Ita was still sitting on her own. She was watching the men talk, her eyes fixated on them as though she could burn a hole through them. I felt sorry for her, being alone here. I knew her husband Yosl was part of the Judenrat in Turka, and that meant he was evil. But he was still a Jew like us.

How long had we been sitting here already? Waiting for nightfall seemed like an endless amount of time to wait. I lay down on my back, with my hands under my head. Maybe I could just pass the time like this, looking at the sky between the trees.

The light was starting to turn orange and the shadows were getting longer. Finally, the day was passing and soon we would be able to do something. Everyone was still huddled as they were in the morning, but now everyone seemed alert and was looking around.

Suddenly, I heard a rustling in the trees. The sound was coming from deeper in the forest, not from the direction of Shanke. Maybe it was a bear. Father and Lieb noticed the sound, too, and had gotten up. They were moving closer to where the sound was coming from, but trying to stay low and unseen. Soon, Father and Lieb were hidden from me by the trees. I could still hear the rustling, now from them walking away, and from whatever or whoever was approaching us. Then, as suddenly as it had begun, the rustling stopped.

For a few moments there was silence. The silence terrified me. It was scarier than if there had been some loud boom or bang; at least then, I would know what was happening. Now, nothing. Then the rustling started up again, getting louder until I could see eight legs approaching. First Father came into sight, and a few steps behind him was Lieb, walking in stride with his brother Chaim, their arms around each other's shoulders. Chaim! My heart jumped to see him. Lieb said he had gotten on the transport in Turka. My mind immediately started racing about what had happened to him. Maybe it was all just rumors, maybe there wasn't really a transport, or maybe they brought everyone back.

A few steps behind them came Yosl, stumbling along through the brush. His face was bruised and swollen with cuts piercing his lips and cheeks. The sight of him shocked me; he always looked so clean and well-dressed. When Yosl came into full view, Ita pushed herself up from her sitting place and immediately ran to him, swinging her arms around his neck so hard that she seemed to knock the wind out of him. I turned away, I was more interested in Chaim and how he had suddenly turned up. I got up and walked over to Lieb and Chaim to say hello.

"Hey, little man!" Chaim said to me, holding out his hand. I slapped his hand hard, squeezing it as I smiled at him.

"How did you get here?" I asked him.

"I knew Lieb was in Shanke, so I decided to come find him," he smiled at me and then looked up at Father who was standing next to me.

"Abi, let us talk," Father said to me. I sighed and rolled my eyes at him. I wanted to know what had

125

happened. I hated that Father sent me away every time he wanted to talk to someone.

I smiled at Chaim and Lieb, and slowly started backing away. When they stopped looking at me, I slipped behind a tree near them so I could listen to what they were saying.

"What happened?" Father asked.

"I went with our parents to Turka," Chaim started. "They lined us up next to the railroad outside of the village. There were huge cattle carts waiting for us there. They just started taking down names and loading us in the cattle carts, without telling us anything. People were saying we were going to some ghetto or some special village for Jews."

"Did you get on the train?" Lieb asked.

"Yes, with Mother and Father," Chaim continued. "They squeezed us in one of the carts with our suitcases. We were so packed in the cart, you wouldn't believe it. Everyone was pressed up against each other, standing on suitcases; some people even had to leave their stuff behind because it wouldn't fit. We luckily got a spot near the edge of the cart—by a window—so we could breathe. People in the middle were screaming that they couldn't breathe."

"So, what happened?" Father repeated impatiently.

"The train started moving, and, well, I don't know, I got a bad feeling," Chaim started. "Father also seemed worried and he, well, he told me to jump."

"To jump?" Lieb said.

"Yea, from the window," Chaim said. "Father lifted me up, and I climbed out. There were some other people also trying to jump out of the windows. The Germans on top of the cars screamed when I jumped and they started shooting, but I ran as fast as I could away from the train. They got some of the others who had jumped."

"What about Mother and Father?" Lieb asked.

"I don't know what happened," Chaim said, his tone had changed. His voice suddenly sounded deeper and hoarse. "I guess they probably stayed on the train."

"I am sorry to hear that," Father said. "Unfortunately, I don't think they are coming back."

"I know," Chaim said. "I think everyone knew once they got on the train."

"What was Yosl doing with you?" Father said.

"That pig!" Chaim spit. "When I was running away, I saw him. He had been riding on the top of the trains with the Germans. Then they tried to push him down to go into one of the carts. He tried to fight them, but then he just fell off. He saw me and just started running after me."

"Why did you bring him here?" Lieb asked.

"What was I supposed to do?" Chaim said. "He kept pleading to me that his wife was here in the forest. That pathetic bastard, I couldn't just leave him. He would have died on his own there or he would have been killed by other Jews in the forest."

I could see Yosl and Ita from where I was sitting. Ita had her hands on his face, trying to wipe away the dirt and dried blood. Yosl's puffy face looked even more swollen now and he had tears running down his cheeks.

"You are an honorable young man," Father said.

"What? No!" Lieb screamed. "What are we supposed to do with him? He can't go to Hungary with us."

"Lieb, he is still one of us," Father said. "It is our duty to protect life, especially the lives of other Jews, even if we don't like them."

"I don't think so," Lieb yelled. "Don't you know what he did to us?"

"To all of us, Lieb," Father said. "He did it to all of us."

"Well, I can't stand it," Lieb said. I could hear him getting restless where they were standing. The leaves were crunching as he moved his legs around, and then, suddenly, he bolted in Yosl's direction.

"Do you have something to say for yourself?" Lieb screamed at him.

Yosl looked up in shock, the swollen parts of his face casting deep shadows on the rest of it.

"Well?" Lieb yelled, just centimeters in front of his face.

"I . . . uh . . . I," Yosl hesitated and started murmuring indistinguishable sounds. "Erh . . . um . . . I . . . uhhhhh . . ."

Chaim and father came running after Lieb and grabbed his shoulders just as he seemed about to raise his arms.

"Enough!" Father screamed.

Suddenly a loud roar rolled through the forest and a heavy rain started pounding down. The rain drops were like bullets pelting us from above, splashing over us and soaking everything in seconds.

The ground quickly turned to mud and my feet started to sink in. I lifted my hands to wipe my face, but every time I wiped the water away it filled my eyes again, sticking to my lashes and running down the dirt on my cheeks.

By now, the sun had set. I hadn't even noticed when it became dark. I could barely see the adults standing in front of me.

"We need to go!" Father yelled to everyone over the roar of the rain.

I could hear Mother, Rachel, and my siblings getting up from where they were sitting. They sloshed through the mud until they were close enough to Father for me to see them. The entire group had gotten up and huddled in close to Father, all looking at him, waiting for him to tell us what to do.

"Let's go," he said.

Father looked around at the group and picked up Yossi, putting him on his shoulders. Then he started walking deeper into the forest and we all followed. With each step I had to forcefully pull my foot from the mud and place it in front of me careful not to let it slide anywhere. The rain continued pounding down on us, and I stopped trying to clean my face. Instead I let the rain clean me, thinking about what my clothes looked like before we came into the forest.

Father was leading the way. His arms were holding both of Yossi's feet in front of his chest. Yossi sat still, with his arms wrapped around Father's head. Yossi's shirt was completely stuck to his back, showing the outline of his thin spine and protruding shoulder blades. It made me wonder if that is how my back looked from behind. Behind Father was Sarah and me. We walked next to each silently, but I noticed she kept looking over at me, as though to check if I were still there. Behind us were Mother and Rachel, followed by Chaim and Lieb. Then, there were Isroel and Ety walking with their daughters between them. I couldn't see behind them, but I guessed Yosl and Ita were in the back.

We walked like that in line for hours, it seemed. The rain continued to pour down on us, but it wasn't cold. In fact, I was happy for the rain. During the walk, I kept tilting my head back to take a drink. The huge rain drops splashed right into my mouth, filling it in seconds. It was so refreshing and quenched my thirst.

We kept moving forward, until a spark of light started coming through the trees. The sun was starting to rise behind the rain. Father stopped and turned around. Yossi was still sitting on his shoulders, his arms wrapped tightly on Father's forehead and his head resting on Father's head.

"We can't move during the daytime," Father said. "There may be Germans patrolling the forest."

I looked around behind me to see the rest of our group. Mother and Rachel were still behind us, as were Lieb and Chaim, and Isroel's family.

"Where are Yosl and Ita?" Father asked the group.

Everyone turned around in surprise, looking for the couple that had been trailing in the back. Isroel turned around and stared behind him for a few moments and then turned back.

"They were behind us . . ." Isroel said in a confused tone. "I don't know what happened."

"Everyone needs to keep up," Father said. He picked up Yossi and laid him down on the ground. "Let's rest here for the day."

We were standing in a large ditch surrounded by trees. Parts of the ditch were covered in puddles so deep they went up to my knees. It was still raining, but the pounding had lightened up. The raindrops were smaller now and the trees around the ditch were large enough that their branches seemed to block some of the water coming down. Everyone sat down around the edges of the ditch, getting comfortable for the day. I looked around at all the faces, wondering if anyone was feeling as hungry as I was. As though she could read my mind, Rachel came over and sat down next to me, handing me a small piece of bread. She had pulled a handkerchief out of her pocket with a few slices that she split with everyone. The bread was soggy—soaked with the rain—but I was so hungry, I had never loved bread as much as I did in that moment. After savoring the small bite, I closed my eyes and fell asleep.

I was woken up by Chaim, who shook my shoulder and told me it was time to get up. When I opened my eyes, I saw that it was evening and the sun was setting. It was time to continue the walk. I saw everyone was getting up, so I followed. I tried to wipe some of the mud off my pants, but it was no use; it just made it worse.

We continued in our formation—with Father leading the group with Yossi on his shoulders. The rain was still coming down, alternating from a slight drizzle to heavy rain drops every few minutes. We continued to walk silently, trudging through the mud until we heard a scream.

"HEEEELLLLLLOOOOO!!!" the scream came out from the forest, spooking everyone. Father immediately turned around and looked at the group, which had started to scatter in different directions. I looked behind me as well, seeing Lieb and Chaim running off to the right, and Isroel, his wife, and children running off to the left.

"HELLLLLOOOO!" the scream came again. My eyes were darting back and forth between the runners and Father, who stood motionless.

"STOP!" Father finally screamed. By then I couldn't even see Lieb and Chaim. On the other side, I saw Isroel's family stop in their tracks.

A few moments later, I could see the outline of two people coming up behind us. From their movements, I could see it was a man and a woman.

"Yosl! Be quiet!" Father yelled. "What are you doing? Are you trying to get everyone killed?"

As the couple approached, I saw that it was Yosl and Ita, who had somehow caught up to us.

"We lost you!" Yosl yelled breathily. "You left us!"

"Everyone needs to take care of themselves and stay with the group," Father said to him. "If you can't, then that isn't my problem. But you can't be acting like an idiot here in the forest, endangering everyone with your screams. If someone else heard you, do you understand what could have happened?"

Yosl looked at Father the way a child does when he is being scolded by his parents. "We were trying to find you," he responded.

"We need to keep moving," Father responded. I could see he was annoyed.

"Wait!" Isroel said. He and his family were jogging back towards us. "Zelda and Ethel lost their shoes in the mud."

I looked over at his two daughters who were both running in their stockings, mud trailing up their legs.

"Both of them lost their shoes?" Father asked.

"Yes," Isroel said. "When we started running. We need to find them."

Father sighed deeply. "All right, let's find their shoes."

We all started walking in the direction that Isroel's family had run, searching the mud all around. I kept looking over to the direction where Chaim and Lieb had run, hoping to see them come back, but that side of the forest was silent except for the steady rhythm of the rain. I looked down at the ground, moving the mud around with my feet to see if I could feel the shoes. Everyone was looking, except Yosl and Ita who looked like they were arguing quietly with each other.

"Found a pair!" Father screamed. "One more to go."

Everyone continued searching. After some time, the night began to turn into day. We were all still searching, but now at least we had some light for help. Finally, Father found the second pair.

By this time, it was already morning and Father decided we would stay here until the next night. I was happy to take a break; looking for the shoes was more exhausting than walking through the forest. I quickly fell asleep, barely noticing the growls coming from my stomach.

Again, at nightfall, I was awoken to continue our walk. I looked around our group and caught the eyes of Father.

"What about Lieb and Chaim?" I asked.

"We can't wait here for them," Father said. "We don't know if they will return."

I nodded. We all got up and continued the trek, walking silently behind Father who continued to carry Yossi on his shoulders. During this night's walk, the terrain of the forest changed. We were no longer walking on flat ground through trees. We were going up a steep hill with fewer trees on each side of us. It was hard climbing up the hill in the mud and rain, and I used my hands to help myself climb up. We climbed for hours and then suddenly we were above the trees. The top of the hill was covered in grass with no trees around to stop the rain. We were on the edge of the rim of a huge mountain range! I could see down on either side of us, the straight line where the trees ended, the endless forest below us and the small villages far away in the distance. We were on top of the world.

We crossed over the peak of the mountain range down to the other side. When we got back to the shade of the trees we stopped to rest until the following night. We continued walking for three more nights, down the side of the hill and again through flat forest, until Father said it was time to stop.

"Hungary is right on the other side of the forest," Father announced. As he said that, the rain started to lighten until it came to a stop. The sun started to shine, sparkling through all the raindrops that were still falling off the trees.

"We're safe here," Father said. He put Yossi down. "Abi, Sarah, go find some sticks—see if there are any dry ones."

I immediately obeyed and ran off looking for sticks to bring to Father. I grabbed as many as I could and brought them to him. Sarah did the same. Father took the sticks and started to build a bonfire. After a few moments, the fire was lit. I was hypnotized by it. The heat of the fire and the brightness of the light was beautiful.

"Abi, get closer," Father said. "Dry off."

I smiled at him and got in close to the fire, holding out my hands to warm them. They were wrinkled and white from the days of rain. The warmth of the fire was starting to roll through my body. Sarah stood next to me, holding Yossi near the fire to dry off his clothes. Zelda and Ethel also stood next to us by the fire, both of them smiling for the first time since we saw them in the forest. They giggled to each other as they waved their hands back and forth, warming their palms and knuckles.

The adults had gone off in search of food in the forest. They returned an hour later with vegetables, berries, and grains that they passed around to everyone. We all sat around the fire drying our clothes and feasting on what the adults had gathered. That is, except Father. He was standing on the side of the fire where the smoke was blowing. The smoke blew right into his eyes, but he stood there, unflinching, watching the group. I couldn't understand his expression, but I wanted him to be happy with us. Happy that we made it through the forest to Hungary. Happy that we were now dry and were finally eating something.

After a few hours, Father and Isroel went off with each other to speak. They were trying to figure out how we would enter in to Hungary. A group like us, coming out of the forest, would likely draw suspicion. I watched the two of them speak animatedly to each other. As Isroel's lips moved, his hands made circles in front of his body and his head shook side to side. Then Father spoke, putting his hands on Isroel's shoulders, causing Isroel's animated arms to go limp. Eventually, the two men came back to the group with an announcement.

"Hinda and I will go with Isroel and his family into Hungary first," Father said. "The rest of you will stay here until I come back and take you."

I looked around at our family—a family that was about to be split up yet again. Father continued, "We will take Yossi. Rachel, you will watch Sarah and Abi here. Yosl and Ita, you must also stay put."

Anger started to boil inside of me. Why should we stay here with Yosl and Ita? Why does Isroel's family get to cross into Hungary first? What are we supposed to do, just sit here and wait?

"Father!" I yelled. "We should stay together!"

"No," he responded. The sad look in his eyes told me he had his reasons to split us up—that he didn't want us all in the same place together. "I promise, I will come back."

It was starting to get dark out. Sarah, Rachel, Yossi, and I stayed next to the fire, watching Isroel and his girls get ready to continue the walk across the border. Father and Mother were sitting together away from the fire, just far enough that I couldn't hear what they were saying. Mother was staring at the ground as Father spoke to her, his hand on her back. I tried to look at her deeply, trying to signal to her with my eyes to look up, to look at me, but her gaze was glued to the ground. When the twilight turned into night, Father and Mother got up and came back over to the fire. Mother first went to Sarah, kneeling down and hugging her tightly. Father's hand then firmly grabbed my shoulder.

"Abi," he said gently, bending down to speak with me. I stood up to face him, so we could speak eye to eye. "You are the man around here. You understand?"

"What about Yosl?" I asked. "He's staying."

"You must be the man," David responded. "I am counting on you until I return."

"Yes, Father." I hugged him, feeling the warmth of his body against mine. He cupped one of his hands on the back of my head and I could feel each of his strong fingers holding on tight. Then it was over, and Father went to hug Rachel and Sarah goodbye.

"Honey, we will be back soon," Mother said as she came over to hug me. "Everything is fine."

She had that smile on her face. The kind of smile that looks like it doesn't belong, like it was slapped on her face to cover up her real expression. I smiled back at her, hoping mine looked a little less forced.

"I know," I responded, hugging her. "Don't worry about us here."

With that, we watched Mother, Father, Yossi, and the Rosenbergs disappear. Our group—the group left behind—sat quietly around the fire that night. The fire was starting to cool, getting smaller as branches we fed it cracked and disintegrated. We watched the fire die down slowly until it was nothing but embers.

By this point, Rachel and Sarah were asleep, holding each other as they lay peacefully on the dirt. Yosl and Ita were also sleeping on the other side of the fire, although with their backs to each other. Eventually, I lay down, closing my eyes with hopes that by the time I woke up, Mother and Father would be back.

I awoke the next morning to the sound of birds humming in the trees above. The sound startled me and my instinct was to try to get them to be quiet; otherwise someone might find us here. I looked around me, and saw that Rachel and Sarah were no longer sleeping where I saw them last night. I jumped up in a panic, but soon noticed them off in the distance collecting berries and other things we could eat from the forest. Yosl and Ita were still sleeping by the ashes of the fire. I got up and went over to Rachel and Sarah to see what they had found.

"Good morning," Rachel said, she handed me a handful of berries she was holding in her skirt. I grabbed them happily, popping each in my mouth. The three of us continued gathering fruits until we were full, and then returned back to the campsite, where Yosl and Ita were now sitting up. Rachel handed them some berries. I wanted to stop her from giving away our fortune. They didn't deserve any; they didn't help at all.

"When do you think David will be back?" Yosl said, his teeth red from the juice of the fruits.

"It's only a few hours walk into Hungary," Rachel responded. "I am sure they got there safe last night and are going to figure out a place for us and then come back. I bet they will be here in a few hours."

We had nothing to do but wait. I started gathering rocks and pebbles and decided to build myself a small castle with leaves sticking out as flags. Sarah and Rachel liked the idea of my game, and quickly joined in finding the smoothest rocks that we could stack together to be the castle walls. The day passed quickly and soon again it was dark. Still, no sign of Mother and Father.

"I think we should go back," Yosl said. "It's been too long, something must have happened."

"No," Rachel responded to him sternly. "David will come back."

"We're waiting here like sitting ducks!" Yosl cried. "Whoever got to them is probably on their way here and we're just sitting waiting for them to come kill us!"

Rachel ignored him and started gathering wood to build a fire.

"What are you doing?" Yosl screamed. "You are going to lead them right to us!"

Rachel continued to ignore him as she stacked together branches in the shape of a teepee.

"STOP!" Yosl screamed again, this time throwing a rock right at Rachel.

Wham! The rock hit her shoulder, knocking her back. She caught herself with her arm, thankfully unhurt. She looked up at Yosl, eyes and mouth wide open. I stood up. This is what Father was telling me about. I needed to be the man here, to watch all these children who needed an adult to lead them. I ran over to where Yosl was sitting and stood above him, hands on my waist.

"You can leave if you want," I said. "We don't want you here. We just let you stay with us because we feel sorry for you."

I stared at him, challenging him to get up and face me. He didn't move. He just looked at me, his lower lip quivering as he tried to decide what to say.

"Do that again, and I will make you leave," I said. I gently kicked his leg to give my threat a little more power and then turned around and walked away. He was so pathetic, so weak. We would have been better off without him, but I didn't want to do anything my father wouldn't have done.

Rachel got the fire going and Sarah and I got in close to watch the flames. Even Yosl and Ita inched closer to warm themselves—those disgusting people. But I quickly forgot about them. Instead, I enjoyed the fire, sitting with my wonderful aunt and big sister, watching them make shadows on the ground with their hands. Rachel twisted her thumbs together and spread her fingers like wings, and the shadow looked like a bird flying far, far away. If only we could do that—just spread our wings and go where ever we wanted.

The crackling of fire and the smell of smoke surrounded us. For some reason it was calming. I enjoyed the feeling of the fire—it was so powerful, so majestic and uncontrollable. Then the crackling started getting louder. And then louder. I instantly became alert and realized the sound wasn't coming from the fire.

"I knew it!" Yosl yelled. "I told you so, your fire will be the reason we never make it!"

Yosl stood up as if ready to run away, but the next moment, Father and Mother appeared through the trees. Father still had Yossi on his shoulders, as if he had been stuck there since they left.

"You came back!" Sarah screamed, running to hug them.

"Of course, we did," Father responded. "There was no other option."

After hugs all around, Father and Mother sat down near the fire. Sarah cuddled Yossi who giggled quietly, happy to be in her arms.

"Where are the Rosenbergs?" I asked when they settled down.

"They found a place to stay in Hungary," Father said. "Tomorrow morning, we will cross the border."

I started thinking about if I should tell Father about what Yosl did, but I decided not to. He had enough on his mind right now. Instead, I told him that everything was fine while they were gone. I told him about the rock castle we built and the berries we found. His eyes shone as he watched me talk and his lips curved slightly up. He patted me on the back before kissing my forehead and telling me it was time to get some rest.

The next morning, we got up to begin the last leg of our trip; it was just a few hours walk and then we would be in Hungary, a place safe from the Germans! Everyone was excited about ending our long stay in the forest. We could find a home, eat bread, maybe even sleep in a bed!

The walk was easy, the ground was flat, but there were streams running through the forest and some places were muddy. We walked slowly, taking breaks every once-in-a-while to catch our breath and find a few berries to stop our grumbling stomachs. Then, finally, I started to see a village through the trees. We had made it! My heart leapt through my chest. I couldn't remember ever being so excited about anything in my life!

We got to the edge of the village and Father stopped. "We can't go in like this," he said. "I am going to find a place for us to stay. Don't go anywhere until I get back."

We nodded and settled down again at the edge of the trees.

"Abi," Father turned to me, waving his finger at me to come over. "You see, over there? There is a shul."

I looked over the direction that Father was pointing, and sure enough there was a large white building with a Star of David on top. A shul! There were Jews here! Jews that still went to shul, no less!

"I want you to go there," Father said. "Tell them you are a Jew and you need help. Tell them you are hungry."

I nodded, excited for this mission. I hadn't been in a shul in forever! We used to go every Friday night when I was little. My father would sing the prayers and I would try to follow along in his prayer book. I looked back at the rest of my family and then ran as fast as I could to the shul. When I got closer, I could hear singing. The Friday evening prayers were roaring through the shul's windows. It was Shabbos! That meant there would be wine and challah at the shul! My excitement grew as I got closer, my heart pounding to the rhythm of the hymns. I recognized the tune they were singing from our own shul back in Butla, but the words were in a language I couldn't understand. I even starting humming along in my head as I got closer.

When I got to the shul's doors, I stopped and looked up. The doors were large and magnificent, made of iron and wood with glass windows cut through the middle. Above the doors was the huge Star of David carved in the building with different colors of painted glass in between each triangle around the star. I took a deep breath, and opened the doors.

Inside were rows and rows of Jews in black jackets, all with a white yarmulke covering their heads. They swayed back and forth as they prayed, feeling the magic of God's prayers. I started humming along louder as I walked down the aisles looking for someone to speak with. As I walked, everyone turned to me and stared. I smiled at everyone, hoping they felt the same connection to me that I did to them. My people.

Suddenly I felt someone grab my shoulders and pull me back. I turned to see a man with a long beard in a suit with tzitzit hanging out. I smiled at him.

"I am a Jew," I said. "I need help."

The man started screaming to me in a language I couldn't understand.

"Jewish," I said in Yiddish, pointing to myself. "Yehudi, Juden" I tried saying Jew in other languages I had heard, but we were in Hungary, and I didn't know Hungarian. I tried to free myself from the man's strong grip, but he wouldn't let go; he kept trying to drag me to the door.

By this time, the entire shul was watching. The prayers had stopped and even the rabbi stood at the front staring at me.

"I am a Jew from Poland!" I screamed. "I need your help."

My scream caused an uproar in the shul and a couple of men got up and came over towards me. Could anyone here understand Yiddish? Did they understand me? Were they coming to help me? No, they came to help the man who was trying to drag me out.

"Please," I yelled, struggling against the three men pulling me towards the door. "The Germans came for us; it is not safe for Jews in Poland anymore."

I was no match for them. They opened the shul door and threw me outside. I fell to the ground, hitting my back on the dirt.

"Filthy," one of the men yelled in Yiddish as he spit on the ground at my feet.

1942—Rachel

Sitting on the edge of the forest, looking out at this new village in this country, I started to feel relief. Here in Hungary, there were Jews still living and practicing Judaism as though they had no idea what was happening just a few days walk into Poland.

I had never been to Hungary before. Starting a new life in this country wouldn't be easy. I didn't know the language, and I knew that Hungarians didn't get along with Poles, but we would make do. What other choice did we have?

The village in front of us looked like it was from a different world than Butla. While the houses were still made of wood, they were larger than the ones we had. In the distance, we could see the village shul. It was grand, not like what we had back home. There was a shul in Turka, but it was just a house that had been designated to be a place for prayer. On the outside it looked like any other house, but on the inside, it had a Torah and pews.

The shul here was massive—a huge white building that could be recognized from all around, with its giant Star of David shining through the wall above the front door. It looked more like a church to me than a shul. Abi was there right now. David sent him, hoping that the people would be more likely to listen to a young boy in need of help, rather than an adult who looked like a beggar.

I was waiting with Hinda, Sarah, and Yossi by the forest edge. David had gone into the village to find out what we would do next. Our companions, Yosl and Ita, sat a bit away from us, always careful to keep their distance, but not too much distance, so they wouldn't get left behind again. They would never get too close, as though they still thought they were different from us. Get too close, and they may realize they were just as Jewish as we were.

Soon, I could see Abi walking back from the shul. He walked slowly, dragging his feet and staring at the ground, as though concentrating on the movement of his legs. The posture was unlike him. He was such a brave child. Only eight years old, but by the way he tried to take responsibility for his siblings, you would think he was closer to my age. He came back to where we were waiting and sat down on the ground silently next to me. He sat slumped over, using his fingers to draw squiggly lines in the dirt in front of him. I rubbed his back and smiled at him. He caught my eye and gave me a defeated smile. I guess the Jews here are different than in Poland.

We sat there a few more hours until David returned. He was walking with a tall slender man in a clean shirt.

"This is the group?" the man said to David as they stopped in front of us. He spoke to David in Polish, although from his accent I could tell he was

Hungarian. The man looked us all up and down. "Do you think they can all make it?"

"Of course, they can," David said. "We're all tough enough."

"It's 175 pengo[8] a person," the man said, resting his hands on his hips.

"A person?" David raised his voice. "That's ridiculous."

"That's the price," the man said. "Otherwise, you can go by yourself. Good luck with that."

"Fine," David said. "There are the three adults and two children. The little one stays on my shoulders—he doesn't count." David motioned to Yossi as he opened his jacket to pay the man. Where David got the money, I will never know. Somehow, he always seemed to have money tucked away somewhere.

"Per person," the man repeated. "I see eight people."

David looked up and glared at the man for a few moments.

"The two of them are not with us," David said pointing to Yosl and Ita.

"What?" Yosl got up and ran towards David. "What are we supposed to do? I don't have any money to pay the guide!"

"You are on your own now," David responded coldly. "We're in Hungary. We agreed to come here together. Now you can figure it out."

_____

[8] Pengo was the Hungarian currency in 1942. In 1941 $1USD was equal to 5 pengo, so the price per person was about $35USD.

David looked back at the guide with finality. Then he shook his head and counted out the money to pay for the six of us. The man grabbed the money greedily and recounted it before stuffing it in his pocket.

"Let's go; we have a long trip ahead of us," the man said. He started walking along the edge of the forest away from the village, and we all quickly got up to follow. David lifted Yossi throwing him over his shoulders.

Yosl stood, his mouth agape as we started walking away, leaving him and Ita alone at the side of the forest. I didn't look at them as we left. I was glad to be away from them.

"Where are we going?" I asked David.

"Munkacz," he responded. "We can't stay in this border village. There are police raids looking for Poles. When they find any, they turn them over to the Germans."

"Where is Munkacz?" I asked.

"Over those mountains," David said pointing to a tall mountain range off in the distance. "It's deeper into Hungary, farther away from Poland."

My heart sank looking at the mountains in front of us. I thought we were done with our trek through the forest, but by the looks of what was ahead, it seems we actually had just started. We walked silently away from the village and entered back into the forest. The forest here was completely different. Instead of walking through thick tree covering, we were now walking along ravines, and climbing up steep inclines covered with rocks and sand. As we climbed, I looked to my side, seeing a deep gorge down below. One wrong step, and I would disappear into the gorge, never to be found. I used my hands to hold on to rocks in front of me, helping me feel steady as we continued up on the side of the cliff.

David was right in front of me, climbing with Yossi on his back. Yossi held on tight, his legs and arms wrapped tightly around David's body. From behind, I could see his face pressed against David's shoulder, his eyes squeezed shut. I looked back down to concentrate on my climb and then, suddenly, there was a thud.

The sound cracked against the rocks, which gave way, sliding down, bouncing off everything in their path. I looked up to see rocks sliding towards me, and above that, Yossi hanging down the side of the ravine, with David's hand wrapped around his small bicep. I gasped, watching David pull Yossi's limp body back up. I was frozen, watching them in front of me. I wanted to call out to David, to Yossi, but I couldn't think of what I could say. David used his one arm to seat Yossi on the rocks in front of him while using his other arm to steady himself along the ledge. I could see Yossi's face, blood running down his lower lip, down his chin and neck, soaking his shirt. Yossi was silent, so silent. Was he alive? Then I saw him blink. David ripped his own shirt sleeve and used it to blot the blood on Yossi's lip.

"It's OK," he said calmly. "You're fine. Everything's fine."

I looked ahead of David, who had been climbing behind our guide. The guide didn't seem to notice the commotion, or maybe he didn't care. Either way, he didn't stop; he was still climbing higher, getting smaller. Then I looked down behind me, Abi and Sarah waited patiently, followed by Hinda.

"Is everything OK?" Hinda called. By her tone, I was sure she hadn't seen what had happened. Better that way, I thought.

"Yes, fine," I called back. "Just taking a little break."

David sat still, holding his shirt sleeve over Yossi's lip for a few more minutes. Then, he whispered something to Yossi, who nodded and climbed back on David's back. We continued the climb, more cautiously this time, moving slowly in the direction the guide had gone. Eventually we got to the top of the steep ridge we were climbing. We were on a flat peak surrounded by mountains all around. The guide was there, lying on his back, waiting silently for us to catch up.

"Dear God!" Hinda screamed when she pulled herself up to the top of the peak and saw Yossi's blood-soaked shirt. "What happened?" She started to sound frantic, and tears swelled up in her eyes.

"He's fine," David snapped. "Don't worry."

Hinda grabbed Yossi off David's back and held him tightly. At that moment, Yossi started to cry. His wails pierced the air and echoed across the mountains. The sound coming from him was so foreign. I was surprised that Yossi was even capable of making those noises. During all of our travels, this was first time Yossi had cried.

Hinda held him close to her chest, brushing her lips against his forehead. I walked over to her, wrapping my arms around her and Yossi, and started humming an old tune from a song I had once sung in choir. Wrapped in our embrace, Yossi's cries started to soften, and soon he was just breathing deep uneven breaths into Hinda's chest. I kissed his head and smiled to Hinda, who was still holding Yossi tight as though her arms had the power to heal.

As Hinda continued to comfort Yossi, we all sat to rest on the mountaintop. I wiped my brow that was soaked with sweat and covered in dirt. After a break that was much too short, we continued, down this mountain and then up another one. Down and up. Down and up. We trekked through the mountains for about ten days, until we arrived at a small village called Roztoka. The guide said he had arranged for two taxis to come take us the rest of the way to Munkacz and then he disappeared into the village.

Soon, one taxi appeared. It was an old car, with just two seats – for the driver and the passenger. David told Hinda to get in first with Sarah and then Abi jumped in, sitting on the car floor at Hinda's feet. The driver scrunched his nose as he looked at them, and then turned to David who was standing at his window.

"Take them to Aaron Koenigsberg," David said to the driver.

The driver nodded and quickly drove off, leaving us to wait for the second taxi to arrive. Aaron Koenigsberg was a friend of a friend of David's and probably the only person he knew of in Munkacz. I don't know if Aaron was expecting us, but I didn't know what our other options were.

The taxi soon disappeared. David and I were left waiting. I sat on the ground with Yossi on my lap. His lip was covered in dried blood, which he kept trying to peel off. I held his hands trying to distract him.

"What are we going to do in Munkacz?" I asked David, who was pacing around, looking for the second taxi.

"I don't know," David said.

"Are we staying there or is it just another stop?"

"I don't know, Rachel," David sighed. "For now, it's where we're going. We'll see."

"What about going to Palestina?" I asked. The thought had followed me throughout our trip from Butla. I thought about the boy from my class who so proudly announced that his family was making Aliyah. How lucky he was, that his family was there, safe from the Germans. He left just in time.

"How would we get there?" David responded.

"I don't know," I said. "How does anyone get there?"

"You don't even know if it is any better there," David said. "We have the Germans here, but they have the Arabs to deal with."

I sighed, smiling at Yossi. His arms and legs were so skinny that they looked like toothpicks sticking out of his round body. His light hair was matted to his head, slick with grease and mud.

"Where is that damn taxi?" David snapped, as he continued his pacing.

The sun was starting to set and we were still waiting on the edge of Roztoka. Not one car had passed us since the first taxi had come and whisked away Hinda and the other two children.

"That scum Hungarian," David yelled. "I bet he ripped us off and only sent one taxi. We're going to be waiting here forever."

I sat quietly as David paced. His breathing was getting deeper and louder with each stride. It was now pitch black, except for the stars that lit up the road around us. I held Yossi in my arms. He was fast asleep, breathing rhythmically in and out. I watched his chest softly rise and fall with each breath as I rocked him. I too, must have fallen asleep, because the next thing I realized was that the air was getting warmer and the sun was coming up. I looked up to see David still pacing. His hair was now sticking up in all directions as though he had spent the night scratching his head.

Then, finally, we heard a rumbling in the distance. Chugging along, getting closer, until we saw two beams of light approaching. The taxi!

"Hm," David snickered as the taxi pulled up. This taxi was a bigger car than the first one. It had a backseat, which I slipped into as David pulled himself into the front seat.

"We've been waiting a while," he said to the driver.

"Busy day," he responded nonchalantly. "Where to?"

"Munkacz," David responded. "And make it quick—the rest of our family is already there."

The driver looked over and smiled at David. He then stepped on the gas and started to drive. We sat silently in the car, driving through the Hungarian countryside and through small villages for several hours. Until the driver stopped.

"You can get out here," he said.

I looked around. In front of us was a small wooden bridge. Around us, just fields of untamed grass and weeds.

"Munkacz is just a thirty-minute walk down the road," the driver said.

"You are supposed to take us all the way," David said. "That's what you were paid to do."

"I'm not taking some Polish Jews right to the middle of the village," the driver responded. "No one will ever ride in my taxi again."

David grunted. "Come, Rachel," he said, glaring at the driver. We climbed out of the cab, which quickly drove away, blowing dust into our eyes. David grabbed Yossi from me and started walking over the bridge. We walked silently down the road until we saw the small village in front of us.

We entered the village near a small market place. People were bustling around from stand to stand, buying fruits, vegetables, and even meat. I looked around at the people in the market—about half of whom were wearing dark clothing—with long beards and peyot[9] hanging from the sides of their heads in front of their ears. Their heads were covered

---

[9] Peyot are the sidecurls or the hair in front of the ears that religious Jews do not cut.

with dark hats, the wide brims casting shadows over their faces.

I stared at every stand that we passed. There was a vegetable stand with a mountain of tomatoes stacked neatly next to a huge basket of carrots. Shoppers crowded around inspecting the tomatoes and carrots, one by one, before stuffing them in large bags and paying the seller. Then we passed a butcher, with chickens hung up by their legs on a bar above the stand. Here, women crowded the station, yelling to the butcher which chicken they wanted as he carefully untied and wrapped the naked birds for them. I started thinking about the chicken soup we used to eat on Fridays, with the carrots and potatoes in it. I wondered what these women would be making—did the Jews here eat the same things we did? Did they make cholent to eat on Saturday mornings or bake fresh challah? My mouth was starting to water.

We got through the market and entered a part of the village with small houses seated next to each other in long rows. I noticed some of the houses had a mezuzah[10] nailed neatly next to the front door. Aside from that, all the houses looked the same.

"We need to find Aaron Koenigsberg," David said to me. "Start knocking on doors."

We walked on opposites sides of the street, each of us knocking. The first door I knocked on, there was no one home, so I moved on to the next. That one, a small boy answered my knock. It was a Jewish home,

---

[10] A small scroll that Jews hang on their doorposts to remind them of their connection with God.

and the young boy already had peyot growing from his sideburns. He looked up at me, eyes wide. I could feel his eyes tracing my skin, dirty from weeks in the forest.

"Do you know Aaron Koenigsberg?" I asked him in Yiddish. The boy looked fearful, as though paralyzed and unable to answer. After a few moments, he shook his head, and then looked to the ground and closed the door.

"Rachel," David called me. "Come on, we found him."

David pointed down the road and started walking in that direction. I followed him as he walked purposefully through the rows of houses, down several different streets, until he stopped in front of a small house and knocked. The house was white, made of bricks and cement with a tiled roof.

A woman answered the door and stood quietly looking at David and me.

"Mrs. Koenigsberg?" David asked.

"Yes," she said. "David?"

David nodded. The woman stepped aside to let us in. Immediately, I saw Hinda, Sarah, and Abi sitting at their table. Sarah jumped up, rushing to hug me.

A man was also sitting with them at the table. He stood as we walked in and approached David.

"Aaron," David said. "Thank you for opening your home."

Aaron smiled. "Are you hungry?" he asked, then turned to his wife. "Zelda, get them some food."

His wife immediately came in with bowls of soup and placed them on the table in front of two empty chairs. I sat down quietly, next to Hinda, who rubbed my shoulder as I looked into the bowl in front of me. The bowl was filled with a clear broth, with just a couple pieces of carrots and potatoes inside. The steam rose up into my nose, smelling delicious and instantly I started to slurp it up.

"What happened to you?" Hinda asked me quietly. "We've been here since yesterday."

"The taxi didn't come until this morning," I responded. "We were just waiting."

Aaron and David then sat down at the table with us. David looked at the soup and kept his arms in his lap.

"We're sorry to have come like this," David said.

"You aren't the first Poles to show up here with nowhere to go," Aaron responded. "Look, we don't have space here, you can see. I've found you a room you can rent nearby. I'll help you find work; you can chop wood, or work for one of the farmers."

"Thank you," David said, extending his hand to Aaron. Aaron shook his hand firmly. Then David picked up his spoon and started to eat the soup.

When we finished eating, Aaron led us down the street to another house that looked almost the same as his. He knocked and a stout woman answered.

"Anna," Aaron smiled, reaching out for her hand. "This is the family I told you about yesterday."

She smiled at us. "Come in," she said, wiping her hands on her apron before she shook Aaron's.

"I have some space here, but this isn't a bed and breakfast," she said. "You share a room, and you be quiet when you are here."

"Yes, ma'am," David responded as all of us nodded.

"Follow me," Anna led us out of her house to a small shed nearby. She opened the door, revealing one square room with two cots in the middle. The room was dark and empty aside from the two old cots which looked like they were probably older than I was.

"You will be sharing this room with Mr. Cohen as well as Mr. and Mrs. Weizmann," Anna said. "They are out right now, but they will be back in the evening."

"Thank you, Miss," I said to her, nodding my head down.

"It's Anna," she smiled back at me. "Don't thank me so quickly. Rent is 500 pengo a week and must be paid promptly on Sunday morning. If you can't pay, you're out. No exceptions."

"Don't worry," David said. "We will pay on time."

"That's what everyone says," she smiled. "Anyway, get some rest before the others get back."

Anna slipped out of the room, leaving us alone. Abi and Sarah immediately went over to one of the cots and lay down next to each other. Hinda, holding Yossi, went to sit down on the second cot. I stayed standing, looking around the room. The room had concrete walls and small windows near the ceiling. The windows barely let in any light, and it appeared that it was almost night, although I knew there was probably still a few hours until sunset. The floor was dirty, covered in mud and dust, probably from all the misplaced travelers who had come here before us.

"Let's all get some rest," David said, sitting on the cot next to Hinda. The two of them lay down and closed their eyes, hugging Yossi tightly in between them. I went over to the cot with Abi and Sarah, who were already fast asleep. I lay down on the cot with my head at their feet and stared at the ceiling. Although I was exhausted, I couldn't sleep.

Later, I heard the door open, and a couple came in—Mr. and Mrs. Weizmann, I guessed. They had been talking, but quickly hushed their voices when they noticed us sleeping on the cots. The two of them quietly lay down on the floor, the woman resting her head on her husband's chest. A few minutes later, another man entered, Mr. Cohen. Mr. Cohen was carrying a bagged loaf of bread under his arm. He sat on the floor with his back leaning against the wall. He stared at us on the cots while he slowly took a piece of bread from his loaf and ripped it with his teeth. I pretended to sleep while watching him slowly chew the slice of bread and then another one. Soon, he lay down on his back and put his hat over his face. He started snoring loudly, breathing in and out into his hat.

I still couldn't sleep, so I continued staring at the ceiling. Everything was dark, but I could still make out the outline of the room and the cracks along the wall. Suddenly, I felt a rustling at my feet. I slightly lifted my head to see Abi trying quietly to get off of the cot without disturbing Sarah or me. He moved in slow motion, inching his body from the center of the cot to

160

the edge before placing his feet on the ground. I still pretended to be asleep, watching to see what he was doing. He stood up slowly and looked around the room, as though checking if he had been caught. Then he started creeping towards Mr. Cohen. What was doing? Should I stop him? When he got to him, he knelt down slowly and reached his hand into the bread bag that was lying next to Mr. Cohen's head. Abi dipped his hand carefully, without touching the bag or making a sound. Then, he slowly pulled his hand back up, his thumb and index finger pinching a slice. With his slice, he quickly stood up and tiptoed back to the cot and then slowed his pace to make his way back into the bed trying not to make any sudden movements. I soon felt his feet back in the cot near my waist. I looked over to see Abi eating the slice of bread as though it were the most expensive delicacy he had ever had. I smiled to myself, thinking about what a brave kid he was. Then, finally, I drifted off to sleep.

When I woke up, there was light coming through the small windows. David was speaking with Mr. Cohen and Mr. Weizmann, who were both standing next to the door. Hinda was awake, rocking Yossi. Abi and Sarah still slept curled together on the cot. Our three roommates soon left, leaving us alone again in the room.

"I'll be back in a little bit," David said, heading out the door.

"Wait," I said. "I'll come with you."

I didn't want to stay sitting around in that room. It felt suffocating, especially after spending the last few weeks outside.

David looked at me as though deciding what to say. "Fine," he finally responded. "Let's go. Hinda, stay put with the children."

Hinda nodded as we walked out the door. We hiked silently back through the village, walking down the streets until we got back to the village center, where the market was bustling, looking even more crowded than it had been the day before. David reached into his pants pocket and pulled out a few coins.

"Get something for dinner," he said to me, putting the coins in my hand. "Try to bargain, get things that look a day or two old, and see if you can get a cheaper price."

I nodded. "Where are you going?" I asked.

"We're going to need more of that," he smiled and then walked away, leaving me at the start of the market. I looked down into my hand at the coins. There was about ten pengo altogether, about the amount I used to spend on one pastry. I started walking through the market. This time I was looking at the sellers, trying to see who looked like they would be willing to help me. I saw a woman selling cucumbers from a small stall tucked between two larger vegetable stands. The woman stood patiently, watching the passersby. I approached her stand and started looking through the cucumbers to try to find the ugliest ones. The woman's eyes were glued to me as I searched. I found three that looked like they would probably end up in the garbage and showed them to the woman.

"Tizenöt," she said to me coldly in Hungarian.

"I don't speak Hungarian," I responded to her in Ukrainian. "How about two pengo?"

The woman laughed. "You Poles are so cheap; don't think I don't recognize your accent," she said in Ukrainian. "I'll agree to seven."

Spend almost our entire money on three cucumbers? I shook my head at her, put the cucumbers back down, and moved on. A few stands down there was an old man selling potatoes. He waved at me when I came by.

"Kell segítség?" he said to me.

I looked down at my hands, one clenched tight on the coins.

"Do you need help?" he repeated himself in Ukrainian.

I looked up at him and smiled.

"You can work with me here," he said. "I'll pay you in potatoes. Come." He motioned to me to come behind the stand.

"What's your name, dear?" he asked.

"Yanina," I lied. Yanina Krasokova was a girl in my class back in Turka. She was blonde, blue eyed, and Christian.

"Nice to meet you, Yanina," he said. "I'm Elek. I grew up here in Munkacz and lived here my entire life. My father was a potato farmer and sold his crops here every week. I took over when he got old, and I am hoping my son will one day take over. But so far he hasn't been so helpful."

I smiled at Elek as he spoke. His voice was calming and rhythmic as though he were singing his story.

"Now, selling potatoes is easy," he said. "You just need to know the numbers in Hungarian because people here, they don't like foreigners—they don't want to hear you speak Ukrainian. One is egy, two is kettő, three is három, ten is tíz. It costs about one pengo a potato, so just count what someone is buying and collect the money. Very simple."

I nodded. As we spoke a woman approached Elek's stand and started collecting potatoes from the pile. She inspected each one before putting it in her bag. I watched her closely, counting each one . . . one. . . two. . . three. . . four. . . five. The woman looked up at Elek, who motioned her to me. Five. . . what is five? I raised my hand, spreading my fingers to silently tell the woman. She handed over five pengo and went on her way.

"You're a natural," Elek said. "Five is öt."

Soon, more customers came and Elek stood back as I counted each one's purchase and collected the money. After a few hours, the market started to quiet down. Some of the stands had already packed up and left, and Elek was almost out of potatoes.

"Well, Yanina, you did great," Elek said. "Why don't you take yourself some potatoes and go along home? I'll be here next week; you are welcome to join me." He handed me a small cloth bag.

"Thank you," I said. I grabbed a few of the small potatoes left in the stand and dropped them in the bag. I waved him goodbye and walked through the emptying market. I still had the ten pengo from David in my pocket and walked to a stand where a baker was packing up. There were still a few loaves of bread sitting out on his stand. The baker looked at me and I pointed to one of the loaves

"Tíz," he said. Ten, perfect. I handed him the coins I had and put the loaf in my new bag. I left the market and skipped back to our room we were renting, humming the whole time.

When I got there, David and our roommates were all there. Everyone was sitting around, and looked up when I walked in the door. I couldn't stop the big smile that was growing on my face as I showed everyone what I had.

"You bought all of this with ten pengo?" David asked, counting the potatoes from the bag.

"You are not the only one who can work," I laughed.

"Good job, Rachel," David said. "What a perfect feast for Rosh Hashana."

I had completely forgotten. Tonight was the Jewish new year, one of the most important holidays in our religion. When I was younger, we would cook huge feasts with turkey and lamb and soup to celebrate Rosh Hashana.

Hinda took the potatoes to boil them on a small burner that was sitting in the corner of the room. Mr. Cohen shared a bottle of slivovitz, and the Weizmanns had carrots and potatoes that they cooked along with ours. Together, we celebrated the beginning of a new year.

As the weeks went by, I was starting to get used to Munkacz. The season changed and it got colder. Once a week I went to work with Elek at the market and David often found odd jobs around the village.

165

We got along well with our roommates and continued to share and work together.

The only thing I didn't like in Munkacz? Well, there was a Jew named Meyer who would come and visit me every week at the market. He was not like the other Jews in Munkacz—he was clean-shaven and didn't wear the typical black garb. Instead, he dressed like everyone else but wore a yarmulke on his head.

The first time I met Meyer was during my walk to the market one morning.

"You're not from around here," he said in Hungarian as he approached me.

I smiled at him politely. By then I could understand some Hungarian, although I wasn't confident enough to speak any except when reciting the numbers to customers at the market.

"You are too beautiful to be Hungarian," he said, this time in Yiddish.

I blushed, but still didn't answer him.

"Where are you going?" he asked. He was walking next to me, as though accompanying me to work.

"To the market," I said.

"Shopping?"

"I work there."

"You shouldn't be working," he said, putting his hand on my cheek. "If you were mine, I would never make you work."

I quickly moved away, creating some space between his hand and my face. "I like working there."

"You are too young to know what you like," he said. "I'll show you." He smiled, baring his teeth that looked slimly and dull.

I started walking a little faster, but he kept up and continued walking next to me until I arrived at Elek's stand. From then on, Meyer would catch me on my walks to the market or come visit me while I was working. One day on my walk home from the market, he was waiting for me.

"Come back with me," he said, trying to grab my hand. I pulled it away and continued walking on my normal route. "How ungrateful you are! I am offering you a better life and you don't want it!" He yelled at me as he tried again to grip my hand.

I lowered my head and began to run. He stood there unmoved, watching me run all the way to our room.

That evening, we were sitting in the room eating a typical dinner of bread and potatoes when there was a knock at the door. We all stopped, and David stood up to see who it was. The door had a small peephole that he looked through and then let out a big sigh. He slowly opened the door, and there was Yosl and Ita standing on the other side.

"Thank God!" Yosl yelled. "We found you!"

"What are you doing here?" David said, blocking the doorway.

"We were looking for you!" Yosl gasped. "We didn't know where to go. We stayed in that town in Hungary and there was a raid, and we almost got caught! Thankfully, I found the man who brought you here, and he offered to help us. He said you were in Munkacz."

"But why did you come here?" David asked.

"We didn't know what else to do!" Yosl said. "Did you hear me say we almost got caught? They are doing raids in Hungary to find Jews! We came to Munkacz and asked around until we found someone who told us you were here."

David breathed deeply and stepped aside to let them in. A moment later, Anna, our landlord barged in.

"What is the racket here?" she yelled. "Remember, I asked for quiet!" Then she saw the two newcomers. "Who are they?"

"They are going to be staying with us," David said to her.

"That will cost more," she said, putting her hands on her hips.

"What's the difference, it's the same room!" David snapped back at her.

"Then you can leave," she said. "Or it's another 200 pengo a week."

"Fine," David said.

"Good," she said. "Now keep it down." Then she turned around and left.

"Thank you, David!" Yosl said, grabbing David's arm. "You always do the right thing."

David looked at him and then came back to where he had been sitting. Yosl and Ita joined us, sitting on the edge of one of the cots. I stared at them as they greedily accepted the invitation to join our dinner.

Now, there were eleven of us sharing that room with two cots. That night, as we went to sleep, David, Hinda, and Yossi slept together in one of the cots, and the Weizmann's took the other. Mr. Cohen and Yosl and Ita slept on the floor. With so many of us, there wasn't even much floor space left. Abi and Sarah cuddled together under the cot their parents were on, and I slept next to them on the floor.

I fell fast asleep, getting used to sleeping on the dirty floor here. Then, suddenly I was awoken by David, who jumped up off the cot, almost turning it over.

"We're caught!" he screamed. He took a blanket and quickly threw it over the side of the cot, covering the children below it. I slid under the cot also, holding Abi and Sarah tight. Then I heard it—footsteps outside the door, and then suddenly the door slammed in, shaking the whole room as the lock was broken.

"EVERYBODY UP!" one of the intruders screamed. I quickly placed my hand over Sarah's mouth; she had started to cry.

"LET'S GO!"

I peeked under the blanket to see two policemen standing in the doorway. They had feathers in their helmets and were carrying revolvers in their white-gloved hands. There was a third person with them, but he waited outside.

"Please," David said. "Take us, but leave our son."

Hinda, now standing up next to David, was holding Yossi tight in her arms.

"He is too young—he won't make it," David said.

"EVERYONE, LET'S GO," one of the policemen pointed the gun at David.

I held Sarah's mouth tight and stopped my own breathing. I watched David and Hinda with Yossi in her arms follow the policemen out. Mr. Cohen, the Weizmanns, and Yosl and Ita followed.

"That's all of them?" the man who had been waiting outside said.

"We got them. Good work."

"You are missing one," the mysterious man said. "A young girl, blue eyes, brown curly hair. . ."

"No."

I listened as the footsteps, which echoed through the room, and the argument between the mysterious man and the policemen got fainter as the policemen marched the captives away, leaving us, hidden, alone in our room.

1942—Sarah

"We're caught!" Father screamed suddenly in the middle of the night. I was under the cot he was sleeping on. I was awake because I couldn't sleep. I hadn't been able to sleep for a long time, but every night I pretended to. When everyone else was sleeping, I lay awake, thinking about what life would be like if we weren't Jewish. Actually, I was waiting for this moment, I knew things couldn't stay like this forever. We were getting too comfortable here in our little room.

Nevertheless, his exclamation caught me by surprise. My heart started racing, I wanted to scream; everything inside of me felt like it was going to pop out. Suddenly I felt Rachel's cool hand on my mouth, holding me tight. Father threw a blanket over the side of the cot, and everything went dark. I tried to bite my lips, I knew I needed to stay quiet, but I had no control. Over anything.

The door broke in like thunder unannounced by lightning. I could hear Father's strong voice and the screams of the policemen who had come to take my family away. I wanted to get up, to go with them. Wherever they were going, I couldn't bear to think of not being with my parents again.

Abi was also under the cot with me and Rachel. He squeezed my hand, as though trying to send me a message. Stay calm, he was saying. How could I when my parents and little brother were being taken away? I heard their footsteps move out the door while the soldiers yelled and screamed. Then, as quickly as everything started, everything went silent.

We stayed still for a few moments, and then Abi loosened his grip, and Rachel took her hand off my mouth. I exploded. Tears flowed from my eyes running into little pools on the dirty floor. My nose stuffed up and my breath flew out of me like gusts of wind.

Rachel wrapped her arms around me. "Shhhh" she quieted me. I wanted her to tell me that everything would be OK, but, how could she? Even if she did, I knew it was a lie. "Come on," she said instead. "We have to leave."

"And go where?" Abi retorted. "Maybe Mother and Father will come back looking for us."

"It's not safe here anymore," Rachel said. "Let's get up."

Rachel slowly rolled out from under the cot and got up, brushing the dirt off her clothes. Then she reached her hands down to help me. I grabbed on, pulling myself up with her arms, and taking a glimpse at our empty room. The door hung loosely from its hinges, looking as if it would fall off in a light breeze. The two cots sat side-by-side, the same as they did when we first came here. In fact, everything looked just like it did when we had just arrived. It was like we had never even been here, completely erased from memory. Like we had never even existed at all.

Rachel walked out of the room to the dark street. I followed, suddenly realizing how cold it was. The air seemed to have dropped in temperature and then I felt something brush my nose and then my cheeks. I raised my hands in front of me with my palms up, and watched the snowflakes start to fill them up.

I used to love snow. Back in Butla, when it snowed, we would put on our mittens and coats and try to catch the snowflakes as they fell. Abi and I sometimes made snowmen, and, if we were lucky, we would find a few stones to make a face in it. Once Abi took Father's hat and put it on top of the snowman's head. We laughed and pretended the snowman was Father until dinner time and forgot to bring the hat back inside. When Father realized his hat was missing, it was already soaked through. Father got so angry, but Mother reminded him it was just a hat, and she left it next to the stove all night to dry. We never touched his hat again, but every time it snowed I remembered that day.

"Sarah, put your hands down! You will freeze!" Rachel woke me from my memory. She had her hands clasped tightly under her arms. It was like she reminded me to feel cold, and suddenly I felt a shiver crawl up my spine. I wiped my hands on my shirt, which by now had also collected some snowflakes in the creases and then rubbed them together to warm up.

"Where are we going?" Abi prodded Rachel as she walked briskly down the street. Abi and I both were almost jogging to keep up.

"I don't know." She stopped and looked at us. "We have nowhere to go."

She then picked up her feet again and started walking. Soon, we found ourselves at the market. The market was empty except for the wooden stands that lined up along the sides. Some of the stands were boarded up, or covered with tarps, while other stood naked and bare. The market was dark and eerie, as though it had been abandoned a long time ago. It was hard to imagine that this place was full of life just hours before and would be again when the sun arose.

Rachel went up to one of the naked stands and sat down leaning against it. She motioned to us to join her, so we sat, me on her left, and Abi on her right. She wrapped her arms around our shoulders and kissed the crowns of our heads. I snuggled into her side, feeling the warmth of her body near mine.

I don't know how long we sat there, but soon a man came through the market pushing a big cart. He walked right past us and stopped at a nearby stand. I watched him slowly start to unpack his cart, carefully placing baskets of fruits on the stand. Then, another man came by with his cart of food. Then another, and another. And suddenly the market was alive again.

I tapped Rachel, who seemed to have fallen asleep, or at least she had been closing her eyes. Her eyes bolted open and, as she watched the sellers starting to set up their stands, she gently woke Abi. She motioned to us that we had to go; we couldn't stay here like homeless people in the middle of the market. It would attract attention.

We got up and left the market. We wandered around until we got to a little park. The grass of the park was covered in patches of snow that were starting to melt as the sun warmed up the air. We found a wet bench and Rachel tried to wipe the water away so we could sit. The bench was still wet when I sat down, and I could feel the water seep into my clothes. But by now, I didn't feel as cold. I was either numb or the sun was strong enough to warm me.

We sat there a few hours, watching people walk through the park, some on their way to the market while others were leaving it, carrying sacks of fruits and vegetables. I couldn't help trying to imagine what was in each of those sacks. One man, I imagined, really loved bread and bought three different kinds of loaves for his family. Another woman, well, she looked like she was carrying meat to make a big stew. My mouth was watering.

Then a man came by carrying nothing, even though he was coming from the direction of the market. He must have been Jewish, because I could see the yarmulke on his head, but he didn't dress like the other Jews in Munkacz. All the Jews in the Munkacz wore black suits and had long beards, peyot, and big hats. But this man dressed like a Christian, except the symbol on the crown of his head. He was walking through the park, and then suddenly, he seemed to be coming towards us.

"I was hoping to find you here," he said as he approached us. Rachel's eyes narrowed and she stood up and walked towards the man. The two of them walked together away from where we were sitting and began to talk. I couldn't hear what they were saying, but I watched them closely. I had never seen the man before. Rachel scrunched her brow as she spoke to him and stared at him with her deep blue eyes. He looked at her with a half-smile on his face and spoke calmly.

After a few moments, they walked back over to us.

"Listen carefully," the man said. "I am taking you on a bus ride to Beregszasz. But you don't know me. If anyone asks, you never saw or spoke with me in your life." The man looked both Abi and me in the eyes as he spoke. "If anything happens, you are on your own. Do you understand?"

"Yes," Abi nodded in agreement. Then the man looked at me, his eyes burrowed deep into my face. I couldn't keep his gaze, but I nodded.

"Follow me," he said.

We got off the bench and followed the man who walked a few strides in front of us. Rachel walked with the two of us as we curved through the village, down streets I had never seen before. I couldn't help thinking about this man. "Who is he?" I asked Rachel, but she just shook her head. He seemed to know his way around this village, but also seemed like he didn't belong here. There was something about him that scared me, but he was Jewish. He was supposed to be on our side, and it seemed like he was helping us.

After a short walk, we arrived at a bus station on the edge of the village. It was just a bench and a tall pole with a wooden sign on the top. Rachel, Abi, and I sat on the bench, while the man stood a few meters away from us. We waited there for a while, until a cloud of dust appeared down the road. The dust got closer, and I realized it must have been a bus. When it arrived at the stop, the man jumped on and spoke to the driver for a few minutes. Then he waved at us to board.

We entered the bus, which was already full of people. There were three people to a seat, it seemed, and even more sitting on the floor. Rachel sat down on the floor and Abi and I followed. The man stood near the front holding on to a seat as the driver started the bus again. I looked around at all the people. There was a man sitting in the seat next to us carrying a cage of chickens on his lap. On our other side, was a woman with three young boys sitting around her on the seat. Everyone sat quietly as the bus toddled along, bumping over every little stone on the road. My bottom started to ache from hitting the bus floor over and over with each bump.

Two hours later, the bus stopped again. The man who brought us jumped off the bus, and then the rest of the passengers began to file out. We were near the back of the bus and were the last to get out. When we stepped out, I didn't see the man anywhere. We were on the edge of a busy street, lined with stores on both sides. We stood there for a few moments, watching the other passengers from the bus disperse into the crowds. We must be in Beregszasz.

I looked at Rachel, who was staring down the busy street. She looked down at Abi and me and then started walking. We walked slowly, looking into each store—one had big candles in the window, while another had mannequins with fabric draped over their naked bodies. Then we came to a store with jewelry in the window. Rachel stopped and faced the window, looking in. My eyes slowly moved from Rachel to the store window, where slanted shelves were covered in gold and shiny jewelry for everyone to see. I became mesmerized with the glitter that shone as the sun hit the jewelry. There were beautiful rings with large stones in different colors, giant necklaces with gold and silver intertwined and dainty bracelets, like ones my mother used to have. I wasn't sure why we were stopped here. The jewelry was beautiful, but what could Rachel want with it? We had no money for food, let alone jewelry.

But then I saw it. On the side of the window was a small grid, each box had a necklace with a small trinket on it. Some of the trinkets were Stars of David. Seeing the symbol of Judaism displayed in the window made my heart flutter and start beating faster. I used to have a necklace like that when I was young, but Father had taken it back when we lived in Butla.

The door to the store suddenly swung open and I realized that Rachel and Abi had gone inside. I quickly followed. The woman working at the store looked at us, up and down, as we entered. She stared at us, her eyes darting from Rachel to Abi to me, as though she was trying to focus on each one of us at the same time. She had been sitting when we came in, but now she was standing, walking towards us, her fingers fiddling together in front of her chest.

"Can . . . can I help you?" she stuttered out in Hungarian. I had picked up Hungarian over the last few months we lived in Munkacz. Rachel still had trouble with the language.

"Hi," Rachel responded to her. "We are Jews from Poland," she responded in Ukrainian. "We need help."

The woman nodded. "I am sorry," she said in Ukrainian. "I cannot have you in my store."

Rachel bowed her head and turned as though to leave.

"But I can help you," the woman said. "My neighbor has an empty room. Let me speak with her. Maybe you can stay with her."

"Thank you!" Rachel exclaimed, overexcited with what the woman had offered.

The woman smiled, looking at us with pity. She motioned us out of the shop and followed us outside. She locked the door.

"I will come right back," she said. "Please, just, please don't stand in front of my windows. It is not good for business, you see."

"Of course," Rachel said. "We'll wait over there." She pointed to a small patch of dirt on the other side of the street.

The woman rushed off and we went to go sit on our small patch of dirt. I suddenly realized it was cold here, now that we were not moving. Although the sun was shining brightly, the air chilled my bones. Rachel, Abi, and I snuggled together to keep warm as we

179

waited. I continued watching the people walking down the street, going to and from the stores, carrying large sacks with them on the way out. Nobody seemed to notice us sitting alone here. An hour later, the woman returned and came over to us.

"Please, come with me," she said. We got up to follow her as she led us through the village to an area with little brick houses scrunched up next to each other. She knocked on one of the doors, and a tall, slender woman opened it. She looked past us, to see if there was anyone else on the street, and then motioned us inside. The woman from the jewelry store left us.

"I'm Franci," she said in Ukrainian. "And this is my son, Rudi." She pointed to a small crib in the corner of the room. "You can stay here with us, but it is best for you to stay inside during the day. If people see you coming and going, they will ask questions."

"Thank you," Rachel responded. "I'm Rachel, and this is my niece Sarah, and nephew Abi. We really appreciate your help."

Franci smiled. "I live alone here with my son; you can help me with him."

I walked over to the crib and peered inside. A little baby was curled up on his side sleeping, breathing deeply in and out. He looked like what Yossi used to look like, two years ago. I wanted to pick him up and hug him, but he was so clean. I was so dirty, I didn't want to get any of my filth on him.

Looking at him made me a little sad. Where was Yossi? And Mother and Father? I knew Rachel didn't want to talk about it, but my imagination ran wild.

Were they in jail? Were they even alive? I probably would never know.

Franci brought us water and cookies to eat and showed us into her bathroom to bathe. She seemed a lot like Mother—kind, caring, and gentle. As I sat in her bathtub, watching the water around me turn black, I started to wonder where Rudi's dad was. Why was Franci here alone?

I sat in the bath longer than I should, but I couldn't help it. It had been so long since I had a bath. When I got out, I was shocked by the color of the skin on my arms. My skin was light, but rough with little bumps and scratches on it. I rubbed my arms and legs with my hands, feeling my clean skin all over before putting on the clothes that Franci had given me.

When I finally got out of the bathroom, I saw Rachel sitting with Franci at their table.

"I like to cook," Franci said slowly in Hungarian. Then, in Ukrainian, "Now, repeat it."

Rachel smiled and repeated her sentence in Hungarian, blushing slightly.

Franci clapped. "You will learn Hungarian in no time," she said.

"I can help!" I walked over to them. "Thank you for the bath and the clothing," I said to Franci in Hungarian.

She smiled motherly at me and gave me a hug. I already liked her and felt comfortable here—a feeling I hadn't had in a long time. Franci liked taking care of people and liked having more people in her house. A few days a week she worked in one of the shops in the village. Rachel, Abi, and I would stay in her home, and cook, clean, and play with Rudi. Abi and I also worked with Rachel to teach her Hungarian. I always held Rudi when we practiced Hungarian, hoping maybe he would learn some, too. Mostly, he just giggled at us, or slept in my lap.

We stayed with Franci for a couple months, never leaving the house during the daylight. Sometimes, in the evenings, we would go out on little walks down the street, but mostly we stayed in. Sometimes I heard Franci speaking with Rachel about other Polish Jews being caught in Beregszasz. While the Germans still hadn't conquered Hungary, the Hungarian police was conducting raids to find runaways from Poland. No one knew what happened to the Jews who were caught. They were put on trains and no one saw or heard from them again.

Soon it became colder. One evening, Franci told us it was Christmas and she made a special meal with turkey and potatoes. I had never celebrated Christmas before, but it seemed like a nice holiday—in fact, similar to all of our holidays. I asked if we would be celebrating Hanukkah as well, but Franci told me it would be dangerous to light candles—we wouldn't want anyone to see the lights through the window.

One cold, snowy night we were sitting around the stove to stay warm. I held Rudi in my lap. We were getting really close and he often wanted to be held by me when we were all together. Rachel was singing softly and Franci sat quietly knitting. I could get used to this, I thought. The night was quiet, except for the wind and the occasional sound of someone walking down the street. I felt calm, relaxed.

KNOCK, KNOCK. Someone was at the door. I jerked up, looking to Rachel and Franci, who both became instantly alert. Franci dropped her knitting needles and placed her hands to her heart.

"Who could it be?" Rachel whispered.

"I . . . I . . . I don't know," Franci said nervously.

KNOCK. KNOCK. KNOCK. The person at the door knocked harder this time.

"What do we do?" Rachel asked.

Franci shook her head, her mouth open as though someone had taken the words out.

KNOCK. KNOCK. KNOCK. KNOCK. KNOCK. The knocking was quicker, harder now, and the person wasn't giving up.

I held Rudi tight, not wanting him to be alarmed. Franci slowly rose from her chair and started to walk toward to the door. The knocking was more like pounding now, and the sound matched the rhythm in my chest. KNOCK! KNOCK! KNOCK! KNOCK!

I held my breath and looked at Rachel, who held both her hands in front of her mouth and shook her head. Then I looked to Franci, who placed her hand on the door handle.

Europe 1939

GERMANY

POLAND

SLOVAKIA

UNGVAR

TURKA

BUTLA

BEREGSZASZ

MUNKACZ

BUDAPEST

HUNGARY

ROMANIA

CONSTANTA

BUCHAREST

Shwartz family circa 1946. From left to right: Hinda, Rachel, Yossi, David, and Sarah.

Rachel 1945

Rachel and Victor, circa 1947

Rachel, Victor, and son Nahum circa 1948

Rachel and author Aviva, 2001

Hinda and David, 1980

Sarah, Hinda, and Yossi, circa 1945

Abi, 1945

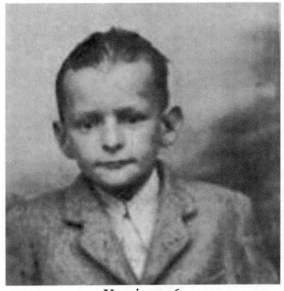

Yossi, 1946

Sarah, 1947

Hinda and David, circa 1960

Abi and Yossi in Israel, 1947 or 1948

Mrs. Freuden, Yossi, and Hinda, 1947

Abi and wife, Esther, returning to Butla in 2005

Butla 2005

1942—David

"We're caught!" I screamed, jumping off the cot I was lying on. I wasn't sleeping. I was never sleeping. I always had my eyes open and now I saw them coming. I saw a faint light coming through the window of our small room. The light was so faint, but I was sure it was a lantern of someone coming towards us.

I jumped from the cot and threw the blanket over the side the cot, covering the children who were underneath. Hopefully, the police would be too stupid to check. Then I ran to the window, and sure enough, there were two Hungarian policemen in their silly hats coming towards us. With them was another man, dressed in black. Probably the scum who gave us away.

The next second, the door to our room swung open, almost falling off the hinges. I stood tall, hoping they would focus on me when they came in.

"EVERYBODY UP!"

I gave a hand to Hinda, helping her up as she held Yossi tight into her chest. Yosl and Ita, Jon Cohen and Daniel and Edda Weizmann all stood up and lined up behind me.

"LET'S GO!" the two policemen were inside, holding their revolvers ready.

I stepped forward. "Please," I said. "Take us, but leave our son. He is too young—he won't make it."

One of the policemen smirked. "EVERYONE, LET'S GO," he said, lifting his revolver to my face. I stood in front of him, without letting my eyes drift, and ensured that Hinda and Yossi were behind me. We walked out of the room silently and the policemen followed. The man in black was waiting outside.

"That's all of them?"

"We got them. Good work," one of the policemen said.

"You are missing one: a young girl, blue eyes, brown curly hair . . ."

"No." I glared at him. "You got us all." His face was shadowed by his hat and I tried to make out who he was. This rat. But I don't think I had ever seen him before.

They walked us towards a cattle cart and stuffed us in. The cart was dark and smelled like the animals it had been built for. The bottom was covered with straw and shit and we had to sit on it. The cart rattled along for an hour or so and we sat silently, bouncing around with every turn. I had my arms on Hinda, who was holding Yossi tight to her chest.

Then we stopped and the policemen came around and let us out of the cart. They walked us into something that looked like a prison, but worse. They led us into the concrete building and threw us all into a cell with no windows. The cell was much smaller than the room we had all been living in together and it was empty. It was just three concrete walls and a gate that locked us in. Guards stood outside the gate, pacing with their rifles, ready to shoot.

There was nowhere to sit but the floor. I motioned to Hinda to sit down against the wall. We faced the wall across from us, not wanting to look at the guards. The Weizmanns and Jon Cohen sat down with us, while Yosl and Ita paced around the cell, stepping over our feet to get from side to side.

"Hmpfff" Yosl kept sighing loudly as though looking for attention. He continued like that for who knows how long, until he got the attention he was asking for. Just as a guard was walking by, Yosl was standing by the gate of our cell. Yosl looked at the guard and caught his eye for just a second. Before Yosl could turn around and pace the other direction, the guard had reached his hand through the gate and grabbed Yosl by the collar. He tugged him back, crashing his head into the metal bars of the gate. Upon collision, Yosl's eyes looked like they were about to pop out of his head. Before Yosl could slide down to ground, the guard turned him around to face the gate, and jabbed his gun through the bars right into Yosl's head. The crack of his cheekbone was as loud as a gunshot. Then, the guard let him slide down. As he walked away, he took out his handkerchief and wiped the butt of his gun clean.

The whole thing happened so fast that we all just stayed where we were for a few moments, watching Yosl collapsed on the ground. When the spell was broken, Ita gasped and ran to her husband. She started to sob and tried to shake Yosl awake.

"Quiet!" I snapped at her as I got up. "Do you want them to come back?"

I put my hand on Ita's shoulder and moved her out of the way so I could get to Yosl. He was lying on his face, his arms and legs spread out around him. I flipped him over and put my ear to his mouth.

"He's breathing," I said. "Let's move him to the corner." Jon and Daniel got up and helped me carry Yosl to the far corner of the cell. We propped him up to sit, leaning him in the corner of the cell. Ita came and sat next to him, holding his hand in hers and rubbing it as though to keep it warm. From then on, whenever a guard came by, we all kept our heads down.

The guards ignored us for several hours after that. But then, one came by and unlocked the cell. "You," he said, pointing at me and motioned for me to come over. I walked to the gate and he handcuffed me. Then he led me out and locked the gate again. He led me down the hall where I realized there were other cells just like ours. Some were empty, but some had people in them that looked so thin they were almost transparent. I couldn't help but wonder how long some of them had been in there. With his arm on my shoulder, the guard guided me to a small door at the end of the hall. He unlocked the door, revealing a small, dark room with a table and two chairs inside. He locked the door behind us and offered me to sit down.

"What were you doing in Hungary?" the guard asked in Hungarian.

"I live there," I responded. I could speak Hungarian well enough.

"You are Polish."

"I was born in Poland, but spent most of my life in Hungary," I responded. "I was repatriated to Poland in 1934 for a few years, but then my family came back to Hungary."

The guard looked at me skeptically.

"Do you mind if I smoke a cigar?" I asked. I always carried old cigar stubs in my pockets, in case I ever needed one. The guard tilted his head in agreement and I started searching through my pockets to see whether there was a stub anywhere. While I searched, the guard reached into his own pocket and took out a package of cigarettes. He put one in his mouth and handed another to me.

"Why were you all together in that little room we found you in?" he said as he lit our cigarettes.

"Times are tough, you know," I responded. "We didn't always live like that. We used to have a nice house in the village. I had a shop, but it went out of business, so we moved in with some friends to save money."

The guard seemed bored with my story.

"Who are you spying for?" he asked.

"I am not a spy."

"This place—here—is for spies. That is why they brought you here," he said, leaning forward.

"Then there must have been a mistake," I took a drag on the cigarette. I closed my throat to make sure I wouldn't cough.

He just watched me and continued smoking his cigarette. When we finished the cigarettes, he asked, "Can you chop wood?"

"Of course," I responded.

"Great, you and the other men with you can go out and chop wood for us," he said.

"Thank you," I responded, grateful for the opportunity to get outside. The guard led me out of the room and walked me back to the cell with the others. He motioned to Jon and Daniel to come, and then he led the three of us out of the prison. The sun was bright; it was probably midday by then, but it was cold. There were patches of snow on the ground and puddles where the snow had melted. When I looked up, I saw the prison was surrounded by forest. There were huge trees all around, although many were bare. The guard led us to a fenced-off area outside on the edge of the prison. Inside the fence were tree stumps and blocks of wood stacked neatly around the edges. He let us free in the fenced area and said he would be back in an hour.

I looked around, hoping to make myself useful, but there really wasn't any wood to chop. All the trees were on the outside of the fence, and all the wood inside was already cut and put away. Anyway, it was a good opportunity for us to stretch our legs and see the sunlight. After an hour the guard returned and took us back to our cell. This time, as we walked down the hall, I saw another one of the guards beating a prisoner in a cell nearby. Too weak to cry out, the prisoner writhed on the floor, barely flinching with each kick. I kept my head down and prayed that would never happen to me.

They put us back in a different cell than we had been in before. This new one was on the other side of the prison, away from the women and Yosl. Then, a guard brought a pot of soup and handed us each a bowl. I looked into the bowl, it had a dark broth and chunks of what looked like meat inside. The smell was strong, powerful, unlike any soup I had ever had before, maybe even rotten. We were all starving, so we gulped it down without a second thought.

We sat in that cell for what seemed like a long time. With no windows, it is impossible to guess how time passes. It could have been minutes, or even days, but eventually a guard came by leading the women past us. Hinda and Ita were holding Yosl, who limped between them. Yossi walked quickly next to his mother, his little legs racing to keep up. When they passed our cell, Yossi paused and put his hands on the metal gate.

"Father," he said. I was suddenly afraid. I looked up at the guard outside our cell and he quickly looked away, as though giving me permission to say something to my son.

"Are you taking care of Mother, Yossi?" I asked him, kneeling down in front of the gate.

He nodded, and then quickly let go of the gate, following Mother, Ita, and Yosl out. Then the guards let us out and walked us to a small courtyard in the middle of the prison where the women were already standing. I ran to Hinda.

"Are you OK? How is Yossi? Have they fed you?" I asked.

"We're fine," she said. "We had soup sometime yesterday."

Based on the light outside, it must have been early morning. I told her about the questioning from the guard and told her that no matter what happened, she had to stick to that story if it ever came up. She nodded.

I went over to check in with Ita and Yosl. Yosl was sitting on the ground while Ita stood above him. He was conscious at least. The left half of his face was purple and his eye was swollen shut, crusted with mucus and blood.

"Are you all right?" I asked both of them.

"Do I look all right?" Yosl whined.

"You're alive. Be happy about that," I said and then went back to spend this time with my wife and son.

Soon the guards brought us back to our cells and handed out black coffee to everyone. The coffee tasted stale and burnt, but I wished I could get another cup.

That was our routine for a week. Every morning started with a short time out on the courtyard, followed by black coffee. In the afternoons the men went out to "chop wood" and we had some sort of soup before the cycle repeated itself.

Sometimes we would see the other prisoners in the courtyard in the morning. Some of the prisoners had swollen faces like Yosl's. Most were thin and walked hunched over as though their heads were too heavy a burden to carry. I guessed that many of the prisoners were Jewish like us. The question was, what were they going to do with us?

One morning when the guards brought us coffee, I decided to ask. "What's going on?" I asked the guard, but he stared at me silently, daring me to open my mouth again. I took the coffee and started pacing nervously in our cell. Another guard came and opened our cell, leading us and the women to the entrance of the prison—the opposite direction of the courtyard.

When we got outside, there was a small bus waiting out front. "Where are we going?" I asked the guard who was walking us out. It was the same guard I had shared a cigarette with back when we first arrived.

"Back to your home," he said. "Your real home."

We were going back to Poland. While my story about being Hungarian might have been believable, the rest of the group being deported was definitely Polish. The bus drove through Munkacz, where a few Jews were waiting on the side of the road. One young Jewish boy threw a loaf of bread through the bus window. It landed on my lap and I ripped it apart to give each person a bite. I tried to look back to see who this generous boy was, but all I saw behind us was dust.

After a few hours we arrived at a real prison. We pulled up in front of a tall stone wall with guard towers on top. In the tower nearest us, I could see a big man in an army uniform carrying a huge gun, unlike one I had ever seen before.

There were guards waiting outside for us when our bus arrived. As we stepped out, they had their guns pointed and ready. They barked at us to line up. I stood behind Hinda and held Yossi to my chest. Hinda wanted to hold him, but she didn't seem like she had the strength.

We entered the prison and were led to a big concrete courtyard somewhere in the middle. There, the guards left us alone and stood around the edges of the courtyard—their guns still erect.

There were lots of people in the courtyard. Different groups scattered around the place, each group huddled together, keeping to themselves. Our group of newcomers was standing near the middle of the courtyard, and some people from other groups had started to look at us. I looked around at the other prisoners, trying to figure out anything about them. Are we in a prison of Jews? Or are these people real criminals?

Suddenly I caught eye contact with a prisoner standing on the other end of the courtyard. Instead of looking away, we both stayed still, our eyes locked together. I recognized him. But from where? Suddenly the man walked away from his group and started walking towards me, our eyes still locked. Who is he? He didn't blink even once when he walked towards me, and I tried my best to hold my gaze without moving.

"David!" he said when he approached me. Then it hit me. He worked in the quarry in Turka.

"Itzik!" I said lifting my hand to shake his. "What are you doing here?"

"I guess the same as you," he smiled. "We just arrived yesterday."

"So, what is the deal here?" I asked him.

"Most people here are Polish Jews," he said. "We were caught a few days ago trying to cross over into Hungary. I don't know everyone else's story."

Itzik pulled something out of his pocket to show me. It was a little green booklet with the Hungarian crest on it.

"We paid a lot of money for these," he said, showing me the passport. "One look, and they knew it was forged."

I looked at the passport and back at Itzik. "So now what?" I asked him.

"We didn't come here empty-handed," he said. "We all have money hidden somewhere in our clothing. I convinced a guard to let us speak with a lawyer. The lawyer said he would make sure we were released for 500 pengo a person."

"Released to where?" I asked him.

"To Hungary," he said. "For the right price, they will agree to let Polish people stay. David, do you want to join our case? The lawyer could get you out, also."

"They think I am from Hungary," I said. "I can't now join your case and say we are Polish."

"Suit yourself," Itzik responded. "Better to say whatever you need to say and have them free you here in Ungvar than to return to Poland." He shook my hand again and then returned to his group.

Ungvar. At least now I knew where we were. We weren't so far from Munkacz that it wouldn't be too hard to get back there from here. I was still holding Yossi to my chest. I rubbed his arms to try to keep him warm. With every breath, I could see the little puff of air come out of my mouth. It wasn't much longer until the guards took us inside. They crammed us in empty cells where we sat on the floor and waited until the next time they would take us out or give us a small piece of stale bread to eat.

After a week, we were still sitting in that prison. Itzik and his family were still there, too, but he was optimistic that their lawyer would succeed in getting them out soon. Then one day the guards came and pointed to me and Yosl. The guard said to get up and have our families follow him out. Jon, Daniel and Edda were still with us, all the way from Munkacz, but this was where we were parting ways. There was no need for goodbyes. I never gave them much thought anyways.

I held Hinda's hand as we followed the guards out. Yosl and Ita walked behind us. By now, Yosl could walk on his own, although his face was still swollen. It didn't look like he would ever go back to how he looked before.

The guards put us in a small bus with a few other prisoners. "Where are we headed?" I politely asked the driver.

"Shanke."

Shanke? We had come all this way, and now we were going back to Shanke? Back to the beginning of our journey. I sighed deeply as we got on the bus and sat down on the dirty seats.

"What did he say?" Hinda begged me.

"We're going to Shanke," I responded. "But don't worry, we will get back to Munkacz and find Rachel and the children."

Hinda's face turned white and she leaned over onto my shoulder. "Don't worry," I repeated. "I will make sure we get back to them no matter what."

The bus rolled along for the next few hours. Not one prisoner made a sound. All we could feel in the air was defeat, despair, and disappointment. But Shanke wasn't so terrible. We would figure it out.

When we arrived in Shanke, I recognized the little huts of all the workers. But now, there were little towers around the edge of the village with German soldiers inside. Two soldiers told our bus to stop before we got too close.

There were two Hungarian policemen on the bus with us. They got up and went to speak with the soldiers. I couldn't understand their conversation, but the German soldier kept shaking his head and motioning to the policemen to turn around. The policemen looked exasperated, gesticulating towards our bus and the camp in Shanke behind the guard.

"The soldier is telling him they aren't accepting any more deportees," one of the other prisoners translated to Polish. "He said to just kill us in Hungary."

The women in the bus all gasped.

"Shut up!" I said to the prisoner. "Do you think you are helping by saying something like that?"

"I am just repeating what they are saying!" the prisoner said. "It doesn't matter. Either they will kill us in Poland or in Hungary. What's the difference?"

I glared at him. Yossi sat quietly on my lap. He had barely made a sound since we left the prison in Ungvar. Sometimes it worried me how quiet he was.

He listened to everything, even when it would be better if he didn't understand.

The policemen stomped back on the bus and said something to the driver. I could hear them cursing under their breath as we drove away from Shanke and stopped a few minutes later at a nearby train station. The guards put us in one of the luggage carts of the train.

"Don't sit on anything," a guard said as he locked us in. "You'll get the passengers' luggage dirty."

The luggage cart had no windows so we stood in darkness during the short train ride. Thankfully it was winter, and the cart was cool. Otherwise we all would have died inside from the heat. When the train stopped, the guards opened the cart and led us out. It was snowing and already the ground was white as though it had been snowing for a while. The guards looked at us impatiently. I could see they just wanted to get rid of us and go home. We sat at the train station for a while, letting the snow start to cover our shoulders and heads. Hinda and I huddled around Yossi, while the policemen smoked cigarettes.

"The damn bus isn't coming!" one of the policemen said. "We better walk."

"Walk?" the other responded. "We'll freeze! You're out of your mind."

"Aren't we already freezing?" the first said. "Let's go."

The second policeman complied and the two of them rounded us up and started walking us away from the train station. The policemen were wearing thick boots, coats and tall hats, while we, the prisoners, were wearing just our shirts and the same shoes we had on since we left Butla months ago. How could they be worried about freezing?

We followed the main road from the train station, but it was hard to even see the road in front of us with all the snow on it. With each step, my feet sunk a little deeper into the snow, and my shoes started to get wet. They got wetter and wetter, until I couldn't even feel my feet anymore. Hinda stared at the ground as we walked, her shoulders hunched forward and arms wrapped in front of her chest. I held Yossi close, hoping he could feel the heat from my body.

We continued walking as the sun started to go down, taking the temperature down with it. I kept looking at the policemen, but they didn't seem to care if we all froze to death here. Around nightfall, we arrived at yet another prison. Here the policemen quickly handed us over and got in a car to take them back to the train station.

The guards at the new prison threw us into a small cell, where it was dark and the air was dank. We all sat on the floor close together, trying to warm ourselves up. When morning came, I was awoken when someone unlocked the cell, letting in bright light from the hall.

"Where are you all from?" the guard asked politely. He was young, just a boy really. Maybe twenty years old. He had clear skin, light eyes, and brown hair that was combed neatly to the back.

"Munkacz," I responded.

The guard smiled. "I've been there," he said. "I used to work for someone there named Meyer. Do you know him?"

I shook my head. I didn't really mix with the Jews in Munkacz, all of them so religious.

"Oh, too bad," the guard said. He stood silently in the doorway of our cell for a while, as though he wasn't sure what he was supposed to do.

"What's your name, Son?" I asked him.

"Erh, Christophe?" he responded, hesitating. He looked at me as though waiting for confirmation. And then it hit me—he was a Jew.

"Nice to meet you, Christophe," I smiled at him. I hoped my unquestioning of his response would give him a little more confidence. Christophe then went and brought us coffee. He was polite, but not too friendly, keeping enough distance that the other guards wouldn't get suspicious.

The next morning when Christophe came in, he asked, "Can you help me with something?"

I nodded and got up.

"Maybe he can help too?" Christophe said, pointing to Yosl, who had been hunched over on the floor. Yosl looked up with his good eye. The other eye barely fluttered when he tried to move it, but at least it wasn't dripping mucus all the time anymore.

"Him?" I asked. "He can barely walk."

"Yea, him," Christophe said. Yosl stumbled to his feet and walked to the front of the cell. "Follow me," Christophe responded, leading us through the halls of the prison. He took us outside of the prison, around to the back where there was a ladder that led to the roof and motioned us to climb up. I let Yosl go up first and then followed him to the top. Christophe came up third.

On the roof was a large water tank and a small pump. "Maybe you guys could pump some water for us?" he asked.

I looked at him in confusion. Something was strange. There were no buckets around. No way to carry the water down from the roof.

"I'm going back inside," Christophe said, looking over to the ladder. "I'll come get you in an hour." Then he disappeared down the ladder and went around the building to enter the prison, leaving the two of us alone on the roof.

"Come on, David! What luck!" Yosl shrieked. "Let's get out of here!"

I looked around the prison. There were no guards around, no one watching us, no fences blocking us. We could easily climb down the ladder and just walk away, down the road until we got somewhere else.

"David!" Yosl pleaded. "We have to save ourselves! We are responsible for preserving our own lives! We can leave now and be free! Otherwise, we are most likely facing death."

"Save myself?" I asked disgusted. "What about my wife in there? About my son? You expect me to run away and leave them here? Don't you think they would punish them if we ran away? What about Ita?"

"We're all dead anyways," Yosl responded. "We should do whatever we can to preserve any life possible."

"You only think about your own life, Yosl," I said. "I'm not leaving here without my family. Whatever happens to them, happens to me."

"You are giving up this opportunity?" Yosl barked.

"Why don't you go, Yosl?" I said, challenging him. "You are free to do as you like."

Yosl looked at me and looked at the ladder. He took a few steps towards the ladder, still staring straight at me. Then he stopped and sighed.

"That's what I thought," I said. I went to the water pump and opened it into my hands, washing my face and taking a drink. Yosl shut up then and sat down on the other side of the building. It was cold up there, but I enjoyed getting the sunlight. Exactly an hour later, Christophe climbed back up the ladder.

"Oh," he said, as though surprised to see us there. "Um, thanks for your help with the pump. Let's go back inside."

We climbed back down the ladder and walked around the building to the front of the prison. Before we walked inside, I put my hand on Christophe's shoulder and gave him a quick nod to show my gratitude to him that he tried to give us an opportunity to go free. He smiled back at me.

He led us back to our cell, but we didn't stay there long. A few hours later another guard came and opened the cell door.

"Time to go," he said, and led us out of the prison, where another small bus was waiting for us. We once again piled in the bus, without knowing where we would be taken to next. We drove along quietly for a few hours and then stopped at a command post along the border between Hungary and Poland. I had never been to this border crossing before. It looked abandoned and, during the drive, we had seen nothing around for at least an hour.

The guards on the bus got out and walked over to the command post. They knocked on the door and yelled, but there didn't seem to be anyone there. It was too cold to wait outside, so they came back into the bus, and there we sat. Soon it got dark and we were still waiting in the bus. I held Hinda tight, felt her shiver against my skin, and tried to rock her and Yossi to sleep.

In the morning, a car pulled up next to us. It was the border patrol station commander; I could tell by his uniform. He lazily walked from his car to the command post and unlocked the door. Startled awake, the guards on our bus scrambled up and ran out to catch the commander.

I could hear them yelling at the commander, who stood calmly, listening to them. Then he nodded, and the guards motioned to us to get off the bus and line up. The commander looked us all up and down and escorted us into the command post, leaving the guards outside, free of their charge.

"Men over there, women over there," he said in a deep voice, pointing at the sides of the room. I kissed Hinda's head and went to the men's side, watching Hinda glide across the room. A woman escorted the women into another room, while the commander took us through a small doorway.

"Strip," he said.

I looked around at the other men with me—Yosl, still injured, and a few other men I did not know. Some of the men quietly started taking off their clothing, while Yosl looked to me, questioning what to do next.

A few other border guards came in and started searching through the clothes the men had stripped off their backs. The man next to me stood shivering so violently he looked like he could explode. The guard held onto the man's clothing with his thumb and index finger, trying to search through the pockets with minimal contact with the fabric. He found a few coins and some cigarettes that had been smashed and ripped, which he confiscated before returning the clothes to the poor man. Then, the guard moved to me.

"STRIP!" he yelled, his eyes glaring at me as I quickly pulled my shirt over my back and lowered my pants to hand him. I had money sewn in the collar of my shirt. Before we left Butla, Hinda had hid money in different places in our clothing. She also hid money in the hem of my pants, and in the lining of my jacket. That money, I had already used, but, luckily, I hadn't needed to rip open my shirt collar yet.

The guard wrinkled his nose at my clothes and started to search through the pockets. He found a few cigar stubs and noticed the ripped open lining of my jacket. He stuck his hand in the lining, ripping the seam even more but his hand returned empty. Then he threw the clothes down on my feet and walked to Yosl, who was already standing naked with his clothes in his hands. I picked up my clothes and quickly put them back on, watching the guard standing in front of Yosl. Yosl's clothes were so stained with blood, the guard didn't even want to touch them. He took them from Yosl, shook them for a second and then dropped them on the floor at Yosl's feet.

After the guards finished searching us, they led us through the command post where the women were already waiting. Before walking over to Hinda and Yossi, I walked over to the commander.

"Perhaps, if we can give you a little cash, you can let us free in Hungary," I said to him.

"Where do you have cash?" he said, his eyes scanning my body.

"Well, I don't," I said. I didn't want to give away that his guards' search had failed. "But I have money hidden in my home in Hungary. The minute I get there, I will send it to your home. No one has to know."

The commander guffawed. "Right."

It was worth a shot. A few minutes later the back door of the command post opened and two German guards came in. I could see by their uniforms that they were the German border police. Not exactly Nazis, meaning they likely wouldn't be the ones to kill us, even if they were escorting us to that end.

The German guards looked us over and were ready to take us back into Poland.

"This one has money," the post commander said to the Germans, pointing at me. "Search him."

One of the German guards approached me and started patting me down above my clothes. He patted my back, sides, my chest, down my legs and then stood up facing me.

"Wo ist das Geld?" he screamed at me in German. I didn't understand, but I could see he was angry. He slapped me across the face and stepped closer to me. "Where is the money?" he yelled again, but I stood there, acting like I was deaf and dumb. But then he gave up and walked away from me.

The Germans shook hands with the post commander and then led us out to Poland, where they crammed us into a cattle cart and drove us away. My heart sank as we drove deeper into Poland, farther away from my sister and two other children. I knew Rachel would take care of Abi and Sarah, but the farther we got, the harder it was for me to imagine finding them again.

When the cart stopped, the guards led us into a house. The house looked like the houses in Turka, small, wooden, and practical. When they let us inside, I noticed that on the door frame there was a small sliver of wood that was darker than the wood around it. The sliver was a shadow of a mezuzah that had once blessed this home, a Jewish home. Now, the house was an office for the German guards. There was a large desk in the middle, made of wood with gold trim and behind the desk was a huge flag with a swastika hanging up on the wall. The man sitting at the desk looked at us and screamed something in German to the other guards.

The other guards in the room stood tall and grabbed their guns, motioning us to follow them out of the command post. They started walking us away from the house, towards a forest with tall trees that were bare from the winter.

"They are going to shoot us," Yosl whispered to me. The one good thing that came out of Yosl working with the Germans as part of the Judenrat was that he could understand and speak German. "The commander said the village people dug a new trench yesterday."

Yosl, who had been walking next to me, then moved over to one of the guards. He started speaking with the guard, in German. His tone filled with desperation. The guard looked at him and then looked straight ahead, continuing to walk at the same pace.

Please, I thought in my head, shoot me first. I couldn't bear the thought of watching them shoot Hinda and Yossi. I looked around at the guards walking us towards death. The guards were expressionless, holding their guns in front of their chests, walking with us as though they did this walk every day. I guess they probably did.

1942—Hinda

"Yossi, my darling," I whispered to my baby in my arms. "You are strong, you can survive."

This is the end. I knew it, as the guards walked us towards the forest. Yosl was pleading with them, trying to bargain for our lives, but what was the use? I already had a plan. When we got to our grave and they fired the first shot, I would throw Yossi down into the trench, and then when they shot me, I would make sure to fall on top of him, shielding his body. Then, when the guards were gone, Yossi could get up. Hopefully when the village people came to bury us, they would find him and take pity on him—a three-year-old alone in the forest. Hopefully they would take him and raise him, or at least help him get away. I know he is only three, but by now, I am sure he could take care of himself in the forest for a few days if he needed to. Enough time for someone with a heart to find him.

We entered the forest and I started to notice fresh mounds of dirt on either side of us as we walked. Graves. We were walking through a forest of death, where many people just like us were buried—shot for the crime of being Jewish. Soon we got to an open trench.

One of the guards screamed something at us in German and some of the other prisoners started to line up against the edge of the deep hole. I looked at David, who couldn't take his eyes off Yossi. Then I looked down into the trench, it was just about two meters deep. Not too deep—Yossi would be fine on the fall.

"*Yit'gadal v'yit'kadash sh'mei raba. Amen,*" David started muttering the mourner's Kaddish under his breath. For some reason, hearing that was what made me start to cry. No one would say the Kaddish for us when we were gone. Sarah and Abi would never know what happened to us.

Yosl was still pleading with the guards as the rest of us lined up. I couldn't understand what he was saying, but one of the guards at least seemed to be listening to him. Suddenly, the guards huddled together, speaking to each other quietly. Then, they faced us and screamed something in German.

I looked to Yosl, whose expression immediately changed. He raised his hand to his face, placing his palms together in front of his mouth. Then he looked over at David, his expression softened. I didn't know what Yosl said to them, but it seemed to work. The guards pointed their guns at us, telling us to get moving and marched us back past the graves, out of the forest and to the command post.

Thank you, thank you, I kept saying over and over in my head. I was never very religious, but if there ever was a point that I thought God had intervened, this had been it.

The command post didn't have a place for prisoners, so instead they took us to a local police station that was run by Ukrainians. There, they threw us in a small cell to wait for whatever came next. Soon a young boy and girl carrying a pot of soup came to us. They were about the same ages as Sarah and Abi and immediately my heart started to hurt for them.

The boy and girl were covered in dirt and had lice crawling through their hair. The lice were so big, I didn't even need to get close to see them. They smiled at us meekly as they handed out soup to all of us.

"What are your names?" I asked them in Ukrainian.

"I'm Shmuel and my sister is Rivka," the boy responded.

"Where are you from?"

"Here, Baligród," the boy said. Baligród was a small village in Poland. I had heard of it, but had never been here before.

"What happened here?" I asked him.

"A few months ago, the Germans came and raided the village," the boy told me. "They took all the Jews and put them on trains. Rivka and I ran into the forest and were hiding there. Then it started getting too cold so we had to figure out something else to do. So, we came here to the police station. They told us we could stay here if we work. Rivka does all the cooking and I chop wood, clean the furnace, or whatever else they need."

I started to imagine Abi chopping wood—he was only eight years old. "What about your family?" I asked the boy.

"I guess they got on the train," he smiled sadly at me.

"You are so brave," I told him. "I am sure your parents would be so proud of you."

He looked up and I could see a small twinkle in his eyes. Or maybe it was a tear. I grabbed his hand and squeezed it. When the two children finished passing out our soup, they left.

Suddenly one of the policemen came to the cell and pointed at Yosl. Yosl scrambled to the door and the policeman escorted him out of the cell. He took him to a nearby room and shut the door. The rest of us in the cell were quiet, unsure what was going on.

Then I heard a large roar from the policeman. He was screaming something at Yosl in Ukrainian, but the sound was muffled by the closed door. Then we heard a SMACK, it sounded like the crack of a whip on a hard surface. The sound startled me and I jumped, almost spilling my soup on Yossi, who was sitting quietly in my lap. Luckily, the soup wasn't hot at all. Yossi looked up at me with fear in his eyes and I kissed his forehead. "Don't worry," I whispered to him. "We're OK; everything is OK."

The screaming from the room continued—as did the sound of the whip—for a half an hour and then the door to the room opened and out limped Yosl, back to our cell. His shirt was ripped and fresh stains of blood were soaking through it. His face, which still hadn't healed from his last beating, had new cuts on it and somehow it was even more swollen than before. Then the guard pointed at David to follow.

"No!" I panicked, grabbing David's arm. I didn't know what to do. I wish they had just killed us in the forest. Now, they were just going to beat and torture us before we met the same end.

"It's OK," David said, pulling his hand from mine. He walked stoically to the guard who was calling for him and followed him into the room where they shut the door behind them. Tears instantly ran down my face. I looked at Yosl, who was crying himself in the corner of the cell. His wife Ita looked at him with pity.

"Yosl, what do they want?" I asked him.

"The partisans," Yosl responded.

"What are the partisans?" I asked. I never heard that word before.

"The Jews that hide in the forest and kill Nazis and anyone who collaborates with them," Yosl said. "They've gotten pretty strong lately. I think they have even killed a few of the Ukrainian police officers from this station."

"How do you know?" I asked.

"Just overhearing things," Yosl responded.

"Why do they think we know where they are?" I asked.

"Because I told them we do!" Yosl said. "Why do you think they didn't kill us in the forest? You think they would have spared us if we didn't promise something they wanted?"

"Do you know where the partisans are?" I was unsure if I wanted to know the answer.

"Of course not," Yosl said. "But I figured that would at least buy us some time."

I could feel the anger bubbling up inside of me. "So, they are going to kill us anyways when they find out you lied!" I burst out.

"Maybe," Yosl said. "You should be thanking me. Without me you would be dead right now."

"I am as good as dead," I said, through my tears. I looked over to the room where they had taken David. This time, there was no sound coming from the room. I didn't know if that was a good or bad sign. A few minutes later, the door opened and the guard brought David back to our cell. With my eyes I searched his face and his body, but he seemed untouched.

"David!" I cried out, standing to hug him. "What happened to you? Are you all right?"

"Yes, Hinda," he said. "Look at me; I am fine."

David looked at Yosl, who was staring up at him with his mouth agape. They stared at each other for a few moments before David broke the silence.

"Did you tell them we could help them find the partisans?" he asked.

Yosl swallowed and nodded his head.

"Well, I told them, we have no clue where they are," David continued.

"They believed you?" Yosl stuttered.

"Well it's the truth, isn't it?" David responded. Then he kneeled down on the floor, putting Yossi in his lap. He hugged our little boy and kissed his cheek.

The guards didn't take anyone else from the cell for questioning, and they left us sitting there quietly for some time. The next morning, the two children from the day before, Shmuel and Rivka, came, bringing coffee to us. I smiled at the children, happy to see them again.

"Hey," Shmuel whispered. "I just heard the station commander speaking on the phone to someone. He said they are taking you back to Hungary."

"What?" David responded in shock. "How did that happen?"

Shmuel shrugged, handing over a cup to David. I instantly felt a wave of relief. We wouldn't have to illegally cross the border again. They were going to take us back! Later in the day a couple of the policemen came and escorted Yosl, his wife, David, and me out of our cell to a horse-drawn sleigh outside the police station. We got in the sleigh and the policemen drove us to a German command post near the Hungarian border. When the sleigh stopped, my ears and nose were frozen from the ride.

Two German border patrolmen were waiting for us when we arrived. They went inside the command post to get the commander.

The Ukrainian policemen who had brought us went to speak with the commander.

"We have orders from the Gestapo to release these prisoners back in Hungary," one of the Ukrainian policemen said.

"I'm not letting them free in Hungary," the German commander responded. "What am I supposed to do with them?"

"Shoot them, for all I care," the Ukrainian policeman said. "They are yours now."

"So why don't you just shoot them?" the German commander said.

"We're just following order from the Gestapo," the Ukrainian policeman said.

"I'm not taking them," the German commander retorted.

The two sides continued arguing our fate. I watched them carefully, trying not to miss a word. Then one of the other guards from the border post ran out.

"Fayge is coming from the Gestapo," he said when he approached the two arguing. The commander raised his eyebrows and shrugged.

"Well, it's out of our hands now," he said. "We have to wait for Fayge."

We were still sitting on the sleigh, waiting for orders of what to do next. I started to wonder about this Fayge. There was a girl from Butla named Fayge. She was about Rachel's age and very beautiful. She didn't look Jewish at all, with her light skin, straight golden-blonde hair and deep-blue eyes. Her beauty was as much a curse as it was a blessing. From a young age, men used to stare at her and it made her parents angry. They always wanted her to cover up, but she liked the attention. One day, when she was fourteen, she disappeared. There were all sorts of rumors then. Maybe a man had raped and killed her or maybe she had run away all on her own. We never knew. Her parents were devastated after she was gone. I had tried to console her mother, but there really was nothing that could make her feel better.

The German commander lit a cigarette while waiting outside the command post. The Ukrainian policemen were obviously annoyed and kept their distance. Soon a fancy car pulled up and a woman stepped out. The woman was dressed in a red suit with a wide-brimmed hat covering her head. Under the hat, I could see her full blonde hair, neatly styled so that it curled perfectly above her shoulders. She lightly brushed her hair back with her hands, which were covered by white leather gloves that came midway to her elbows. Gracefully, she walked over to the German commander, who handed her a cigarette and lit it for her as she placed it to her lips.

As I watched this woman, I realized she was the Fayge from Butla. She was almost unrecognizable, but something inside me told me it was she. Maybe it was the way she walked, or the slight curve of her nose, but it had to be the same Fayge. I guess she wasn't raped and killed after all.

"I'm coming from Gestapo with strict orders that these prisoners be released in Hungary," she said, blowing out the smoke from her cigarette.

The commander gave her a confused look. "Why does the Gestapo care about these prisoners?"

"I don't make the orders," Fayge said, her tone sounding annoyed by the commander's question. "Do as I say, and there won't be any problems." She threw her cigarette down to the snow and walked back towards her car, passing the sleigh on the way. She looked up at us and I caught her eye. She smiled and winked at me before getting back into her car and driving away.

I looked at David, his eyes wide with shock.

"That was Fayge, from Butla!" I whispered to him. "Can you believe it? Do you remember her?"

"Fayge?" he responded. "The girl who was murdered?"

"I guess she wasn't murdered," I said. My heart was pounding and I wished I could have run over and thanked her. I have no idea how she knew we were in Poland, or how she got them to release us in Hungary, but she must have seen our names somewhere and remembered we were once from the same village.

The German commander breathed deeply. I could see the cold puff of air come out of his mouth. He said something to the guards with him and they quickly came over to us and motioned that we get into a different sleigh. A German sleigh, to take us to the border crossing. I felt nervous getting in the German sleigh, even knowing that they were supposed to be taking us back to Hungary, and the chances were, they wouldn't disobey orders from the Gestapo.

The next sleigh ride was short, and we arrived back at the border crossing where we had been just a few days before. The German guards spoke with the Hungarian border patrol, who looked at us skeptically, before conceding to the Germans.

Just a few minutes later, we were back in Hungary, on the other side of the command post. They rushed us through and closed the door behind us, leaving us there in the snow. There was barely a road visible, let alone a car, or a bus stop or anything else to give us direction of where to go.

"Hinda, do you remember which way we came from?" David asked me. I looked around the post. There was fresh snow covering everything. The ground, the trees, even the sky looked white like it was draped with lace made of snow. Even if I knew which direction we came from, was that the right direction to go? We had been in a prison before we were here.

I knew the basic direction from which we came. There was a road there at least, even if it was covered in snow. I looked to David and pointed him in that direction, and the five of us started walking. David had Yossi up on his shoulders, I walked next to them, and Yosl and Ita followed behind. We walked for several hours, trying to follow the road. There were trees on both sides of us, and as the wind blew, snowflakes fell from the branches onto our shoulders.

Yossi was getting restless atop David's shoulders, so eventually David took him down and let him walk himself. He walked in between us, his little legs swinging back and forth to keep up. But I could see he was comfortable walking for now.

Then, we heard a rumbling coming towards us and soon we saw the headlights of a car. The car had a small flag hanging off the back, a Hungarian flag. It must be guards coming to the command post.

"These guards don't know we are supposed to be free!" Yosl whispered hurriedly. "They are going to take us back to the border! After all this time walking."

"Shut up," David retorted. David looked at me, and I could see he had the same concern. When the car approached us, it stopped.

"Where are you heading?" one of the guards asked.

"Polonye," I answered before anyone else could speak. Of the four of us, my Hungarian was the best. I was able to pick up accents quickly. Polonye was a small village that I knew was somewhere around this area.

The guards looked at each one of us suspiciously, then tipped their hats and continued driving. Within seconds they had disappeared behind us into the snow. Both David and Yosl sighed with relief. Now at least, there would be tire tracks along the road, making it easier for us to follow. We continued walking down the road, and, finally, we saw a village on the horizon. It must be Polonye.

When we approached the village, we saw there were Hungarian guards everywhere. It looked like there was an army base here where the guards must have been quartered. Of all the people walking down the street, at least a third were wearing the Hungarian police uniform. The other two thirds looked like normal people, going about their business in the village.

David was hesitant to walk around. He stopped the five of us near the village edge and we stood there, unsure of what to do. There was a constant stream of people walking by, guards, village people, children. None seemed to notice us. Then, I noticed a Jew walking in our direction. The Jew, identifiable by his thick beard and big hat, was walking with a non-Jew and they were deep in conversation. Then they stopped, shook hands, and parted ways. Immediately

David raced over to the Jewish man. The man noticed David running and approached. The two of them started talking and then walked over to us.

"So, can you help us?" David said in Yiddish.

"It's broad daylight now," the man said. "If it were night, I would happily invite you to my home, but, as you can see, there are guards everywhere here. And there are punishments for helping Jewish refugees. The guards here already don't like us Jews, but for now, there is nothing they can do. If I bring you in, it will endanger my own family; surely you understand."

"What about your friend?" David asked. "The man you were walking with? Is he dependable?"

The man smiled. "Yes, very. You can approach him."

David quickly looked up, trying to see which direction the man had gone. The Jew told us where he would be and David ran off to find him. Soon he came back and motioned us to follow. We followed David through the village to a small house, where the door was open. We walked inside, and there was the Jewish man's friend and another much older man.

"Please, come sit," the younger man said in Hungarian. He had a small wooden table with a few rickety chairs sitting around it. The chairs didn't look like they could hold a person's weight, so I held my breath as I sat down. The inside of the house was mostly empty. There was a small rusty pot sitting on an old stove and a tattered cot in the corner of the one-room home. The floor was made of clay and dirt and the ceiling of straw.

David pulled a few cigarettes out of his jacket—I have no idea where they came from, but he handed them to the two men, who greedily grabbed them from David's hand. They lit up and quickly sucked in the smoke as though they had been craving cigarettes for years.

"Do you have anything to eat?" David asked. "For the child."

"We have no money," the man said.

"But we do," David said. He raised his hand to the collar of his shirt and ripped it open. The money that I had sewn in there was still waiting for us. David pulled it out and handed the man a few bills.

"Please, go to town and buy some bread," David said. The man smiled and agreed, heading out the door. We sat there with the older man, who didn't say a word. He must have been at least seventy years old, his face creased and hair thin and white. I smiled at him, but he seemed to look right through me. It wasn't long before the younger man came back with a loaf of bread, which we split among all seven of us.

"Do you have a horse?" David asked the man.

"I do," he responded.

"Can you take us to Barezna?" David asked. Barezna was a village halfway between here and Munkacz. If he could take us there, we would be that much closer to reconnecting with Rachel and the children. "I'll pay you three hundred pengo."

At the offer of money, the man immediately lit up. "I can take you, but my wagon only fits three people. My horse couldn't pull any more than that."

"Fine," David responded. "So, take the women and my son first, and then we can take a second trip."

"Three hundred pengo per trip," the man said. He was getting greedy now that he saw an opportunity to extort us. "You know this is very dangerous for me."

"Fine," David responded.

"We will go at 3:00 a.m.," the man said. "Until then, I don't want the neighbors to see you here. You can go up into the attic."

I looked up. What attic? The ceiling above us was straw but then I noticed in the corner of the room was a small wooden square. The man went over to it and pushed it up, revealing a crawl space above. He moved a ladder to the little hole in the ceiling and told us to go up. We climbed up and squished into the space above the ceiling. It smelled moist and the air was dank. I could hear mice scattering around when we came up, probably wondering who had come to disturb their living space. Sitting there, I immediately started to feel itchy, as though bugs were crawling all over me. I held Yossi on my lap, not wanting him to touch anything.

We sat quietly in the attic. It was dark and I had no idea what time it was or how long we had to wait there until 3:00 a.m. I could hear someone's deep rhythmic breathing, but I couldn't sleep. I couldn't even close my eyes.

Eventually David got up and crawled down from the attic to the house. I could hear the muffled sound of his voice, likely waking up the man and telling him it was time for us to go. I smiled to myself, thinking I was lucky to have a husband like him. So resourceful, so assertive. I knew whatever happened, I could count on him to take care of everything.

Then I heard footsteps and David popped his head back up into the crawl space. "Hinda, Ita, come on. It's time for you to go."

I handed Yossi to him, and then Ita and I crawled down the ladder to the house. The door was open and the man was outside, hitching his wagon to his horse. David handed me a raggedy sheet. "Wrap Yossi in this," he said. I looked at the sheet and looked at David. "It's cold outside."

I took the sheet and wrapped it around Yossi, praying to myself that it wasn't full of bugs. I carried my sleeping child out to the wagon and climbed in with Ita. The man sat up front, and then we were off. David was right—it was cold. My ears burned from the chill, but at least Yossi was wrapped up tightly in this rag. The village was silent, except for the trotting of the horse and the roll of the wagon. Everyone was asleep, and we slipped out of Polonye without being noticed at all.

As we continued on the journey, I couldn't help but look up at the stars. They glittered the sky, sparkling bright. Every once in a while a shooting star flew across the sky, slicing the darkness. Watching the sky seemed to calm me. It was so beautiful. I started to think that mankind didn't deserve this covering.

I looked over at Ita, to see if maybe she was seeing what I was, but she was hunched over, asleep, her head nodding with the movement of the wagon. Sometimes I felt sorry for her. It must have been hard for her back in Turka. Everyone hated Yosl as part of

Judenrat, but at the same time I understood him. He was doing what he thought best for himself and his wife. Could we judge him for that? And poor Ita, she was hated as much as he was, just for being married to him. I remember her from before the war. She was always unassuming, modest, quiet, but respected among the women. Once the war started, she was shunned. If anyone from the area around Turka knew that our family was still traveling with Yosl and Ita, they would probably judge us as well.

I don't know how long it was, but eventually the sun started to rise. We were still trotting along slowly when we saw the village in front of us. Barezna. I had never been there before and knew no one there. Where would we go when we arrived? The man we were with seemed to have a plan. He drove us through the village, navigating the streets as though he had a specific destination in mind. Barezna was much smaller than Polonye. There weren't many people on the street and the buildings looked older and smaller. Soon we pulled up to a small stone cottage in an alleyway. I immediately noticed a mezuzah on the door frame.

"We're here," the man said. "Go in there."

I looked at him and looked at the cottage. "Do you know them?" I asked.

"It's a mikveh,"[11] he said. "Surely they will take you in."

"You'll tell David we are here when you bring him?" I asked.

---

[11] A Jewish ritual bathhouse.

"Of course," he said. "I have a long journey back, I have to go."

I thanked him as Ita and I hopped out of the cart. He quickly drove off, leaving a cloud of dust behind. I looked at the door of the mikveh. I had only been to a mikveh a few times in my life. Once, before David and I got married, and a few other times scattered over the years. I always thought it was a nice tradition, but unnecessary. Right now, I felt ashamed that I didn't go more often. I also felt that I was too dirty to be allowed to enter into a mikveh.

I knocked and immediately heard movement from inside. A few moments later, a woman answered the door. The woman was plump and had a scarf covering her head. She looked at us silently, her mouth dropped open.

"Hi, I am Hinda and this is Ita," I said in Yiddish. "Can we please come in?"

The woman moved aside and let us in. The room inside was clean and white and I could see the bath of the mikveh through a doorway at the back of the entryway. The woman brought us water to drink and told us to sit down at her table. I looked at the table, feeling guilty that my sitting would dirty the chair.

"Please," the woman said, noticing my hesitation. Ita had already sat down and was drinking the water the woman had poured. I sat down next to her, still holding Yossi in my arms. He was awake now, quietly taking everything in.

The woman offered us a shower and let us enter the mikveh after we were clean. It was a Thursday, she told us, meaning that the next day there would likely be many women coming in for the mikveh before Shabbos.

"I hope we aren't bothering you by being here," I said to her after having cleaned myself. I took a short dip in the mikveh, but it felt like just a normal bath to me. I didn't feel blessed or cleansed from the ritual.

"It won't be a problem," the woman said. "Fridays here are always packed with many women. They won't think anything of there being two more here."

I was hoping that the man would return with David and Yosl by then, and we wouldn't be here when the wave of women came. For some reason, I felt like all the religious women coming for their ritual bath would see me as an imposter—not a real Jew.

We spent the day at the mikveh. Ita and I helped the woman clean and prepare for the following day. Yossi played quietly by himself with a few toys the woman had lying around. Finally, it became evening, and still there was no sign of David. The woman lived behind the mikveh, and eventually she left us to go to sleep. She said we could stay there and sleep on the couches so long as we made sure to keep it tidy before the women arrived.

I felt bad imposing on her, but I didn't know what else to do. We couldn't go anywhere; otherwise, David may not know where to find us. So, we slept there in the mikveh and stayed the next day as the women started pouring in. All the women were friendly and smiled at us as they came. All day there were women coming in and out, and there were always at least twenty to twenty-five women there at a time. They entered into the mikveh separately, but sat around for hours before and after, gossiping and chatting about their children and what they were cooking for Shabbos. They were obviously unaware, or unconcerned, of what was happening to women like them in Poland and even other parts of Hungary. I felt sad for them, and I hoped they wouldn't be displaced one day like we were.

As the day went on, the number of women coming in and out started to dwindle. I could see that it was becoming evening and that it would soon be Shabbos. And still, there was no sign of David. The woman who ran the mikveh gave us some food and told us not to worry, that we could stay there as long as we wanted, but that she would be with her family for the Shabbos, and we wouldn't see her again until Saturday evening. I thanked her and prayed to myself that we would be gone by then.

"What do you think happened?" Ita asked me when we were alone at the mikveh.

I shook my head, not wanting to think about it. They should have arrived by Friday morning, and now it was already Friday evening. How long do we wait here until we need to figure out what to do? My question was answered by a quiet knock on the door. I jumped up and ran over to open it.

A wave of relief hit me when I saw David and Yosl there. They were with a young boy, who David handed a little money. The boy ran away. "Where have you been?" I burst out.

David sighed. "They set up a guard post on the road half way to Barezna. We had to come on foot through the hills. We got here and found the shul, where services were going on. I found that boy waiting outside and told him we would pay him to take us to the mikveh."

"We were starting to get worried," I responded.

David smiled. "Well, we are here now. The boy is bringing us a taxi to take us to Munkacz. If all goes well, we'll be back with the children and Rachel by morning."

My heart started to flutter. It had been weeks since we saw them, maybe even months. I hoped they were all right in Munkacz. I was sure Rachel was taking good care of them. We waited there for a little while until a taxi arrived. David told the taxi driver that Yossi was sick and that was why we urgently needed to go to Munkacz in the middle of the night. There was a hospital in Munkacz, the closest hospital to where we were.

The driver agreed to take us for five hundred pengo. It was, after all, a drive of several hours. The five of us—Yosl and Ita, and David, Yossi and me—crammed into the taxi and we were off! My heart pounded, knowing we were closer to reuniting with our family. The taxi drove through Ungvar, where we had been a few weeks ago. There were guard posts along the road whenever we approached a village, but the driver explained to everyone that our child was sick and we were going to the hospital. Afraid that the boy was contagious, none of the guards bothered us. Sometime around mid-day Saturday, we arrived at the hospital in Munkacz. David paid the driver and we waited for him to drive off. Then, we started walking towards the room we had rented from Anna.

It wasn't a far walk and we quickly arrived. We knocked on the door of the room, but there was no answer. Then, we went to the main house, where Anna lived. She came out when she saw us wandering around her house.

"Are Rachel and my children here?" David asked her.

Anna looked at us, like she didn't know who we were. David walked up to her, and it must have jogged her memory.

"They left the same day you were arrested," she said. "I haven't seen them since. You know, I had to pay for the door that was broken in the room."

David ignored her, and my heart dropped. Where did they go? What happened to them? Tears started to well up in my eyes, even though I tried to hold them back. David looked at me, staring into my eyes for a moment, and then started walking down the street. I hurried after him, leaving Yosl and Ita behind. At this point, I didn't care what happened to them. They could stay there, rent from Anna, and they would be fine. David and I, we couldn't stay. We had to find our children and Rachel. Yosl and Ita yelled at us to come back, but we ignored them. That was the last we saw of them.

David and I started wandering around Munkacz, unsure where to go. We went to the market, where Rachel had worked, and started asking around. "Did anyone know Rachel?" "Did anyone see a young girl about twenty years old with two children with her? A boy and girl?" We went through the market, asking everyone we saw, but no one seemed to know who we were asking about.

At the end of the day, we found ourselves sitting near a small park by the edge of the market, defeated. I held Yossi in my lap; he was the only thing bringing me comfort. David looked around tirelessly, as though looking for a clue. I don't know how long we sat there, but eventually it started to get dark. We couldn't stay there at night. We would freeze outside.

David was still sitting alert. I noticed that he seemed to be looking at something off in the distance. I looked over and saw he was staring at a man coming towards us. The man was tall and wore a yarmulke on his head, but he wasn't dressed like the Jews in Munkacz. This man was clean-shaven and seemed to blend with the rest of the village people, except for the small circle covering the crown of his head.

"I hear you are looking for someone," he said. David stood up.

The man continued. "A pretty girl about twenty years old? She was with a boy and girl, about ten years old. In fact, they may have looked like you."

"Where are they?" David said sternly.

"They are no longer in Munkacz," he said. My heart skipped a beat. That could mean so many things; how would we know if they were safe?

"I helped them get out of here," the man continued. "My name is Meyer."

"Where did they go?" David asked.

"Beregszasz," the man smiled. "They are safe."

I had heard of Beregszasz. It was a nearby village that we could easily get to. I looked at David, who was staring at Meyer.

"How do we get there?" David asked him.

"Well, there is a bus on Monday, or you can take a taxi," Meyer said.

David looked at me. I could feel an expression of panic hardened on my face. I couldn't hide my feelings about having to wait another day to see them.

David then turned back to Meyer. "How much is a taxi?"

"You don't look like you have any money left," Meyer said.

I looked to David, surely there was something left? David stuck his hand in his mouth, and squinted his eyes, pulling out a gold tooth cap. He had three gold tooth caps in his mouth, I never would have thought of that as currency.

David held up the tooth cap in front of Meyer. "Will this get us to Beregszasz?"

Meyer smiled. "Maybe half way, if you are lucky."

David then pulled his two other gold tooth caps from his mouth and held them up. "Meyer, can you get us to Beregszasz tomorrow?"

"Come with me," he said. "You can spend the night at my house, and we will go in the morning."

He led us to the other side of the village, to a big house surrounded by a white wooden fence. He took us inside and gave us a room to stay in. "I'll have a taxi come in the morning," Meyer said, leaving us for the night.

I looked around the room he gave us. It was almost bigger than our house had been in Butla. It had hardwood floors and a tall ceiling with gold trim where it connected to the walls. The room made me nervous. Who was this Meyer? With such a fancy house, he had to be someone important, but I had never heard of him before.

David sat back in a chair and closed his eyes. I watched him, unable to rest. I hugged Yossi tight and waited there throughout the night. In the morning, Meyer came with coffee and told us the taxi was outside. We got in the car, starting the next leg of our journey. Meyer came with us, sitting in the front, while David, Yossi, and I sat in the back of the taxi. We didn't speak the entire car ride, which seemed to drag on forever. During this ride, we passed through guard posts, but Meyer tipped his hat at each one and they let us pass without question.

We arrived in Beregszasz in the early afternoon. The taxi dropped us off at the edge of the village and Meyer and the driver turned around. We were on the edge of a long street with stores all around. It was Sunday though, and many of the stores seemed to be closed. We wandered down the street, until eventually we saw a shul.

David went inside and after a while came back out again, a smile plastered on his face. "I know where they are," he said. "Let's go."

He started walking through the village at a fast pace. I almost had to run to keep up with him. We walked through neighborhoods with little brick houses, until suddenly David stopped in front of one.

KNOCK. KNOCK. David knocked on the door. We could see there was a light on inside, but there was no sound or movement.

KNOCK. KNOCK. KNOCK. David pounded a little harder this time. Again, no response. What if they are not here? Why won't they open the door? It wouldn't be smart for us to be standing out here for a while for the whole neighborhood to hear.

KNOCK! KNOCK! KNOCK! KNOCK! KNOCK! David pounded again, trying to look inside the small window in the door.

Suddenly, there was a click. A tall, slender woman cracked open the door, her face stunned like she was about to turn into a rock. Her mouth dropped open as she stood in the space between the door and its frame, blocking whatever was behind her.

"Sorry to bother you," David started in Ukrainian. "I am looking for my sister and children."

The woman's face softened and she turned around, creating more space between the door and its frame. And there they were—Rachel, huddled on the floor, her arms around Abi and Sarah, all three of them looking shook up and frightened.

1943—Rachel

There were a few times that I felt paralyzed with fear—fear that was so strong it coated me like rust that makes metal, that was once limber and flexible, brittle. That moment, with my arms around Abi and Sarah, was one of those times. I was sure that was it. We had been hearing about raids every day, and I knew it was only a matter of time before we were caught in one. We were too lucky, always getting away in the nick of time, and always finding someone who was willing to help us, for who knows what reason. All of that was coming to an end, I thought, when I heard that knock on the door.

"Sorry to bother you," I heard when Franci peeked through to see who was knocking. The voice was stern and familiar, but the paralyzing fear had not yet lifted. "I am looking for my sister and children."

Then the door swung open, showing David and Hinda, carrying Yossi in her chest, standing there out in the cold. My first thought was that it was an illusion, that my mind was playing tricks on me, showing me what I wanted to see, instead of the evil guards standing there, ready to cart us off. But slowly, as they entered the house, I started to study their features, and was finally convinced that it was really them.

"How did you get here!?" I said in Polish, realizing that I was still gripping Sarah and Abi at my sides. I lifted my hands from them, but they sat still, also shocked and still absorbing that we had, once again, evaded capture. I nudged Sarah and Abi, waking them from their trance.

"Mother! Father!" Sarah screamed, scrambling up to go meet them. Abi quickly followed, throwing himself into David.

"Let's just say there are miracles," David said, hugging Abi and Sarah. Sarah reached up to grab Yossi from Hinda's arms. Hesitant at first, Yossi quickly warmed up to Sarah, hugging her back as she held him and kissed his face all over. I also hugged my brother, Hinda, and kissed Yossi on the forehead, while he was in Sarah's arms. I could see that Sarah wasn't going to let go of him any time soon.

Franci made tea for everyone and we sat down at the table. Hinda wrapped her hands around the teacup, staring at it, as if she were just imagining the flavor. David, on the other hand, gulped his down without giving it a moment to cool off. We sat for several hours. First, David told us about what they had been through over the last month, from the time they were captured. He told us about the different jails they had been to and how they were deported to Poland. He told us about Fayge. Did I remember her?—the beautiful young Jew who had now somehow become influential in the Gestapo and had saved them. Then he talked about Yosl and Ita. How Yosl was the same pest he always was and had been beaten up a few times. But it turns out he had come in handy once, saving them from being executed by a firing squad. The four of them had been freed together and traveled to Munkacz, hoping to find us there. When we weren't there, they didn't know if they would see us again, until they met a Jew with a shaven face who told them we went to Beregszasz. David didn't trust the man, but decided they had no other choice but to listen to him. Meyer, I thought, feeling anger towards that man, even though I guess we owed him thanks for bringing us back together. Meyer had brought them to Beregszasz and here they asked around until someone told them where we were.

I realized I had been squeezing Hinda's hand the whole time David was talking. Listening to his story, I kept thinking, David is right, there must be miracles. From his story, it didn't make sense that they were here—safe and alive. Then Hinda asked me how had we gotten here. I laughed a moment, thinking about how easy our trip had been compared to theirs. "That beardless Jew; his name is Meyer," I told them. "He helped us get here." I told David he was right not to trust him; there was something about him, even though he had brought us here and reunited our family. We had been here with Franci the whole time, staying in her house because there were continual raids here in Beregszasz. The police were constantly looking for Poles. We heard daily stories of people being caught and taken away. We didn't know to where, but I thought—best case scenario—they were deported back to Poland. Worst case scenario, I didn't want to think about that.

We spoke late into the night. The children had all fallen asleep, but Franci, David, Hinda, and I continued sitting at the table, long after we ran out of things to say. I looked over to Franci who had been quiet this whole time, but absorbing every word. Her eyes were wide, but tired, as though she were fighting hard to keep them open. For the first time, I thought about how much we were imposing on her. She was just a kind woman, who had agreed to help strangers, and suddenly a month later, even more strangers had barged into her house. Strangers with nowhere to go, and the only thing they brought with them were horror stories.

"I deeply apologize for coming into your home like this," David said finally, as though he had read what was on my mind. "You have been too kind already, helping my sister and two children. I cannot ask you to help us anymore."

"Oh," Franci responded. She looked relieved, and I could understand why. Imagine what was running through her head right now, three more people sleeping in her house? Three more mouths to feed. "Your family is a pleasure to have here," she said politely.

"In the morning, I will go back to the shul," David said. "I will find us another place to stay."

We all tried to get some rest, but I knew there was no way I would be able to sleep. My adrenaline was high and my heart was still pounding from the fear and relief of not being caught.

Early in the morning, David got up and left the house, likely to get to the shul before the morning prayer begun. He arrived back in the afternoon with good news.

"There is a Jew who lives just outside the village," David said. "He has a barn that he offered me to stay in. I also found a job at the sawmill nearby. Abi will be able to come work there with me as well."

"I want to stay with you in the barn," Abi said. "You shouldn't be there alone."

"Fine," David said, but I could see he was happy that Abi would be with him. Then David turned to me. "Rachel, there is a rich family in town looking for a nanny. I got you the job; you will go live with them. They have two nice children that you will take care of."

I lit up with the news. As much as I was comfortable here with Franci, I did not feel great about staying with her all this time and doing nothing. Yes, I helped around the house, cooking and cleaning, and helping with her son, but it had been hard feeling like I was just a burden this whole time.

"Franci, if you don't mind," David continued. "Hinda, Sarah, and Yossi will stay here. Hinda can work at the local mikveh and Sarah will take care of Yossi."

"Aren't you worried about everyone going out to work every day?" Franci said. "Someone could get caught!"

"If anyone asks, we are Hungarians," David responded. "We were just living in Poland until recently."

David didn't waste any time. He got up, and motioned to Abi and me that it was time to go. They would take me to the house of the family where I would work and then head outside of town to the barn where they were going to stay. The three of us walked briskly, quiet as David led us to another part of Beregszasz, where I hadn't been before. Here, there seemed to be a lot more space. The houses didn't touch the ones next to them and they were much farther away from the main street. Far enough that I couldn't see in the windows and, although I could tell that there was décor around the front door, I could not tell what it was. Here, houses seemed to be less practical, and much more beautiful. Suddenly David stopped and turned to me.

"That is where you are going to stay," he said. "I will come visit you when I am in town."

I looked at David and at the house. Then I looked back to Abi, who was staring up at me with wide eyes. I kneeled down to hug him and kissed his forehead. David started to look impatient, so I got up and started walking towards the house. I didn't turn back, but I could hear David's and Abi's footsteps continuing down the road.

When I got to the front door, I paused. What do I say to them? Which language do I speak? My Hungarian was still not so great, but I was sure this family didn't want to hear Polish or Ukrainian. Definitely not Yiddish. My head told me to stand at the doorstep a little longer, but my hand decided to knock. I held my breath as I waited there, counting the seconds. One, two, three, four. Maybe they aren't home. That thought actually made me feel relieved, that maybe it was a sign that I shouldn't be here. But then the door suddenly swung open.

"You must be the new nanny," said the woman in Hungarian. I smiled and nodded politely. I tried not to stare at her, but I almost couldn't help it. She was tall and curvy, probably around Hinda's age. Her hair was styled fashionably pulled back, each hair in place as though it was afraid to move. She wore makeup, her lips were dark red, and her eyes lined so they looked like they could pop out. Around her neck she had a thick gold necklace with diamonds on it. It covered her chest like armor. "Well, come in already." She didn't seem to notice my stare.

"I'm Mrs. Kovacs," the woman said. I followed her through the foyer of the house and down a hallway. "My husband is Mr. Kovacs; he'll be home in the evening. He likes a clean house when he returns. And, of course, that the children be washed up by then."

The ceiling in the house was higher than I expected. I looked up around the walls, covered in portraits and paintings of nature. The frames around the paintings were what really struck me. They were as elaborate as the paintings themselves, large, gold with designs carved into them.

"Here is the children's playroom," Mrs. Kovacs said, turning around towards me. "You can stay with them here, or take them to the yard to play. If you take them out, their coats and gloves are over there." She pointed to a small closet in the corner of the room.

In the middle of the floor sat two young children. A girl, maybe about six years old, with long blonde curls, puffy cheeks, and a wide-open smile that showed her tiny teeth with gaps in between. The other child was a boy, who looked about three years old. Also blonde, he had rosy cheeks as though he had been running around in the cold. He sat up straight surrounded by wooden blocks that his sister had placed. Building a fort, to protect him from the outside . . . or maybe to lock himself in.

"This is Kristoff and Vivien," Mrs. Kovacs said. "They are cute, but they are a handful. I expect you will keep them entertained and behaved."

"Of course," I mumbled.

"Great," Mrs. Kovacs said, swinging her hips as she continued walking down the hall. I stood by the door of the playroom, looking back and forth between the kids watching me, and the back of Mrs. Kovacs. She turned back around. "Come on, I want to finish giving you the tour so you will know everything you need."

I quickly followed her as she led me through to a large dining room with a big round table and heavy chairs placed equally around it. "We eat here," she said. "And the kitchen is through there." She pointed to a door on the other side of the living room. "You will prepare meals for the children. For me and Mr. Kovacs, we have a cook who comes five days a week. You will share the kitchen with her."

Mrs. Kovacs turned away from the dining room and continued walking. I guess going into the kitchen is not part of the tour. I followed her to a large room with couches and a bar that ran all along one of the walls. On the other side was a glass door to the outside, revealing a large yard surrounded by a tall white fence.

"There is your new home," Mrs. Kovacs said, pointing to the yard. "It's right off the kitchen, so you can go in and out from there. Keep it tidy. I don't need any mice coming in here because your quarters are dirty."

"Yes, ma'am," I said, looking through the yard to the small hut where I would be living. It looked more like a storage shed, but at least it had four walls and roof. More than I could say about some of the places I had slept in the last year.

"Well, if you need anything, please ask," Mrs. Kovacs said. "I am usually home in the mornings and then I go out for lunch in the afternoons."

"Thank you," I smiled to her. "I think I'll head over to the playroom to introduce myself to the children."

"Wonderful," Mrs. Kovacs said and swiftly walked through a corridor that was not included in our tour. I headed straight for the playroom, where Vivien was trying to balance blocks on top of her brother's head.

"Hi, I am Rachel," I said, as I got down on the floor in front of them.

"I'm Vivien," the girl said. "Are you our new nanny?"

"I am," I said, thinking that my Hungarian was probably at the same level as Vivien's. "And I am very excited to be here with you."

"Where are you from?" Vivien asked me. "You talk funny."

I laughed. "I am from Poland. I am just learning Hungarian. You can help me if you want."

"Sure," Vivien said. "Why did you leave your home?"

"I wanted to come be with you," I said quickly, unsure how to answer Vivien's questions. I could see she had more coming.

"Are your parents still in Poland? And your brothers and sisters?" she asked.

I sighed. My parents? I was actually glad they weren't around to witness what was happening to Jews today. My brothers? Aside from David, I had no idea what had happened to the others. Shlomo, Meir, Itzik, Zeilig, and Chaim had all moved away from Butla. Chaim, Shlomo and Meir had been in Krakow. Itzik and Zeilig had been in Warsaw. When we were in Turka I had tried to contact them. I sent them all letters telling them about what was happening at home and asked them what was happening where they were. But I never got a single response.

"Yes, they are still in Poland," I responded to Vivien. Better to keep things simple for her.

"Do you miss them?" she fired back.

"Yes," I said.

"Do you know how to build castles?" Vivien said motioning to the blocks around her and Kristoff.

"I sure do," I said, thankful that she had changed the subject so quickly. "Every castle needs a tower where the princess sleeps. We can start by building that."

Vivien's eyes lit up. Together we constructed a big castle with a tall tower, thick walls and a moat around it to protect it from intruders. Kristoff kept knocking over the tower, making Vivien scream with anger. The more she screamed, the funnier Kristoff thought it was, causing him to knock it over again and again until Vivien was red-faced and kicking the floor. I tried to distract Kristoff with the other toys they had in the playroom. There were just so many: cars, trucks, a train, a play kitchen, puzzles, but Kristoff was only interested in what Vivien was playing with.

Mrs. Kovacs walked by the playroom, raising her eyebrows at me when she heard the crying. She walked by silently, but I got the message. They hired a nanny so they wouldn't have to hear any screaming. I quickly decided maybe it was time for a snack and ran into the kitchen to see what I could find. I grabbed a loaf of bread and some jam and brought it back to the playroom for the kids. They were excited for the snack, so I spread the jam on the bread quickly and handed them each a slice. Vivien immediately cried that Kristoff had more jam than she did. This of course made Kristoff smile and tease his sister with each bite. I gave Vivien a little more jam on her bread and then Kristoff complained that he wanted more jam too. I told them they should be happy to have any jam, and bread for that matter, and then I went back to the kitchen to put the snack away. When I came back, I saw that there was jam on all the blocks they were playing with, on the carpet, and all over them. Vivien had jam in her hair and dripping down the front of her sweater, while Kristoff's face was also covered with the berry spread. I hadn't even given them that much jam; how could it have gotten on so many things?

I quickly decided it was bath time and took the children to their bathroom and started filling up their large tub. They cried they didn't want a bath, that they were clean, but I stayed firm and scrubbed the jam out of their hair and off their skin. They were tired, so I put them in bed for a nap and then I washed their clothes and ran to clean the playroom, scrubbing jam from the toys and the carpet, and then putting everything away. By then, I could hear Vivien getting up, so I ran to her room and braided her hair to keep her quiet so she wouldn't wake up her brother. I made a deal with her that I would braid her hair whenever she helped me with her brother and played nice with him. She liked having a special deal with me. It made her feel important that I trusted her with a secret agreement and didn't have one with Kristoff. When he woke up from his nap, she offered to read him a book in the playroom, so we all went to sit there and she read us her favorite story.

Eventually, Mr. Kovacs came home and was surprised to see the children sitting so quietly together. He came in to give them hugs and then went to the dining room with Mrs. Kovacs for their dinner. I forgot that the kids didn't eat dinner with their parents, and realized I now had to feed them before taking them to bed. I snuck into the kitchen, where a woman was standing over several steaming pots. The cook, I thought, smiling to her. She was an older woman, with gray hair tied up at the back of her head and a white apron covering her from her chest to her knees. She stared at me, confused, as I burst into the kitchen.

"Hi, I am Rachel, the new nanny," I introduced myself. "I just came to grab some dinner for the children."

"I'm cooking now," the woman said. "You should feed them before Mr. and Mrs. Kovacs are having their dinner."

"Right, yes," I said. "It's my first day."

"There isn't enough room in here for two people cooking," the woman said.

"The kids are hungry, and they need to go to sleep soon," I said.

"You know what," she said. "Go back to the playroom, I will whip something up for you and bring it to you there. OK? And tomorrow, you can help me when you are making their food."

"Sure, thank you," I smiled at her and rushed back out to the children. I could smell the food she was cooking, it smelled delicious. There was borscht and meat and fresh bread being baked. From the playroom, I could hear her serving the Kovacs in the dining room. Then, she came into the playroom, carrying bread with melted cheese and bowls of soup for the children. She placed the food down on their small table and looked over to me. "You bring me back the dishes, and once the kids are asleep. There are leftovers for you in the kitchen," she winked.

"Thank you so much," I said, watching Vivien and Kristoff slurp up their soup, tearing and dipping the cheese bread in it. My mouth watered from watching them, but I didn't dare eat from their plates. I was thankful the cook had invited me back to the kitchen for leftovers later. When they finished, I ran the dishes back to the kitchen and took the children to bed, tucking them in again. With lights out, I sighed with relief and went back into the kitchen where the cook was just finishing up putting all the dishes—now clean—away.

"How was your first day?" the cook asked me, putting a bowl of borscht in front of me. The beet soup was deep purple with a big dollop of cream in the middle. It was rich and delicious, and I couldn't slow myself down when eating it.

"They are sweet children," I said to her, deciding not to speak too much to the cook. She was nice to me all right, but I still didn't know who she was.

"Yes, very sweet," she smiled. "That's what the last few nannies thought as well."

I finished the soup quickly and the cook immediately refilled my plate with more. "Where are you from, dear?" she asked me.

"From here, Hungary," I stuttered out. I was afraid to tell her I was Polish, and I immediately regretted that I said so to Vivien. What if she told someone and I was caught because of my carelessness?

"You don't sound like it," she said. "You from the Ukraine? Poland?"

I shook my head, afraid to say anything more.

"All right," the cook said, getting the message. "When you finish eating, wash your plate. I'll see you tomorrow." She left the kitchen, and I was alone there.

When I finished eating, I washed my plate and walked out to the shed where I would sleep. There was a small bed and stove. It was freezing in there, so I went out to find a few logs to light in the stove to keep me warm. Behind the shed was a small outhouse, where I relieved myself before I pushed the bed in front of the stove and fell asleep.

Every day at the Kovacs got easier. I got to know Vivien and Kristoff better and was able to keep them entertained and happy most of the time. I also found a good partnership with the cook—Soma, her name was. I would get up early and help her cut vegetables and she would often make food for the children. I was starting to love the Hungarian food she cooked— goulash, paprikash, and all kinds of soups.

It was two weeks before I heard anything from my family. I was starting to wonder what was happening with them, and the wonder was already turning into worry by the time David came knocking on the Kovacs' door. It was a Saturday morning, and he came to pick me up and walk with me to Franci's house, where we would have lunch together.

David showed up at the Kovacs with Abi, the two of them having come from the barn they were staying at outside of town. David's eyes were sunken in, tired-looking, and his face was pale. Abi looked older than I remembered, and more muscular, too.

"You look well!" David exclaimed when he saw me. I smiled, wishing I could say the same back to him. I hugged him and Abi and we started on the walk to Franci's. "Are they treating you well? Do you have enough to eat?" David started with the questions immediately.

"Yes, very well," I said. "And yes, there is plenty. I am even learning to cook Hungarian food!" Maybe one day I could have my own kitchen, and cook for them, I thought. "How are you doing?"

"Just fine," David responded quickly. I noticed Abi looked up at David when he said it, but Abi didn't say anything.

"Things are fine at the barn?" I asked, hoping to get more information.

"Yes," David responded. "There are a few cows there, and Abi learned how to milk them, so we are living like kings."

As we continued to walk, Abi told me about working at the sawmill—how David would cut wood and Abi would carry it and stack it up. He said there were other children working at the mill, some even cutting the wood themselves, but David wouldn't let him hold a saw. I told them about Vivien and Kristoff, and Mrs. Kovacs, who had no patience for her children. Soon, we got to Franci's house. My heart started racing. I was excited to see everyone, to be with my family again, even for just a little while.

Hinda opened the door, wearing an apron. I hugged her tightly, and then walked in, looking for Yossi and Sarah. The house seemed quiet. Franci's son, Rudi, was playing by himself in the corner, and Franci was setting the table.

"We sent them to Budapest," David said to me. What? I thought, confused. "Yossi and Sarah," he continued speaking. "They are in Budapest."

"Why?" was the only thing I could say.

"The Jews in Budapest want to help people like us," David said. "We sent Yossi and Sarah to an orphanage for Jewish children there. The Jews in Budapest adopt the children, and they will be safe there. There are no raids, or Germans there."

"When did they go?" My heart sank as I asked; it was hard enough being away from them, thinking I would see everyone soon. Now, who knows when I would ever see them.

"A few days ago," David said. "We paid a smuggler to take them on a night train to Budapest and they have already arrived at the orphanage. It is supposed to be safe there for them."

"Actually, Sarah wrote us a letter," Hinda said. "One of the smugglers brought the letter back here yesterday. If you want to write back to her, we can send a letter with him when he goes back tomorrow." Hinda handed me the letter.

I quickly opened it and read it aloud to everyone.

Dear Mother, Father, Aunt Rachel, and Abi,

I already miss you now that we are here in Budapest, but I don't want you to worry about us. The man you sent us with on the train was very nice and even made sure we had enough space to sleep during the train ride! At first, I was really scared, but Yossi kept reminding me that we will be safer there, even if we are away from you.

We were on the train all night and then, when we got off, the man took us in a taxi to a campsite in the forest where there are a lot of other children. All the other children are Jewish. Some are Polish like us, and others are Ukrainian, Czech, and there are even a few German children here. Those poor German children; they have come such a long way, and they seem the loneliest of everyone here.

We have three meals a day. Usually it is just some watery soup with vegetables. Every day everyone gets 180 grams of bread. I save mine every day, to make sure Yossi is getting enough to eat. When he finishes his, I give him mine if he is still hungry. Don't worry about me—I'll manage. As long as Yossi has enough to eat, I know we will be fine.

Jews from Budapest come here every day to look at all of us and sometimes they take a child home with them. We're always so happy for the children that get adopted. They are going to live in a real Jewish home, like we used to in Butla! I know someone will adopt Yossi soon. The younger ones seemed to get adopted more often.

We both miss you very much and hope to hear back from you soon!

Love,

Sarah and Yossi

I could see that Yossi scribbled his own name at the bottom of the letter. I rubbed my hand across the messy handwriting, missing them even more now that I had a glimpse of how they were doing. Hinda's eyes had welled up with tears when I was reading the letter. I handed the letter back to her, and she kissed it before folding it back up and putting it in her pocket.

We sat down to eat. Hinda and Franci had made vegetable soup and bread. It was delicious and reminded me of home, of the Shabbos lunches we used to eat before we left Butla. We ate quietly, nobody having anything to say. I wanted to ask what they had heard about the raids in Beregszasz. I sometimes heard the Kovacs muttering about them. There were raids almost every day. Police would come to people's houses and tear them apart until they found evidence of hiding Jews. If they caught Jews, the Jews and the people hiding them were shipped off—probably to Poland, or worse, to special prisons the Nazis built for the Jews. Everything I knew was just from overhearing Mr. and Mrs. Kovacs, or from the cook Soma, who sometimes talked to me about what was happening. I still wasn't sure if they knew that I was Jewish, so I always pretended like I wasn't interested in hearing about the raids even though I was desperate for information and in constant fear that Franci would be raided. I could never forgive myself if Franci was arrested because of us.

When we finished eating, I helped Hinda clear the table and went with her to the kitchen to clean up. With the two of us alone, I wanted to find out if everything really was fine with David and Abi.

"David has been really sick," Hinda told me as she was washing the dishes. "Sleeping in the barn—in the cold—hasn't been good for him. Abi has been taking care of him; he has been really strong." She handed me a dish to dry and put away.

"Is he OK?" I asked.

Hinda smiled. "We're getting older, it's getting harder for us, but David will be fine. He is strong."

Hinda continued. "I think we will have to go somewhere else soon. It is becoming too dangerous in

259

Beregszasz. I can't continue endangering Franci. She has done so much for us. David wants all of us to go to Budapest eventually."

I started thinking about the Kovacs—were they knowingly endangering themselves for me? Or did they think I really was Hungarian?

After lunch, David, Abi, and I left. I watched David as they walked me back to the Kovacs' house. He walked hunched over, his arms folded tightly in front of him. He definitely looked older than I remembered him, but I guess that is what happens when you live on the run for as long as we have.

When we arrived at the Kovacs, I said goodbye and walked around the back of the house to enter through the kitchen. It was already evening, meaning the kids were probably already asleep. I wanted to check the playroom, to see if I needed to clean it up before I went to my shed and went to sleep. I could hear Mr. and Mrs. Kovacs in the living room, talking softly to each other. I passed by them while walking to the playroom, trying to eavesdrop on their conversation. My Hungarian had improved significantly already, to the point where I could usually understand entire conversations.

"I am just shocked," Mrs. Kovacs said. "I mean, the Molnars—they were such pillars in our community. Such standup people."

"They were just doing what they thought was right," Mr. Kovacs responded.

"Yes, but to put your own family in danger. I mean, for what purpose? To help someone you don't know? A Jew?"

"It's tragic."

There must have been a raid today, I thought. The Molnars were a family that lived a few houses down. Mrs. Kovacs was friendly with Mrs. Molnar; sometimes she would send me to bring them things she bought, or to pick up cookies Mrs. Molnar had baked. I had been to the Molnar's home a few times. They also had a girl like me working there, but I never suspected she was Jewish.

The Kovacs must not know I am Jewish, I decided. On one hand, that meant they would never turn me in. On the other, that meant they were unknowingly risking their lives for me. I suddenly felt guilty for being there.

The playroom was a mess. Toys everywhere, crumbs strewn across the floor. I quickly cleaned it up and then went straight to my shed to go to sleep.

From then on, I kept my head down while I worked. I was afraid the Kovacs would somehow figure out I was Jewish and throw me out, or worse, turn me in. Part of me thought I should leave, but I wasn't sure what else I could do. I knew Hinda wanted to leave Franci's place, so I couldn't go back to staying there.

The next week, David and Abi again came to pick me up for a Shabbos lunch at Franci's. This week, David looked a little better. His eyes were a little less hollow, and his cheeks were pink from the cold. We walked quickly to Franci's house, eager to find out if there was another letter from Sarah. Sure enough, there was. I again read it aloud to everyone.

Dear Mother, Father, Aunt Rachel, and Abi,

We were adopted! We are now living with Mrs. and Mr. Freuden. They came to the orphanage last week and they just fell in love with Yossi. They came back the very next day and adopted him. He was sad when they took him, but I told him to be strong and not to worry about me! He promised me he would, but then two days later they came back to the orphanage. I was afraid they were coming to return Yossi; maybe he did something wrong, or they changed their minds. But no, they came back to get me. They said Yossi didn't stop crying from the moment they left the orphanage with him. They tried everything, gave him chocolate, took him to play with other kids, but the only thing that made him stop was a promise that I could come live with them, too. So that is what happened—they came and picked me up, and now we are both staying with them.

They are a very nice couple. They don't have any children, but I can tell they really want them. I guess that is lucky for us. They have a really big house, and even wanted to give Yossi and me our own rooms, but we told them we would rather stay together. Next week, they are going to take us to school.

We miss you very much and hope we get to see you soon!

Love,

Sarah and Yossi

Hinda again cried as I read the letter aloud, but these must be happy tears, to know two of her children were now safe, living in a big house in Budapest. We all hugged and then sat down to eat. We sat in silence eating together, but then started to hear the gentle rhythm of horses on the street. David ran to the window and yelled, "We have to leave! Now!"

The police were coming. They must have gotten a tip about Jews on this street. We didn't know if they were coming for us, but there was no time to wait and see. Franci's house had a back door, and we all rushed to quietly slip through it and run. We exited the house in a quiet alleyway and ran together as fast as we could without looking back. I prayed they weren't coming to Franci's house, but at least if they did, they wouldn't find us there. I knew we could never go back there now. We kept running until we got to the mikveh where Hinda was working. It was closed on Saturdays, but she had a key and we slipped inside.

1943—Abi

We didn't go back to the barn that night. Instead, when it got dark, Father took me to the train station. He told me to sit in a corner and keep my head down, while he went to go find someone. A few minutes later, he came back with a man dressed in dark clothing with a brimmed hat that covered his face.

"Son, you are going to Budapest, to the orphanage where Yossi and Sarah were," Father kneeled down and said to me. "You be a good boy and try to connect with your brother and sister when you are there."

I nodded. I didn't really want to go. I didn't want to get on the train and leave my father. He needed me with him. He had been sick the last few weeks since we had been staying in the barn. The nights were cold, and even bundling ourselves under the straw was not enough to keep us warm at night. I knew my father was strong, but the cold was wearing him down. He needed me to help him. I milked the cows at the barn and made sure Father had something to drink. At the sawmill where we worked, I worked extra hard to make sure we cut and stacked enough wood to get our pay. Even though he wouldn't let me use the saw, I would pick up the wood and put it in the right spot for him to swing at, and then I would pick up the pieces and stack them away. When Father was tired, I made sure he sat down, drank some water, and I checked to make sure he didn't get caught sitting on the job. What would he do without me now?

But I knew I had to listen to him. There was no use arguing with him if he decided I was getting on the train. So that is what I did. I kept my head high and boarded the train with the smuggler. We sat in a cargo car, with boxes stacked up all around us. There were a few other children in the car as well—other Jews the smuggler was taking to the orphanage. All of us squeezed in between or on top of the boxes, trying to find a comfortable position for the long train ride. In front of me, there was a girl who I couldn't stop staring at. Even though it was dark in the car, I could see the girl's sunken face, her dirty hair. She sat leaning against a box, her knees bent up to her chin, and she was biting her nails—aggressively biting them. Her fingers were already covered in dried blood and fresh blood was started to seep from her finger tips. We were probably about the same age. I looked down at my hands and started to wonder if maybe I looked like her. My hands were also not in great shape. Rough, calloused, with dirt tucked under my nails and in every crease around my knuckles. I clenched my fists and then leaned my head back. I should try to sleep. The smuggler said it was long train ride.

With my eyes closed, I concentrated on the rhythm of the train. My whole body vibrated on the boxes that I was lying on, and, every once in a while, there was a bump that sent my body up in the air a few centimeters before landing back down on the hard surface. I started thinking about Yossi and Sarah on this trip. I hoped they were more comfortable. This wasn't so bad for me, but for them, it would have been really difficult.

I must have drifted off to sleep, because it seemed like no time had passed when the train came to a sudden stop, making the boxes all slide from their places, hurdling into us. I watched as a box flew towards the girl in front of me, hitting her legs and knocking her knees into her face. Not a great way to wake up.

The smuggler opened the door of the train car, letting in the bright sunlight. The car had no windows, just a few small holes that let in enough light for us to see. I was suddenly blinded by the bright light and was surprised that enough time had passed since we got on the train for the sun to become so strong. I followed the smuggler off the train car. He stood as four other children climbed out and stood with us. Then, he motioned all of us to follow and we started walking. Instead of walking through the train station, he led us next to the train tracks, back the way we came for a few meters and then we turned into a forest. The ground was covered in snow and my feet sank with every step. I could feel my shoes getting soggy from the walk.

I looked at the other kids walking, following the smuggler. Aside from the girl who sat across from me in the train, there were three other boys, one about fourteen, and the other two were probably a little younger than I was. The two younger boys seemed to be brothers. They spoke quietly to each other, and even held each other's hands. All of us walked with our heads down, moving our feet as fast as we could to keep up with the smuggler. We walked for about an hour before arriving at a big campsite. There were little cabins all around, a big fire pit, and lots of children running around. A big Hungarian woman came to greet us when we arrived, shaking hands with the smuggler, who then disappeared, leaving us there with the woman.

She looked at all of us and said something in Hungarian. ". . . dirty . . . clean . . . there . . ." she pointed over to a small building. I still only knew a few words in Hungarian, but I understood that we needed to go wash ourselves. I motioned to the other kids to follow and we walked into the building that the woman had pointed to. Inside, there were soap and showers. The boys all started peeling of their clothes immediately, but the girl stood still, her arms crossed in front of her chest. I looked at her, and then at the three other boys.

"Wait," I said to them. "Let her go first." I pointed to the girl and made eye contact with all boys. I spoke in Yiddish, hoping that maybe that was a universal language for Jews. The others weren't Polish, so I didn't know what they would understand. My message seemed to be received. The boys stopped undressing, and even put their shirts back on and we all walked outside to let the girl shower first.

We all sat outside the washroom, looking around the campsite. "I'm Abi," I introduced myself to the other boys. I suddenly wondered why I didn't do it sooner.

"Ivan," one of the brothers said. "He's Josef," pointing to his brother.

"Boris," said the older boy.

"Where are you from?" I asked.

"Czechoslovakia," Ivan said.

"Ukraine," said Boris. "You?"

"Poland," I responded. "Have you heard anything about this place?"

Boris chucked. "They won't be here long." Boris motioned to Ivan and Josef. "People like cute kids like them. They'll get adopted before we finish showering."

The brothers looked hopefully at each other and held each other's hands a little tighter.

"Me? I'll be here until they kick me out," Boris continued. "No one wants to adopt someone like me."

"Why not?" I asked.

"I'm fourteen! Basically, an adult. I don't even know why I am in this place," Boris said.

The door of the washroom opened, and the girl came out. Her face was red from scrubbing, but it was clean. Her hair, which before had looked short and ratted, was now sitting neatly on her shoulders, shining in the sunlight. I smiled at her as she came out. "I'm Abi," I said. "I hope you had a good shower."

"Thanks," she said. "Dafna."

The boys all filed into the washroom and I followed, peeling off my wet clothes. I grabbed a bar of soap and turned on one of the shower heads. The water dripped out and was freezing cold, but I held my breath as I forced myself under the stream. I scrubbed my face, my arms, my legs, and finally my hands, which were stained so dark they didn't seem to get any cleaner. My body was starting to go numb to the cold water when I finished. I was shivering when I turned off the water and looked at my dirty clothes that I would have to put back on. I used my hands to try to dry myself off a bit and then slipped back into the clothes I had.

Outside the washroom, the Hungarian woman was waiting for us. She walked us around the campsite, showing us where we would be sleeping, where we would eat, and giving us the rules of the place. We had to wash up every day. When visitors came, we had to be polite and never speak to them unless spoken to. Everyone had to help keep the campsite clean and help in the kitchen at least one meal a day.

Ivan, Josef, and I were all staying in the same cabin. There were six cots per cabin. The other three were occupied by other Jews around our age. Everyone at the campsite was Jewish. There were probably a hundred kids running around this place, between the ages of four and fourteen. I was actually surprised that there were so many kids here separated from their parents. What happened to their parents? Were they all like mine? Hiding somewhere?

During the day, the younger kids would usually play in the snow or sit around the big fire pit which the older kids would take care of. Every day, new kids would show up, and every night, kids would disappear. In the morning, everyone would look around their cabins to see if there were any empty cots and then at breakfast everyone would talk about who had gotten adopted the night before.

"Simon got adopted last night . . . it must have been that old couple that was here yesterday. They seemed really nice." Or "Daniel disappeared last night. I was surprised, I never saw him talking to any of the visitors."

Boris was right; most of the kids who got adopted were the younger ones. The four-year-olds, the five-year-olds—they were what people wanted. If one of the fourteen-year-olds disappeared, everyone assumed he or she had just run away in the middle of the night. I was right in between. I was nine, meaning I wasn't as sought after as the little ones, but there was hope for me.

I spent a lot of time with Ivan and Josef. They were seven and five. Ivan, the older one, was blonde, had deep blue eyes, and a toothy smile. Josef had dark curly hair and rosy cheeks. He always looked scared and didn't smile as much as his brother did. One day I asked them about their parents.

Ivan looked to the floor. "We were all hiding under our neighbor's house. One day, some soldiers came, and there were really loud noises, shots. They got our parents and our neighbors. Josef and I stayed under the house for a few days until we decided to leave. We wandered around until we got to the train station where the smuggler was. We had a little money on us. We gave it to him and he brought us here."

Most of the children had similar stories. Many saw their parents get shot or die slowly from hunger or sickness. One boy said his parents were shot execution-style in the forest. He was lined up next to them and pretended he had gotten hit. He lay in a mass grave with bodies all around him until he was sure it was safe for him to move. He told me that what struck him the most when he was lying there was the expression on his mother's face. He lay in front of her dead body, staring at her staring back at him. "She looked surprised," he said, "like she was about to say something, but got stopped right before the words came out."

Dafna, the girl who sat across from me on the train to the orphanage, had been in prison with her family in Poland. She said the guards would touch her, make her touch them, sometimes making her parents watch at gunpoint. One day, her father had enough and sprang up to protect his little girl. That was the end of her family. The guards tortured her parents and little brother in front of her eyes. She stayed in the jail for a few more weeks and then somehow, she escaped.

When people asked me about my family, I would just shake my head and say I didn't want to talk about it. Honestly, I was ashamed to say that my family was all alive and healthy. I didn't belong there with those real orphans, the ones who really deserved to get adopted by families that would take care of them. It wasn't fair.

My silence about my family made the other children assume that something really bad had happened. Everyone was really nice to me and would warn others not to ask me about it. I guess I liked it that way.

I tried to help out at the orphanage as much as I could. I volunteered to clean the washroom, the cabins, or the kitchen after the meals. The Hungarians who ran the place always appreciated it, and I felt like it was the least I could do there. I also made an effort to get to know all the children and was the first to introduce myself whenever new children arrived.

One morning, about a week after we arrived, I woke up to see that Ivan's cot was empty. The sheets were gone, as if no one had ever slept there. I looked over to Josef, who was still sleeping in his cot, breathing heavily in and out. Ivan must had been adopted, I thought. Good. I was happy for him. I stayed in my cot, watching Josef sleep until he finally woke up.

"Ivan?" he said softly when he blinked open his eyes to see the empty cot. "Ivan!" he said again, a little louder, as though maybe Ivan just didn't hear him the first time. "Where is Ivan!?"

"Shhh," I hushed Josef. "He must have been adopted."

"No, he wouldn't go without me!" Josef started to cry. His eyes instantly turned red and tears started to stream down his cheeks. "No, no, no, no, no, no!" he cried, the tears becoming fiercer and his face puffier.

I hopped off my cot and went over to him. "It's OK," I said, putting my arm around his shoulders. "This is a good thing."

"No, no, no, no, no!" Josef screamed. "We have to stay together!" He started wailing. The sound pierced the air, making my eardrums vibrate. How could such a sound come from such a quiet boy? Josef started pulling at his hair, his hands contorted and shaky. I grabbed his arms and pulled them down, holding him tight so he couldn't move. But his wailing just got louder.

The other boys in our cabin looked at me holding Josef, and quietly slipped out of the cabin, but I stayed there. Holding Josef as strong as I could, even as my arms seemed to get heavier and heavier. I couldn't let go. I started to imagine it was my younger brother, Yossi—how he would feel if he were abandoned here, all alone. I wanted to comfort Yossi, but Josef was all I had.

You would think Josef would start to get tired after a while, his voice would get hoarse, or he would just lose his strength. But he didn't. His cries continued at the same tone for hours and hours. My arms became like lead holding on to him. My fingers filled with blood and started to tingle like they were about to go numb. I didn't want to leave him. I was all he had. What if this had been Yossi, with another boy? Would I forgive the boy for leaving Yossi to cry alone?

We skipped breakfast. I wasn't hungry, but I did feel bad not helping to clean up after the meal. Then it was lunch. Josef still hadn't stopped. Then it started to get cooler and I could see through the windows that the sun was starting to go down. It would be dinner time soon. I had to get up, had to move, had to go to the washroom. I patted Josef's shoulder and told him

I would be right back, feeling the wave of guilt hit me as I loosened my grip around him. He nodded, as if he was just noticing me now for the first time. His cries still echoed throughout the cabin and my ears.

I ran out of the cabin and to the washroom as fast as I could, relieving myself just in time. Then I ran to get dinner, hoping there was something good to warm my stomach. After dinner, I stayed in the kitchen to help clean up. When I was washing dishes, I noticed that the Hungarian woman who ran the orphanage was staring at me. She stood tall, her hair tied up, arms crossed in front of her chest, watching me clean. I avoided her eyes and finished my chores. Part of me wanted to go back to check on Josef, but the other part of me was afraid of going back to see him. My guilt of abandoning him still held me captive. When there was nothing left to do, I started to walk back to the cabin.

The Hungarian woman was still watching me. When I walked past her, she stopped me. "Abi," she said. "Come with me." She turned and started walking towards the main entrance of the orphanage. The entrance where visitors came through. Standing there was a man and a woman, neatly dressed in fancy coats and hats.

"Abi," the woman who ran the orphanage said. "Please meet Mr. and Mrs. Seigel. They want to adopt you."

I looked at the couple. They were older than my parents. They were both smiling at me, their arms linked together. Then I looked at the orphanage's caretaker, confused. I had never seen this couple

274

before. Usually when someone comes to adopt, they visit the orphanage and meet with several children, sometimes spending a whole day at the orphanage before choosing which child they wanted. Why did this couple choose me? There were younger kids, cuter kids, like Josef, that they could have taken.

That reminded me. Josef was still in the cabin, probably still crying. "I have to go check on Josef," I said. I nodded to the couple and then started to turn around.

"Josef is fine," the Hungarian woman said, grabbing my shoulder and stopping me from going anywhere. "You leave him to us. You need to meet with your new parents."

"It's very nice to meet you, Abi," my new mother said in Yiddish. "We would be very happy for you to come home with us."

I smiled at her, at her husband—my new father— these strangers. How could they just become my parents? They motioned me to come with them, and walked me to a car where they opened the back door and told me to get in. I complied, staring at the orphanage as it disappeared when we drove away.

We drove for a few hours. It was dark around us and I wondered how they could tell where they were going. Eventually we arrived at a city—I guessed Budapest—and the car pulled up at a hospital.

"Let's go," Mr. Seigel said, helping me out of the car. We walked into the hospital. The building was huge. There were people running around everywhere, back and forth, people sitting on the floor and in chairs, waiting for whatever reason. Mr. Seigel knew where to go. He navigated through the people, through the corridors, and took me to a small room with a hard, cold bed where he told me lie down. I hesitated. I had never been in a hospital room like this before. I had seen doctors before, but the doctors we had in Poland worked from their homes, not sterile rooms in giant fortresses like this one.

I sat quietly on the bed, looking around the room. There was a big desk with a cabinet above it. Each drawer filled with little vials and needles. Above the bed was a big light that, if turned on, would shower me with its bright bulbs. Mr. and Mrs. Seigel stood quietly together against the wall of the room. I looked down at my hands, pinching each of my fingers as I waited there.

Suddenly the door opened and an old man in a white coat came in. He shook hands with Mr. and Mrs. Seigel, greeting them like old friends.

"And who do we have here?" He asked in Hungarian as he turned towards me.

"This is Abi," Mr. Seigel said. "He will be staying with us."

"Nice to meet you," the doctor said, extending his hand to me. "I'm Dr. Weizer."

I looked at the doctor's hand. It was so white and his knuckles were so round. I slowly lifted my hand to shake his. Dr. Weizer grabbed my hand quickly, first shaking it for a moment, and then, with his grip holding it tight, he flipped his hand down and started looking at the top on my hand. Then he took his other hand and started lifting each of my fingers, examining each one.

"What I thought," Dr. Weizer said. "Abi, can you please take off your shoes?"

I looked at Mr. and Mrs. Seigel, trying to read their expressions, but I couldn't figure out what they were thinking.

"Abi?" the doctor repeated. I leaned down and slid my shoes off my feet. My shoes were still wet. They hadn't been dry since before I started staying in the barn with my father. The doctor grabbed each of my feet, pinching my toes.

"We have to operate," he said to Mr. and Mrs. Seigel. "Abi has severe frostbite on his fingers and toes."

I pulled my feet away from Dr. Weizer. "No!" I screamed, staring at him in horror. I would not let him cut off my hands and feet!

I stood up, picking my shoes off the ground. I had to get out of there. I didn't know these people, why they adopted me, why they took me to this doctor who wanted to cut off my limbs. I started towards the door of the room, but Mr. Seigel blocked me.

"Abi," Mr. Seigel said. "It's OK. Don't worry. It won't hurt, the doctor is just going to make you better." He spoke to me in Yiddish.

Better? I thought to myself. I looked down at my hands. The tips of my fingers bulged out like marbles. Through the dirt caked under my nails, I could see that the skin was dark red and even blue on some parts. My toes were worse. The skin around the edges of my toes was black.

"But I need my hands and feet," I pleaded out loud. "How will I walk? How will I work?"

Mr. Seigel smiled. "Abi, the doctor is just going to cut off some of the dead skin. Once you heal, you will be able to walk and work even better than before."

I decided I had no other choice but to trust him. After all, what were my other options? I put my head down and went back to sit on the bed. The doctor ruffled my hair and went over to speak with Mr. and Mrs. Seigel. They spoke quietly in Hungarian, which was still hard for me to understand. The three of them looked at me and then they finished talking. The doctor went over to the desk and took a vial out of one of the cabinet drawers. He walked over to me and smiled.

"This will all be over before you know it," he said, pulling a cap off the vial to reveal a long needle. "Now hold still."

The doctor put the needle in my arm and told me to lie down. I did, and then I closed my eyes. When I opened them, I was still lying on the bed. Mr. and Mrs. Seigel were sitting in chairs next to me. The doctor wasn't in the room anymore. It seemed like I had just closed my eyes for a second, maybe even two seconds, but I noticed that my hands and feet were now bandaged and aching.

"How are you feeling, Abi?" Mr. Seigel said to me when he noticed my eyes open.

"Fine," I said.

"The surgery went really well," Mr. Seigel said. "You will be back to normal in no time."

And I was. I stayed in the hospital for a few days, where every day a nurse would come and put new bandages on my hands and feet. Dr. Weizer also came to check on me daily. Mr. and Mrs. Seigel took turns staying with me. I told them I would be fine on my own, but they said they wanted to be there.

When the doctor said I could leave the hospital, I was excited. He warned me not to stay out in the cold too long and to make sure to keep my hands and feet dry. I thanked him and left with Mr. and Mrs. Seigel, who were finally taking me to their home. When we left the hospital, I no longer had bandages. My hands and feet were red and raw where the doctor had cut off frostbitten skin. But they were clean. I couldn't remember ever seeing my hands and feet so clean.

The car ride to the Seigel's home wasn't very long. We pulled into a quiet neighborhood and they parked the car in front of a nice-looking house. When they stopped the car, Mrs. Seigel turned around to me in the back and said, "Abi, we have a surprise for you!"

I smiled at her, unsure what the surprise could be. They walked me into their house and opened the door. Inside, sitting on the couch, were Sarah and Yossi! When they saw me, they screamed and ran over to hug me. I was in shock, unsure if I was imagining this, or if it were really happening. I hugged them back and decided that it must be true—it must really be happening.

"What are you doing here?" I asked them.

"We were adopted by Mr. and Mrs. Freuden," Sarah said. "When we heard that you were at the orphanage, Mr. Freuden convinced his friend Mr. Seigel to adopt you!"

I looked over to Mr. and Mrs. Seigel, who were speaking now with another older couple who had been in the house. Mr. and Mrs. Freuden, I imagined.

"You will like it here, Abi," Sarah said. "It's a lot safer. Father even said he will come visit soon, and they may even move here as soon as they can. I wrote to Mother, Father, and Rachel that you were going to be adopted by Mr. Freuden's friend. I will write to them again to tell you are here!"

I was happy to see that Sarah and Yossi were doing well here in Budapest. Maybe everything would be all right now, and we would start a new life here, one that wouldn't feel so temporary. We spent the day together and then, when it got late, the Freudens took Yossi and Sarah back home. They promised we would see each other every weekend.

The next day, Mr. Seigel woke me up early and told me I would be going to school. I told him I didn't need to. I hadn't been to school in a while and I didn't want to go, but he told me I had no choice—that as long as I was staying with them, I would go to school.

"Going to school gives you a lot of opportunities," Mr. Seigel told me. He then told me about his two sons, who both had studied hard in school and now one was a doctor and the other was a lawyer. Both of them lived in Budapest. I would meet them soon.

Mr. Seigel walked me to school and took me to my new class. Everything was in Hungarian. The teacher spoke Hungarian, as did the other children. All the writing on the chalkboard was in Hungarian and so were the books in the room. I pretended I understood everything the teacher said to me and took a seat in the back of the classroom. I thought a lot about what Mr. Seigel had said: that if I studied hard, maybe one day I could be a doctor or a lawyer. I decided then that I would try to become the best student in the class—as soon as I learned Hungarian.

Every hour in school, the teacher switched subjects. We had Hungarian lessons, math lessons, reading time, and then in the afternoon, a different teacher came in. This teacher taught German. When the lesson started, I raised my hand.

"Ja?" the German teacher said.

"I would like to be excused from this lesson," I stood up. I didn't want to learn German. The language of the Nazis, the murderers who were killing Jews.

"Why is that?" the German teacher responded.

I looked around the room. All of the students were staring at me. "Germans are murderers," I said, watching all of the mouths in the room drop open. "I don't want to learn their language."

The teacher smiled. "That doesn't happen here in Budapest," the teacher said. "Now, please sit down."

I sat back down quietly. I decided I wouldn't learn German. I would work hard in school at everything except that. I became a great student; math was my favorite, and within a few weeks my Hungarian was just as good as the other kids in the class—even though I mostly just spoke with my teacher. The other kids stayed away from me. During breaks and lunch time, I would sit alone, usually with a book I took from the classroom, and eat quietly by myself. I didn't mind it. I didn't come to Budapest to make friends.

After school, I would help out in Mr. Seigel's textile store. He sold fabric for clothing, furniture, and everything else that could be imagined. People would come from all over Hungary to buy textile from him. I think my Hungarian improved the most just from working there.

The weather was starting to get warmer and soon it would be Passover. Mr. and Mrs. Seigel were planning on having a Seder[12] together with Mr. and Mrs. Freuden. We even got a letter from Father that said he would come visit for Passover and do the Seder with us.

We were more than excited for Father to come visit. Sarah spent a whole week thinking about what she wanted to cook for him and Yossi worked on decorations for the table for the Seder. I helped Yossi make decorations with scraps from the textile store. On the day of the Seder, we all worked together to clean up the house, set the table, and create a huge feast.

The most recent letter from Father said he would be on a train that arrived in Budapest in the morning. Mr. Seigel took me to the train station to go pick him up. My heart was pounding hard the whole drive to the train station. Would Father still look the same? Would he recognize me? It had been months since I had seen him. We waited on the platform as the train

---

[12] The traditional feast for Passover during which the story of how the Jews were freed from slavery in Egypt is told.

pulled into the station and people started pouring out. I was studying everyone's faces . . .was that Father? Did he change so much? No, that wasn't him. Maybe over there? After a few minutes, the platform started to empty, and I still hadn't seen Father. Did we miss him? Did he not recognize me? I looked over at Mr. Seigel, who stood patiently next to me, looking at the emptying train.

"He's not here," I said to Mr. Seigel. "He didn't come."

"Let's wait a few more minutes," Mr. Seigel said. We waited. We waited more than just a few more minutes. We waited until the train left the station and we were the only two people standing on the platform.

"He didn't come," I said again, my head starting to spin with thoughts of what could have happened.

"Maybe he missed the train," Mr. Seigel said. "There is another train coming in a few hours. We can wait and see if he is on that one."

I nodded and we found a bench to sit on. It felt like a day had passed before the next train pulled in to the station. I stood up on the bench to try to see everyone as they piled out onto the platform. Father? Nope. Maybe there? Nope. Again, within a few minutes we were the last people standing on the platform. I stared at the train pulling away from the platform. Where is Father?

1943—David

Knowing that my children were safe in Budapest made things much easier for us in Beregszasz. Yes, we were in hiding, and there were raids every day, but, somehow, I wasn't worried about us getting caught. Hinda and I were staying with Hungarian Jews that agreed to hide us. Hinda and Rachel had learned Hungarian so well they could pass as Hungarian Jews, and they could mostly go about their day without raising any suspicions. Me, on the other hand, I was not so good with languages. I struggled. When I spoke, my accent was a quick giveaway that I wasn't Hungarian. If I had to say more than a few words, then it was obvious that I barely grasped the language.

I spent most of my days at the local shul. The Hungarian Jews there were nice to me, mostly out of obligation, it felt. I knew they preferred that I wouldn't hang around, but what else was I supposed to do?

Sarah wrote letters to us a few times a week. The letters were brought back and forth by smugglers taking Jews out of Beregszasz to Budapest. For a few pengo, they were happy to carry a letter during their trip. Whenever I would go meet the smugglers to pick up my mail and give them new mail, I would ask them about what they had heard about what was going on in Budapest and in other places. As the most mobile people, they usually had a good grasp of the status of the war and what to expect. One day, when I went to go give the smuggler letters from us to the children, he told me that I also should think about going to Budapest.

"The Polish resistance is in Budapest," the smuggler told me. "They can provide you with fake papers that will make you a legal immigrant to Hungary."

If I were legal, it would be easier to find work—not to mention, I couldn't be deported in raids. I decided I would go to Budapest and find out about getting papers to be a legal immigrant. It would also be a good opportunity to visit the children, whom I hadn't seen since they had left. Passover would be a good time to visit. I could spend the holiday with them, and then when I had legal status, I could work in Budapest and save up enough money to bring Hinda and Rachel. Then we would all be safe.

I bought a train ticket to Budapest for the morning before Passover begun. The day before my train, I went to the local mikveh with a new friend of mine, Herzl Singer. Herzl was a Hungarian Jew whom I had met at shul. A nice man, about my age. At the mikveh, we both took the ritual bath and said the prayers, cleaning ourselves for the holiday. After the ritual, we went to sit in the steam room they had there. We sat there, naked, with just towels wrapped around our waists.

"Have you heard about what is happening in Warsaw?" Herzl asked.

I had heard rumors, but shook my head. "What has been happening there?" I asked. I got all my news from word of mouth. All the newspapers here were in Hungarian. Even if there were papers in Polish, I wouldn't be caught reading one.

"At the ghetto in Warsaw, some of the Jews there have been resisting. Rumor has it there is going to be a big uprising there. Last summer they emptied out half the ghetto," Herzl said. "Took them to those camps they built."

"Camps?"

"Yes," Herzl responded. "Forced labor camps, where Jews work in factories with smoke burns all day long. There are rumors that the camps are used for killing Jews, but that seems absurd."

"Why absurd?" For some reason, hearing this from Herzl made me feel angry. "Those Nazis want to kill us all! Just wait, they will come for you, too, one day!"

"Relax, David," Herzl said. "It will all be over soon. I am sure you will be able to go back home before you know it."

"Ha," I scoffed. I didn't think I would ever go back to Butla, maybe never even to Poland. More than that, I didn't think this would all be over soon.

"How do you know that there will be an uprising?" I asked.

"Smugglers," he responded. "They are making a ton of money taking weapons and explosives there."

"Good!" I yelled. "I hope those Jews give them . . ."

Suddenly the door of the steam room flew open revealing four Hungarian policemen standing tall with their guns out.

"Hands up!" one of them yelled, pointing their guns right at us.

Herzl and I were the only people in the steam room. Herzl was legal, meaning it was me they came for. I looked over at Herzl and raised my hands.

"Excuse us, sirs," Herzl said with his hands raised. "We're just here having a bath, if you don't mind."

I couldn't say a word. I was afraid they may have heard me speak when they burst in. If they did, they would surely know I was not Hungarian.

"Papers," one of the policemen said.

"Sir," Herzl responded. "We are naked in here, we have nothing on us. Our papers are not with us."

The policemen looked at Herzl and me and then at each other, and then, by some miracle, they walked out, leaving us alone in the steam room. I let out my breath.

"I need to get out of here," I whispered to Herzl. He nodded. I wrapped my towel tight around me and slipped out to the shower room where I quickly put on my clothes and ran to the home where we were staying. That was too lucky.

We were staying with an older Jewish widow. She lived alone in a small house near the shul, where her husband had been a member until he died. After his death, his friends would come by to spend time with her, but eventually that stopped and she was alone. She had no children, and it seemed like no relatives around. We were grateful to her that she let us stay with her, knowing the danger it brought her.

When I got to her house, there were two policemen standing on her porch speaking to her. She was sitting out front on a rocking chair, knitting as she often did all day. The policemen towered over her, speaking to her as she nodded. Before I was close enough to hear, I stopped and crouched down behind a tree, afraid to get any closer. I watched as the woman got up and led the policemen inside. My heart was racing, I didn't know if Hinda and Rachel were there, inside, about to be arrested by the Hungarian police! I wished it was me who was getting arrested. I slowly crept towards the house and peeked inside the window. The two policemen were sitting at the woman's kitchen table eating matzah. Eating matzah! I ducked down so they wouldn't see me through the window. Were they waiting for me? What was going on?

I waited outside the house for about fifteen minutes, and then the policemen came out. They shook the woman's hand and left, walking right past me without noticing me. I waited until I was sure they were gone and went inside.

"What was that all about?" I asked the woman.

"Hm?" she raised her eyebrows.

"The police!" I yelled.

"Oh, such gentlemen," she smiled. "They come every Passover for a bit of matzah. It's not just us Jews who like it!"

"Do they know we are here?" I asked.

"Of course not."

Two close calls in a day. It was too much. I was afraid I wouldn't be so lucky the next time. I started to worry about my train ride the next day to Budapest. The train station was always filled with policemen randomly checking people's papers. I would need to be careful.

When I arrived at the train station the next day, sure enough, at the entrance was a policeman, checking the papers of every person who walked in. I stood there for a while, wondering what I should do. After a few minutes, I turned around. I couldn't risk it. I would have to go to Budapest another day.

I spent Passover with Hinda, Rachel, and the widow, the four of us leading a quick Seder and sharing a small meal. I was sulking, angry that I had broken my promise to the children. They must be upset with me—or more likely, worried about me that I didn't make it like I had said I would.

All through Passover there seemed to be heightened security around Beregszasz. There were more policemen than normal roaming the streets, more arrests and deportations every day. We mostly stayed inside now, afraid of being caught ourselves. After about a month, I decided I had to go to Budapest. I made my way to the train station, praying the whole time that there wouldn't be so many police there. Again, I was lucky. There was no one checking papers at the station entrance, so I easily slipped inside, bought a ticket, and took a seat on the train. I sat next to a man wearing a yarmulke, a fellow Jew making the trip. Obviously, a Hungarian Jew;

otherwise, he wouldn't so boldly be showing off his faith.

"Excuse me, sir," I said to him in Hungarian. "Could I please ask your help?"

The Hungarian Jew was reading a newspaper, but looked up at me when I spoke.

"I am not from around here," I said. "If anyone comes up to us, and tries to speak, will you please speak for us?"

The Hungarian Jew nodded in understanding and went back to his newspaper. And suddenly, the train was off! We were moving. I was on the way to Budapest. I sat back in my seat, looking at the other passengers as the train hummed along. After about twenty minutes, some sort of official entered in to the train car. He wasn't a policeman—his uniform was different. He had on a dark coat with white buttons and a round hat that sat straight up on his head. He was walking through the carriage, carefully looking at each passenger. My heart started to pound. He will find me out! I quickly got up and started walking as fast as I could—without looking suspicious—away from the official. I walked through the car, into another train car, hoping I could stay ahead of him until we stopped somewhere and I could hop off. I looked back, and the official had entered the car I was now in. I rushed to the back, switching to another car, and then another, the official following me all the way, scrutinizing each train passenger as he passed them. I kept going farther and farther back, and then, I was at the back of the train. There were no more cars, and the official was getting closer to me. I looked around.

What do I do? Jump? No. I couldn't. I noticed an empty seat in the back and slipped into it, breathing deeply to try to calm myself. Stay relaxed. Don't look suspicious. Now the man was just a few rows in front of me, going side to side, checking each passenger. Three rows in front of me. Two. One. I shut my eyes.

"Ticket?" I heard someone say. I opened my eyes to see the man standing over me. He was just collecting tickets! I smiled as I pulled my ticket out of my jacket pocket and handed it to him. He looked at the ticket and looked at me. Then he handed it back and turned away, walking back towards the front of the train. I laughed at myself. How paranoid I had become!

I made it safely to Budapest. When I got there, I went straight to where Abi was staying with the Seigels.

"Father!" he yelled when I arrived. "Where have you been?" I explained to him that it wasn't safe for me to come, and I wasn't able to write to him, either. I told him not to worry, that Mother and Rachel would join us in Budapest soon. Mr. Seigel helped me find the Polish resistance that was making papers for Jews here. They were stationed in a small hut near the edge of the town. I went there on my own.

When I arrived, I knocked on the door, which quickly opened, revealing a dark room with several young men inside. The man who opened the door was tall—a head taller than I— and stood silently waiting for me to speak.

"My name is David Shwartz," I said in Yiddish. "I am from Poland."

The man who opened the door stepped aside. "Have you heard about our brothers in Warsaw?" One of the young men asked me.

"I heard there may be an uprising."

"There was!" another of the young men said. "On the first night of Passover, our brothers rose up to fight when the Nazis came to burn down the ghetto! What heroes!"

"What happened?" I asked.

"What do you think?" another one of the Poles said. "The Nazis destroyed the ghetto anyway, but at least we took down some of them. We are not cattle that can be killed so easily."

Another of the men started talking. "We just received news yesterday that they destroyed the great synagogue in Warsaw and liquidated the ghetto."

My heart dropped. I had been wondering if any of my brothers were in the Warsaw ghetto. A few of my brothers had lived in Krakow, some around Warsaw, and I hadn't been able to get in touch with any since the war started.

"But this is the beginning of the end for the Nazis," one of the Poles said. "This will inspire other uprisings, more resistance. We will beat them!"

I smiled at the young men. I was not so optimistic, but I was glad they were. We needed more young Jews who were willing to fight for us. Me, I had to protect my family. Ensure our survival. If not, I would have instantly joined the resistance.

"So, what do I need to do to get papers to be here legally?" I asked, changing the subject.

"We'll make the papers," one of the Poles said. "David Shwartz, you said?"

"Yes."

"It won't take long. Come back in an hour."

I thanked the young men and left the hut to wander around for the next hour. I thought more about the uprising in Warsaw. Why hadn't we resisted when the Nazis came to Butla? To Turka? Why did most people just do exactly as they said? I wondered if any of our neighbors were in the Warsaw ghetto, the ones that got on the train when we were in Butla— when we decided to run away.

The hour went by quickly and I went back to pick up my papers that said I was a legal immigrant to Hungary. According to the papers, I had immigrated to Hungary in 1938, when Jews could still pass freely across borders. I put the papers in my pocket and left to find a place to work and a place to stay.

I found and was hired at a sawmill where logs were cut into boards. The owner of the sawmill was a Hungarian Jew—Haim Levitt—and it seemed many of the workers were Jewish, too. Several of the workers lived together in a small apartment and agreed to let me live with them if I shared the rent. Working at the sawmill was harder than I expected. I felt weaker than I was before. Even though I had been doing manual labor for the last few years, my body didn't feel as strong as it used to.

We would saw the logs into boards, sand them down, and then package them up. Packing was done outside the mill, in the sun. As spring turned into summer, packing became harder and harder. The bright sun beat down on us while we packed up the boards for shipment.

One day, I sat down to take a rest while packing. The other workers who were packing with me also sat down for a break. We sat in silence, catching our breath, when Haim noticed us. He was usually inside his office at the sawmill, but sporadically made rounds to check the different stations.

"What are you doing?" He yelled.

"Just need to catch our breath," I answered for everyone.

"Do I pay you to sit around?"

"We'll finish our packing, don't worry. We just need a minute," I spoke firmly while trying to stay calm.

"You lazy Poles!" Haim yelled. "I'm not paying you for this!"

"We're just taking a short break," I stood up.

"Lazy Poles," Haim muttered again as he turned around and left. "This is coming out of your pay!"

Sure enough, that week, we were only paid for four days of labor instead of five. When I received my pay, I wanted to break Haim's neck, but I needed the job and the money. Even with my legal papers, many places didn't want to hire Polish Jews.

In a few months I had saved enough for Hinda and Rachel to come join me. They came on the train and I got them legal papers from the Polish resistance. Hinda and I rented a small room to live in and Rachel stayed with Yossi and Sarah at the Freudens' home. I started to think that staying in Budapest could be a permanent solution for us, until the authorities decided there were too many immigrants and we had to leave.

The police came one day to the sawmill and said anyone who was not a Hungarian citizen would be deported from Budapest. We would be taken to other neighboring villages. The police knew where we lived and there was no getting around it. The next day, Hinda and I got on a train. The children were allowed to stay since they had been legally adopted by their families. Rachel was also able to stay; she could pass as Mr. Freuden's daughter.

We were sent to Grosswardein, a five-hour train ride east of Budapest. We got off the train with a few hundred other Polish immigrants who had been deported. Grosswardein had a large Jewish community that wanted to help us, but they were as poor as we were. I went to the shul to try to talk to some of the local Jews, to find out what we could do.

"David?" I heard someone call my name. I turned around to see a thin man, his skin gray, eyes sunken in. It was Isroel Rosenberg! I had not seen him since he had crossed the forest with us from Butla into Hungary. We had parted ways when we got to Hungary, and I did not know what had happened to him.

"Isroel!" I said in disbelief. "What are you doing here?"

"I think I should be asking you that question," Isroel laughed. "How did you end up here?"

"We were deported from Budapest," I told him. "How long have you been here?"

"After we arrived in Hungary we travelled to Budapest and then came here," Isroel said. "Grosswardein was very accepting of Polish Jews."

"I am happy to hear that!" I remarked, and I was happy to see a familiar face. "How are Ety and the girls?" Isroel had two daughters—Zelda and Ethel—who had traveled with us in the forest. He had two other daughters, Rosa and Pesil, who had both died before we left Butla.

Isroel broke eye contact with me and looked down at the floor. "Zelda and Ethel didn't make it. It's just me and Ety here."

"I'm so sorry," I said.

"Tuberculosis," he said. "Traveling during the winter was tough. First Zelda got sick, and then Ethel. Ety also started to get sick, but she recovered."

I put my hand on Isroel's shoulder. There was nothing I could say to him, so I changed the subject.

"Isroel, I am sorry to ask you, but I am here with Hinda and we have no money and no place to stay," I said.

"Of course," he cut me off before I could finish speaking. "Stay with us. Please. We don't have much, but we can share with you."

We left the shul and Isroel led me and Hinda to his home. He and Ety lived in a small one-room wooden hut with a straw roof. Ety was home when we arrived. She looked twenty years older than the last time we had seen her. She half smiled when we arrived, as though she wanted to be happy to see us, but couldn't remember how.

Isroel worked at a factory that made cloth napkins. He took me to the factory with him the next day and helped me get a job there, too. I would pack the napkins into boxes, like I did with the wood boards back in Budapest. Packing napkins, though, was much easier.

In Grosswardein, we had to report to local authorities every fourteen days. They wanted to keep track of all immigrants and our movements. We were allowed to travel, but we didn't have enough money for train rides, so we kept in touch with the children via letters. The children did well in Budapest. Abi was working hard in school and Sarah was turning into a fine young lady. Yossi was growing up, too, and learning to read and write. Nothing eventful happened as we stayed in Grosswardein through the fall and winter.

One morning in March, I received a letter from Mr. Freuden, who had adopted Sarah and Yossi.

Dear David,

I am sorry to write to you with such news, but the German army has arrived in Budapest. City officials have agreed to peacefully settle with the army and hand over all Jewish citizens. The Germans are setting up a ghetto outside the city and we must report there within a week. I am writing to you on behalf of myself and my dear friend Mr. Seigel, who has adopted Abi. We will be moving into the ghetto as required, but are making arrangements for the children. We have Christian friends who have agreed to take them in so they do not need to move

*into the ghetto with us. I will write with more
information when I can.*

Abner Freuden

I reread the letter. Hungary was no longer safe.
If the Germans were in Budapest, it would not be long
before they came to Grosswardein and moved all of
the Jews here into the ghetto. My family would not be
moving into any ghetto. Not after what I had heard
about them in Warsaw. Not ever. I wrote back.

Dear Abner,

*Thank you for letting me know and for making
arrangements for the children. Please let me know
how I can reach the children, as I believe it would be
best for us to get out of Hungary as soon as possible.
I believe this would be best for you as well, but that is
a decision you need to make for your family.*

David Shwartz

I wanted the children to come to Grosswardein
and together we could cross the border into Romania.
Grosswardein was close to the border. We just needed
to find smugglers who could get us across. It's not so
easy to find smugglers. You can't just ask around for
references or find them in a storefront.

Isroel and Ety agreed to come with us to
Romania. In the evenings, Isroel and I would go out
and walk towards the border, hoping to run into a
smuggler or meet someone who could point us in the
right direction. The border was through a forest right
outside of town. There had to be smugglers hiding in
it. We walked in the dark, without bringing a light.

There were border guards, and we needed to make sure we weren't spotted by any of them.

"You know, David, sometimes I wonder what is the point," Isroel said to me one night when we were out searching. "We go to Romania, and the Germans will follow. Then we go somewhere else, and again the Germans will one day show up and we will have to keep moving, or admit our defeat. It won't end."

"No Isroel, it can't be like that," I said. "There are already Jews starting to resist. To fight back. Did you hear about the uprising in Warsaw? A group of young men fought the Germans for a month! We may not be as strong as them, but we have to fight. We have to fight for our lives."

I continued. "And if we keep moving, one day, we will make it Palestina. To a country for Jews, where the Germans won't be able to get to." Even I wasn't convinced by what I was saying, but it was what Isroel needed to hear.

"Palestina," Isroel said. "It's a fairy tale."

"You have to keep hope," I said. "It's—" I stopped. I heard a noise in the trees. Footsteps. Someone was walking near us. I grabbed Isroel's arm, pulling him down on the ground. The sound of the footsteps was getting stronger. I looked up, but still I could see nothing, just a few meters in front of me, and no clues of who was walking. Then, suddenly, a light shone on our faces.

"What are you doing here?" a voice said in Hungarian. "Get up."

We stood up in front of two Hungarian border patrolmen, armed with lanterns and guns. I looked at

Isroel, hoping he would speak. His Hungarian was better than mine.

"Are you trying to sneak over the border?" one of the guards asked. Isroel stood frozen as ice.

"Please, sirs," I said, trying my best to sound Hungarian. "We're from Grosswardein. We were out here hunting during the day, and we got lost."

The two guards looked at each other. "You're Jews, aren't you?" one asked. "Trying to sneak into Romania." It was more a statement than a question. Both guards raised their guns at us.

"No," I said. "Like I said, we were hunting—we got lost and we're on our way home."

"Prove it," the second guard said, holding his gun pointed at my face.

I looked at Isroel. We didn't have any hunting gear with us. We didn't have anything with us. I started searching my head for a response.

"There is one easy way to identify a Jew," the first guard said. "Pull down your pants."

I froze. Isroel was looking at me, waiting for me to tell him what to do. If we pulled down our pants, it was a dead giveaway. We were stuck, there was no way of pretending we weren't Jewish. So, I changed my strategy.

"Look," I said. "You are right, we are Jews. And you can arrest us, report us, deport us, or do whatever you are supposed to do with us. But if you do, remember this. That we will most likely be killed. And that will be because of you. You will have murdered us. Our blood will be on your hands."

The two guards looked at each other. I could tell they were listening.

"Now, you have another option," I continued. "You could leave us here, pretend like you never saw us. No one would know. You continue guarding the border, and we will continue on our way, and we will be careful not to get caught by you again. No harm done."

Again, the guards looked at each other, still holding their guns up. I could see the guards were young. Probably just twenty years old. New guards who still hadn't turned cold from years of patrolling the border.

"Get out of here," one yelled. "Before we change our minds."

"Thank you," I nodded my head to them. "You are doing the right thing." I hit Isroel's shoulder to wake him from his trance, and we both turned around to run back to Grosswardein. We ran through the forest, without stopping until we were back at Isroel's home. When we got there, I suddenly fell forward. I was hit from the inside with a pain in my stomach so strong it felt like it would rip through my skin. My hands hit the ground in front of me, and I was stuck. The pain overwhelmed me, captivated me, held me hostage.

"David?" Isroel said. "What's wrong?" I couldn't respond. The pain held my vocal cords still. "We have to go to a hospital!" Isroel said. I couldn't protest. I still couldn't move, the pain ripping through my insides like a ping pong ball hitting all directions.

Isroel ran to his neighbor, a gentile who had a horse and wagon. A few minutes later, he returned with the neighbor and the wagon. The two of them picked me up and gently placed me in the wagon and rode off. I didn't want to go to the hospital. I could be stuck there. What if we needed to run?

The hospital was a short ride from Isroel's home. When we arrived, Isroel and his neighbor carried me in and a doctor ushered them to put me on a bed in a huge hall. There were probably thirty beds there, most of them filled with groaning and bandaged men. They brought me to a bed at the end of the hall and left me there with the doctor.

"I'm Dr. Cohen," the doctor said. "What's your name, Sir?"

A Jew, I thought. What a fool working here as though it were safe for Jews to still live like this. When the Nazis came, and they definitely would come to Grosswardein, they would surely deport him to the new ghetto in Budapest, or worse to one of their extermination camps.

"I'm Jan Kolochinsky," I said, thinking of the most gentile name I could.

Dr. Cohen started to press his hands down on my stomach. Each press sent a bolt of lightning through my body.

"Your appendix is inflamed, Herr Kolochinsky," he said. "We need to operate right away." Before I could say anything, the doctor put a shot in my right arm, and started wheeling my bed out of the hall. I started to get tired and in seconds, I blacked out.

When I awoke, I was in a different room with just five other beds filled with patients. Dr. Cohen was standing at the foot of my bed, writing something on a notepad.

"Herr Kolochinsky," he smiled. "Surgery went perfectly. We had to take out your appendix. It was full of pus and extremely swollen. I am surprised you lasted this long with that inside you."

I felt a dull pain in my stomach and reached my hand up to touch the bandages around me.

"Are you a Jew?" the doctor asked in surprise.

"Of course not!" I responded, looking around to see if anyone had noticed the doctor asking me that question. What a fool. How can he ask such questions in a public place? Dr. Cohen looked at me skeptically.

"Well, Herr Kolochinsky, you will need to stay here until you recover," the doctor said.

"Danke," I responded, thank you in German, trying to make my denial of being Jewish more believable.

The next day, Hinda came to visit me in the hospital. I almost cried seeing her. Maybe it was the pain medicine, or the adrenaline from the past twenty-four hours, but I was overcome with emotion. She held my hand and told me she was trying to get the children to come to us in Grosswardein. She told me not to worry—that they would all be with us soon. After a few hours, I told her to go back home. I was tired and needed to rest.

Soon after she left, an alarm went off. The shrill sound echoed through the hospital room making my ears vibrate. From my bed, I could see doctors and nurses running down the hall past my room. One nurse came in and screamed. "There are American planes overhead! If you can walk, you need to run down to the cellar!" The nurse then continued down the hall, without bothering to help the patients in my room. I looked around at the five other patients. All five of them peeled themselves off their beds, grabbed their IVs, and walked out of the room, leaving me alone in the room. I lifted my head, trying to test if I could get up, but I couldn't. My lower body still felt numb from the anesthesia. What could I do? I closed my eyes and then I heard the scream of thunder. A bomb falling; the windows of the room shattered, showering me with glass. The ceiling shook, pieces of it falling on top of me. I kept my eyes closed, better not to see what was going on. The room shook, my ears were ringing, and debris was falling all over me.

"Herr Kolochinsky!" I heard a faint sound of a voice. I peeked open my eyes to see Dr. Cohen hovering over me, throwing the debris off my body. "What are you still doing here?" He wrapped his arms around my chest, pulling my limp body from the bed, and started dragging me down the hall towards the stairs to the cellar. I wanted to help, wanted to make my body feel lighter, but I was powerless. My feet dragged as the doctor struggled to pull me. We got closer to the stairs, closer to the cellar, and then there was another explosion. BOOM! It echoed as the walls of the hospital began to crumble.

1944—Hinda

BOOM! I felt the ground shake below me and a cloud of smoke shot up from the ground. The smoke grew bigger, expanding across the sky, blocking out the sun. What was that? The shake echoed out from my heart, along my bones, all the way to the ends of my fingers and toes. I had barely just arrived back at Isroel and Ety's home, when the boom came. And then there was another one. I turned around, following the smoke with my eyes. Where did it come from?

I started to shake. I looked up and saw there were planes overhead. Did they drop a bomb? Was it near the hospital? Why would anyone bomb a hospital? I couldn't stop the questions from exploding in my head. I needed to go back! David! I started to run back towards the hospital. It was a few kilometers, maybe six or seven. I could be there fast if I ran. I needed to see if he was all right. He must be all right. No one would bomb a hospital—that would be barbaric.

I ran as fast as I could, the smoke above me getting darker as I got closer. Soon I felt dust and ash falling down on me, hitting my shoulders like hail. I kept rubbing my eyes to wipe the dust away. There were other people running. But running away, the opposite direction as I was going. Cars also sped away, not stopping even with the ash blocking their vision.

"Lady! What are you doing!" someone yelled at me from a car window. "You can't go there; get in the car—I'll help you!"

I ignored the man and continued running. Soon I got to the hospital. The building looked like it had been smashed into the ground. The walls, which an hour ago stood a few stories high, now stood like jagged teeth coming up from the ground, barely rising a few meters. Outside the hospital, doctors were hustling patients into cars. I looked over to see one man, a huge gash in his head being thrown into the back of a truck just as the truck started to drive away. I noticed other patients sitting and lying on the ground, some barely moving.

I got closer to the patients, looking at each one. Part of me prayed I would find David, but the other part of me wished maybe he wasn't here. That somehow, he had left the hospital before the bombing. That was possible, right? I started studying the patients. There was a man in a hospital gown that was now black with soot. His left arm ended right before where his hand should have been. His arm was black and red, as through the explosion had clotted the blood. My eyes were drawn to his blackened arm, but I forced my eyes to look up to his face. This couldn't be David! No, thank God, it wasn't. I moved to the next patient. A younger man, also covered in dirt and ash. Too young to be David. I moved on. Then I noticed a nurse coming over to me, or rather to the patients.

"Excuse me, Miss," I said, grabbing her arm. "My husband was here at this hospital! Do you know where he is? David—I mean, Jan Kolochinsky?"

The nurse shook her head and started to pull away, but I didn't let go of her arm.

"Please, Miss," I begged. "I need to find him."

"Ma'am," she said. "As you can see, there are a lot of patients here. We're trying to evacuate everyone that survived." She nodded her head towards the cars that were being filled up with patients.

"Where are you taking them?" I asked.

"Other clinics and hospitals nearby," she said. "Anywhere we can take them."

I let go of her arm and she bent down in front of the man with the missing hand. She took his pulse under his chin, and then marked his forehead with a blue pen before moving on to the next patient. I ran over to the row of cars and yelled over to one of the drivers.

"Where are you going?"

"To the hospital on the other side of town," he said.

"Can I come?"

The man looked at me for a moment, deciding, and then agreed. I hopped in his car and waited as doctors filled the backseat with injured patients.

"Why do you want to go to the other hospital?" the man asked me.

"My husband is missing," I said. "He was here. I need to find him."

The man didn't respond. He didn't say anything for the entire drive over to the other hospital. It wasn't far, but it felt like hours before we pulled up. It was chaos at this hospital, too. Cars were dumping patients at the front door, and doctors were running in and out to bring people in. I thanked the man and rushed out towards the hospital.

"David?" I screamed. "David? Are you here?" I ran through the patients lying on the ground outside the hospital, into the hospital, where the corridor was filled with patients sitting on the floor. "David?" I yelled, as I ran down the corridor. The hospital was loud, with doctors' footsteps clacking on the floor, patients moaning in pain, or even screaming. I wondered if he was here, if he could even hear me.

Then I heard the faint response. "Hinda!" I could hear David's stern tone cut through the noise. I stopped. Where was he? "Hinda!" I heard again and then I caught his eye. There he was sitting at the end of the corridor, holding an empty IV bag still attached to his arm. I ran to him.

"David!" I screamed, throwing my arms around him. "Are you all right? What happened?"

"I'm fine," he said, patting my back with his arm that didn't have the IV in it. "They evacuated us from the hospital, brought us here. How did you find me?"

"I went back to the hospital when I heard the bomb. I was so worried!" I said. "I heard they were bringing patients here, so I came. I didn't know what to do! I'm so glad you are safe!"

"Everything is fine," David said. He had soot on his face, but seemed mostly unharmed. "No need to worry."

I sat down on the floor next to him and held on to his hand. We sat there in silence for hours, just watching more patients come in, and very few going out. I could see it was starting to get dark outside— dark from the sun setting, not from more smoke.

Then, an alarm went off. A siren blew through the walls of the hospital and everyone started to scramble. What was happening?

"Get up," David said. "We have to go down into the cellar." I watched David struggle to push himself up, using the wall to help him. "Come on!"

I stood up quickly, and we made our way towards the stairs where patients, doctors, and nurses were all pushing to go down. David seemed to have trouble walking, but he held my hand tightly and leaned on me for support. We finally found ourselves in the cellar, in a hall with a group of nuns kneeling with their hands pressed together in front of their hearts. Their lips were all moving as if they were singing together in a choir, but there was no sound. David motioned to me to kneel as well. We both got down on our knees and crossed ourselves with the nuns.

Please, God, I prayed, still hearing the echo of the siren. Please save us. Please take us away from here. I can't keep running like this. This is no life for us, for our children. Please, save us, our children. Please help us to find a better life somewhere, where we can all live together in peace, without fear, without being persecuted. Please, take us to Palestina. To our own homeland, where Jews can live in peace.

The siren stopped. I waited for a boom, for some sort of explosion, but it didn't come. We stayed there in the cellar with the nuns, nonetheless, for a few hours, unsure of where to go. All the patients who were here with us stayed put. No one knew what to do. Sometime in the middle of the night, a doctor came into the room and started talking to each patient. He spent a few minutes with each one, writing notes on a clipboard and handing people a piece of paper. Patients with the paper left the cellar, going back upstairs.

Soon the doctor arrived at us. "Name, please?" he said.

"Jan Kolochinsky," David responded.

"Why were you hospitalized?"

"I had surgery to remove my appendix."

"And how are you feeling now?" the doctor asked.

"I'm all right."

"There is no room for you in the hospital right now," the doctor said. "You can go home to recover. Please come back in a couple days so we can check up on you." The doctor scribbled on his clipboard and ripped off a piece of paper to give to us. "When you come back, bring this."

The paper had David's fake name on it and instructions for cleaning the incision area from the surgery. Soap and water and rebandage every day. I helped David stand up and we walked through the cellar, up the stairs, and out of the hospital, where we found a taxi to take us back to Isroel's home.

Now I was more desperate than ever for us to get out of Hungary. We needed to get the children and get over the border to Romania. From there, I wasn't sure. We would be safe there for a little while, but I knew we couldn't stay. We needed to go to Palestina. To a place far enough away that the Nazis wouldn't get to. Everywhere in Europe, well, it was just a matter of time. I was sure of it.

David and I started to talk about what we should do. We couldn't have all the children stay with us and the Rosenbergs in this tiny house. It would be cramped, and also suspicious. Even though there were Jews living freely here, people were wary of Poles on the run. No one knew when the Germans would arrive. It could be any day, especially now that we knew they were setting up a ghetto in Budapest. We needed to get all the children and Rachel here, and then we needed smugglers to take us across into Romania. And we needed to do this as soon as possible.

That evening, Isroel went out to go talk with some of his friends to see if he could find out anything about smugglers. David was still too weak from the surgery, so we stayed home, talking quietly about what we should do.

"Can't Rachel bring them on the train?" I asked.

"People will know they are trying to escape the ghetto," David responded. Then, there was a knock on the door. I felt alarmed. Are the Germans here already? No, the knock was too soft. It must be a woman, I thought. I got up and opened the door.

"Mrs. Shwartz?" a young woman said. She was blonde and pretty, probably around Rachel's age, early twenties. I hesitated. Saying yes confirmed I was Jewish, and I wasn't sure who this young woman was. She continued speaking.

"My name is Kristina Andras," she said. "I am friends with Mr. Freuden in Budapest. He asked me to come see you."

Kristina, I thought, a gentile. I smiled at her and let her in.

"Mr. and Mrs. Freuden have been like parents to me, and when the Germans came, I asked if there was anything I could do to help them," she said. "You see, I was engaged to a Jew. He was arrested and taken to a forced-labor camp a few months ago. He was arrested for trying to help other Jews who came from Poland. Anyway, Mr. Freuden, he asked me if I could help bring your children here to you before they move into the ghetto. He said you didn't want your children going into the ghetto with them, and because I am not Jewish, it is much easier for me to travel around. I can bring the children here on the train."

"We would be happy if you could help us," David said.

"Of course," Kristina said. "Tomorrow evening, I will bring them here."

We hugged and thanked this gentile stranger, who was willing to risk her life to help us. Then she left, leaving us alone again in the house, waiting for Isroel to come back, hopefully with news about smugglers. Sure enough, Isroel returned with a smile on his face. Several other Jews in the community had found smugglers to help them over the border the following night. Suddenly, it seemed everything was working out. The children would be with us and together we would all go into Romania, where we could be safe again for a little while. Everything went as planned. The next evening, Kristina returned with the three children. I was so happy to see all of them. They looked healthy and well-fed, even though they seemed worried about their adopted parents who were moving into the ghetto now. I was worried about Rachel. She decided to stay in Budapest, on her own.

Later in the night, we got ready for our trip to Romania. We left the house with Isroel and Ety and met up with fifteen other Jews who would be making the trip with us. We gathered with the smugglers at the edge of the forest. There were four smugglers. They explained to us how it would work. One would walk with us, and the other three would be up ahead, one straight in front of us, one ahead to the right and one ahead to the left. They would signal to us if they saw anything, if we needed to hide. They seemed to know what they were doing. They had a system, like they had done this every night. The smuggler who would be walking with us was a woman. She was tall and thin— beautiful. From the way she looked at David, and the other men in our group, I could see she was no stranger to men. She beckoned them with her eyes, her mouth open just wide enough to show the tips of her teeth. David didn't seem to notice, but the other men did.

We started on the walk. It wouldn't be long, just a few hours, they said. Sarah held Yossi's hand—he wanted to walk alone. He was, after all, five years old. Abi walked next to his father and I stayed behind them.

"Why do they hate us?" Abi asked David.

"They are jealous of us," David said.

"Why?"

"Because we are the chosen people," David said.

"But have we done anything wrong?"

David looked at Abi and shook his head. "There is no reason for them to hate us."

Abi looked up at his father, as though unsatisfied with the answer. Of course, he was. There was no real answer to his question at all. No real reason any of this was happening. Abi was getting older, more independent, less like a child. That was what really struck me when Kristina brought the children to us. Sarah and Yossi hadn't seemed to change as much, but Abi, he was different. It was like he wasn't a child anymore, even though he was just ten years old.

We walked along in the darkness, mostly staying quiet except for the crunch of branches under our feet. I could feel the thick layer of fear that covered everyone, like a blanket on top of our heads. The air was cool in the night—not cold, but a nice temperature. The kind of temperature I would like when sitting outside on a nice spring evening.

It wasn't long before we were safely across the border. It had seemed almost too easy to cross. When we arrived in Romania, the smugglers took us to a barn. The barn was full of people, all likely Jews who had snuck into Romania. I looked around the room at all the faces, and then there was one I recognized. It was the beardless Jew from Munkacz, the rich one who had helped us get to Beregszasz.

"Look, David," I whispered to my husband, pointing out the man in the barn. David looked over to him and smiled.

"Guess he is no better off than we are now!" David scoffed. I looked over at the man, Meyer was his name. His face was no longer clean-shaven. Instead, he had scruffy tufts of hair stuck in different places and dirt smeared on his face. His clothes weren't clean and pressed as they had been last time we saw him. David was right; he was just like we were now.

With the smugglers gone, we were in the barn without a plan of what to do next. Then, an older man approached us.

"Welcome to Romania," he said. "I am Constantin and this is my barn. I will help you move on and get settled here in Romania. I don't recommend you go wandering around on your own. Police here are very wary of illegal immigrants, but you don't have to worry about being deported. Worst case scenario, you will be jailed, but whether that is better than deportation is still up for debate. So, I recommend you listen to me."

Constantin would take us to Bucharest, where he would help us get apartments. There, we would need to pretend to be Romanian and we could live and work there as we pleased. We would be taking a train the next evening. Better to travel at night, he said. I was starting to feel more comfortable about being in

Romania. It did seem that this place was safer than anywhere we had been before.

We stayed in the barn for a day with all of the other runaway Jews. We found a small corner where we could sit and I played with Yossi while Sarah and Abi walked around meeting other children their age in the barn. I was happy to see them making friends, meeting other Jewish children. I felt so much hope and optimism about our new life in Romania. Maybe Romania wasn't just another stop on our journey— maybe this would be it.

The next evening, Constantin led a group of about twenty people to the train station. We took a midnight train to Bucharest. The train was mostly empty except for us. We arrived in Bucharest in the morning and Constantin led us to the city where he had already arranged apartments for us. Our family would be staying in a small one-bedroom apartment in the basement of an old building. The apartment had a few cots, a small kitchen table, and a little stove to cook on. I was excited to have a place of our own again. No more imposing on other people or sharing a space with other families. This apartment was just for us.

Living in Bucharest, nobody questioned us. Of course, I was still afraid that something could happen, that we could be found out to be Polish or that we could be deported, but the war hadn't seemed to touch us here. Yes, there were German soldiers in town, but they never bothered us. They never seemed to bother anyone. I started to think they were also here to get away from the war, just like we were.

Over the next few months, we became very comfortable living in Romania. We all started learning Romanian, David found a job in a local factory and I took care of the home. Sarah helped me and spent a lot of time caring for Yossi, who was starting to blossom and laugh. Abi wasn't home much. He seemed to be making a lot of friends and was becoming more independent with every day. And one day when he came home late in the evening, he asked David and me to sit with him at our small kitchen table.

"I'm going to Palestina," he told us. It was a warm July evening. Abi had been out all day, all week even; he mostly only came home to sleep.

"But we're safe here; things are going well," I said to him.

"I'm going to Palestina," he repeated. "I have a ticket for the MV Mefküre, a boat that is leaving from Constanta on August 3. The boat will stop in Istanbul and then go on to Palestina."

"But where will you live there?" I asked again.

"They have communities there for people like me, young people who come alone," Abi said. "Don't worry, I already have a place to live."

"How did you buy a ticket?" David asked.

"I just got it," Abi said. "I have my own money."

I was shocked that Abi had planned this all on his own. That he had decided that he was going and leaving us all behind. I was also proud. Palestina was the dream, and I was happy for him to be achieving it, even though part of me wanted to tell him not to go. But even if I did, he wouldn't have listened.

"I'm leaving in a few days for Constanta," Abi continued. "I am going with a bunch of friends; we're all going to Palestina together."

The next few days Abi spent a lot of time with his brother and sister, telling them about his decision to travel. I tried to listen to what he was saying to them, but even in a small apartment it isn't always easy to eavesdrop. He was telling them about Zionism, about a group he joined, Hashomar Hatzair—the Young Guards—who were dedicated to establishing a Jewish homeland in Palestina. Maybe they would join him one day, he asked them. Sarah and Yossi just looked at him in awe.

When it was time to go, Abi said his goodbyes to us. He told us the boat ride to Istanbul was about twenty-eight hours and that there was a small office for the Zionist movement here in Bucharest where we could go to get information about his trip. I hugged him tightly and told him I loved him, and then he was gone.

I was nervous the next few days. He was taking a train to Constanta and then on August 3, the MV Mefküre would be departing for Istanbul. I went to find the office Abi had told us about, for the Zionist movement. The office was just a twenty-minute walk from our apartment. It was a small room in a basement with maps and black and white pictures pinned up on the walls. The pictures showed men and women smiling in sand dunes, of people kissing the ground, and of flags with the Star of David hanging up tall and fluttering in the wind.

"Can I help you, Ma'am?" a young boy said to me when I entered the office. The boy was probably just a few years older than Abi.

"My son just left for Palestina," I said. "He told me to come here to get news of his travels."

"He's going on the MV Mefküre?" the boy asked. I nodded and the boy smiled. "They should be getting on the boat tomorrow. We'll get a list of everyone onboard after departure."

"Do you know Abi Shwartz?" I asked the boy.

"Abi is your son?" the boy asked; the smile grew bigger on his face. "You must be so proud."

I suddenly realized my son had a whole life I didn't know about. Yes, I was proud of him, but I knew nothing of who he really was.

"Come back in a few days," the boy said. "We'll let you know when they got to Istanbul."

I thanked the boy and left the office. It was August 1. I decided I would go back on August 5 to see that he arrived safely in Istanbul. The next few days dragged on. I was nervous and anxious for any news about Abi. Then, August 5 arrived and I got up early to go to the office where I had been a few days before.

This time, the office was packed. There were people pushing and shoving outside the front door, trying to get in. Everyone was screaming, yelling, at no one in particular.

"What's going on?" I asked one of the women in the back of the crowd also trying to push in.

"A boat sank," the woman said.

"Which boat?"

"One of the boats going to Istanbul," she said.

"What do you mean?" My heart dropped.

"It sank," the woman repeated.

Abi, please, he couldn't have been on the boat that sank! I looked over the crowd of people trying to get into the office.

"They have a list of passengers," the woman said.

A young boy—not the same one who had been at the office the last time I was there—came out carrying a big piece of paper. He pushed through the crowd, guarding the paper as though it was a precious artifact. I guess it was, if it had the names of the boat passengers.

Standing outside the office, the boy asked everyone to gather around. The crowd hushed to hear him speak. "On August 3, three ships left Constanta carrying about a thousand Jews on their way to achieve the Zionist dream of establishing a Jewish homeland in Palestina. Two of the boats arrived safely in Istanbul as planned. Passengers on those boats are now headed to Palestina where they will dock in Haifa. The third boat, the MV Mefküre, unfortunately, didn't make it. At about one o'clock this morning, the boat was seen caught on fire, and it sank about forty kilometers away from Istanbul."

The crowd now started screaming at the boy. "Who was on the ship?" "What happened?" "Why did it sink?" But all the questions got mashed together in a loud scream. The MV Mefküre—was that the boat Abi said he was getting on? It sounded like it, but it couldn't be. It just couldn't.

The boy continued talking, raising his voice over the screaming crowd. "This is terrible news, but we have to be happy that there are still about seven hundred young, strong Jews who are now one step closer to Palestina!" The crowd roared even louder now, almost drowning out the boy's speech.

"We have the passenger list for all three boats here," the boy continued, screaming now to try to be heard over the crowd. "I'm going to hang it up here." The boy pushed through the crowd to pin the list on the wall outside the office. The boy quickly moved away, allowing the crowd to rush the list. Everyone was screaming louder now, yelling out names, asking the people in the front to check for certain people. The people in the front were searching down the list looking for names. Some people sighed with relief when they pinpointed a name. Others cried out in pain. I pushed forward patiently, waiting for my turn to get to close enough to the list. I was afraid of getting too close, of seeing Abi's name on the passenger list of the sunken ship. The longer I was waiting here, the longer there was still hope that Abi was alive.

"Hurry up!" "Move!" "Check for Moshe Zinger!" "Is Chaim Leavitt there?" the crowd's screams were getting more impatient as the minutes passed. People checked the names and then moved out of the crowd, still standing around the street. Women were crying, sobbing, holding their chests. I willed myself to keep moving forward, getting pushed in the crowd towards the list. Soon, I was close enough to see it. Then, close enough to barely read the names. Then, close enough to touch the list. I looked at the three columns, one for each boat, and looked at the column for the

MV Mefküre. I put my finger on the list, moving it down with every name . . . Zelig Cohen . . . Jonathan Katz . . . Michael Rosenberg . . . Abi Shwartz. There was his name. On the list of the sunken ship. My whole body suddenly started to feel hot. No, it couldn't be! Abi was going to Palestina to start a new life. After everything we had been through, everything we had done to keep him safe and alive, and now, when I thought the danger had passed, he was dead.

There were 270 names on the list under the MV Mefküre. Two hundred and seventy people at the bottom of the sea. Most of them young children who had left their families for their dreams. I pushed out of the crowd. I couldn't breathe, I was going to faint. I kneeled down on the street, still surrounded by men and woman who had either just found out their child was alive or at the bottom of the Black Sea. My heart was going to stop. I couldn't go on. I sat there on the street, paralyzed for hours. The crowd had dispersed. Several people had asked me if I was all right, but I didn't have the strength to answer them. I didn't know what to do. I had to tell David, I realized. I forced myself up and walked back to our apartment. I was in a daze, completely blind to everything around me. Back at the apartment, Sarah and Yossi were playing together on the floor. I sat at the kitchen table and stared at the walls.

"Mother?" Sarah asked.

"Not now," I said to her. She understood, and she took Yossi to the bedroom, away from me.

A few hours later David came home from work. I told him the news and he bowed his head. He had never been an emotional man, but even he couldn't stand this new reality. He went into the bedroom, kicked the children out, and slammed the door.

For the next couple weeks, every day seemed to melt together into one. I didn't sleep, I could barely eat. Sarah took care of Yossi, making sure to stay out of my way. I didn't tell them about their brother. I couldn't. I didn't know what they knew, but I didn't want them to feel this pain I felt. David also sunk in his pain. He continued going to work, but when he came home, he would shut himself in the bedroom.

Then, one day we were forced out of our trance. A siren wailed through the city. Explosions sounded in the distance. David powerfully opened the bedroom door, emerging as though coming up for air after being under water. We looked at each other and at the children.

"We're in a basement, we're safe here," David said. "I'm going out to find out what is going on."

"No! You can't go out," I screamed. "It's bombs; we're being bombed!" I was starting to feel frantic.

David didn't listen to me. He stormed out of the apartment, slamming the door behind him. The siren screamed louder, warning people to get into shelters, basements, or to say their last prayers, and instead David was now out in the street doing who knows what.

Yossi started to cry. I ran to him, picked him up, and held him in my arms. "Mother! We have to leave! We have to get out of here!" he screamed.

"Shh," I tried to hush him, but he just started to scream louder.

"We have to get out of here! We have to get out of here!" Yossi cried, louder than he had ever cried before. "Mother!"

I didn't know what to do, Yossi's cries got louder as the seconds passed. The siren whistled in my ears.

"OK, let's go," I yelled, grabbing Sarah's hand and pulling her towards the door. I didn't know where we were going, but I couldn't stand being there another moment with Yossi screaming in my ear. We ran out of the apartment, out on the street, and then suddenly, I was pushed forward, as though carried by God in the air. Then I heard the explosion, louder than anything I had heard before. Louder than the siren, louder than Yossi's screams. An explosion so loud, it was like it swallowed up every other sound around it, leaving only silence behind. Then, I fell to the ground, still holding Yossi in my arms. Rocks started to rain down on my back, hitting me, as I held Yossi under me and Sarah at my side. After a few moments, I lifted my head and looked back. Our apartment building had been hit. The building was decimated, entirely crushed down into our basement apartment.

I had just lost one son, and my second was the reason we were still alive.

1944—Abi

I don't remember exactly when it was, but there was a moment when I decided I had to take care of myself. That my parents just couldn't do it on their own. It wasn't their fault. They wanted to, they tried, but it was impossible. Maybe it was when Sarah and I were first alone in the forest, or maybe it was when I went to the orphanage. At some point, I started to feel that I had to be responsible for myself.

That was definitely the case in Budapest. Living with Mr. and Mrs. Seigel, I tried to be an adult and do everything I could to prove that I was. I worked hard in school, knowing that it would be important for me long term. I worked hard at Mr. Seigel's textile store, making sure I was contributing and would never be a burden on my adopted family. I kept thinking the harder I work, the better I will become, and the sooner I will be able to be fully independent.

But then the Germans came to Budapest. I first found out about this when I was in school. A few soldiers came to our German class—where, by the way, I was one of the top students even though I detested it—to revel at the Hungarian children learning their language. The teacher had us recite a few German poems we had learned, but, of course, she had only called on the gentile students so as not to bring attention to the Jews. Those gentiles butchered the German poems—I would have done much better—but the soldiers seemed impressed anyway.

That afternoon in the textile shop, I overheard Mr. Seigel speaking with one of his regular customers—a Mr. Levy—who came weekly for upholstery for his furniture factory. Mr. Levy said he was running away, that he wouldn't stay here under German command. Mr. Seigel tried to calm him, saying they were just asking the Jews to move to a different neighborhood so we could all live together—that there really was no harm in it, and, in fact, it could even be better for us. And besides, it would only be temporary. Surely the German soldiers would leave Budapest soon. What business did they have here?

I wanted to tell Mr. Seigel about what I knew about German soldiers. About how they emptied my home town of Jews, how I was pretty sure all of the Jews from Butla were dead, and most of them thought the same way he did when they obeyed orders to get on the trains. But I knew it was no use. From the few months I had lived in Budapest, I learned that the people here didn't believe what was happening in Poland, and probably in other places in Europe. They all thought that if they just followed orders, they would be fine, and when the war ended, they could continue their lives like normal. I guess that was easier to believe than the truth: that the Germans were trying to get rid of the Jews, once and for all.

In the evening, Mr. Seigel sat me down and told me that his family was moving into the new Jewish ghetto that was being setup in Budapest. He already had a home picked out and there was enough space in it for me to join them if I wanted to. But, of course, I didn't want to. So, Mr. Seigel said he would help me go meet my parents. I told him to speak to Mr. Freuden also—that I wanted Sarah and Yossi to come with me. They also would not be going to the ghetto. Mr. Seigel nodded.

A few days later, Mr. Freuden arranged for his friend Kristina to take Sarah, Yossi, and me on the train to Grosswardein, where our parents were. I knew that my parents would want to leave Hungary now that the Germans were here. And while I knew I could take care of myself, get myself out of Hungary safely, I didn't think I was capable to taking Sarah and Yossi with me. So, I knew we needed our parents.

Kristina pretended to be our mother, buying us train tickets and telling everyone we were all going to visit our sick grandmother in Grosswardein. The policemen at the train station—whose job it was to make sure Jews weren't trying to leave the city— smiled at Kristina and patted Yossi's head, while commenting on what well-behaved children she had.

Sarah held Yossi on her lap during the train ride. I sat next to them, staring at all the other passengers. Next to us were a couple of businessmen in suits. They both had newspapers in their hands. The cover had a picture of German soldiers carrying the Nazi flag.

"Finally," one of the men said. They spoke quietly, but leaning over, I could make out their conversation.

"I'm glad they're here now; they will bring some order to this place," the other man said. "I'm sick of those Jews just doing whatever they want, thinking they are better than us."

"We really have been suffering enough."

My blood started to boil. They have been suffering? Why? Because the Jews in Budapest have successful stores and work hard to make a living? Because we study hard in school to get the best grades? Why? What did these two men know about suffering? I could feel my face getting hot and then, suddenly, I felt a cool hand on my arm. It was Sarah. She looked at me with her soft eyes, calming my nerves.

The rest of the train ride, I tried not to listen to anything. I couldn't handle hearing any more. If I heard one more thing, I didn't know if I could control myself. When we arrived in Grosswardein, Kristina took us to a small hut where our parents were staying with Isroel and Ety Rosenberg. I wondered where their two daughters were. The ones who had crossed the border into Hungary with us, but I figured it was better not to ask. Our parents had arranged for us to cross the border into Romania and we left with a big group of Jews to be led by a few smugglers over the border. We crossed the border without incident and ended up in a barn that seemed like a way station for Jews on the run. The barn was filled with Jews of different nationalities, all sneaking into Romania to escape the Nazis. A lot of the Jews were Hungarian, Polish, or Ukrainian, but there were also German Jews, and people from Austria.

From the barn, we moved on to Bucharest, where we lived in a small basement apartment.

Bucharest had a lot of Jews. Some who had always lived there, and a lot like us, people who had just immigrated.

I didn't want to go back to school. It would have been in Romanian, and I wasn't really ready to try to learn another language just yet. Another language that would probably only be useful for a few more months until we had to run away to somewhere else. Instead of going to school, I wandered around the city during the day.

A few weeks after we arrived in Bucharest, when I was sitting in a park one afternoon, a boy approached me. He was probably a few years older than I was and wore a yarmulke. "Hey," he said, sitting down next to me. "You Jewish?" He spoke to me in Yiddish.

"Yes," I responded.

"Where are you from?" he asked me.

"Poland."

"And where are you going?"

I thought about it for a moment. "To Palestina," I said. "I want to go to Palestina."

"That's great," he said. "Me too."

"Really?" I asked him.

"Yes, I am a member of Hashomer Hatzair," he said. "Do you know what that is?"

I shook my head.

"You really should—you seem like you belong," he said. My interest had been piqued and I looked at the boy, waiting for him to continue.

"You know, Palestina needs young people like us to come and build the country from the ground up," the boy said. "Right now, the place is mostly sand dunes and Arabs, but with the right people coming, it could become an oasis in the Middle East—a real country, just for Jews. It's people like you and me who will build it."

"So how do we get there?" I asked.

The boy laughed. "Well, let's first get you registered for Hashomer Hatzair."

And just like that, I became a member of Hashomer Hatzair, the young guard, a Zionist movement that recruited idealistic teens who wanted to build the Jewish state. Like with everything I did, I fully invested myself in the movement. I started working at the local office for the movement and received a small weekly stipend for my efforts. I also helped recruit new members and organized classes for us to learn Hebrew and survival skills that would help us build the new Jewish state. I organized sessions about agriculture and farming, first aid, even sailing, but that was more just for fun. In the meantime, I also learned Romanian, just from talking with other members of the movement.

One day, when I was working in the office, an older couple came in, likely parents of one of our members. It happened a lot, parents would be interested in learning about the movement their son or daughter was getting involved with and they would want to learn more. We had pamphlets and could talk all about the great things we were doing for members, all the things they were learning, and how important it was for young people to feel like they belonged to something. Generally, parents would be impressed with what we told them, and leave feeling proud of what their children were doing.

The couple walked around the office, looking at the pictures on the walls. They stopped in front of a large map of Palestina, where we had drawn blue circles on the kibbutzim, or villages, where we would settle when we got there.

"Are you interested in pioneering the Holy Land?" I asked them.

The couple turned around and smiled at me politely.

"It's a thought that has crossed our minds," the man said.

I grabbed a few pamphlets from the desk in the office with information about settling in Palestina and held them out to the man. He smiled again and shook his head.

"You are David Shwartz's son, aren't you?" the man asked me.

I didn't respond. I just looked at him and my mouth dropped a little, unsure of why this man would bring that up.

"I know your parents," the man continued. "They are very traditional, conservative people. What do they think of your involvement with Hashomer Hatzair?"

"You must be mistaken," I said. I hadn't told my parents about my involvement in the movement. It didn't seem important for them to know and I didn't think they would have any thoughts about it anyway. When I joined, I really knew nothing about the movement's beliefs, other than it wanted to form a

Jewish state in the Holy Land. As I got to know it better, I learned that the movement wanted to form a socialist Jewish state. My father, once one of the wealthiest men in our hometown, was a firm believer in capitalism, in everyone working hard for themselves and their families, without thinking of the greater good of the community. Maybe that worked in Poland, but we Jews needed to work together and support each other in the new country. We couldn't have different classes. We all had to succeed, or we would all fail.

"Are your children in the movement?" I asked the man, hoping to change the subject.

The man again smiled at me and thanked me for my time. The couple left without answering my question. I hoped he wouldn't say anything to my father about seeing me here. But even if he did, what did it matter?

Later that day, I went sailing with some of the other members of Hashomer Hatzair. There were several lakes in Bucharest and when the wind was right, we would close up the office for the afternoon and spend it on the lake. We could rent a sailboat for just a few lei[13]. Moshe, the boy who had brought me into Hashomer Hatzair, was an expert sailor and was always the captain of our boat. He would teach me how to steer and adjust the sail. Moshe was older than I was—he was fourteen. In fact, almost all of the members of the movement were older than I was. I

---

[13] The lei is the currency in Romania. In 1944, 1 lei was worth about half a US penny.

was ten, but if anyone asked, I said I was thirteen. No one questioned me.

"I'm definitely not going to miss this place," Moshe said when we were on the lake that day. There were four of us on the sailboat: Moshe, me, and two other boys, Haim and Itzik.

"Is there sailing in Palestina?" Haim asked.

"Palestina has the best lake in the world!" Moshe responded. "The Sea of Galilee—it's huge! We'll go sailing there all the time."

The wind blew on my face, ruffling back my hair. I closed my eyes for a moment, trying to imagine that we were sailing on the Sea of Galilee. It must somehow feel different than sailing here in the middle of Romania.

Itzik laughed loudly. "Sailing all the time? Who is going to farm there? We go sailing all the time, there won't be anything to eat!"

"We'll all work together, you'll see," Moshe said. "If everyone is working hard, we'll have time to farm, build our kibbutz, and still be able to go sailing."

Moshe then looked at each of us, making eye contact in the way he did when he had something important to say. It was like he was preparing us to listen for some announcement.

"You will see soon enough," he said. "Because it's time for us to go to Palestina."

"What do you mean?" Haim asked.

"We're sailing there right now?" Itzik joked.

"I'm serious," Moshe said. "I got us all tickets for a boat leaving next week. The boat goes from

Constanta to Istanbul and then from Istanbul to Haifa. It's really happening!"

The three of us looked at Moshe.

"You ready?" Moshe asked.

"Of course," I was the first to respond. I was ready.

Haim and Itzik smiled. "Yes!" "Let's do it!" they both affirmed.

We spent the rest of the afternoon talking about what it would be like to finally be in Palestina. About the kibbutzim. Moshe said that in the kibbutzim, children all live together, without their parents. He said there would still be adults there, who would be our new families, but we would be independent to make our own decisions. I couldn't wait!

When I got home that evening, my parents were sitting quietly like they always did. I asked them to sit down with me at our kitchen table.

"I'm going to Palestina," I said to them.

"But we're safe here, things are going well," my mother responded, quickly without hesitation, as if she had been ready to try to convince me to stay.

"I'm going to Palestina," I repeated. "I have a ticket for the MV Mefküre, a boat that is leaving from Constanta on August 3. The boat will stop in Istanbul and then go on to Palestina."

"But where will you live there?" Mother asked.

"They have communities there for people like me, young people who come alone," I said. "Don't worry, I already have a place to live." I didn't want to tell them that I would probably have a new family there.

"How did you buy a ticket?" my father asked.

"I just got it," I said. "I have my own money." I had paid Moshe back for the ticket he bought me. I had been saving my stipend every week for this.

My parents were speechless. They both stared at me as though I had grown a second head, suddenly had horns, or was speaking a foreign language.

"I'm leaving in a few days for Constanta," I continued. "I am going with a bunch of friends, all going to Palestina together."

Then I told them good night and went to bed. I tried to spend some more time at home during the next few days, mostly for Sarah and Yossi. I told them both about my upcoming journey and about how excited I was to live in Palestina. They both stared at me wide-eyed, but for different reasons. Sarah, for one, looked almost sad when I spoke about it, like she felt I was abandoning her. Yossi, on the other hand, looked at me with admiration. I was his big brother going on to do big things. I told them both they should come. That I would write to them when I got there and that if they wanted to, I would help arrange for them to come to the same kibbutz as me. We could all be there together, I told them. They both nodded and smiled. I knew they didn't share my dream, but maybe I could plant the seeds in them and one day they would join me. I promised them I would always be there for them and would do anything I could for them.

Then the day came. I said goodbye to my family and hopped on a bus with my friends to Constanta where we would catch the boat. When we arrived at the docks, my excitement suddenly turned into fear.

There were several boats lined up, some big ones that looked like oil tankers, and other smaller fishing boats that looked old and rickety. And there was chaos. The docks were full of people running around, pushing, trying to get to or away from the boats.

Moshe put his hand on my shoulder. "This is it," he smiled at me. Moshe handed each of us our tickets and started walking towards the docks. We all tried to follow him, weaving through the crowds, hitting shoulders with strangers. Most of the people on the dock were young boys like us. Some were there with families, hugging their parents goodbye. Others came in big groups of boys led by other boys who were probably just a few years older than they. I could still see Moshe up ahead of me and I tried to push harder to keep up with him. Haim and Itzik were also up ahead of me, doing a better job of staying close to Moshe.

I held my ticket tightly in my hand. It was the only thing I had with me. The other boys each came with a small backpack, but I had nothing to pack. I didn't even have a backpack. All I had were the clothes on my body, in which I had hidden any money I still had saved, and my ticket for the second boat from Istanbul to Haifa. Suddenly I was pushed forward by someone moving more aggressively through the crowd. I would have fallen on my face if there weren't several other people in front of me who I bumped into instead. "Hey!" I yelled looking around me, but I couldn't see who had bumped into me. Whoever it was, he had already been swallowed into the crowd.

I looked ahead for Moshe, but now I couldn't see him. Was that him? No, just another boy weaving through the crowds. Haim and Itzik were also gone. I continued to push forward. I'll meet them on the boat, I guess. I kept pushing forward until I saw the boat, the MV Mefküre. The boat was big, but nothing like what I expected. I expected to see a big passenger boat, with windows along the sides. This boat looked like a mix between a pirate ship and a fishing boat, one that had already travelled around the world many times before. The sides were rusted over, the yellow paint was cracked and dull. There was a huge crowd around the boat, some people waving tickets trying to push on, while others just stood in wonder watching the boat fill up with passengers. I looked around for my friends, but I didn't see them.

I started pushing my way through the crowd to get on the boat. When I got to the entrance, there was a dirty sailor standing there collecting tickets. The man smelled like fish and had a cigarette that looked like it was about to fall out of his mouth. I handed him my ticket. He grabbed it from me, looked at it, ripped it in half, and let me on. I stayed near the entrance of the boat, waiting to see if my friends got on. Maybe, somehow, I had passed them. More and more people kept getting on the boat, handing over their tickets to the sailor and pushing past me to find a place to stay for the journey. There were families, adults, and a lot of boys my age, but not my friends. The boat was getting more crowded. People were pushing me, yelling for me to get away from the entrance, but I didn't budge.

Then, someone yelled something from up above. Another sailor, screaming down to the man collecting tickets. I couldn't understand, but the ticket collector started yelling back. The two sailors screamed at each other back and forth, and then the one up above stopped and turned around. Suddenly the ticket collector grabbed me around the shoulders and threw me off the boat. I landed with a thud on my back.

"Hey, sir!" I screamed at the ticket collector. "I gave you my ticket! I paid for this boat ride! My friends are on the boat!"

The ticket collector ignored me and started throwing other passengers off the boat. Each one landing with a thud on the dock.

"You can't do this!" I screamed, but he still didn't pay any attention to me. I ran up to the side of the boat, trying to get the sailor's attention. "Hey! I need to be on the boat!"

Then I felt an arm on my shoulder. I turned, it was another boy, probably about fifteen years old. "There are too many people on the boat," the boy said.

"But I had a ticket!" I yelled.

"Come with me," the boy said, grabbing my arm and pulling me away from the boat. Away from my promised journey to the Holy Land. My heart started to sink. What would Moshe think when he realized I wasn't on the boat? Maybe he would think I changed my mind, that I was scared. But I didn't! And I wasn't! I had to be on that boat!

The boy was pulling me down the dock further away from my boat. We turned past another boat that looked a lot like the MV Mefküre. At this boat was another sailor collecting tickets as passengers pushed on. The boy pulled me and we ran past this boat's ticket collector to the other side of the boat, where the ticket collector couldn't see us. Then the boy stopped.

He looked at me and looked at the boat. "Come on," he said as he grabbed on to an iron step on the side of the boat. The step was the first of several that climbed up the side. The boy followed the steps and then swung himself into the boat. I looked up to where the boy had disappeared and then looked around me. No one was looking. I took a breath and then grabbed on to the iron step, pulling myself up the rusty ladder until I was on top. I pulled myself over the edge and fell into the boat. I was in! It wasn't the boat I was supposed to be on, but this boat was also going to Palestina. I would find my friends when we got to Istanbul and tell them what happened.

I got up quickly to go find a place to stay for the journey. I didn't want to stay where I was in case someone had seen me sneak on. I couldn't risk getting thrown off this boat, too. The boat was just as crowded as the docks. I pushed through the people to find a space for myself to sit down. There were people everywhere, mostly in groups. There were families huddled together with blankets and pillows. Boys stood around smoking cigarettes and laughing. I found a small space near a column, between two groups of young boys, and sat down.

People kept pushing in, crowding closer to me. I pulled my knees into my chest, hugging them tightly as people started stepping on my toes. Then, suddenly, it was like the boat breathed and everyone spread out a little. A horn blew and then I felt the boat heave forward, pushing away from the docks. We were off! The boat moved slowly, rocking side to side. I tried to look towards the outside, to see the sky, or the sea, but all I could see were the legs of the other passengers around me. After about a half an hour the boat started to pick up speed. As it moved faster, the rocking side to side turned into a bouncing of up and down. The boat lurched forward and then crashed down on the waves. Lurch forward, crash down. Lurch forward, crash down. The rhythm started to make me feel a little nauseated. Lurch forward, crash down. I could feel my stomach flop with each movement. My stomach turned around, going up into my chest and back down. Stomach acid started spouting into my throat and mouth, but I kept my mouth shut tight, swallowing it back down. Good thing I hadn't eaten in a while; otherwise, I may not have been able to control the food from coming back up.

People in the boat were starting to move around and suddenly I had air around me to breathe and room to stretch my legs out. I looked up around me, trying to see if maybe I recognized anyone, but I didn't. I tried to listen to the conversations around me. People were speaking Yiddish, Hungarian, and Romanian, but the boat was so loud I couldn't really hear anything that people were saying.

I sat still for a few hours, trying to close my eyes and hope that the ride would go by quickly. But the hours felt like days as my head started to spin and my whole body felt weak from the movement of the boat. Then, I felt something hit my leg.

"What's your story?" Someone said in Yiddish. I opened my eyes to see a tall boy standing in front of me. He kicked my leg again. He was tall, older than I was, and much bigger.

"I'm going to Palestina," I said. "My friends got on one of the other boats." I felt like I should explain myself, for some reason.

The boy looked down on me, his hands on his waist. Then another boy ran by, holding a cup that he turned upside down over me. The water hit my left shoulder, stinging as it rolled down my back. It was boiling, burning my skin under my shirt. The two boys laughed and walked away, without looking back at me. I raised my arm to touch my shoulder where the water first touched me. The skin was sore and red, already blistering from the burning water. Where did they even get hot water? My skin burned and I held my hand over my shoulder, but my hands were hot and sweaty and did nothing to calm the skin.

"Here," a woman said, handing me a wet handkerchief. The woman seemed to appear out of nowhere. I took the handkerchief and slid it under my shirt on my shoulder.

"Thank you," I said to her. She smiled at me and disappeared in the crowd, leaving me alone again.

I kept my eyes open, scanning the crowds, afraid that the boys would return, but I didn't see them again. I was scared to move, scared to go anywhere in the boat, in case I would lose my little spot, so I sat there, unmoving, without sleeping, for two days, until the boat slowed down again, getting ready to dock in Istanbul. Finally, the boat stopped. I could feel the rocking as the sailors tied the boat up to the dock and the crowd started spilling out. I waited, watching the boat empty. Then, I got up and walked off the boat onto the dock, which was even more crowded than the docks in Constanta. Here, there were huge ships parked all around. The boat I came on looked like it could easily have been smashed by any of the other boats in the harbor.

I needed to find where the other boats from Constanta were docked. I had to find my friends, and then we could all get on the next boat together. I had my ticket for the next boat stuck safely in my pants, and I kept my hand over it, making sure it didn't get lost somehow. I started pushing through the crowds on the dock, trying to see where the other boats could be. Soon, I saw one of the other boats. In front of it was a large crowd of people who had just pushed off. I tried to get closer to see if it was the MV Mefküre, the one that I was supposed to get on, the one where my friends were. I slid through the crowd up to the boat. The MV Morina, it said on the side. Not the boat with my friends.

"Come on," I heard someone yell. "We have to get to the next boat." I looked around, seeing the crowd move like a wave down the docks towards a larger boat, where everyone would be getting on for the second leg of the journey towards Palestina. I let the crowd move around me, and I stood still, trying to decide what to do. Where was the MV Mefküre? Should I just get on the bigger boat and wait for my friends there? I decided to follow the crowd towards the bigger boat. I could get on, find a spot, and my friends would get there and find me.

As I approached the bigger boat, the crowd got thicker. They weren't letting people on the boat yet, someone in the crowd said. They were waiting for the third boat and then they would let all the passengers board. People started to sit down on the docks to wait.

I still had some money on me, so I decided to see if I could go buy myself something to eat. I started to move away from the ship towards the end of the docks where there were stands selling food. As I approached I could smell smoke from meat being cooked. I took a deep breath in, enjoying the smell, but then my stomach clenched and I almost fell forward from the force of my stomach acid coming up my throat. I hadn't eaten in almost three days.

I approached one of the stands and smiled at the man. He looked at me, his eyes traveling from my head down to my toes, and then he leaned back, crossing his arms in front of his chest. I pulled my money out of my pocket; a few Romanian coins was what I had. I lifted my hand to show the man, who looked at me and said something I couldn't understand. Turkish, I guessed.

"Can I buy anything with Romanian money?" I asked him, speaking Romanian and hoping he would understand.

"No," he said, shooing me away from his stand. I clasped my hand around my money and walked over to the next stand. This one was selling fruits and vegetables. Above the stand, a swarm of flies flew around, landing on the food until the seller waved his hand to push them away.

I smiled at the man and held out my coins to show him. He looked at me and then my coins, as though thinking about what to do. Then he reached up to a yellow tree branch that was hanging from the top of his stand and pulled off one of the yellow fruits and handed it to me. The fruit was long and thin, curved like a smile. Even though we had farmed a lot of different fruits in Butla, I had never seen this one before. But I was happy to have something. I held out my money to the man, who took a few coins from me. I held the fruit in my hands and raised it to my nose. It had a sweet smell, and I put one end in my mouth to taste.

Suddenly the man yelled something at me and grabbed the fruit from my hands. I started to feel panic—did I misunderstand something? Didn't I just buy this fruit? The man held the fruit in one hand and used his other hand to rip the top of the fruit open, peeling it from all sides to reveal a white inside. With the peel halfway down, he handed it back to me. "Banana" he said. I couldn't understand what he was saying, but I smiled and took a bite of the white inside of the fruit. It was creamy and sweet and felt good in my upset stomach. The man handed me a second one. I tried to give him more money, but he waved me away. I finished my open fruit and held the second one tight in my hand as I went back to the boat that would take me to Palestina.

The crowd was still waiting there, unable to board the boat. I looked around to see if there were more people; maybe the third boat had arrived, but it seemed that the size of the crowd had stayed the same.

"What's going on?" I asked a man who was standing near me. He was older, like my father, and I figured he must know what was happening.

"The third boat hasn't shown up," he said. "They think it may have sunk."

The words hit me. Sunk? It couldn't have. My friends were on that boat! "What do you mean?" I asked the man.

"Sorry, Son. That's all I know," he said.

It was morning when my boat had arrived in Istanbul, and we waited on the docks until it was dark before they started letting people on the ship. I spent the day pushing my way through the crowd, hoping that somehow my friends would be there. As I walked around, I listened to the rumors buzzing around me.

"The Germans blew up the ship."

"The ship was old and had a hole in it."

"I'm telling you, it was the Russians."

"Maybe it got stuck somewhere."

"We should wait a little longer."

But whoever was running the place had decided that we wouldn't wait any longer. They started hoarding the crowd onto the boat. I lingered by the back of the crowd, but moved forward slowing, while continually look back, and hoping to see more people arrive.

I was one of the last people to get on the boat before they shut the doors and started to sail the ship away from the dock. This boat was much bigger than the one I was on before. There was more space to move around and the rocking wasn't so bad. As we pulled out of the harbor, I stood near the edge of the boat looking out to the sea. It was dark, but the moon was bright. I looked around. Maybe the other boat was still coming. Maybe I would meet my friends in Palestina. Eventually, I decided to find a place to lie down and I closed my eyes. My back still ached from the burns, but my stomach remained calm and soon the swaying back and forth started to feel comforting.

The boat ride took six days. This boat was much more bearable than the one before it. On this boat, there was drinking water, and one meal a day of bread and watery soup. I kept to myself on the boat, always thinking of my friends who I had left behind. Finally, we saw lights in front of us. The boat slowed down and the lights got brighter. It was morning when we approached, and I stood by the edge of the boat watching the city get closer and closer. The sky was bright blue, without a cloud, and the water looked deep and calm. Soon, I could see the docks and the city behind them. My heart started to race. This was it—this was Palestina.

We got even closer and then I saw the flag. A great white flag with a blue Star of David in the middle. I was here, in the Jewish country! When the boat docked, I rushed out to docks that were crowded with soldiers, woman, and children, all looking like they were waiting for us to arrive.

The soldiers smiled at us, saluted us, and guided us off the docks. Behind them, the women and children were screaming and clapping. "Welcome home!" they said. I heard them scream in Yiddish, Polish, Romanian, Hungarian, Hebrew, and other languages I didn't understand. "Welcome home!"

Suddenly, it came over me. I was finally home. As I walked down the dock, I felt a rush of emotion and looked at the crowds on either side of me. I was home; these were my people. I finally was where I belonged.

It was then, at that moment, walking down the docks, that I decided that from then on, I would focus on my future. I would perfect my Hebrew, I would fight for this country, and I would dedicate my life to building this land. I decided then that I had no past.

1945—Rachel

Suddenly, it was all over. The Germans were gone, and I was told they were no longer rounding up Jews. They had fallen—their pursuit was over. The news came after months of bombings in Budapest. The bombs rained down, destroying the city, and then one day, there was silence. And it was over.

I was alone in Budapest. When my brother took his children to Bucharest in Romania, I decided to stay behind. I was tired of running and had started to find my place in Budapest. I was living with a nice Christian couple. Their children were grown up and out of the house, so they let me stay there, along with two other girls—Bianca and Ruth—who became my friends. The three of us would stay up all night talking, telling each other about our lives before the war, and daydreaming about what our lives could have been. I was twenty-two then. I had always imagined that by twenty-two, I would have a house of my own with a husband, maybe even a baby. I never expected to be living under someone's stairs with two other displaced Jewish girls. But, it had been a long time since I had been around girls my age—a long time since I had had any friends, and I was happy to be with them.

I kept in touch with David and his family through letters. Sarah wrote to me often, telling me about where they were staying and what things were like in Bucharest. Hinda wrote to me at first, but after Abi left on that ship, her letters became less frequent. After their apartment was bombed, they bounced around from place to place, unable to find shelter for more than a few days at a time. I thought maybe they should come back to Budapest, but crossing the border again would have been too dangerous. Especially with the constant bombing.

In Budapest, the couple my new friends and I were staying with treated us like their own daughters. In fact, if I went outside with them, people often thought I was their daughter. With my blue eyes and soft features, no one ever suspected I was a Jew. Bianca and Ruth, on the other hand, had to be more careful. They didn't blend in like I did.

In the fall of 1944, before the bombings in Budapest started, I watched the city's Jews who had moved into the ghetto get deported. Every week, trains came and loaded up families and carted them away, slowly emptying the ghetto, neighborhood by neighborhood. I thought of Mr. Freuden, whom I had lived with before. When I moved to live with this Christian family, he moved his family into the ghetto. I didn't know what happened to him—if he was deported—and I had no way of finding out. Asking questions was the same as announcing to everyone that I was also a Jew. Bianca, Ruth, and I tried to keep our spirits up, but it was hard. Bianca and Ruth didn't know where their families were. At least I knew mine was safe, for the time being—except for Abi.

Fall slowly became winter. And then it was Christmas. The couple we were staying with planned a big celebration and wanted us to join them. In the morning, the husband slaughtered and butchered a pig. His wife took the meat and started grinding parts into sausages and threw other cuts in the oven with potatoes and carrots. The three of us girls worked in the cellar to bottle wine for the celebration. The cellar had a strong smell, like sweet musk mixed with oak barrels. We had a bunch of bottles to fill, and started off working quietly, until Bianca took a sip.

"What are you doing!?" Ruth yelled at her.

"Taste it! It's delicious!" Bianca giggled and handed me the bottle she was holding. I smiled at her and took it. First, I lifted it to my face to smell it and then took a sip on my own. The wine was tart and made my throat feel dry. I had never had wine before, except the sweet wine we used on Friday nights for Kiddush, back before the war had started.

"Rachel!" Ruth screamed. Both Bianca and I giggled. I took another sip before handing the bottle back to Bianca, who held the bottle up to her lips and took a long drink. "Bianca! Stop!" Ruth kept screaming.

When Bianca did stop, not because of Ruth, but because she needed some air, she smiled and held the bottle out towards Ruth. "Try it." She said.

Ruth hesitated and looked at us back and forth, before slowly reaching out and clasping her fingers around the neck of the bottle. Bianca let go, and Ruth pulled the bottle towards herself. Again, she looked back and forth between us, and then, for just a second, she put the bottle to her lips.

Bianca squealed with laughter and clapped her hands as Ruth's face turned red with embarrassment. Ruth handed the bottle to me quickly, as though she was afraid of holding it for too long. I took another drink, and before long the three of us had finished the bottle completely. We refilled it and continued to drink from it as we filled up the rest of the bottles for the evening Christmas celebration. The rest of the day was a blur of giggles that lasted through the evening feast, until a piece of the ceiling fell right on top of the roasted pig in the middle of the table. My first thought, I knew we shouldn't have eaten the unkosher meat.

The ceiling fell with a loud thud, silencing everyone sitting around it. We had all been laughing and talking so loudly that we didn't hear the planes overhead, which had started to drop bombs right then in the middle of our Christmas celebration. Once we realized what was happening, we abandoned the dinner and spent the rest of the evening sitting silently in the basement.

The bombings continued for several months, through the end of 1944, destroying more than half of the city. But then, one day, they stopped. The Nazis left and the remaining Jews in Budapest were free. The ghetto, which had once been overcrowded with 200,000 people, had just 70,000 Jews remaining and they were now free. We were now free. When it happened, my first feelings were of confusion. What am I supposed to do now? I had been running for so long that I couldn't imagine not running, or not living in hiding in someone else's house. Where should I go? What do I do? Could I now find my other brothers who I had lost track of before the war?

While I had hoped this day would come for many years, I had never thought about what I would do when it did come. I felt even more lost than ever. And then, I received a letter from my brother David in Bucharest.

Dear Rachel,

It is time for you to come to Bucharest. The war is over, and you cannot stay in Budapest on your own. I have started a new business with a few other men and the business is going well. My partners travel between Budapest and Bucharest often. I am sending one to come get you and bring you here.

David

The note was short and direct, and it was exactly what I needed—someone to tell me what to do, without asking what I thought. So, I said goodbye to my friends and the couple I was living with and met my brother's business partner at the train station in Budapest.

"You must be Rachel," he said when he approached me. The man was older than I was, but not that old, maybe thirty. He wore a brown suit with a tie and a brimmed hat on his head. He had a large briefcase that he held tightly with his left hand. "I'm Aaron," he said reaching out his right hand to mine. I took his hand, and he lifted it to his mouth, kissing my knuckles. "Very nice to meet you."

"You, too." I blushed, pulling my hand away.

Aaron already had train tickets for us and he led me through the station, onto the train, and to our seats. He kept the briefcase on his lap without letting go of the handle. We sat quietly until the train started to move.

"So, you're David's little sister," Aaron said, more like a statement than a question.

"Yes," I responded.

"Why were you in Budapest alone?"

"I liked it there, I guess," I really didn't have a good answer.

"It must not have been too bad for you," he said, his lips creeping up into a big smile.

"What do you mean?"

"Well, look at you," he said. "No one would have ever thought you were Jewish. You look as Christian as they come."

I smiled at him. I hated when people told me I looked Christian. But he was right. I could get away with things because of my looks.

"What are you going to do now?" he asked.

"I want to go to Palestina," I said.

"What? Why?" Aaron said. "Do you even know what it is like there? The Jews there are fighting on the streets. If there are Arabs, they fight with them. If there are no Arabs, they fight each other. It's a war there. Aren't you done living in a war?"

I looked down at my hands. "Maybe it's not like that."

Aaron laughed. "You'll see. We Jews are always in a war. The question is just with whom."

We sat quietly the rest of the train ride. I stared out the window, looking at the green farmlands, and small broken-down houses along the tracks. When we got to the Romanian border, the train stopped and border patrolmen entered our car. When I saw the man in uniform, my heart stopped. Was he going to throw me off the train? Is there any way I can hide? Maybe under the seat. I suddenly felt Aaron's hand on mine.

"Relax," he said. "We're going to be fine."

My heart pounded as the patrolman walked through the cart. The patrolman stopped at every row and examined every passenger's passport. Then, he opened each suitcase or bag in the train car aisle and carefully combed through the contents. It seemed to take ages for each person, and then he got to our row.

"Passport?" the patrolman said to us. Aaron smiled at him and handed him our passports. My heart was pounding so loud, I was sure they could both hear it. When the patrolman opened Aaron's passport, his eyes bulged open slightly. He looked at it intently, then looked at Aaron, who was smiling, and then he looked back at the passport. There's something wrong, I thought immediately—we're caught! They are going to take us off the train! Where will they take us? Aaron squeezed my hand. I was still watching the patrolman, who took something out of Aaron's passport and shoved it in his pocket. Then, he handed us back the passports before even looking at mine. "Have a nice trip," he said, and turned to passengers on the other side of the aisle.

"He didn't check your briefcase," I whispered to Aaron.

Aaron laughed. "No, he didn't."

"Or my passport."

Aaron shook his head.

"Why?" I asked. My heart was still pounding.

"We have an agreement," Aaron said.

"What does that mean? What is in the briefcase?" My mind was hammering out questions as fast as my heart was pounding my blood. "What was in your passport?"

"In the passport, there was money," Aaron said. "As for your other questions, it is probably best for you to talk to your brother when we get to Bucharest."

What does that mean? Did this have something to do with my brother's new business he mentioned? I sat quietly, the questions piling up in my mind. After a few hours at the border, the train started moving again, and we were off to Romania. When we got to Bucharest, Aaron and I took a taxi to a small house outside the city. When we pulled up, the door opened and Sarah ran out.

"Rachel!" she screamed, running to the car. She looked taller than I remembered. She was still thin, but her cheeks had a healthy glow to them. I jumped out of the car to hug her, noticing Yossi running behind her. Now six years old, Yossi didn't look like such a baby anymore. I bent down to hug him, squeezing him tightly in my arms. Then there was Hinda in the doorway. She looked older, her hair seemed lighter, and her forehead was lined from years of suffering. She smiled at me, but it was a different smile than she had had before. I stood up to embrace her, my arms wrapping all the way around her.

After letting go, I looked back to see if Aaron was still there, but he had disappeared, along with the taxi that had brought us. Then, I followed Hinda and the children inside the house. While it seemed small from the outside, the house inside was spacious and bright. My eyes followed Hinda to the kitchen, where she grabbed a shiny tea pot, filled it with water, and placed it on the stove. On the other side of me was a living room, with a big rug on the floor surrounded by plush couches. There were even toys on the rug, like the ones the Kovacs had when I was a nanny in Beregszasz.

"Hungry?" Hinda asked, carrying cups of tea and cookies to a wooden table near the kitchen. I walked over to the table, where we both sat down. The table was smooth and I ran my hands over the knots of wood that flowed down its edge. "How was your trip?" she asked me.

"Fine, good," I responded, taking a sip of the tea and grabbing a cookie. I was still looking around the house. There was a bookshelf in the corner, organized neatly with a few large books and small gold boxes. "Where's David?"

"He'll be back soon," Hinda said. "He's at work."

Before I could ask her what was work, I heard his loud voice from outside. "Those damned Russians again! Who do they think they are? Do they think we work for them? That we do all this so they can make money? Hmpf, back in the old days, I never would have let this happen."

Then the door swung open and David walked in with another man. Both men were wearing suits and brimmed hats that shadowed their faces. The man with David was slightly taller and had broad shoulders that looked like they were built perfectly for his suit jacket. He had a wide smile and when he removed his hat, his light blue eyes caught mine.

"Rachel!" David yelled when he saw me. "I'm happy to see you made it. I hope the trip was fine with Aaron." He came to hug me and then grabbed himself a cup of tea.

"Yes, fine," I said, still looking at my brother's friend.

"Is everything all right?" Hinda asked, getting another cup of tea for David's friend. He thanked her quietly as she handed it to him.

"Fine," David said. "The Russians caught Martin in Czechoslovakia. They took all of his merchandise! He just came back completely empty-handed."

"But he came back alive," David's friend said.

"Ha," David scoffed and took a loud sip of his tea.

"At least Aaron completed his run successfully," David's friend said, his eyes focused on David, who was pacing around the kitchen. "Martin will be more careful next time."

Then, David's friend turned to look at me. "I'm Victor." His face softened when he said it, his eyes twinkling as they looked into mine.

"Rachel," I responded. "I'm David's sister." I held his gaze for a moment, or maybe it was a full minute, before David cut in.

"Well, Victor, we should get going," David said. "We have a pick-up tonight, and we have to get the packages ready for the run tomorrow. You're going to Budapest tomorrow, right?"

"Right," Victor responded, still holding my gaze. David placed his hand on Victor's shoulder and the two of them handed their tea cups to Hinda and turned towards the door.

"Nice to meet you, Rachel," Victor said, as David guided him out and shut the door behind them.

The kitchen was suddenly quiet again, as though David and Victor had sucked all of the sound out of it. Hinda stood by the sink washing the cups, while I sat still at the table. I watched Hinda, trying to decide how to break the silence and what exactly to ask her. Before I said anything, she dried her hands and sat back down at the table with me. "David is very busy," she said. "This business takes a lot of time."

"What is his business?" I asked.

"He exports merchandise from Romania to Poland," Hinda said. "He and his men travel back and forth to Budapest. They have other men that take the merchandise from Budapest to Czechoslovakia and onto Poland."

"What happened with the Russians?"

Hinda smiled at me, as though deciding how much to tell me. "Well," she started. "The business is not exactly legal. They are smugglers and they often get attacked by Russians who steal their merchandise. And really, since the business isn't legal, there is nothing they can do about it."

"What are they smuggling?"

"Cigarettes," Hinda answered. "You wouldn't believe how expensive cigarettes are now. No one wants to buy them legally. There are huge profits for selling them on the black market."

"But how . . .?" I wasn't sure how to ask what I wanted to know. How did David get into this business? How did he smuggle cigarettes? How did they go from living on the streets to living in their own house like this?

Hinda must have understood my confusion. "After our apartment was bombed, we were homeless, you know. Every night we stayed in a different place. Nobody would let a family of four stay with them for long. Sometimes we slept on the street if we had no place to go. One evening, when we were looking for a place to stay, David met Victor. He let us stay with him. David and Victor spoke the whole night. By the morning, David said they were going into business together. Not long after, we moved into this house."

Who was this Victor? Why was he so eager to help my family?

"He's also from Poland, you know," Hinda said, reading my mind. "From Kalwaria. Like us, he was forced to leave his home when the Nazis came. When we met him here in Bucharest, he already had a whole network set up for smuggling cigarettes to Poland. But then, it was just a small operation—he and a few guys traveling back and forth. With David, they turned it into a bigger business. Every day, they have men taking cigarettes to Poland and coming back with briefcases full of money."

I thought back to my train ride with Aaron. How he held his briefcase tightly, not putting it down for a second. And how he paid the border patrolman not to check the bag.

"He's a very nice man," Hinda continued. "A little older than you are . . ." she trailed off.

I smiled, thinking about Victor's blue eyes. I started to think about what his life could have been like before the war. Did he live comfortably like us? What about his family? Did he have brothers and sisters? Or maybe even a wife and children? Where were they?

Hinda and I sat quietly in the kitchen as the sun set and it became dark outside. We prepared a light dinner, fed the children, and put them to bed. They set up an extra bed in the children's room for me, and I was eager to sleep.

The next day, David didn't come home at all. Victor didn't come by, either. Hinda told me it was normal, that sometimes he would disappear for a few days at a time when he was going to Budapest to drop off cigarettes and pick up payment. Of course, she worried, she said, but this was life, and things were less dangerous now than they were last year. The day after that, David came home, alone. I was a little disappointed; I had hoped he would return with Victor. They had just gotten back from a successful run to Budapest and David was tired from the trip. We had a quiet dinner together and he went to sleep. The next morning, he was gone again.

After a few days, I started to get used to living in Bucharest. Hinda and I took care of the children and the house and David would come and go, usually just stopping by to sleep or eat a meal with us. One evening, after dinner, I decided to ask him something.

"Maybe I can help with the business," I said to David. I was bored in Bucharest, really. There wasn't much to do, I didn't know anyone, and I wanted to feel useful. The fact that I might run into Victor also crossed my mind.

David studied my face silently. I started to worry that maybe he would understand my intentions and decide to keep me as far away from the business as possible. Maybe he would get angry!

"Sure," he said. "We could use you at the warehouse. We pack up boxes for shipments and, of course, take care of all the accounting. You can come with me tonight."

I smiled, surprised at how easy it was. I started to feel excited, not just about seeing Victor, but about doing something, anything but sitting in this house all day. Later that evening I walked with David to a small warehouse nearby. The warehouse looked completely dark from the outside. On the door was a large chain and a lock that David grabbed and swiftly unlocked with a brass key he had. He undid the chain and led me inside where several men were working, some carrying boxes and organizing them in different places, others slipping smaller boxes into the lining of suitcases. In the far corner, I saw Victor, counting money that had been piled onto a small table.

"Go over there with Aaron," David said, pointing to a small group of men stuffing small cartons into a suitcase. "They could use your help sewing the lining closed. It always looks tampered with when the men do it."

As I walked over, Aaron looked up and smiled. "Joining the family business?" he said.

"Whatever I can do to help," I responded. "What are you doing?"

"Well, when you take illegal cigarettes somewhere, you can't just carry them like normal luggage," Aaron said. "We hide them under the lining of the suitcase. See?" He bent down to the suitcase and lifted the lining, showing several cartons of cigarettes lined up tightly. "Now we just sew the lining on, and it's a normal suitcase. Every night we repack suitcases like this that the men will take in the morning on the train to Budapest." Aaron smiled at me. "That's what I was doing on my way to Budapest when I came to get you."

I smiled back at him. "So, you need help sewing the lining?"

"Yea," he responded. "As you can imagine, after you rip out the lining of a suitcase a few times, it starts to get harder to sew it in so that it looks new. We can do the packing, and you can do the sewing." He handed me a needle and thread. I took it and bent down to the suitcase to start sewing. After standing around watching me for a couple minutes, Aaron and his team moved on to another suitcase. They ripped the lining out of it and methodically started packing in cigarette cartons. I watched them as I sewed, every once in a while taking a glance at the far corner of the room where Victor was organizing the pile of money.

He was focused, his lips moving as he gently stacked bills and placed them in a small safe.

We worked like that for several hours. Each time I finished sewing a suitcase, Aaron brought me another one and inspected my work. "Looks great!" "You're a real natural." "No one can tell this was ever resewn!" He complimented me on every one. At the end of the night, each of the men grabbed a suitcase that he would be taking to Budapest on the train in the morning. David gave each person instructions of whom to meet, and what to do when he got to Budapest. He took vigorous notes on each man and the suitcase he was carrying. After all the suitcases were gone, it was just David, Victor, and I left in the warehouse. Victor had also finished. All of the money was locked in the safe he had. After locking the safe, he bent down, lifted one of the floorboards, and placed the safe in the space below. After replacing the floorboard, he brushed his hands on his pants and looked up to the front of the warehouse where David and I were standing. I could see his eyes widen as he noticed me; his eyebrows jumped up and his lips curled into a smile. David was still going over the notes in his notebook and didn't notice that Victor was walking towards us.

"Rachel," Victor said when he got to the front of the warehouse. He was in a suit and tie—like David— but no hat on his head. "How are you doing in Bucharest?"

My heart raced as he said my name. It sounded so melodious coming from him. Like each syllable was a note that was chosen and composed as part of a symphony. "Good," I responded. "I just came to help out." I wanted to continue a conversation, but wasn't sure what to say.

"That's great, the guys could really—"

"We done here for the night?" David looked up from his notebook.

"All finished," Victor turned to David.

"Great, let's get some sleep before we have to do a pickup of new merchandise tomorrow," David responded. We walked out of the warehouse, which David locked with the chain and padlock. He pulled on the padlock a few times before being satisfied that it was closed. Then, we said goodnight to Victor and began walking back towards the house. Victor walked the other direction, and I watched his back as he got farther down the street. It was almost dawn when we left the warehouse and the sun started to rise quickly on our walk home. David didn't say anything to me during the walk. When we got home, all he said was "You can help again tomorrow night," and with that, we both went to our rooms and went to sleep.

The next evening, I again went with David to the warehouse. But this time, Victor wasn't there. I spent the night sewing in the lining of suitcases and staring at the door, hoping he would come, but the night ended and he didn't. The same thing happened the next night, and the night after that. For a whole week I went to the warehouse every evening with David, but Victor didn't show up. I was itching to ask David where he was, but I couldn't. He would wonder why I was asking. Maybe he wouldn't even tell me. Maybe I didn't want to hear the answer.

But I continued working at the warehouse. If nothing else, it was something to do—something to fill my time while I figured out what to do with my life now. I didn't want to stay in Bucharest, that I knew. I wanted to go to Palestina. But even so, that seemed like a far-off dream.

Then, one afternoon, when I was alone at the house, there was a knock on the door. I opened it, and there was Victor, standing tall, holding his hat in front of his chest. He was in a brown suit with a dark tie running down his chest. The breeze ruffled his wavy hair and his eyes twinkled in the sunlight.

"David's not here right now," I said to him.

"I know," he responded. "I came to see you."

"Oh," I was startled. "Come in." I led him into the house, to the living room, and then ran into the kitchen to make tea. As I stood there, waiting for the water to boil, my palms started to sweat. What was he doing here? What do I have to talk to him about? Maybe I made a mistake sewing one of the suitcases, and he was here to reprimand me. Maybe my sewing got him in trouble during one of his runs to Budapest! I pinched each of my fingers, trying to calm myself down.

"How are you doing, Rachel?" Victor was suddenly in the kitchen behind me.

"Oh, fine," I said, startled by his presence.

"You know, you are really helping out at the warehouse," he said. "We're all lucky to have your help."

I blushed. I was at a loss for words. What do I say to him? I used to know how to talk to boys. I used to be able to be coy and funny and flirty, but now, I was stuck. I couldn't even have a regular conversation.

"What's it like, taking the cigarettes to Budapest?" I finally asked, immediately regretting it. I was being too pushy, too nosy. What was I doing?

Victor smiled. "Well, it's just like taking a regular train ride, but you have to be more alert."

"Is it dangerous?"

"Probably less dangerous than the things you have been through over the last few years," he said with a smile.

The water for the tea was boiling. I poured us two cups and we sat down at the kitchen table.

"You are from Butla, right?" Victor continued.

"Yes," I responded.

"Do you think you will ever go back?"

"No," I said without hesitating. The answer even surprised me. I had never thought about it before, whether I would go back to Butla. But once I said it, I knew I never would.

"I don't think I will ever go back to where I am from, either," Victor said. "I just want to keep moving forward."

"Which way is forward?" I asked.

"Well, I guess, eventually, to Palestina," he said. My heart jumped as he said it. "We have no place here in Europe anymore. Don't you think?"

"Yes," I said. My heart was screaming, Yes! Let's go! Let's go now! "I also want to go to Palestina."

"We will," he smiled at me, and placed his hand on mine. "Rachel, I know we just met—you barely know me, but I feel like I know you." He paused. "And

I want you to get to know me, and then, one day, we will go to Palestina together and start over." Again, he paused. "If that is what you want."

Yes! Yes, that is what I want! My heart screamed. But I just responded quietly, "That sounds wonderful." Victor lifted my hand and kissed it. Then, he left, asking me if he could come by tomorrow to take me on a walk. "Of course," I told him. I couldn't wait to see him again.

That evening at the warehouse, Victor was there. He smiled at me and we spoke briefly, but we both had work to do. I did catch his eyes a few times, staring at me while he worked. It was like we had a secret conversation going through the warehouse— that no one could hear but us. Then the next day, he came by and we went for a walk near the river. We talked about our lives before the war, what we were like, what we wanted to do, what our families were like. He knew about my brothers. He said David had been trying to find them, but hadn't had any luck so far.

Victor told me that he had ten siblings—like me, he was the youngest—and all of them were married and had families before the war. Some even had grandchildren. But he had never married, even though he was already thirty-five when the war started. He said he just never met the right one, and he had always been focused on business rather than family. He had worked at a local train station, which gave him access to all kinds of people, and from there he had started a small smuggling business before the war. He was smuggling cigarettes from Poland to Germany when the war started and that had originally kept him safe. At first, the Germans allowed him to continue his business, so long as they benefited from it. But then, things got worse, the Germans started deporting Jews, and he had to run away. Like us, he spent most of the war in hiding. He went to Hungary and then, when he tried to cross the border into Romania, he was caught and sent to prison. Eventually, he was released, and he made his way safely into Romania, where he again started smuggling cigarettes. Shortly after that he met David. Now that the war was over, he also was trying to find his siblings, but so far, he had found no one. He wanted to find out what happened to all of them, and, then, he would go to Palestina.

I told him about how I used to love to dance and sing and about how I used to sneak out of the house to go dancing with my friend Bina. Now, I didn't know if I could remember how to dance or if I could still carry a tune. I told him about hiding in the forest and the different places I had stayed along the way. We continued our walks every day; each day, I discovered more about him and told him more about me.

The next week, Victor surprised me with tickets to the opera. He even took me to buy a dress, because I didn't think I had anything nice enough to wear. He told me I was beautiful and held my hand through the entire show. It was magical. The singing, the dancing, and Victor's soft hand gently wrapped around mine.

Afterwards, he walked me home, my arm threaded through his. When we arrived at my door, he stood in front of me and placed his hands on my cheeks. I looked up into his blue eyes, getting lost in them, feeling my knees getting faint, and then he kissed me. His soft lips locked onto mine, as though they were made to fit together perfectly. I raised my hands to his face, placing them on his warm cheeks and falling into his embrace. I didn't want it to end, I didn't think I would have the strength to stand on my own once he let go. But after a moment, he pulled his head back, leaving his hands still on my cheeks.

"Are you ready to go to Palestina with me?" he asked.

I nodded. At this point, I would have followed him anywhere.

Afterward

Rachel and Victor did not go Palestina right away. First, they moved to Budapest and got married in June, 1946. Shortly after they were married, Victor returned to Poland to search for his siblings. He found one brother in Bielsko, Poland. That brother, Zigmunt, had lost his wife and two daughters in the war. After finding Zigmunt, Victor and Rachel moved to Bielsko to be near him. Victor later found another sister and brother in Poland. The rest of his family had been murdered by the Nazis.

In 1947, Rachel and Victor had a son, Nahum. They were still in Bielsko and while they were doing well there, they hadn't let go of their dream of moving to Palestina. When Israel became a state in 1948, the dream became even more attainable. In 1950, they decided to leave Poland behind and restart their lives in Israel. That journey is another story in and of itself. They traveled via Italy by boat and arrived in Haifa where they first lived in a tent until they were able to move into a small apartment. From there, they moved south to Ashkelon in order to help populate the country's periphery. They were settled in the neighborhood of Barnea, a place that could hardly be called a neighborhood by our standards. Rather, it was a few sand dunes, several kilometers away from the next family.

David, Hinda, Sarah, and Yossi also made it to Israel. They arrived in 1947 after finding out that Abi was alive and living in Kibbutz Ein Shemer in the north of Israel. Abi went to the port of Haifa to meet his family upon their arrival. He said he was afraid that he wouldn't recognize them when they got off the boat, after not seeing them for so long, but he did, and they were happily reunited. The family settled in Netanya, but Abi chose to stay in the Kibbutz where he felt he most belonged. He also tried to convince Sarah and Yossi to come live with him there. Sarah lived there for a year, but decided she preferred living with her parents. Yossi used to visit often. He said that Abi, even until his last days, made it a point to be there for his siblings, and help them in any way he could.

As for the rest of the Shwartz family, they were all murdered. David and Rachel's five other brothers were likely murdered in the camps. No one else from their family survived.

Interested in learning more about the Shwartz family's journey?

Go to my website: www.avivagatauthor.com to see more pictures.

Sign up for my newsletter to get update about future books and a sequel to My Family's Survival.

Other books by Aviva Gat:

- My Heart from Inside
- The Evergreen Life Experiment
- She Had To Kill Him

Acknowledgments

I want to thank my husband, Ori Koskas, for his continuous support and for encouraging me to follow my dreams and write this book. Without him, I never would have had the confidence to sit down, write, and pursue this project.

I would also like to thank my father, Nahum Gat—the son of Rachel and Victor. Nahum compiled tons of pictures, maps, timelines, a family tree, and other materials that helped me put together this book. Without his thorough research, I would not have been able to put together a comprehensive story. Also, thank you to my father and mother, Linda Papermaster, for reading the manuscript and giving me valuable feedback and comments.

The biggest thank you goes to my grandmother Rachel for inspiring me. Not only was she strong, she was also kind, compassionate, and extremely loving. She dedicated her life to helping others—not only taking care of her family, but volunteering fulltime at a hospital until she was unable to do so. Thank you to her for recording her story about her life in Butla and her experience during the Holocaust. The recording she made appears to be the only time she spoke about her experience. Unfortunately, she never spoke to her children about it.

A huge thanks also goes to Yossi Shwartz, who spent a lot of time speaking with me about his family and providing significant insights and anecdotes.

Yossi also recorded his sister Sarah speaking about her experiences before and during the war, so thank you Yossi for that, and to Sarah for speaking with him. Additionally, a huge thank you goes out to David and Abi for telling their stories in recorded testimonies that were the main materials on which this book is based.

I also want to thank the very talented Marianna Cohen, who created the beautiful cover for this book.

Want to help Holocaust survivors?

The Blue Card is an organization that provides financial assistance to Holocaust survivors in the U.S. The Blue Card was established by the Jewish community in Germany in 1934, to help Jews already being affected by Nazi restrictions through loss of jobs, forcibly closed businesses, and other forms of oppression.

In 1939, The Blue Card was reestablished in the United States to continue aiding refugees of Nazi persecution resettling in America.

After the Holocaust, the mission of the organization was expanded to help survivors of the Shoah from all European countries. The Blue Card continues its work in the United States to this day, providing:

- financial assistance, on a monthly basis as well as for emergencies, such as medical and dental care
- week-long vacations in a rural setting
- special holiday grants
- health precautionary services that permit survivors to live with dignity in their own homes
- As the number of survivors still alive declines, their needs for financial assistance increase.

To make a donation, go to
https://www.bluecardfund.org.

Made in the USA
Columbia, SC
06 September 2021